Archer
of the
Lake

Kelly R. Michaels

Published by
Little Owl Publishing

Cover by
Sarah Foster
Sprinkles On Top Studios

Map by
Arbor Winter Barrow

Edited by
Kelsa Warner
Andy Arnold
Halley Hampton

2018 Edition

ISBN: 0-9894685-1-8
ISBN-13: 978-0-9894685-1-0

For my darling Mamaw
And my beloved Papaw,
Whose souls retired before I finished

And also—
For dearest Halley
Who helped bring this story to you

CONTENTS

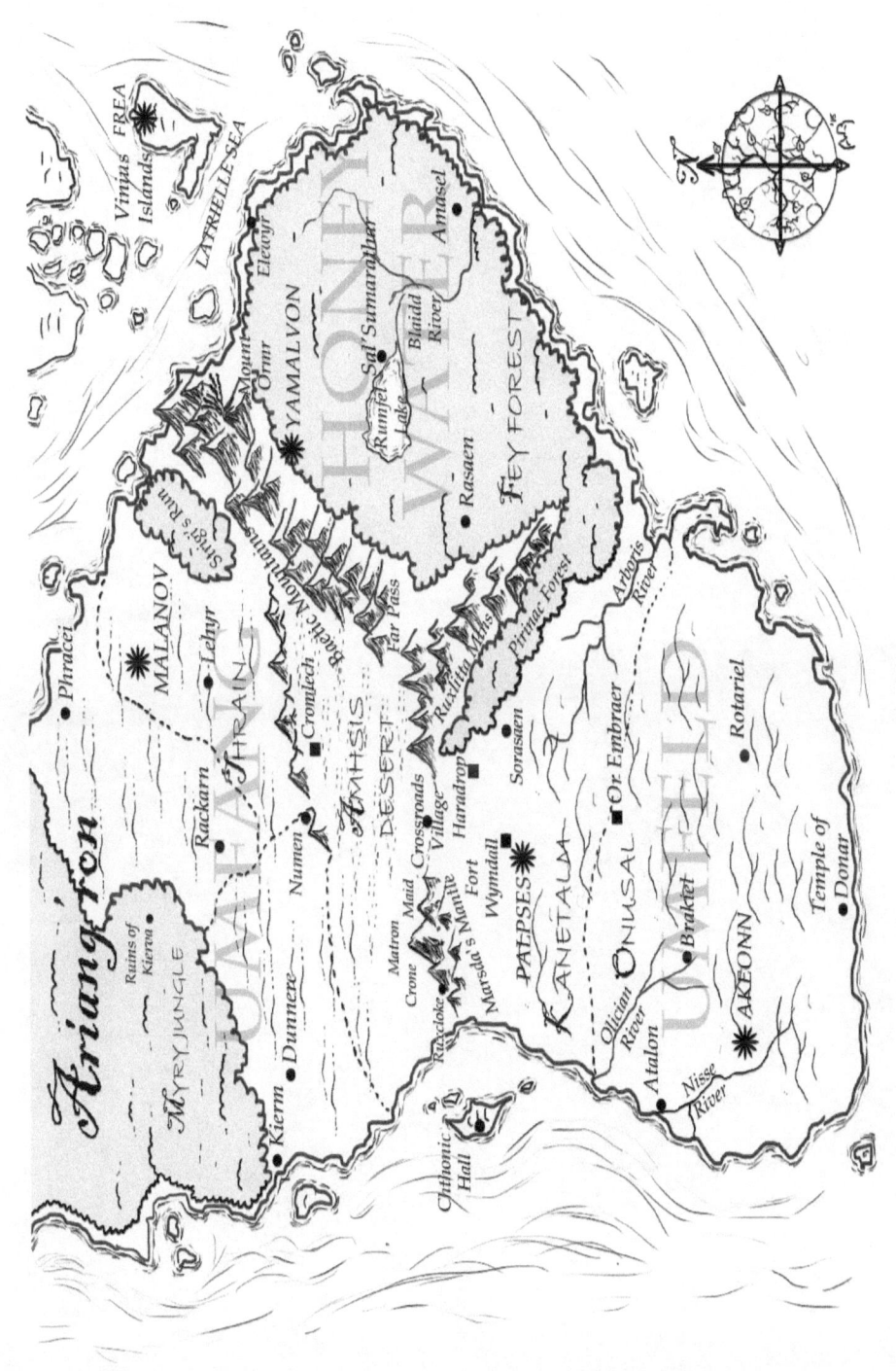

Prologue

"**T**ake an army with you."

"Where am I going to get an army?" Feraan asked. Lividia, the Mistress of the Chthonic Order, leaned back in her chair. Sharp fingernails drummed metronomically on the table. Feraan calmly noted the woman's expression of impatience. Humans were always impatient, but he supposed they had a right to be because their lives were so short. But Feraan did not understand the Mistress painting her lips blood red, just as he did not understand why she insisted on branding her followers with tattoos on their shoulder blades. For an order that prided itself on secrecy, membership markings did not make much sense to him.

"You are the Wandering Elf. You are famous for solving such problems," Lividia pointed out, arching a dark eyebrow. Feraan thought her dark hair and bright red lips made her skin look shockingly pale, which only made her look like a blood drinker.

"My problems never required an army."

Lividia looked down the long table at the other officers of the Order. Her eyes fell on Lycaon, head of the Dirus Clan of werewolves. "I hear there is no shortage of mercenaries in Haradrop."

Lycaon returned Lividia's gaze with a cold glare but said nothing. Feraan asked, "Does the Order plan to fund these mercenaries for me?"

"The Dirus Clan would not need funding. They would only be repaying what is rightly owed to us. Would you not agree, Lycaon?"

Lycaon did not answer Lividia and instead turned his attention to

1

Feraan. "My family will always assist you with whatever you need, old friend."

Feraan's mouth twitched into a half-smile for Lycaon.

"Good," Lividia said, rising. "Take the werewolves to the east and destroy whatever stands in your path."

"The east?" Feraan repeated. "There is only one thing in the east—"

"We are well aware of your race and heritage, Feraan," Lividia interrupted. "It shows well enough in your pointed ears and the bare skin on your back where you did not take the tattoo." Lividia went to inspect a map tacked to the wall, tapping her fingers on the forest of his youth.

"Surely the Order has better things to do than send me on missions filled with mindless destruction. What is the point of all this?"

"Those are your orders, elf. You will do well to follow them."

"I make a point to not follow orders blindly."

"These orders do not come from me," Lividia said, turning to show him a condescending smile.

"Then who gave these orders?"

"They came from me," rumbled a voice from the shadows of the Chthonic Hall. The figure stepped into view, and Feraan had no difficulty recognizing the half-naked female with blank, white eyes that had no iris or pupil. Each step she took sounded like the rolling of distant thunder. It made everyone in the room but Lividia nervous.

"You are the Blind Seer," he said.

She smiled though her face looked past him. "Feraan Auvrearaheal. You do not trust me though I can bring only absolute truth."

Feraan looked to Mistress Lividia, having difficulty keeping his face smooth. "You take counsel from the Seer?"

"Sibylla sought me out. The future has told her something disturbing."

"Sibylla? I did not realize you were personally familiar with the Traitor of the World," Feraan hissed. Lividia faltered.

The Blind Seer pointed two fingers at him. "Calm yourself, Wandering Elf. You must keep focus now. There is a great evil brewing in your forest. Confront it, destroy it, and bring the one responsible to justice."

"What evil? Who is responsible?" he asked.

"It kills your people as we speak. I cannot see who causes this. They are cloaked by a great energy. Be cautious, Wanderer."

Feraan checked himself, and his hand went to the hilt of the sword sheathed at his waist. "There's more to this than you're letting on."

She smiled. "There will be consequences, Wanderer. You will save your people from their own destruction, and they will hate you for it. Attempts will be made against your life, but if want your life to continue, you must defeat this great evil. Do not leave until you have secured the one responsible. There will be a lake, and your life's worth will be tested there."

"Are you threatening me?" Feraan asked, stepping closer with his hand tight around his sword.

"I am not threatening you. I only recount the truth shown to me."

"What is your payment for telling us this? What does Mistress Lividia owe you for such valuable information?"

"Mistress Lividia owes me nothing, but I want your sword, Wanderer. I will have it one day," she promised.

Feraan only scoffed, turning his back to take his leave of the Chthonic Hall.

80 Years Later

In a hollow mountain, a desert princeling with an insatiable need for vengeance approached the Blind Seer. Though she could not see him, the oracle knew the exact hour of his visit and was prepared for his questions.

"He has slighted me," was his explanation.

"He has slighted many. You are not the first and you certainly will not be the last.'

"Perhaps not, but I *will* be the one to defeat him."

The oracle tilted her head curiously. "Do you seek to kill him?"

"No, I do not. I wish to torture him. His demise will be his eternal agony, a scar that I will leave him with," the princeling said. She turned her head the other way.

"But?" she prompted, luring him.

"But he has cursed me. I cannot see him unless he decides to reveal himself to me." The oracle knew this already.

"I cannot lift the curse for you. That is beyond my abilities."

"Then how am I to exact my revenge if I cannot even see him?"

"Draw him out and have him come to you. Take something precious."

The princeling paused at this. "Do as he did to me?"

The oracle slowly nodded. Eager, the princeling began pacing.

"Is there something he loves so dearly, he could not bear to be parted from it?"

The question, when asked, brought forth an image to the oracle, a vision of fierce beauty.

"Is there?" he asked impatiently.

"No," she answered, smirking. "But there will be *someone*."

1. Injustice

Elves were a secret race. Highly protective of their lands, they often sent small battalions to confront enemies that lurked at the borders of their beloved realm, the Fey Forest. They rarely ventured outside these borders and did not involve themselves in the problems of the other races. They lived in seclusion but not in ignorance. They were well aware when forces began mobilizing to strike against them, and the elves of the Honey Water Empire met and eliminated each danger that approached their home. As a result, they were largely left alone.

Goblins were the one exception. The nasty creatures lived underground and were stupid beings that often liked testing the prowess of their elvish neighbors, typically attracting attention by setting fire to trees. The elves always responded in kind, sending out small hunting parties to eradicate the pests. Blaes Llychlin, military adviser to the Empress Haelyn, was responsible for handling such matters. He charged the elvish city Sal'Sumarathar to deal with the latest goblin sighting, since they were the closest to the treeline border and the goblins. He determined the number of archers and swordsmen that were required, and the assignments were handled by either Sal'Sumarathar's Head Councilor or Chief Executor.

Caelfel Gyssedlues, at the age of seventy-six, was a young she-elf that had been called to the day's hunting party. She had been assigned a partner, an elf veteran named Tahlmus, and they would each be responsible for ensuring the other's safety.

Caelfel noted that the hunting party was not large. There were three other pairs in their group, and she knew of two other groups that roamed the forest with them. They had spent the majority of the morning searching for the characteristic fires of the goblins and they presently spotted the billowing pillars of smoke that were the telltale indicator of their location. They spurred their horses in the direction of the thick smoke.

The suffocating haze made Caelfel's eyes burn and water. She tied a scarf around her face and had just raised her sword when a green, leathery goblin suddenly came hurtling towards her out of the blinding smoke. Her eyes met the bulbous black orbs of the creature's before her blade impaled its compact torso, and the creature's corpse fell limply to the ground, leaving trails of black blood on her sword. She wiped it off on the back of her leather bracers before sheathing it to pull out her bow.

Three more goblins descended from the trees, and Caelfel nocked three arrows to meet them. The arrows pierced their tiny skulls, and Caelfel rode on, following Tahlmus through the ambush.

They hacked their way through the swarm of goblins. During the the midst of the fray, a goblin fell onto Caelfel's shoulders, digging its long nails into her cheeks. Her horse pranced sideways in surprise. She reached behind her head to throw it from her back.

It held onto her arm and bit down on her elbow. Caelfel cried out in pain, and Tahlmus dispatched the pest without hesitation. Its corpse fell to the ground with the others.

Within the hour, most of the goblins had fled or been dispatched. She compared her kill record with that of Tahlmus, reporting that she had taken the lives of sixty-three goblins. Tahlmus had little over forty.

They regrouped with the others of their division, and Caelfel realized with some embarrassment that she was the only one bleeding, and elves could easily detect the blood of their own kind. She wiped her dripping cheeks with a sleeve.

When the shrieks and the cries of the goblins had quieted, the mages of the hunting party went to work extinguishing the fires. Caelfel found it easier to breathe after that, but the odor of scorched trees and corpses still hung in the air.

Before they returned to Sal'Sumarathar, Caelfel and another elf named Winwaloe searched the piles of goblins to ensure there were no survivors. They left their horses with the group to do this, while

Caelfel went in one direction and Winwaloe in the other.

The trail of goblin corpses led her a distance away from the others, and soon she was surrounded by the silence of the forest. As she kicked over piles of goblins, Caelfel's thoughts wandered to her induction examinations that were scheduled for the following day and would determine whether she would be permitted to study magic at the College of Sal'Sumarathar. The thought made her stomach give a nervous flip, and Caelfel fretted over the task of performing simple magic in front of Headmaster Nimuath.

Her thoughts were interrupted when a sudden, shrill cry pierced the silence that had surrounded her. Caelfel's head snapped up to see a wounded goblin scampering towards her. Having left her bow with her horse, she quickly reached for her sword but before she had time to draw it, an arrow whizzed towards the goblin. The creature toppled back to the ground.

Caelfel turned to look for the archer, thinking Winwaloe had ventured in the opposite direction. She was surprised by what she saw.

There was another elf riding toward her on a black horse, a bow in his hands. Caelfel recognized the dark hair that fell past his face and knew that his name was Feraan Auvrearaheal and that he was reputed to be the most hated elf of the Honey Water Empire. She had never met him but as the dark-haired elf continued to approach, she thought that she soon might.

"You can claim that one as your kill, if you want," he said, nodding to the goblin at her feet

Caelfel attempted a smile but then realized it was hidden by the scarf tied around her face. She did not know why he had his reputation, only that other elves generally gave him a wide berth.

Feraan looked pointedly to the scratches on her cheek that still leaked blood and arched an eyebrow. "Did one of them bite you?"

Caelfel's fingers gently touched the marks on her face. Feraan turned to rummage through one of his saddlebags. While he was thus distracted, Caelfel noticed that his horse had peculiar milky red eyes but she thought it might be rude to inquire.

At that moment Feraan turned back to her and tossed a small, rubber-stoppered bottle. "Here."

Caelfel caught it, wondering how someone who was deserving of the reputation as the most hated elf of Honey Water could possess such generosity. She examined the bottle for a moment.

"It's not poison," Feraan said. "Put it on your cheek. Do you have a name, youngling?"

She straightened her back. "I'm not a youngling—"

"Caelfel?" Tahlmus answered, calling for her. "Caelfel, where are you? We should not tarry." She looked around for Tahlmus, but the veteran was not yet in sight. She turned back to Feraan who looked surprised by her name, but the expression was gone as quickly as it came.

"Gyssedlues?" he said. But Caelfel was not given a chance to respond. The sound of a rapidly approaching horse came from behind Feraan and distracted him. Caelfel only saw a glint of silver before a goblin that had escaped the earlier massacre jumped her.

"*Caelfel?*" came Tahlmus again. She fell to the ground, struggling to get the creature off of her. She reached for her sword and heard the wet sound it made as she hacked into the goblin. It stopped moving, and Caelfel looked at its wide, lifeless eyes. The scarf she had tied around her face had slipped off, and Caelfel picked it up from where it lay near her feet.

The goblin's high pitched shrieks had momentarily rendered her deaf, causing the world around her tilt slightly. She waited for the ringing to cease before she turned to Feraan again, tying her scarf around her belt.

But Feraan was no longer towering above her. His horse was gone, as was the mysterious glint of silver, and an elf lay face down on the ground before her, streaks of blood staining the back of his cloak.

"Feraan?" she said tentatively, wondering if it was silly to expect a response. She crouched above him to turn his face over. His closed eyes and shallow breath indicated he was unconscious.

Someone had obviously attacked him, and Caelfel wondered what sort of weapon could render its victim unconscious so quickly.

"Caelfel?" Tahlmus was beside her now. "What kept you—" But the veteran fell silent when he saw the answer to his own question.

"Someone *just* attacked him. He was talking to me only moments ago. A goblin fell on me, and I didn't see what happened." Caelfel was shocked and alarmed and she looked to Tahlmus for answers, but none of her panic seemed to penetrate him.

"Let's go. We should not keep the others waiting," Tahlmus said, taking the reins of his horse with a tighter grip.

"What of him?" Caelfel asked, wondering how Tahlmus could

miss the sharp scent of elf blood that overpowered the stench of goblins around them.

"That is no one, Caelfel," the veteran answered coldly.

Caelfel looked to him, confused. "Are you blind? He is someone, and we cannot leave him here to die."

Something dark flashed through the veteran's eyes, and Caelfel was suddenly reminded of Feraan's infamous reputation and wondered about the reason behind it. "He is condemned, Caelfel. There is nothing to save."

"Don't be ridiculous. He is still breathing."

But Tahlmus leveled his gaze in a way that made Caelfel think he meant the word differently. "Come. You've wasted enough time on him." Tahlmus extended his hand to her, but Caelfel backed away from it and offered him only a hard stare.

"You want him to die," she guessed slowly. She saw the truth of her statement flash in Tahlmus's eyes, and this realization sent cold shivers down her spine.

"He will die, Caelfel, and Honey Water will be rid of his burden."

"But *why?*" she insisted in a hollow voice. The glass bottle Feraan had given her was warm against her fingertips when she touched it. Caelfel was surprised she had not dropped it when the goblin attacked her. "He is an elf, and he was kind to me. This is murder."

"You should not let his handsome face fool you. He is a clever liar who only bodes ill for the rest of elvenkind. An execution is not murder."

Caelfel's mouth fell open slightly. "Execution?" she repeated. "You mean that this was planned?"

But Tahlmus would answer no more of her questions. "It is time to return to the others. Forget what you saw, Caelfel. It is for the best."

Caelfel imagined herself leaving with Tahlmus and forgetting her meeting with Feraan in the forest and found it was not an easy task. She had met him, and he had given her medicine. Caelfel could never leave him to die alone in the forest.

"Go without me, then, because I cannot leave him."

"You don't understand! There is no help for him—"

"I am *not* going to argue the matter of another elf's life," Caelfel hissed, her rage suddenly swelling at Tahlmus for his cruelty.

Her resolution seemed to surprise him, and Tahlmus left her

surrounded by dead goblins and the most hated elf of Honey Water. She waited until the sounds of his departure were gone before she went to further inspect Feraan's condition. Still unconscious, he hadn't much changed. Caelfel whistled for Rowan, her faithful mare.

It did not take long for Rowan to appear from the trees. Caelfel wrapped her arms under Feraan and lifted him, vaguely aware of how Feraan's congealing blood stained her clothes. When she had secured Feraan to her saddle, Caelfel stowed the bottle he had given her inside her cloak. Then she settled herself in the saddle behind Feraan and raced back to the city of Sal'Sumarathar, frantic thoughts whirling through her head. It seemed that elves were not only a secret race but a vengeful one.

It was almost spring, but as Rowan sped past trees, the air felt as cold as the deepest part of winter. The rushing wind pushed Caelfel's hair back and exposed the stinging cuts on her face. They had not been far from Sal'Sumarathar, and as they reached the woodland city, Caelfel wondered what she could possibly do to help Feraan. She knew nothing about the magical art of healing or of alchemical potions that would revive an elf. Feraan needed a healer, but based on Tahlmus's initial reaction to the elf, Caelfel doubted she would be able to find one willing to help.

Her father had trained as a healer and was fluent in the language of alchemy, but Caelfel knew he was not home. When they entered town, Caelfel tested her luck with the first healer's door she passed. Elves that walked the streets stared, but Caelfel didn't know if it was because she brought her horse into town or because she brought a particular passenger. Her instinct leaned toward the latter.

Awen Baeltylar answered the door when Caelfel called. The healer took one look at the patient and immediately slammed the door in Caelfel's face. Caelfel was not surprised but loudly cursed the she-elf all the same. By the time she turned from the closed door, the elves of Sal'Sumarathar were openly staring. Caelfel did her best to ignore them, irritated with their curiosity and their indifference, and urged Rowan forward to find another solution.

They turned when the dirt street veered to an empty path, and Caelfel paused to check on Feraan. His skin had taken on an alarming gray sheen and was ice-cold to the touch. She threw her weather cloak over his recognizable face to prevent others from staring but wondered at the usefulness of her efforts. Gray skin did not bode well for a living elf.

But he was still breathing, so she decided to try another healer, one close to her home. Caelfel was friends with this healer and knew him to be kind and a trifle handsome. When she reached his dwelling, Caelfel dismounted and approached the wooden door painted the signature green color of a healer. She heard latches opening and recognized the elf that came to the door.

"Caelfel?" said Thoroth Orletylar when he opened the door. "Is there something wrong?"

Caelfel struggled for words. "I need your help. I have someone who needs your help."

"What is wrong? Who needs my help?" He craned his neck to see who was with her, but Caelfel moved to block his line of sight.

"You must promise you will do everything you can to save him," she insisted. Thoroth's expression turned doubtful, and she touched a pleading hand to his arm. "Please? I would be very grateful for your help."

"Save *him*?" Thoroth repeated suspiciously.

"Promise," she insisted severely.

Thoroth gave a half-smile. "If I don't, it would not affect me either way. You can let me see him, or he will stay to die where he is while I will be none the worse for it," he pointed out.

Caelfel deliberated and nodded. She stepped out of his way, and Thoroth went to retrieve the unconscious elf from Rowan. Before he reached his house, Caelfel's cloak shifted, revealing Feraan's face. The sight made Thoroth freeze, and for a moment, Caelfel feared that he would just drop Feraan where he was.

Thoroth turned to her. "What business do you have with the most hated elf of Honey Water?" Thoroth tried to keep his voice neutral, but Caelfel detected a hint of bitterness from the healer.

She shook her head. "No business. He was attacked in the forest. I couldn't just leave him."

"Everyone else would have," Thoroth muttered darkly. His tone surprised her.

"You would abandon an elf to die?" she asked, appalled.

"I would not abandon any other elf. I *would* abandon him."

"I don't care who he is. I'm going to save him."

"Caelfel, he is a murderer."

Caelfel was taken aback by the statement but she did not let it visually affect her. She remained resolute, "He was kind to me. I'm going to at least repay that kindness. You can help me or not, but if you don't, I shall not know what to do."

Thoroth exhaled sharply through his nose, and Caelfel knew that he disapproved. "This is a mistake, but I will look him over. Mind you, I'm not doing it for him."

Caelfel beamed at Thoroth and stretched to kiss his cheek to show her gratitude. Thoroth lingered for a moment when her lips brushed against his face and then turned away towards his home. Caelfel picked up her fallen cloak and followed him inside.

It was not uncommon for healers to refashion the front room of their dwelling for their occupation, and Thoroth was no exception. The raised examination table was visible from inside the doorway. Glass bottles lined the shelves and dried plants hung from the ceiling. Caelfel suppressed the urge to look curiously around the home of Thoroth. There had been occasions when she had been inside this room to deliver alchemy ingredients from her father, but despite her curiosity on those occasions, Caelfel never had had the chance to examine everything. Now she focused her attention on Feraan as Thoroth gently placed him on the pallet. Thoroth checked him over, pressing two fingers at specific points on Feraan's chest. After a moment of this, he looked up.

"I'll have to turn him over. The entry wounds are on his back." Caelfel helped him do this and began to surreptitiously inspect Thoroth's home while the healer began cutting away Feraan's tunic. She preoccupied herself by naming the various plants Thoroth had hung from nails in the walls and rafters. She easily recognized stinging nettles and some calendula next to that but Caelfel wasn't sure if the berry cluster beside them was honey dew berries or something else.

She braved a glance back to Thoroth and saw he was busy poking around Feraan's wound. Caelfel continued roaming around the room. She was about to set the cloak on a table when she felt the glass bottle protruding from its pocket. Caelfel kept her back to Thoroth and took it out as discreetly as she could. She dabbed a few drops of the medicine on her fingertips and applied it to the scratches on her cheek. There was the slightest tingling sensation, and then she felt a small amount of warmth spreading across her face. She briefly checked her dim reflection in the bottle and saw that the ragged marks had disappeared without a trace.

She wondered if she could have just used Feraan's medicine to save him but thought it better if a proper healer looked him over. "It was strange," she commented, stuffing the bottle back into her pocket before turning to Thoroth. "He had been talking to me before *that* happened. A goblin fell on me, and when I looked at him again, he was unconscious on the ground. I don't know of any weapon that could bring him down so fast."

"I'm assuming you killed that goblin in the same amount of time. Something else could have done the same to him," Thoroth said as he glanced up at her.

Caelfel gave a noncommittal shrug. "It was still strange."

Thoroth produced something from his examination, and held it up to the light for her to see. "We know what weapon was used."

Caelfel took the piece of flint covered in congealed blood with a thumb and forefinger. "It's an arrowhead." She tilted it and wiped some of the bloody mess away with her thumb. "It's an elvish arrowhead." At Thoroth's indication, she dropped it in a metal dish on the nearby table.

"That's not all. He's been poisoned."

"*Poisoned?*" Caelfel repeated. She turned back to Thoroth. "Someone really wanted him dead, then."

"Are you surprised? There's nothing I can do for poison. I'm sorry, Caelfel."

At this, Caelfel whirled around to face him. "You cannot cure poison? Why not?"

"The base ingredient for the cure of any poison was a flower that is now extinct. It was native to Amasel and the flower died with the city."

Caelfel looked away and merely said, "Oh."

Amasel had been an elvish city in the Fey Forest that had been destroyed nearly a century ago. All of the Amasel citizens were discovered dead one day, without explanation. It was a mysterious tragedy, perhaps the largest of elvish history.

"Is there not another plant you can use in its stead?" Caelfel asked.

"There's no way of telling what sort of cure he needs without dissecting his *dead* body."

Caelfel turned her devastated gaze to Feraan's face. She touched his cheek again, and it felt cold as ice and hard as stone. "You won't help him, then?" she asked mutely.

"There's nothing I can to do to help him, Caelfel. I am truly sorry."

She looked around the room. "There's nothing you have that can draw out the poison? And no other healer has anything?"

"We have not had anything for poison in the last half-century. I'm sorry, but there is no hope for him."

"You mean all he can do is die?" Caelfel asked, turning her back to Thoroth. When he turned around to replace his instruments on a shelf, a curling scroll caught her attention with its shimmering ink. The heading of a Royal Decree made her pause, and Feraan's name spelled out in bold letters made her slip it secretly under her cloak.

"You don't have to watch him. You can leave him here, and I'll take care of all the rites," Thoroth said, facing her again. He bent down and began covering Feraan's face with a black veil.

"No," she said quickly, ripping the veil from Thoroth's hands. "He'll come with me. I will take care of him."

"Caelfel, there's nothing you can do."

She dignified him with a hard stare. "I still have to try, Thoroth."

"And what will you do?" he asked, straightening from his hunched position over Feraan.

Caelfel sighed, avoiding his gaze. "I don't know."

Thoroth was obviously reluctant to allow Caelfel to take off with Feraan, but she was irritable and impatient. Soon, Thoroth bent to her manner and became obliging, carrying Feraan back to her horse and securing him there. Caelfel couldn't stand to look at the still face as a panic began rising in her throat. If Thoroth could do nothing as a healer, there was little she could expect to do instead.

She hesitated on Rowan before taking off, and Thoroth stood below her, as if waiting for the right words to come to his lips.

"Will you be applying at the college tomorrow?" he finally asked.

Caelfel had a vague recollection of fretting over the entrance exams, but that was far from her concern now. She merely nodded.

"I have a friend coming down from Yamalvon tonight who will be too. She'll be staying with me while she attends the college. Her name is Garvanna. You should speak to her if you meet."

Caelfel gave Thoroth a blank stare and said nothing more to him, choosing instead to spur Rowan away from the dwelling of the useless healer. Her eyes burned as she wondered what she would do and where she should take him.

She eventually decided to take the most hated elf of Honey Water to her house, because it was not far from Thoroth's and she assumed every other useless healer would reject him, just as Thoroth had done Caelfel didn't take Feraan inside, though. Instead, she stopped Rowan just inside her family's garden. She carried Feraan all the way to the bathing area and set him on the low stone platform next to the water fountain before closing the gauzy curtains around them. She knelt on the ground beside Feraan, increasingly aware of the longer gaps between his short breaths.

He would be dead soon, she knew, but Caelfel didn't want that on her conscience. She thought back to their first and incredibly brief conversation and wondered how anyone could hate an elf who so willingly offered help. He did not seem like a murderer to her, because she did not suspect murderers would give away medicine without prompting. Although, they might. Perhaps if he was awake, Feraan would know what to do about his situation, but then Caelfel realized he would not wake ever again. She would never speak to him. Caelfel restlessly combed anxious fingers through her hair as the hopeless despair crushed her chest. She rocked herself back and forth as a small wail escaped from her throat.

She had never killed an elf and she considered herself responsible for Feraan's life. If he died under her care, that was a loss she could not bear.

She pushed her hair to one side of her neck, and her hand brushed against the chain of her amulet. Caelfel looked down at the grape cluster shape of her charm and felt as though she had her answer. She quickly unfastened the amulet and put it around Feraan's neck. It was a protective amulet given to Caelfel by her mother, and Caelfel's father had modified it specifically to shield the wearer from certain intrusive evils, poison included. She wasn't sure if this method would work on Feraan but Caelfel held her breath as she waited.

It was nearly an hour before she saw any effect. His breathing regained measured consistency, and his deathly pallor was slowly replaced by a more healthy and natural color. Caelfel sighed, and it was a relief that unknotted her stomach. She realized he would live now, and Caelfel was glad.

With the immediate danger out of the way, she went to read the scroll she had pilfered from Thoroth's counter and saw it was indeed a Royal Decree issued by the Council of Sal'Sumarathar. Caelfel felt her fingers grow cold as she slowly learned that by saving Feraan's life, she had committed a very serious crime. The decree ordered every healer to refuse their service to the elf Feraan Auvrearaheal. Healing him would be considered as an act against nature, a crime of high treason.

Caelfel transferred her gaze to Feraan's seemingly innocent face. Saving his life had been a crime, and she realized the objective of the entire hunting party was to kill him. That was why Awen Baeltylar shut the door in her face and why Thoroth was so reluctant. But Tahlmus had seen, as well as the masses of Sal'Sumarathar. They would know of her crime, and strangely, Caelfel was unafraid of the consequences. She had saved a life, and that was all that mattered to her. But the notion that the Council of Sal'Sumarathar would organize such measures to eliminate him astounded her.

She continued staring at Feraan's face. "What did you do to deserve such injustice?"

2. Eye of Ewyn

Feraan awoke when it was dark, and it felt as though a bolt of lightning coursed through him. He sat up panting and struggled to name where he was. The bathing fountain and the floral scents around him were unfamiliar. Feraan was sure that he had been in the middle of the hunting party, but the garden around him suggested he was back in Sal'Sumarathar. Nothing suggested how.

He remembered a girl. A name came to him. Gyssedlues. And then—

And then he fell. That was all he had left of the memory.

Feraan looked at the garden around him and the name popped into his head again. Gyssedlues. Eviat and Sylaera Gyssedlues. But that wasn't who he saw in the forest. He had seen their daughter Caelfel. Perhaps it was she who had brought him here. He was at the Gyssedlues home. The familiar cloak and glass bottle at his feet were telling enough. He had given her the bottle of medicine when she was wearing the cloak.

But there was something else in the pile, and further inspection revealed that it was a Royal Decree. Specifically, it was a Royal Decree forbidding anyone to save his life. But it would seem that Caelfel had.

She had also set aside his things—his bow and quiver and a pack—neatly next to the curtain which sealed off the rest of the garden. He quietly gathered these things when he noticed an amulet around his neck. He thought about removing it but decided against it, figuring it had been given to him for a reason. He pushed the amulet from his mind and prepared to leave the Gyssedlues garden for his

17

own home, but then a notion struck him.

Leaving without notice would be rude, and Feraan considered that for a few moments. He shrugged the idea away. He had not bothered himself with manners in nearly a century and he wasn't going to begin now. It was late, an attempt had been made on his life, and he wanted to return to his home. Feraan did not have the patience to ponder on the implications of someone saving his life.

He saw lights inside the house but did not feel up to the task of conversation. He left, then, deciding the Gyssedlues girl could keep his glass bottle.

***

Caelfel had remained by Feraan's side for the majority of the day. She left only when Mother called for dinner for the fourth time, and only then because Father had stuck his head outside to rush her along. She had eaten her dinner so quickly it had made her stomach turn. Her parents noticed her impatience but they did not ask about it. When she had finished, they let her leave without question.

But by the time she had rushed out to the garden again, Feraan had disappeared. This should have been good news because it probably meant he had awoken and felt well enough to leave. But Caelfel was disappointed; she had wanted to talk to him.

"Caelfel?" Her father was a tall, greyling elf with a voice like smoke and ash. Eviat Gyssedlues was an old elf to be sure, much too old to marry her beautiful mother and much too old to have such a young daughter. His age had not stopped him from accomplishing either feat, and Caelfel always felt he had a special store of love, which was reserved solely for doting on his daughter. "He's gone," Caelfel muttered to herself as Eviat stepped up beside her.

"Who is?" he asked.

Caelfel took a single sideways glance at her father and, remembering her actions had been a serious crime, decided not to implicate her parents on the matter if she were discovered. "Nothing," was her answer.

"Are you nervous about tomorrow?" Eviat asked.

Once more, it took a moment's hesitation for her to remember the significance of tomorrow.

"Are you prepared?" he asked when she had said nothing. "The College of Sal'Sumarathar only accepts new students every fifty years."

18

"I know that, Father. If things do not go well, there is always the College of Yamalvon."

Eviat gave her a curious look. "Do you plan for things to not go well?"

Caelfel wondered what the Council did to elves who committed treason and figured that expulsion from magical academia was the least of her concerns. Caelfel imagined herself being thrown into the fiery pits of Mount Ormr. Or maybe an execution would be something as simple as a public beheading. Caelfel was disturbed to find she accepted the mental images of her death with a cold indifference.

"I have no such plans," she answered at length.

"You will make me proud," Eviat mused with a distant smile. Caelfel wondered what her father thought of the most hated elf of Honey Water.

"I hope so."

She decided then that the best thing for her was to get as much rest as she could for her exams the next day but as she tossed in her bed, Caelfel found that sleep eluded her that night. She wondered if she was prepared for her exams and how Feraan fared. Then she speculated when the Council would discover her crime, and every time Caelfel heard an odd sound in the night, she thought the militia had come to take her.

But no militia came, and sleep remained elusive as ever.

Eventually sleep found her, only to be swiftly chased away by the watery light of dawn. She dressed in a short time, belting her long, silver-threaded blue shirt at her hips. The air in her bedroom was chilled, so she donned her cloak as well. Even so, Caelfel felt completely naked without her amulet. She didn't dwell on this and, pausing only to give her parents a brief hug, hurried out of the house to make it to her exams.

The College of Sal'Sumarathar was built like a fortress and stood at the furthest edge of the city. It had its own magnificent gardens that boasted of every known plant, foreign and domestic, the one exception being the flower to make poison antidotes. It was a respectable school of magical academia and certainly comparable to the college in Honey Water's capital Yamalvon.

The headmaster of the college was a patient sort of elf named Nimuath. Caelfel's mother Sylaera had studied with him when she first enrolled in the college. He was there to greet the masses that had come to apply. Since the College of Sal'Sumarathar only accepted students every fifty years, the selection process was hailed as a celebrated event. Caelfel was unsurprised to find a large crowd pushing their way to the front gate. Headmaster Nimuath was there to greet them all individually.

Already, the selection was a matter of filtering. Nimuath looked each entrant over carefully, allowing some inside but sending many more away. Caelfel shoved her hands nervously into her pockets and found she could not meet Nimuath's eyes when her turn had come and she stood before him.

"Caelfel Gyssedlues," he greeted her. She raised her eyes to see him smile. "Your mother was a powerful mage indeed. I sense she has passed her abilities to you. Please enter."

The sudden elation and relief made Caelfel feel dizzy. "How can you tell? You've only just met me."

"When you have studied magic as long as I have, you become sensitive to another's power. Your aura is green, by the way." He winked and ushered Caelfel through.

She passed the gardens, cheeks numb from the late winter cold. Caelfel hurried through the grand entranceway where she had seen others go. When she was inside, she saw that the entrance hall to the college was made of elaborate stonework. Gems of all colors, both polished and uncut, decorated the walls with large deposits and thin veins. A stone dais sat in the center of the room, and on it was a round gem as large as a tree. It was smooth as marble, and colors seemed to shimmer beneath its surface. Caelfel felt a strange urge to touch it but when she noticed the others standing in the room, she suppressed the urge.

They were all silent, all waiting for the selection process to end and for their exams to begin. The room was circular, so there was no corner for her to hide in. Instead she chose a space that did not put her too close to the other elves and waited as they did. Within an hour, a few more elves joined them in the room followed lastly by Nimuath. The doors shut behind him, and Caelfel heard locks falling into place.

A quick estimate told Caelfel that there were only about forty, perhaps fifty elves in the room. Of them, Caelfel only recognized Winwaloe from the hunting party the day before, and Daerad, son of Sal'Sumarathar's Head Councilor and Caelfel's childhood playmate.

Daerad was the second youngest elf of their city, the first being her. Over the years, they had grown distant from each other until, finally, their personality differences severed any bond they might have had.

Headmaster Nimuath strode to the gem centerpiece, circling it to address them all. "The College of Sal'Sumarathar teaches two branches of magic—the mundane and the auric. Each branch of course has their own fields. To be considered for acceptance, your examinations focus primarily on your auric abilities, as the aura is the measure of an individual's magical capabilities. Each of you passed the selection process because of your auras. Please understand, every elf is born with one, but that does not mean they all possess the same strength. I choose only those I felt could safely perform the magical tasks that would be assigned to them.

"As a precautionary warning, you should all be aware that one's aura is not infinite. To perform any sort of magic requires a varying amount of energy, and while energy can recharge itself, it can also be depleted. If you are not cautious, it is quite possible to kill yourself while casting spells."

Many of the prospective students exchanged nervous glances with each other, and Caelfel was one of them. One she-elf across the room from her with a tall frame and long, copper hair did not look the least bit concerned. Caelfel tilted her head curiously at her, but either the she-elf did not notice her gaze or simply chose to ignore her.

Nimuath stopped his circling and continued. "The stone you see behind me is called the Eye of Ewyn. It can store, give, or steal auric energy. This will be how you take your examinations. I will call upon each of you one at a time, and the Eye of Ewyn will test your worth. You will either pass or fail. We will go by age, oldest first and youngest last."

The she-elf with the copper hair was selected first, and the rest of them were herded into another, smaller room. Caelfel thought it looked to be an empty classroom. A greyling named Nadeth Kennyratear stood guard at the door. Caelfel knew him because he was friends with her father and she had been to his house once as a youngling. Now she recalled Eviat mentioning that Sir Kennyratear taught at the college. If he recognized her among the crowd, Sir Kennyratear did not show it.

"What's happening?" someone asked when gold light began seeping through the cracks of the door.

"She is being tested. All of you will have your turn," Sir Kennyratear promised. The gold light fluctuated with strength, waning and waxing. After an hour of the light show, it disappeared entirely, and Nimuath opened the door to their holding place.

"Next."

Each elf was different. There were red lights, blue lights, and a multitude of other colors. Some lasted several minutes, occasionally an hour, while others only lasted a few seconds before Nimuath called for the next entrant. Caelfel lost track of how long she had been waiting for her turn.

Eventually, only three of them remained—her, Daerad, and Winwaloe. But then Nimuath came for Winwaloe, leaving her and Daerad. Winwaloe's light was blue but very brief. Nimuath returned less than a minute later for Daerad, and, predictably, Caelfel was the last, waiting alone for her turn. Sir Kennyratear was with her of course, but with his silence, she might as well have been by herself.

Daerad's light shone brilliantly white and continued for a while. She wondered what became of Winwaloe and suspected that the color of light she produced would be green, since Nimuath had told her that was the color of her aura.

Caelfel waited and waited, picking at threads on her cloak or at her fingernails, and finally, when Daerad's light was extinguished, Nimuath came for her.

"Miss Gyssedlues." She followed him to the room with the Eye of Ewyn. He put a hand on her shoulder as he gave her instructions.

"You will put both hands on the stone, and it will measure the extent of your aura to the point where you *will* fall unconscious. You will be taken to the infirmary until you awake and are told your result. While you are touching the stone, the Eye of Ewyn will show you images. These images may be from your past, present, future, or they may mean nothing at all. Only you can see what the Eye shows you, and everyone sees something different. Do not be afraid. You will not be harmed. You may begin whenever you like."

Caelfel stood in front of the stone, entranced by the waves of color shifting inside it. She reached with both hands and felt its warm surface.

For a moment, all she saw was emerald green light, but then the light faded to the peripherals of her vision, revealing a wolf taller than any elf she had met. Darkness swallowed the image of the wolf, leaving a cold chill in its wake. Then the darkness gave way to show a house, an elvish house. The vision showed her where to find it outside of Sal'Sumarathar but nothing more of its mystery.

The house disappeared within the wingspan of a raven that flew to the towers of an icy fortress that Caelfel had never seen before. She felt very cold at the sight of the tundra landscape.

Then Caelfel noticed a face that melted the ice fortress into a great lake. The face was hidden from her, so Caelfel replaced it with another face from her memory. But before she could focus on the new visage, everything fell away to blackness as Caelfel passed out.

***

Bright lights shining down on her from a tall ceiling brought Caelfel back to consciousness. Her neck felt stiff, and her head throbbed as she struggled to remember details. A glance around her revealed to Caelfel that she was in the college infirmary, surrounded by multiple cots for the other applicants. By now, most of them were empty, Caelfel being the last to take the test. Headmaster Nimuath patiently stood next to her and waited for her to focus on him before speaking.

"Congratulations, Miss Gyssedlues. You have been accepted into the College of Sal'Sumarathar. Try not to exert yourself too much as you are still recovering."

"What happened?" she asked him.

"Your aura is a slightly perceptible field of energy. It is connected directly to you and your life force. The Eye of Ewyn drained the auras of all the applicants until they were an inch from death. It was a test to see how long your aura would hold. Obviously, the college cannot accept students with weak auras."

"Did anyone die?" Caelfel asked quietly, horrified at the thought.

"The Eye of Ewyn has never killed anyone. You are free to leave, Miss Gyssedlues. Return an hour after dawn tomorrow to begin your basic training with Sir Nadeth Kennyratear. Good luck." Headmaster Nimuath stepped away as he moved onto another prospective student. Caelfel blinked and looked around in his absence. She saw Winwaloe in the far corner of the infirmary, knees drawn up to his chest. She slipped off her cot to see him.

"Winwaloe?"

He looked up quickly in surprise. A moment later he remembered her. "You're Caelfel."

"And you are Winwaloe," she said. "How did your test go?"

He looked to his knees again. "I failed."

A strange silence followed. Winwaloe was obviously disappointed, but Caelfel didn't have the words to comfort him. She placed a hand on his shoulder instead.

A few minutes later, he met her gaze once more. "You left the hunting party yesterday. You didn't come back with Tahlmus."

Caelfel hesitated. "Did he say why?"

Winwaloe shook his head. "He would only say that you were lost."

It was Caelfel that looked away this time. "Tahlmus was the one that got lost," she muttered.

She didn't give an explanation, and Winwaloe didn't press her for one. She took a deep breath, drawing the strength to leave the infirmary. She didn't object when Winwaloe silently followed her out of the college grounds. Caelfel wondered if he would even be allowed inside again and pushed the thought from her mind. He followed her until they parted ways at the Hall of Court, and Caelfel paused momentarily to watch his solitary figure pass down the wide avenue. He stepped out of sight, and Caelfel prepared to return home when a faint memory stopped her.

The Hall of Court stood before Sal'Sumarathar's grand center plaza, which was dominated by an ornate fountain that shot streams of water into the sky before splashing down into its vast pool. Beyond that, Caelfel noticed the shops of spinners and goldsmiths closing down for the day. The fletcher packed his arrows, and the jeweler locked his valuables in a metal chest. They didn't notice her, too focused on returning home for the evening.

There was an empty forge, abandoned for several decades. Caelfel only vaguely recalled that the armorer was a she-elf who had moved to the elvish capital of Yamalvon. There hadn't been anyone to take up the forge after her departure, or perhaps she still owned it and planned to return one day. Caelfel wasn't sure; a lot of armorers seemed to leave for Yamalvon in the end, finding better pay in outfitting the imperial army. But it wasn't the forge that drew Caelfel's attention. She saw the cramped alleyway beside it that ran alongside the fletcher's stall.

She knew that if she took that path and turned left at the river, she would find a house. She wasn't sure whose, but it was the house the Eye of Ewyn had shown her. It might mean something, or as Headmaster Nimuath stated, it might mean nothing at all. But there was one way to find out.

She took the path through the narrow alleyway, past the ring of shops, past the houses of the hunters to reach the edge of the River Blaidd, the river that ran alongside Sal'Sumarathar before it joined into Lake Rumfel. The walk to the river took longer than she originally imagined, and Caelfel paused by the bank to check her surroundings.

The Eye's directions suggested she turn left at this point. If she veered left even further, she would reach her home. But the Eye's strict instructions were to follow the river, so she did, following it upstream. There was no road this way, but Caelfel was not deterred by splintered logs or gnarled roots. She traversed the uneven ground effortlessly, wondering whose house the Eye showed her. It seemed outside the grasp of the city, tucked away in the wilderness and hidden away from curious eyes. She decided not to consider the possibility that the owner of the house would object to visitors. Her anticipation made her excited, which only made her impatient, so soon she was running. Caelfel barely noticed the absence of the natural wildlife. She heard no birds nor buzzing insects. Somewhere in the back of her mind, a thought insisted to Caelfel that that was odd.

The thought was banished as she cleared another large boulder to see the house before her. It had a garden, like most houses of elves, and it was tall, sitting against the backdrop of a mound that rose against the river. Caelfel thought it was an odd place for an elf, so far away from others, but then she remembered Sir Kennyratear's house, the distance between it and Sal'Sumarathar was even greater.

She stepped up to the front door and knocked before she could lose the nerve. She heard sluggish movement behind the door before it creaked open slowly, cautiously, and not enough to see anyone on the other side. Caelfel tried peering through the miniscule crack but could see nothing but darkness.

"Hello?" she called.

The door opened fully, and Feraan Auvrearaheal appeared in front of her, leaning against the door frame. "How did you find this place?" he asked.

"You're alive!" she exclaimed, beaming. She experienced a sudden urge to throw her arms around him but she restrained herself and merely stood there, grinning.

He hesitated at her brightness. "Very astute, youngling. What are you doing here?"

"I am not—" she began hotly, before shaking her head. "Nevermind. You were injured in the forest. I brought you home, and—"

"I can imagine the rest," he interrupted, raising his hand. He shifted his weight against the doorway. "But you've done an impressive job of ignoring my questions."

"Can I come in?" she asked, craning to see over his shoulder. "I didn't know you lived here."

"Then how did you get here?" he asked, growing increasingly impatient. Caelfel clasped her hands behind her back and attempted to focus herself enough to answer him.

"The Eye of Ewyn showed it to me."

"The Eye of Ewyn?" he repeated before recognition crossed his face. "I did not realize Nimuath was admitting children through the college gates. You could not have passed, being as young as you are."

Caelfel frowned. "I am seventy-six." Applicants had to be over a half-century old. "And I *was* accepted."

"Well, what are you doing here?" he asked. Caelfel briefly considered admitting she was simply curious but decided against it.

"I wanted to see how you were faring. You left last night without a word. Anything could have happened."

"I went home," he said curtly before moving to shut the door.

She stubbornly held her arm out to block it. "And your injury? Are you still wearing the amulet?"

The mention of her amulet caused Feraan to absently touch a hand to his chest as if just remembering that the amulet was still there. "I was wondering about that. I thought that perhaps some fair lady had meant to claim me but I decided to leave it on, just in case there was an actual reason for it."

Caelfel's cheeks flared. "You had been poisoned, and since there is no antidote, giving you my amulet was the only thing I could do."

"This is *your* amulet?" He said feigning disappointment but doing a poor job at hiding his smirk. "So much for that fair lady."

"It prevents the poison from attacking your body; however it cannot remove the poison from your system. I'm afraid you will have to keep it, though I may not be the fair lady you were hoping for,"

Caelfel retorted, grinding her teeth at his remark.

"How did you know I was poisoned?"

"I'm not a healer. I took you to Thoroth, and he told me."

Feraan seemed to find this bit of news interesting, "How did you convince poor Thoroth to break royal decree for my sake? I would not think you were pretty enough for that sort of persuasion."

"As if the '*most hated elf of the empire*' has any room to criticize," she said, flaring defensively. "He saw that you were poisoned and offered to perform your death rites," she said, her voice rising with her irritation. "You almost died, but *luckily* I thought you were worth saving. *Luckily*, I took you home. *Luckily*, I gave you my amulet. And *luckily*, it worked, though my appearance does not suit you."

He stared at her for a while, looking her up and down, as if reevaluating Caelfel entirely. Breaking the silence, he said, "Would you like to come inside?"

Her irritation instantly evaporated, and she answered with an eager nod.

3. Harboring

Caelfel harbored an odd fascination with how the most hated elf of Honey Water kept his house. So as she moved around his front room, she did little to suppress her urge to look at everything. Feraan, who remained by the door, did not reprimand her for her curiosity. But he kept his eyes trained on her and his back to the wall with his arms folded. There was nothing particularly extraordinary about the room, nothing odd or out of place. Feraan was a messy elf if anything, piles of loose scrolls and open books littered every surface while other ordinary objects poked out from beneath the papers. Eventually Caelfel managed to tear her eyes away from the room.

"How are you feeling?" she finally asked.

He lifted his chin and squinted at her. "As you have already pointed out, I am alive."

"What about your back? Does that trouble you?" She circled around him and reached for the spot on his back. Before she could touch it, Feraan issued a sharp hiss. His shoulders tensed, and when he spun around, Caelfel hardly recognized him. He had the look of a wounded animal fighting for its life. She started to withdraw her hand when he grabbed it, crushing it in his grip. Feraan violently wrenched her arm around her back, causing Caelfel to bend in an attempt to lessen the sudden pain. He twisted her arm, holding it to her back.

Caelfel dipped and spun in an attempt to free her hand. She succeeded for a moment until Feraan, with lightning speed, grabbed onto her wrist and slammed her against the wall. She squirmed under his hold. His grip was like iron as she struggled against him.

"You are hurting me," she said softly.

In the span of a few blinks, he released her, and his pained features hinted at a wound that was proving a heavy burden. His ragged breathing was loud in the silence that followed. She looked up from massaging her wrist where he had grabbed her and saw him blinking furiously at his hands.

"I'm sorry. I did not mean to—" But he couldn't finish.

Caelfel knew from his wild eyes that the outburst was unintentional. She had seen the look many times before when hunting animals during trade season. She cleared her throat to draw him away from the moment. "No, the fault is mine. May I look at your back?" she asked, thinking his permission would be better than provoking another attack. She would keep her hands to herself unless otherwise asked.

Feraan looked surprised and he struggled to speak. "Don't you think you've done enough?"

Caelfel wasn't sure if she understood his question enough to answer it properly. "I found you in the forest. I feel as though I'm responsible for you."

"If I recall correctly, it was I that found you."

"That's right. You killed that goblin." She paused. "What happened to you? I looked away for just a moment, and then you were on the ground, unconscious."

Feraan rolled his eyes. "I was shot with an arrow."

Caelfel sighed.

"I couldn't help but notice that there has been a Royal Decree issued that forbids anyone to save me, yet that didn't stop you."

"It didn't," she agreed. This only seemed to frustrate him.

"I don't understand—"

"You're welcome," she interrupted, smiling.

"That means you've committed treason. You understand that, right?"

"Do you plan to report me?" she countered.

"As if I would sign my own death sentence. I don't think you're worth that."

"No one has to know."

"No one saw you hauling me back to Sal'Sumarathar?"

Caelfel faltered. "Everyone knows there was nothing I could do for you anyway. You were poisoned, and there's no antidote for that. No one knows about my amulet, save for my parents."

"Your parents," Feraan sighed, sounding exhausted.

"They don't know what happened and if they did, they wouldn't say anything."

"I've no doubt of that."

"Do you know my parents? You recognized my name in the forest," she asked.

"Did you not recognize me as well?"

"I don't have your infamous reputation," Caelfel pointed out. This made Feraan look more uneasy. He gripped the nearby table for support, and Caelfel realized his previous outburst must have drained him more than was at first apparent. A thought occurred to her. "May I look at your back?" she asked again.

His face was instantly guarded. "Why do you need to see it?"

"You have an open injury that needs tending," she pointed out flatly.

When Caelfel wouldn't back down, Feraan eventually relented. He begrudgingly lifted the back of his shirt, and Caelfel could tell that he held himself with a tense, almost nervous air. She instinctively wanted to reach out and comfort him, but stifled the urge.

"I promise to behave myself," she said, tapping her chin as she inspected him. "It appears as though you are wearing some bandages, the same ones, I believe, that I dressed you with."

She couldn't see his face but she imagined him rolling his eyes. On the shelf above him, she noticed a pair of snips and instructed Feraan to hand them to her. Caelfel smiled at her command, and Feraan audibly voiced his annoyance, groaning as he reached for the snips. When he handed them to her, she used them to cut away the blood-stained bandages, revealing a deep wound that still leaked multi-colored fluids.

Caelfel frowned. "This is looks rather atrocious and far beyond my abilities," she said, doubting the task she had been so eager to accept. "I don't have a healer's hands."

"I don't doubt that. Describe what you see," he said, thinly disguising his impatience with her incompetence.

Her frown deepened. "Blood. Red, yellow, and green blood."

"Blood isn't yellow or green. You're probably looking at pus or poison. Here—"

Feraan waved his hand in space above his head, creating a floating image of his back as it must have looked before his injury, bare without any blemishes. Caelfel marveled at his use of magic. Nothing more, she told herself. She would not be caught ogling his bare back with its toned muscularity that hinted too broad for an ordinary elf.

"What color is the skin around the infected area?" he asked.

"Dark purple, almost black. What does that mean?"

"I wouldn't know. Unfortunately there is not a healer among us." The remark felt heavily sarcastic and mocking. Caelfel pressed her lips together and didn't say anything. He moved his fingers in circles, recreating a similar but not quite exact replica of his injury on the shimmering image.

"No there's more coloration along the bottom, purplish," she said, pointing.

He corrected the image. "Has any of it healed over?" he asked.

"There's some scabbing." And Caelfel pointed where in the translucent twin of his back.

He cursed darkly to himself as he adjusted the magical image. "You will need to help me clean it, since I can't reach it on my own," he admitted after some time. With another wave of his hand, the image disappeared altogether.

Caelfel tried not to think about how unpleasant that would be. "Of course, just tell me what to do, your greatness."

He ignored the remark and gave her some very specific instructions while fetching a pan of water and a tiny glass vial of a cleaning agent. He got the water from the fountain in his garden and handed her a cloth satchel full of rags and a small but very sharp knife. She was to lance the wound to drain it of any pus or toxins and clean it thoroughly before bandaging.

"Can you handle that?" he asked roughly.

"Exactly how much do you know about healing?" she asked, becoming more and more uncomfortable with the task he had charged her with.

"I have quite a bit of experience, but don't act like you've never done this. You are making me nervous."

Caelfel fell silent and looked at him pointedly.

It didn't take him long to understand her pointed stare. His shoulder sagged against the wall as he eyed her sharply, dumbfounded by her inexperience. "*Never?*" he asked with a scoff.

"Are you sure we shouldn't get someone else to do this? Another healer, perhaps? My father was a healer long before I was born."

Feraan scrutinized her hands that cradled the bundle of rags, and Caelfel knew he was second guessing himself. "You will have to do. There's no point in leaving the house."

His tone was so harsh and critical that Caelfel's eyes fell to the floor. Her stomach flipped uneasily. "My house is only a few minutes away. My father wouldn't mind."

He removed himself from the wall. "If I'm going to stay alive, we cannot go to anyone else. As far as everyone is concerned, I am dead. Do you understand?"

"I understand that you seem to be placing an enormous amount of faith in me to keep you alive," she said in a low voice.

"If only my rescuer had had some proper medical training," he muttered wistfully.

She sucked in a deep breath to prepare herself. "You will need to lie down on your stomach."

Feraan nodded and led her to his bedroom, which was a large room with a vaulted ceiling and a bed in the shape of a perfect circle. Caelfel wasn't sure which was more peculiar, that he so easily took her into his bedroom or that he had a circle bed. She imagined Feraan did not receive many visitors, something that probably came with being the most hated elf of Honey Water.

Before she started, he moved his hands to create another image of his back with the wound. With it he demonstrated the procedure she would have to do to properly clean the injury. Caelfel admired the detail and the perfect likeness he conjured for her. Her mouth fell open in amazement.

"If you live through this, you must show me how to do that," she said when the image disappeared. "I do question your judgment of using magic in your condition."

He gave her a sideways look. "Focus on your task. My magic is helping, and I would risk using my magic over you killing me."

He pulled his shirt over his head, baring his back to her.

Caelfel took the knife into her grip, measuring the width of the injury with her finger. She played the vision through her head, mimicking the movements in the air before performing them. Feraan waited silently for her to proceed, so she began without warning, slicing through the flesh with a quick movement.

Feraan winced beneath her fingertips. She commented, "I don't believe you were so delicate to pain in your vision."

Feraan snarled in response, his back vibrating beneath Caelfel's touch.

"I wouldn't advise doing that again. My knife may slip, and you would be much worse off," she said, biting down on a laugh.

She made quick work of draining the fluid that ran clear and red. She used the cleaning agent and water to wash the wound, scrubbing away the pus with rags. Feraan uttered no word of complaint, but Caelfel could tell how much pain he was in by how he recoiled from her touch. He said nothing throughout the entire process.

She finished soon enough, wrapping fresh, new bandages around his chest. "There we are," she said grinning. "Still alive, aren't you? I did a good job."

Feraan stood, replacing his shirt. "I've had better from other novices. It is obvious you do not have a healer's hands."

Caelfel suppressed a scowl. After all, she had admitted the same herself. "What happened before when you twisted my arm behind my back?"

Feraan scowled. "What happened is that you learned to respect personal boundaries."

A silence followed that Caelfel did not know how to fill. Thankfully, Feraan did.

"You were accepted to the college, then? For everyone's sake, I hope you are not training to be a healer." he asked.

Caelfel remembered mentioning the Eye of Ewyn to him. "Yes, I was accepted. I plan to be a battlemage," she admitted slowly.

He arched an eyebrow at her answer. "Let's hope your aim is better than your bedside manner."

Caelfel rolled her eyes. "Did you study at the college?"

He gave a careless shrug of one shoulder. "I studied there for a short time before I was expelled."

There was a story there, if the casual dismissal was any indication, but Caelfel did not have the chance to ask about it before he changed the subject.

"You realize that if anyone finds out that I'm still alive, or at least if the wrong person discovers the truth, that could mean death for both of us. Do you understand how serious this is?"

She looked at him and his desperately impatient expression a moment before answering. "Someone will find out eventually. Even if your house is tucked away outside the city, you can't hide your existence forever."

"Let's hope that day is so far away from now, it won't implicate you."

"That is rather gallant of you," she remarked derisively.

"You're right, though. It is only a matter of time before someone discovers that I am still alive. When that time comes, I can handle the matter alone. In the meantime, I suppose I shall return your debt by ensuring your safety. Your carelessness has brought danger upon us both."

That stung Caelfel, but she brushed it off. "Why not just leave Sal'Sumarathar? Everyone seems to hate you anyway."

Feraan looked away, and his expression appeared ancient. "I can't leave."

He wouldn't explain why, so Caelfel continued. "Tahlmus knows I took you back from the forest. He's on the Council. If they found out you were alive, he would know I was responsible."

The information angered Feraan. "You let Tahlmus see you?"

"I didn't have much choice," Caelfel said defensively. "He was my hunting partner."

Feraan sighed. "The only thing we can hope for is that my presence remains hidden. Taking me back to the city would mean nothing to them if I died anyway."

"Do you plan to stay locked in your house forever, then?" Caelfel asked. She found slight amusement in his reactions, though perhaps she should take the situation more seriously.

"My plan is to make sure no one sees me," he amended. His eyes lost focus as he mentally engineered some elaborate plan.

"Can I see you?" she asked suddenly.

He gave her a suspicious look. "Do you *want* to come see me?"

"You'll need someone to clean the spot on your back."

Feraan groaned, as if in defeat, and Caelfel inwardly rejoiced over her victory. "Just make sure you aren't being followed."

Caelfel glanced out a window, almost to reassure herself that she wasn't being followed now, and noticed how quickly the sky had darkened. "I should go."

He followed her gaze. "Is there something wrong?"

"No, my parents will just be wondering about me." She pulled her cloak tighter around her shoulders. "Shall I return tomorrow?"

Feraan only offered a blank stare. "Only if you feel it is necessary."

Caelfel thought it was but did not say so as she bid him good night.

She had all but forgotten her entrance exams to the college until she was bombarded with questions upon arriving home. Her parents' questions subsided when she assured them that she had been accepted. Eviat breathed a sigh of relief, but Sylaera only smirked. Her mother's concerns were elsewhere.

"It is dark. Surely they did not keep you at the college so late?" Sylaera asked.

"No," came Caelfel's slow answer. She remembered her promise to Feraan, and struggled to find a suitable reason. "I was visiting a friend. One of the other archers from the hunting party was not accepted. He seemed quite distraught, so I walked him home." Her parents exchanged glances, but the answer satisfied them.

"Thoroth came to visit you," Eviat said later while they were eating.

Caelfel pushed baby leaves around on her plate. "Did he?"

"He wanted to know how your exams went and how well you were faring after yesterday's hunting party," Eviat explained.

Caelfel was suddenly alert. "Did he say anything else?" Thoroth had seen Feraan, so he probably wanted to know what became of the dying elf. Thoroth couldn't know of Feraan's condition either. Caelfel would have to keep it secret from all of them, and the gravity of the ordeal finally seemed to settle on Caelfel. She was not sure how well she could keep secrets.

"He was particularly insistent to see you," Sylaera interjected. Caelfel looked at her beautiful mother and not for the first time in her life, wondered if there was another meaning to her words. With the arrival of this sudden uncertainty, Caelfel was not inclined to respond to her mother. She went to bed that night to dreams filled with daggers and goblins.

***

Dawn came quickly for Caelfel, and she hurried to make it to the college on time. She met other beginner students an hour later as they were admitted inside like a sea of excited whispers. Their classroom contained a great number of benches, and the rows lined the room lengthwise, facing a center pulpit manned by Sir Kennyratear. Caelfel took a seat somewhere in the middle and saw that the left wall was comprised of giant stone columns that exposed the room to the weather outside. The gardens outside were wreathed in early morning mist that curled and danced in slow motion above the ground. Sir Kennyratear called them to their seats and began his lecture.

Caelfel expected her classes would deal with the basics of performing magic, but it soon became apparent that Sir Kennyratear's only concern was with ancient elvish history. His first topic focused on Ewyn, the ancient mother of elves. Her magical powers were passed directly to all of her descendants, to every elf. The elf blood was so powerful it was even present in some half-elves. Her first generation of children allegedly contained some of the most powerful elves. They were famous for conquering the ormr of the Vinus Islands over seven thousand years ago.

A student raised his hand. "What are the ormr?" he asked. Caelfel turned around to see who had asked the question and saw Daerad sitting behind her. She turned quickly to face Sir Kennyratear again.

"The ormr have been extinct since the War of the Firescales. There is the occasional relief painting you'll see of them in the college halls, but they can be described as great flying serpents with impenetrable, protective shells. Otherwise, they are known as dragons."

A murmur of interest rippled through the students.

"It has been said that Ewyn received her power from two enormous diamonds. These diamonds were both called the Eye of Ewyn. One is in Yamalvon. The other resides here in the college, the instrument that measured your auras for the entrance exams. It used to belong to Amasel and was moved here after the city's destruction. Arguably, those two stones are the source of all magic in the world."

"What were the entrance exams here before the Eye was brought to Sal'Sumarathar?" asked the oldest student among them, the she-elf whose aura was tested first.

Sir Kennyratear fixed her with a serious stare. "The Headmaster would attack each student with a number of spells. Their acceptance would depend on how long they could defend themselves." Caelfel thought she preferred the Eye of Ewyn method.

Sir Kennyratear went to continue explaining the original

conquering of the Vinius Islands, a feat completed by a mere five elves. They were the first generation of children Ewyn bore. After the islands were added to make her empire, each of her children went on to found the five major cities of the Fey Forest.

"Her firstborn she named Yamalvon. He led the fight against the ormr and then went on to create our capital. Amasel was next and the oldest daughter, followed by her brother Sal'Sumarathar. Elewyr founded her city near the Latrielle Sea. Can anyone harbor a guess to the youngest of the five?"

Caelfel looked around, knowing of many smaller cities but could only think of the four major ones. The she-elf from before raised her hand. "Rasaen?"

Sir Kennyratear nodded. "Correct. Rasaen is not typically viewed as a large city and in life, its namesake was thought of as Ewyn's weakest child. Rasean is normally depicted as close to one of his older brothers, usually Sal'Sumarathar, which would account for why they are close together geographically."

The same she-elf raised her hand again, and Sir Kennyratear addressed her as Garvanna. "Why did Ewyn not establish the capital herself? What happened to her after the empire was created?" Garvanna asked. Caelfel stared at her, realizing this must have been the friend Thoroth spoke of.

Sir Kennyratear hesitated. "Scholars of Honey Water history still debate over your question today, Garvanna. Some speculate she decided to settle in the Vinius Islands, although there is no indication of her ever being there. There are a great many who believe she gave herself up to fortify the enchantments that protect the Fey Forest. This theory continues to say her residual magic seeped into the bowels of the earth and created the goblins. Another common legend was that Ewyn stepped into the Latrielle Sea to visit her newly conquered land and was swept away by sea foam."

Sir Kennyratear moved on from Ewyn, detailing how the direct descendants of Ewyn formed the noble houses of the Families, one for each city. Caelfel remembered her mother used to belong to the Family of Sal'Sumarathar before they estranged her over some disagreement.

Caelfel raised her hand this time, pausing Sir Kennyratear's lesson with her own question. "Why did the elves conquer the ormr? Why did we attack them in the first place?"

Sir Kennyratear smiled at her question, and Caelfel thought that strange. "The ormr were here long before the elves. They were advanced and powerful. Ewyn and her children saw them as a threat that needed to be taken care of."

Garvanna spoke again, this time without raising her hand. "I had heard that the ormr had attacked various elvish settlements and were preparing for war."

Sir Kennyratear smiled again. "It depends on who you ask."

For the remainder of the day, he had them focusing their auras, instructing them to meditate on protective wards. He said that an elf's aura could be enhanced into a shielding mechanism, but the exercise felt boring and pointless to Caelfel. The benches were cleared from the room, and all the students sat cross-legged on the floor. He wanted them to close their eyes and concentrate but he wouldn't explain what to concentrate on. Caelfel felt as if they were all waiting for something so she kept her eyes open, until she saw Sir Kennyratear staring back at her.

"Eyes closed, Miss Gyssedlues."

So she did, but she opened them again a moment later when a small explosion erupted behind her. To her credit, the rest of the class turned to look as well and saw Daerad flat on his back. It soon became apparent that Sir Kennyratear had attacked him.

"What are you doing?" Daerad demanded, red-faced and scrambling to his feet.

"Before you learn any magic, you must learn to protect yourself from it. Sit down, Master Killelvris."

Daerad sat, and Sir Kennyratear's eyes scanned the room for another target.

"Concentrate," he reminded everyone. He lifted his hand toward Garvanna, and a wave of red flames billowed from his palm toward her. Caelfel flinched when it should have hit the calm she-elf, but Garvanna remained unmoved. The flames parted harmlessly around a transparent, gold bubble that appeared around her. The gold bubble dissipated when Sir Kennyratear stopped his fire. "You have studied magic before, Miss Hunithrae?"

She nodded. "I've been to the College of Yamalvon as well as the College in Amasel, my home before it was destroyed."

"I am not sure what my class could offer you, as you should be a master now," he said.

"I have dedicated myself to study every method of magic that I can."

Sir Kennyratear said no more and turned to the rest of the class. "Everyone should try to achieve what Garvanna has done. She is able to focus her aura into a palpable defense."

He continued with his assault on the rest of them, although Caelfel noted his fire didn't truly harm anyone. When it was Caelfel's turn, she was unsuccessful at blocking his attack and, like many others, was left to rub her smarting face.

By the time class ended, less than a handful of students had been able to accomplish anything with their auras, and Caelfel was not among them. Garvanna remained the only one able to produce a functional shield. Sir Kennyratear dismissed class with the promise that there would be more the next day. Caelfel felt herself anxious to leave the college grounds but instead found herself following someone to the college library.

"Garvanna?" she called tentatively before they reached the doors.

The tall she-elf whirled around instantly, copper hair flying over her shoulder in a frenzied wave. Caelfel felt overwhelmed by her demanding presence, though Garvanna said nothing, waiting with an expectant expression.

"You are Thoroth's friend," she began, uncertain how to voice her question. She wasn't even sure she had one.

"Yes. And who are you?"

Caelfel wouldn't call her tone impatient, but it definitely did not have a welcoming note. "I'm Caelfel. I'm also his friend. I think he wanted us to meet. He told me you would be applying to the college."

Garvanna smiled, but it did not feel at all kind. "Yes, you're the baby."

"I'm sorry?" Caelfel said, confidence shaken.

"You're the youngest, I mean. You were the last one to be tested by the Eye. By the time you started your examination, I was already awake."

Caelfel wasn't sure how to respond to that so she grappled for a subject change. "You studied magic before?"

"Yes, what of it?"

"What was your branch of magic?"

"Branch of magic? I make a point to study all fields, but if you're asking for my *preference*, then that would be Summoning. It's not a well traversed field, but there were many more masters of the art that lived in Amasel." Garvanna faltered at the mention of her home city.

Caelfel tried to be sympathizing. "Did you lose your entire family?" she asked softly.

Garvanna's sharp features turned even sharper. "What sort of question is that? What do you want?"

"I'm sorry. I just wanted to meet you."

"I am not inclined to meet anyone who asks insensitive questions about my family," she snapped.

Caelfel sighed; she rarely got along with moody, temperamental elves. "I did not mean to be insensitive."

"And fools often have the best intentions," Garvanna said, smiling coldly.

Caelfel was at a loss to respond so she merely glared at the she-elf who had probably just called her a fool.

"Excuse me," Garvanna said, continuing to the library.

Caelfel left the college, grumbling. Her mood had soured so much that she did not feel like visiting Feraan. Then Caelfel reminded herself that she had willingly accepted that responsibility so she satisfied herself by entertaining thoughts of putting Garvanna in her place. As is so often the case, she thought of the perfect, clever and scathing responses only after the fact.

"Were you followed?" Feraan waited for her on the branch of a tree that guarded the entrance to his home. Caelfel had to tilt her head to look up at him.

"No," she said, though she had not checked. She had taken the same route through the abandoned alleyway as she had done the previous day. She would remind herself to take a different path tomorrow, one that doubled back to make sure she wasn't being followed.

Feraan jumped down to greet her. "Aren't you cheerful as ever?"

She didn't want to be reminded of Garvanna, so she focused on something else entirely. "How is your back?"

He led the way inside for her to examine his wound in his bedroom. Mostly it had not changed, except that it looked puckered up and swollen. She told him so, reminding him in a disgruntled tone that she was not a healer.

"Must I conjure the image again for you again?" he replied.

"No," she said gruffly.

Feraan remained absolutely patient with her as he talked her through the lancing, the draining, and finally the cleaning. His voice soothed her nerves. His reaction to the pain was minimal, and though Caelfel was sure he restrained himself for her sake, she appreciated it.

It did not take long for her to wrap new bandages around him. She stared at her hands as she tied the ends together. Feraan slipped his shirt back on.

"Can you tell me how to use my aura?" she blurted out suddenly.

He did not give her a strange look like she expected. For that matter, he didn't look at her at all. "Problems on your first day?" he assumed.

"Yes, I can't get my aura to work." She followed him to the front room of his house where he sat down and leaned back in his chair.

"Most people don't accomplish that on their first day."

"Can you teach me?" she asked.

"It's not something that someone can teach you. You have to learn it on your own."

"Then what is the point of Sir Kennyratear teaching us?"

"The college teaches you how to control the aura, not how to call upon it specifically. They can prompt you to use it instinctively to protect yourself if you believe you are in danger."

"Could you help me trigger it?"

Feraan considered her question. "I may be able to do that with my aura. It might come as a shock to you, which is why the college no longer employs that method of activating an elf's aura."

"What sort of shock do you mean?"

"It varies. For some, it can produce a simple, mild shock. For others, it could knock them back quite a bit."

"Can we try it?" Caelfel asked eagerly.

"No."

"Why not?"

"It has the possibility of being quite painful for you."

"But it won't kill me?" she affirmed.

"You're talking as though I would actually consider this. I am sorry but I won't. It will come to you in time at the college."

Caelfel sighed, suddenly finding herself very impatient. "How long did it take for you to figure it out?"

"Not as long as I'm sure it will take you."

Caelfel frowned. "I appreciate your vote of confidence. I haven't produced anything with my aura. Garvanna could form an entire shield."

"Garvanna?" he repeated, sounding as if he recognized the name. "If you mean Garvanna from Amasel, then you should know she already mastered the use of her aura at Yamalvon."

"How do you know Garvanna?" Caelfel asked, curiosity piqued.

"In a way, we grew up together. Is she still as pleasant to be around as I remember?" Feraan asked.

Caelfel folded her arms, not missing his sarcasm. "If by 'pleasant' you mean 'insufferable,' then you will be glad to know she hasn't much changed."

Feraan made a low whistle. "I can only imagine what she has done to offend you."

"She called me a baby and a fool."

Feraan stood up and began searching through his shelves. "Look where the insult came from."

"She walks around like she knows everything. How is that supposed to make me feel better?"

Feraan turned to face Caelfel, a book in his hands. "She is almost as old as I am with the temper of a child. There is no wonder why she is still alone."

"You are older than her and more alone than she is," Caelfel pointed out.

Feraan's mouth twitched into what Caelfel could only name as a smile but it didn't reach his eyes. "Correction. I *choose* to be alone yet I am popular enough for everyone to want me dead."

"I don't want you dead," Caelfel said quietly.

His smile faltered, and Feraan broke her gaze to look at the book in his hands. "Read this and you'll have a better understanding of what Sir Kennyratear wants you to do," he said, handing it to her.

"What is it?" she asked.

"A book," he told her, prompting Caelfel to roll her eyes at him.

She prepared to leave, and Feraan reminded her again to make sure she wasn't being followed. Caelfel waved off his concerns though she did wonder who would be following her. She elected to take a different route home and glanced frequently over her shoulder the entire way. By the time she reached home, the sky had turned a fiery color. Her mother was there to greet her before she even stepped through the door.

"Where have you been?" Sylaera asked. Her tone did not suggest suspicion, so Caelfel forced her shoulders to relax.

"I was at the college. Where is Father?" she asked mildly.

Sylaera stepped slightly to the side to let her daughter to pass. "He went to visit your teacher Sir Kennyratear."

"That's right. They are friends," Caelfel said, forcing a casual tone. She threw a last glance over her shoulder before closing the door behind her.

"Don't look so nervous. I'm sure your classes are going fine," Sylaera said, inaccurately guessing the source of Caelfel's anxiety. "Besides, someone came to visit you."

Caelfel looked around and only then noticed Thoroth standing in the room. He had called on her yesterday too, she remembered. Her mouth went dry, and Caelfel found she could not greet him.

"Caelfel," he said, greeting her instead. "How are things?"

Sylaera left the room, but Caelfel did not feel more at ease with the healer. She knew he was wanting to ask about Feraan and she was not sure if she could lie about what happened.

"Fine," Caelfel finally answered at length. "Things are fine. I was accepted at the college and I have met Garvanna."

At the mention of his friend, Thoroth became distracted. "Did you? She never said anything."

Caelfel seized the subject change. "I suspect she wouldn't have. She is not very pleasant company to keep."

"She does have trouble making new friends," Thoroth agreed reluctantly.

"I wasn't under the impression she wanted new friends. She made it rather clear she wasn't interested in *fools* or *babies*," Caelfel snapped.

Thoroth sighed in a way that made Caelfel think this wasn't abnormal behavior for Garvanna. "I'm sorry if she offended you, but don't be cross with me. There's something I wanted to ask you."

Caelfel turned her back and left for the garden. Thoroth kept up with her, waiting until they were outside before addressing his concerns.

"Where is Feraan?" he asked.

She slowly lowered herself onto a bench, the same one she had kept the wounded Feraan on. Her eyes fell on the book in her lap, and she hoped Thoroth would not recognize it as Feraan's. "I think you know where he is," she hedged carefully.

"Is he alive?" Thoroth tried again. Caelfel detected a tone of panic in the healer's voice.

"I don't see how he would be. No one would save him, and I definitely didn't have the ability or knowledge to save him."

"After you left my house, where did you take him? Did you perform any death rites?"

"I don't know how to perform a death rite."

"Where did you take him?" Thoroth repeated harshly.

"I took him home."

"You took him here?" Thoroth asked.

"I took Feraan to his home."

Thoroth's eyes widened. "How do you know where that is?"

Caelfel's throat tightened, and she clenched her jaw. "Why are you asking me about Feraan?"

He sighed. "The Council is doing an investigation. He was reported dead, and then they couldn't find his body. They started asking all the healers."

Caelfel felt a wave of panic freeze her entire body. Out of the healers, Awen Baeltylar and Thoroth knew who had Feraan. Tahlmus, who was on the council, had seen Caelfel with Feraan's body. "What did you tell them?" Caelfel asked in a hollow voice.

"It was only the Chief Executor—"

"Who?"

"Markis Rilynnzea. He was Feraan's hunting partner that day. He reported Feraan as dead."

"What did you tell him?" Caelfel repeated.

"I said nothing about you."

"What did you say about Feraan?"

Thoroth shook his head. "I need to know what you did with him. I have to turn in the body to the Council."

"*What did you tell him?*" Caelfel asked. Her heart hammered painfully in her chest. She looked around for a spy or an eavesdropper in the garden. She saw none, but still her stomach rolled with a sick feeling.

"I told him that I had taken care of the body that someone had left on my doorstep. I assume he is dead now, killed by poison?"

Caelfel looked straight through Thoroth. This Markis hadn't spoken to the Council. Otherwise, he would have come to her first. Meanwhile, Thoroth claimed her actions as his own, an act Caelfel could not fathom. For that matter, Markis could be following him at that very moment. "I need you to leave," Caelfel told him quietly.

Thoroth appeared stunned, almost hurt. "What about the body?"

"I don't have anything to give you."

"Markis could arrest me, Caelfel." Thoroth's panic returned

"Then tell them it was me. They'll find out soon enough."

Horror flashed through his face. "What have you done?"

She sighed, thinking perhaps Feraan's previous paranoia was not misplaced. "I tried saving his life," she informed Thoroth slowly.

"You tried saving *Feraan's* life?" he hissed. "You must have seen the Royal Decree I was given. I saw you taking it."

"I did see. Now you must leave."

Thoroth's shoulders sagged. "Caelfel, I do not think that you realize—"

"I know what I'm doing, Thoroth."

The healer sighed, and it was a sound of defeat. "I hope that is true. Please, if you need anything, come find me."

He left, but Caelfel did not see him to the door. She remained where she was in the dark garden. The sun had vanished below the horizon during Thoroth's visit, but Caelfel continued staring into the distance, as if expecting someone to be hidden and watching her. She was at a loss for what to do next. Perhaps Markis had followed Thoroth to her home and he was watching her now.

Whether or not she was being watched, Caelfel did not have many options. She could warn Feraan, but that would be careless if someone was following her to investigate his death. It would risk leading Markis or anyone else right to Feraan. Otherwise, Caelfel could wait through the night until something happened.

And so she did, locking herself in her bedroom until morning.

4. Feraan's Dream

Feraan rarely dreamed, so when he did, he was quite conscious of it. The forest around him was too bright and too blue for the late hour. The air was too sweet and the creatures too silent.

And there was music, elven on a human instrument. It was a combination he had not heard in centuries. Trees did not play such music.

And an orb of bright blue light danced around the trees. Its light fluctuated with the music, dimming then shining brightly with each rise and fall of the dynamics. As Feraan drew closer, the light assumed the shape of a miniature she-elf, only a few inches tall. The identity of the apparition was easy to discern, as he had seen her just that day.

The figure of light moved further into the trees, bidding for him to follow, and as the way of dreamrealms, he had no choice but to obey, entranced by her alluring dance. She floated around the trunks of trees and through the low-hanging branches. Feraan followed and listened as the music swelled with voices chanting ancient phrases of sorrow and weeping. Voices cut across the composition in long phrases that added to the melancholy. They were the mournful sounds of a lament.

As the volume of the music increased, so did the height of the she-elf apparition until she retained her normal height. She broke past the treeline and turned around on the surface of a lake. Feraan stood motionless on the shore and watched as the intricacies of her movements matched the growing complexity of the melody. Then he felt an urge, a slight urge to join her in this dance and since it was a dream, he gave in to it before he could allow himself a chance to resist.

The music grew louder, and Feraan found himself dancing with a ghostly, transparent version of the one who had saved him from the forest.

There is a great evil brewing in your forest.

The Blind Seer's warning echoed faintly in his mind. Feraan focused on the faint features of the face before him. Caelfel couldn't be the evil Sibylla spoke of.

They continued their dance, and he lifted her by the waist at the appropriate rise in the music. Feraan gave little thought to the impossibility of walking on the water. It was a dream after all.

Bring the one responsible.

A bellowing bass cut across the tragic composition, and she twisted out of his grasp to the lake's center. She started spinning, slowly at first then faster and faster until she was a glowing blur. Feraan was stunned motionless. He wanted to call out to the Blind Seer that spoke in his head, but he was too enamored by the specter before him.

"Who is responsible?" he asked in a muted voice.

Caelfel continued spinning. He caught a glimpse of her arms lifting above her head and a bow materializing in her hands. At the penultimate moment, she stopped moving and fired a single, translucent arrow that flew through his chest.

The music stopped, and silence followed. Feraan looked down to see a red stain spreading on his chest.

"Who are you?" he asked.

She merely smiled.

He knew who she was. *The Archer of the Lake.*

***

The dream returned with subtle variations and plagued Feraan throughout the night. He gave up on sleep some time before dawn and started rifling through his books. He had not done much research on prophetic dreams, usually dismissing it as folly, but the image of Caelfel on her lake with the Blind Seer's voice troubled him. He had not seen or heard from the Blind Seer in over eighty years. She had charged him with a task that he had only partially completed.

He wondered if the dream was a signal telling him that time was running out. He knew Caelfel could not be the person the Blind Seer meant, since Caelfel was less than eighty years old. Maybe the dream was warning him about Caelfel. She could be in danger or she might be a danger to him.

Or perhaps the dream was simply a conglomerate of experiences he had focused on recently, meaning nothing prophetic or mystical at all. Still, he knew his nerves wouldn't settle until he had seen Caelfel for himself. She would be at the college for most of the day before she came for her visit. Feraan kept time throughout the day, frequently watching out his window for her approach. He expected her around midafternoon and had a rather difficult time keeping himself distracted.

He tried continuing his research on the target the Blind Seer had assigned him, but the past eighty years had provided him with very little results. Feraan doubted he could solve the problem of parasitic energy in less than a day so he changed his focus, tossing aside old maps of goblin tunnels. He couldn't leave his house and risk exposure but he did brave to go as far as his garden, gathering all his blades for routine sharpening.

A small forge sat in the corner of his garden. It came complete with a grindstone and a smaller whetstone with a large barrel of the necessary oil. He lined up all his weapons and set to work with slow and practiced hands. His eyes always strayed to his front door which was visible from his forge. He forced himself to work even slower.

Noon came and went, drifting to afternoon. The trees kept time as their shadows traveled imperceptibly across the garden. Sharpening swords and daggers did not occupy enough time, so Feraan resorted to pacing, not really understanding why he was nervous. Eventually, he settled on practicing his alchemy. His supply of medicine was running low, especially after he had given Caelfel an entire bottle.

Boiling the necessary leaves was a process that required two hours of close attention. Feraan decided to boil the rest of his stores, which divided into two separate boiling batches. Four hours later, Feraan had an obscene amount of boiled leaves, and Caelfel still had not appeared. By then, the sky had turned pink with dusk. Feraan paced some more. He didn't recall Caelfel specifically promising to visit that day. He just assumed that she would. Perhaps she went straight home after her class.

Feraan held all of his tension in his back, and the irritated wound there bothered him even more. Caelfel could be perfectly safe but then again, she might not be. Someone might have discovered her crime. Tahlmus or Thoroth would have easily given her away. He had to find out what happened to her.

He threw on his black, hooded poncho that Lycaon had given him over twenty years ago and left his house just like he had sworn he wouldn't do.

Feraan had had his own training as a tracker, and a quick scan of the surroundings told him that he was alone. At least no one else had discovered his home yet. He remembered where the Gyssedlues house was, but the route he took double backed on itself several times, a precautionary measure to assure himself that he was not being followed. Once he was certain that he was indeed alone, Feraan made his way straight to the Gyssedlues household. He looked down both sides of the street as he approached their front door. Then he knocked.

Feraan started wondering if he was merely being paranoid. Caelfel had only been gone for a day. But then Sylaera answered the door, and Feraan knew something was wrong from her anxious expression.

"Is Caelfel here?" he asked her. It would be annoying to reveal himself to her parents for nothing.

Sylaera glanced at someone inside. "No."

Feraan blinked and waited only a fraction of a second for an explanation. "Where is she?"

Sylaera fixed him with a hard glare, in no mood for his impatience. "Caelfel has been arrested. She will stand trial tomorrow morning. Would you like to come inside?"

Feraan stepped inside and saw Eviat in the room. "What happened?" Feraan asked.

Eviat answered, "Markis came to arrest Caelfel and Thoroth for the crimes of necromancy and treason."

"Necromancy and treason?" Feraan repeated.

"Apparently, you were reported dead. Caelfel and Thoroth are suspected necromancers since they raised you from the dead, which is an act of treason," Eviat explained.

Feraan looked between Caelfel's parents. "Do you believe that?"

Sylaera folded her arms. "I think I would know if my daughter was a necromancer."

"They can't be taking these charges seriously. Caelfel can't even perform magic, much less necromancy."

Eviat and Sylaera exchanged glances, clearly surprised Feraan spoke of their daughter with such familiarity. Eviat spoke. "According to Markis, you had been listed as dead. When they went searching for your body, they couldn't find it. They started asking healers. The Baeltylars said Caelfel was the one to take your body. Then Thoroth confessed he was responsible. They were both arrested. What really happened?"

Feraan sighed, feeling strange having to explain things to Caelfel's parents. "I wasn't dead. I almost died, but Caelfel decided to save me."

"She didn't say anything to us about that," Sylaera said.

"I asked her to keep the incident a secret, particularly since it was a failed assassination attempt."

Sylaera stepped closer to Feraan. "And I suppose you thought it was a good idea to drag my daughter into this?" she hissed.

Feraan clenched his jaw. "I didn't drag her into this. Caelfel made this decision on her own."

"And now she is in some prison cell like a criminal." Although Sylaera struggled to remain composed, her aura betrayed her anger. There was a moment when Sylaera was surrounded in crackling blue fire before she returned to normal. Eviat placed a hand on his wife's shoulder at the sign of her temper. Sylaera calmed instantly.

"We all know what this is really about," Eviat said, maintaining eye contact between Feraan and Sylaera. "You could present yourself to the Council at her trial to show that you're not dead."

"I can't do that," Feraan said, crossing his arms. "As I said, this was a failed assassination attempt. I can't afford to reveal myself to the Council or Markis."

The blue fire flickered around Sylaera again. "You mean it's either you or my daughter?"

"I didn't ask her to save me," Feraan defended in a tight voice.

"But without her, you would be dead. Isn't that right?" Sylaera pointed out.

"She should have been smart and kept it secret. What did she expect to gain from saving the most hated elf of the empire?"

Sylaera's anger dimmed as she turned an uncertain glance on her husband. Feraan didn't miss the exchange. He wondered what he just said that had made the fierce mother bear withdraw.

"You haven't told her why," he guessed at length. He ran a hand through his hair with a humorless chuckle. "You never told Caelfel how she was born or how the infamous Feraan Auvrearaheal earned his reputation."

"Isn't that what you wanted?" Eviat countered.

Feraan didn't have an answer for that so he sighed and paced the room instead. "What do we do about the trial?" he asked.

Sylaera chose her next words slowly. "If Caelfel is found guilty of treason, they will execute her. If she is found guilty of necromancy, they will execute her."

"I won't let that happen," Feraan said in a voice that left no room for debate.

"How?" Sylaera persisted.

"We prove she is innocent," Feraan decided, still pacing.

"No, she has to prove her own innocence. Only Thoroth and Caelfel will be able to speak for their defense."

"I'm still confused about why Thoroth was arrested," said Feraan.

"They consider him the consulting physician. He admitted to being responsible for your death rites before they arrested Caelfel," Eviat said.

Feraan's expression remained blank. He glanced toward Sylaera for an explanation. "I still don't understand why he would volunteer to do something as stupid as confessing to treason."

There was something deviously smug about Sylaera when she answered. "I am under the impression that Thoroth is rather fond of Caelfel."

Feraan felt as though he should suppress the disgusted glare that came to his face, but he didn't. "Perhaps Thoroth is so fond of her that he will take all blame for the crime," he muttered under his breath.

"Please," Eviat said, stepping between them. "This isn't helping. Why did you come here in the first place?"

"My instinct told me something was wrong," Feraan answered carefully.

"And you at least cared about her enough to visit?" Eviat pressed.

Feraan frowned. "I do feel as though I owe something to her for the trouble."

"Then help her. How is Caelfel supposed to defend herself if the Council turns saving someone's life into necromancy?" Eviat asked.

"It's only necromancy if the Council doesn't like the person," Sylaera pointed out.

Feraan let loose a large breath, thinking. "Is there any way we could see Caelfel before the trial?"

"They are going to let Eviat and I into her cell tomorrow morning, before the Council sees her," Sylaera said. "We're supposed to prepare her for the trial."

"Just the two of you? No other visitors?" Feraan asked.

"Would you like to visit her?" Sylaera asked with something of a derisive scoff.

"I would prefer that," he shot back evenly. "And I need to see her tonight."

"The Council will not allow it. Besides, you won't even show your face in court. Why would you even risk facing her guards?" Sylaera asked.

"If you want my help protecting your daughter, you will have to trust me."

Eviat left shortly afterward to see if Caelfel would be permitted any visitors that night. When Eviat was gone, Feraan asked Sylaera to see Caelfel's bedroom, wanting to find the book he had given her. She reluctantly showed it to him.

Caelfel's bed was significantly smaller than his own. It sat beneath a tall, glass-paned window and was surrounded by sheer, white curtains. She didn't keep very many possessions. Books were placed neatly on the shelves that had been carved into the walls. A wardrobe stood against the far wall. The left-hand wall held racks dedicated to her weaponry. It was apparent that Caelfel obsessed over organizing her arrows. They were grouped according to the feathers they were fletched with. Her bow hung on its appropriate hook above them. A small shelf jutted from the wall just below that, bearing a dagger that looked to be more ornamental than practical.

He slowly lowered himself to sit on Caelfel's bed. The book next to her pillow caught his attention. He picked it up and saw it was the one he had given her the day before. He thumbed through it, looking for a specific page.

The book detailed a single theory on the Ewyn creation myth. It narrated Ewyn's efforts to establish the original elvish kingdom before it became an empire. Ewyn prided herself on the species she had created, claiming that they were more powerful and more beautiful than any other race, as well as vastly more intelligent and gifted with longevity. The elves had a flaw though, a problem that proved almost impossible to track genetically. A large percentage of elves were infertile.

Because of this, Ewyn recognized the need to preserve the safety of her people. Violence had been inherently discouraged among elves, and isolation protected elves from interfering in the military affairs of their neighboring lands. But Ewyn was most noted for treasuring the sacred, elvish life. The life debt was born, an unspoken agreement between two elves. If an elf saved the life of another elf, then the second elf was honor bound to return the favor if the need arose.

Because Caelfel had saved Feraan from certain death, he was in her life debt. And that would protect Caelfel in her trial.

***

Caelfel hadn't realized sitting in a prison cell would be so boring. She easily remembered the terror she had felt hours before when Markis had arrested her on her way to the college that morning. It was inevitable and not shocking, but Markis was a frightening elf. He had a wild, untamed air about him that suggested a roguish nature. What was most unusual, Caelfel thought, was that he had decorated his face with silver paint. She didn't understand it but felt it made Markis look that much more sadistic.

But that was hours ago. Her initial fear had ebbed, quickly replaced with boredom. She shared a prison cell with Thoroth who was already there when she arrived. He had attempted to speak to her, but Caelfel had spurned his desire for conversation or explanation. She preferred sulking in silence, even if it was boring.

Their cell had three solid walls, and a fourth wall of metal bars that made up the gate that locked them in. Through the bars, Caelfel and Thoroth could see the forest, as well as the guards that flanked their cell. The chilly evening made their cell drafty.

There was only one bench in their cell, and when it grew dark, Thoroth immediately elected to sleep on the ground. Caelfel didn't argue with him and remained silently on the bench with her knees drawn up to her chin. After a while, she felt her mind go hazy as she struggled to keep her eyes open. At some point in the night, she heard the guards talking, but when she pried her eyes open, she didn't see anyone.

Her eyes had closed again, when one of the guards spoke to her. "Your parents are here to see you."

Caelfel started and felt disoriented when she saw it was still dark. Her parents were not supposed to be coming until morning.

"Please approach the gate," the same guard ordered firmly. Caelfel stood and did as she was told. Thoroth sat up, wide awake at the hint of visitors. The guard told him to stay where he was.

Caelfel stepped closer to the bars, seeing two figures standing just outside her cell, her parents. The slighter of the two drew closer, revealing her mother's nervous face.

"Mother?" Caelfel whispered in the darkness. "What are you doing here? I thought you weren't coming until morning."

Sylaera glanced at the other figure behind her. "Your father and I wanted to make sure you were all right."

Caelfel turned to the figure of her father, squinting through the darkness. "I am," she answered. "Was there anything else?"

It was not until when Sylaera glanced behind her again that Caelfel noticed something out of place. Even standing a few feet away, her father looked too tall.

"Who is that?" Caelfel asked.

Sylaera gave Caelfel a pointed look and offered a weak smile. "Don't you recognize your father? He's come to give you something."

At this, the second figure stepped forward with something in his hands. He discreetly passed it through the bars, and Caelfel saw that the hands were certainly not her father's. She tried to see through the gloom to identify the stranger, but his hood cast the unknown elf's features in deep shadow. Caelfel took the parcel handed to her, and he stepped back before Caelfel's eyes could adjust to the darkness. Sylaera reached through the bars in his absence to stroke Caelfel's cheek.

"Be safe, my daughter," Sylaera whispered before backing away from her cell.

"I don't understand—" she tried calling out, but they were already gone.

She stayed by the bars for a few minutes, using the moonlight to see the gift they had brought her. It was a book, and further inspection proved that it was the book Feraan had given her the previous day. She hadn't told her parents about it, so she speculated that it was Feraan that had visited her in Eviat's stead. He certainly had the correct height. She flipped through the pages anxiously, wondering if there was some hidden message that would help her. Surely Feraan would give her this book for a reason, but as she scanned the pages, all she could read was the creation myth of Ewyn. She had already learned that from Sir Kennyratear.

She sighed and returned to her bench. Caelfel waited until she heard Thoroth's airy snores before continuing her search through the book's pages. Another inspection revealed nothing new, so Caelfel balanced the book on its spine and waited for it to fall open to a random page. She started reading there.

It detailed a story about Ewyn's fourth child, Elewyr. Elewyr loved the sea and the city named for her was a beautiful port. A sailor came to her city one day, visiting from faraway lands. Like Elewyr, he also had a love for the ocean. He called himself Sidhe. Elewyr fell in love with his free spirit and sense of adventure, and Sidhe fell in love with Elewyr's beauty which was comparable even to her mother's. The story went on to say that Elewyr's beauty made many people jealous. There were many attempts on her life because of it. On one particular incident, Elewyr had been attacked by remnants of the resistance from the Vinius Islands. Sidhe saved her life, and there was a great celebration held in his favor. Elewyr granted him many gifts and royal titles. They were to be married.

However before their ceremony, there were many disagreements among Ewyn's children. Yamalvon did not want his sister to marry Sidhe, who was a foreigner who was neither human nor elf. Yamalvon considered Sidhe inferior and unworthy of his beautiful sister. As such, Yamalvon sent assassins to eliminate Sidhe.

Sidhe fended off his assassins well, but there was a moment when he became overwhelmed. Elewyr threw herself in front of Sidhe's attackers, and they killed her.

Sidhe fled the Fey Forest, taking refuge in Umfang. Whatever his race was, he also had the gift of longevity because nearly a century later, he commented on the occurrence. Someone asked him about the depth of Elewyr's devotion for him.

Sidhe responded, "She admired me. She never loved *me*. She sacrificed her life for my sake because of a debt."

Caelfel noticed that Sidhe's quote had been circled with dark ink. She instantly knew Sidhe referred to the life debt. Caelfel leaned her head back on the cold, stone wall.

"Life debt," she repeated to herself under her breath.

5. Trial

Caelfel didn't sleep for the rest of the night, preferring, instead, to remain conscious through the excruciatingly long hours before daybreak. When her mother returned at sunrise, one of the guards escorted Thoroth away to allow them privacy. Sylaera came alone.

"Where is Father?" Caelfel asked.

"He's already in the Hall of Court, waiting for your trial to begin."

"Did Feraan risk coming here for my trial?" Caelfel whispered, eyeing the other guard outside.

Sylaera met Caelfel's gaze and said nothing. Instead, Sylaera gave a slight, nearly imperceptible bob of her head, affirming Caelfel's suspicions. Then she turned her attention to the dress she had brought.

The bodice and skirt were made of azure blue velvet. The sleeves came from a separate chemise that her mother explained was spyder silk. Sylaera helped Caelfel to put it on, tightening the corset as Caelfel tugged at the sleeves.

"Stop that," Sylaera reprimanded. "I worked on this dress all night so I will not have you ruin it with your stubborn distaste for dressing like a lady."

"Sorry," Caelfel muttered.

When she finished with the corset, Sylaera pulled out a swan feather to tie into her hair. "I know how much you like feathers."

Sylaera paused, as if waiting for some response from Caelfel, but Caelfel said nothing.

"You're nervous about the trial," Sylaera guessed.

"You think so?" Caelfel asked. Her sarcasm fell flat.

"If you are innocent, they should have nothing to convict you for."

"Innocent by whose standards, Mother?"

"You know you've done nothing wrong."

"The Council says I've committed treason."

"Then the Council is wrong," Mother answered simply.

"I'm not sure how that's supposed to save me from an execution."

Sylaera turned around to look her seriously in the eye. "You will not be executed," she told Caelfel severely.

Sylaera's tone offered little room for disagreement, so Caelfel permitted herself to believe her mother's words. She gave Sylaera the book on Ewyn and Elewyr. "Here. I don't think the guards would be happy to discover I've had this," she whispered.

Sylaera took it, wrapping it with her weather cloak. "Did it help?" she whispered back.

"It gave me an idea."

Seeing that Caelfel was dressed, her remaining guard turned impatient to usher Sylaera away. Then he escorted Caelfel to the Hall of Court.

It wasn't an actual building. The walls were merely cherry saplings that surrounded the floor space. There was a marble bench at the end that seated all five Councilors. Audience seats were fashioned out of overgrown roots. As Caelfel walked the long aisle, she saw Thoroth was already there, dressed in a tunic of green velvet. Her guard stopped her when they reached the healer and turned around to fasten bronze cuffs around her wrists. A chain ran from the cuffs to a ring solidly embedded in the ground.

"Hey!" Caelfel gasped when he tightened them.

"A precautionary measure for necromancers," was the only explanation the guard gave. Caelfel saw that Thoroth was similarly chained. Silence fell in the Hall of Court.

"Caelfel Gyssedlues and Thoroth Orletylar," said Head Councilor Uthruil, who was also Daerad's father. "The two of you have been brought before the Council accused of the crime of necromancy. Miss Gyssedlues, how do you plead?"

Caelfel steeled herself with a short breath. An urge came to look at the elves seated behind her, but she suppressed it. She kept her eyes on Councilor Uthruil instead. "To necromancy? Not guilty."

The Head Councilor marked something on his paper before

transferring his gaze to Thoroth. "How do you plead, Master Orletylar?"

Thoroth glanced towards Caelfel to meet her steely gaze. "Not guilty," he said, looking back to Uthruil.

Councilor Uthruil sighed. "This presents a problem. I will narrate the sequence of events, regarding the death of Master Auvrearaheal, and then each of you shall have an opportunity to present your own case. Understand?"

Caelfel glared at Uthruil and hoped that Thoroth's features mirrored her expression.

When they said nothing, he continued, "Feraan Auvrearheal was accounted for during the last hunting party, involving our retaliation with the goblins. Upon the return of the party, his hunting partner Sir Markis Rilynnzea reported him as deceased. When officials went to retrieve the body, it was found missing. Our investigation led us to question the healers of Sal'Sumarathar for his whereabouts. One healer, Master Orletylar, claimed under oath the body had been brought to him for last rites. When he failed to provide a body, Master Rilynnzea's investigation concluded that this was false. Lady Awen Baeltylar testified that the body of Feraan Auvrearaheal was brought to her home by one Caelfel Gyssedlues. Is this correct?"

Uthruil paused for their answer, and Caelfel glanced at Thoroth uncertainly. There were flaws and truths to his story, and Caelfel could not wholly confirm it. "I don't—"

"Miss Gyssedlues, was that correct or not?" Uthruil repeated firmly at her hesitation.

"Is what part of it correct, exactly?" Caelfel asked, clenching her jaw.

"It is an observation of events following the incident of Master Auvrearaheal's death."

"It is not a completely correct observation," Caelfel countered. She hoped she appeared menacing to the Councilor, but Uthruil continued as if unconcerned with her dissent.

"Upon receiving the information from Awen Baeltylar and after collecting several eye witness statements confirming the animated state of Feraan Auvrearaheal after his death, the Council sent Chief Executor Rilynnzea to arrest the two of you under suspicion of necromancy."

"We are not necromancers," Caelfel insisted stubbornly.

"Is Feraan Auvrearaheal currently alive?" Uthruil asked.

"Yes—"

"Then it must be a result of necromancy, after the report of his death from our Chief Executor and the confirmation made by Healer Orletylar."

"*He wasn't dead,*" Caelfel hissed, feeling her face grow red.

Uthruil grew silent at the outburst and his eyes bored into Caelfel. "You have two accounts that disagree with you, Miss Gyssedlues, both of whom have a higher form of integrity with the Council."

"The Council asked me to attend the same hunting party, yes? I was there when Feraan Auvrearaheal was attacked."

Uthruil arched an eyebrow and consulted a book he had before him. "The list indicates you were with a separate division for the confrontation with the goblins."

"At the end of the *confrontation*, I was asked to eliminate any goblin survivors along with an elf named Winwaloe. During my search, I came across Feraan, fully conscious and alive. There was a moment when I was attacked by another goblin, and by the time I looked up, Feraan was on the ground, unconscious."

"Dead?" Uthruil asked.

"No, he was still very much alive. I did not see any sign of his hunting partner, so I took him back to Sal'Sumarathar with me to find help for him."

"And this was when you came across Awen Baelytlar?"

"Yes."

"And she refused her service?" Uthruil continued, as if this did not surprise him.

Caelfel sighed through her nose. "Yes."

"So then you proceeded to the dwelling of Master Orletylar?"

"Right."

"Then Master Orletylar confirmed his death."

"No, Thoroth saw he was alive." She looked to the healer desperately. "Tell him, Thoroth."

Uthruil turned to Thoroth who sighed. "It is true. Although unconscious, Feraan Auvrearahel was still alive. He suffered from a wound on his back."

Uthruil suddenly looked very angry and shifted his weight in his seat. "This only gives you an unreliable witness, an elf who claims one thing a few days ago and then admits the opposite now."

Caelfel angled her face to him. "If you would like another reliable witness, just look to your left, Councilor." Caelfel pointed, with chains rattling, to the Councilor sitting next to Uthruil. It was Tahlmus, her hunting partner, who, with all attention focused on him, suddenly appeared very anxious.

"Explain yourself, Miss Gyssedlues."

"Tahlmus was my hunting partner. He was there when I found Feraan. He knew Feraan was alive."

"I saw he was on the ground," Tahlmus defended hastily. "I did not see if he was alive."

"You told me to leave him! You told me he was better off dead!" Caelfel spat, her voice rising dangerously.

"I said he was already dead, and there was nothing you could do," Tahlmus shot back.

Everything grew silent, and Caelfel became acutely aware of her heavy breathing. She pressed her lips together to silence herself as she waited for Uthruil's response. The Head Councilor took his time, considering the two convicted necromancers before him.

Finally, he turned to Tahlmus. "Councilor Tahlmus, I must ask you to leave the Hall of Court at once."

Tahlmus looked as though as he was about to argue, but Uthruil's expression forbade any sort of retort from the veteran, who left without a word. Everyone was silent after Tahlmus was dismissed, so Uthruil returned to asking questions.

"Master Orletylar, would you please relate to the Council your diagnosis of Master Auvrearaheal after Miss Gyssedlues delivered him to your door?"

Thoroth was visibly nervous, but when he spoke, it was in a clear voice. "Miss Gyssedlues brought the patient to my dwelling, and I performed a simple examination. Master Auvrearaheal had received an injury to his back. Further inspection showed that the wound had been inflicted by an arrow."

"Is this all your diagnosis yielded?"

"No, the patient had also been poisoned with the arrow."

"Miss Gyssedlues, since you claim to have been present during Master Auvrearaheal's attack, you were able to identify his attacker, I presume?"

Caelfel took a deep breath, remembering. She had only seen a flurry of movement before falling to the ground. "No, I was attacked by a goblin."

"So the great Feraan Auvrearaheal was taken down by a goblin, of all things."

Caelfel pressed her mouth together. She did not think Feraan had been bested by a goblin. "Councilor, I was there when Feraan was conscious, I was there when he was attacked, and I was there afterwards. You said Markis had reported him dead? But I did not see Markis there at all."

From the corner of her eye, Caelfel saw someone shrug themselves off the wall and approach the raised dais. A glance told her it was the Chief Executor with the renowned silver markings on his face. He approached her with the slippery stealth of a snake, and she couldn't help but associate him with a deceptive serpent, the paint on his face glinting like scales. He stared at Caelfel with unnerving, wild eyes. She wanted to stop looking at him but was afraid to do so.

"Sir Markis? What is your response to this allegation?"

"I saw the attack," Markis explained in a smooth voice, his back still turned to the Council as he continued staring at Caelfel intently. "Even from a distance, it was evident that Master Feraan would not survive the incident, so I hurried for aid. Miss Gyssedlues must not have seen me." His cheek twitched as he leaned closer to Caelfel, whispering only for her to hear, "I must have missed you somehow."

Caelfel's body went very cold even after Markis backed away to return to his position on the wall. She balled her hands into fists to keep them from shaking, and the trial continued as if nothing had happened, the others in the room completely oblivious to the waves of terror Markis had sent coursing down Caelfel's spine.

"Feraan Auvrearaheal was poisoned, and as we all know, there is no longer an antidote for such a thing. Nothing could have saved him," Uthruil said. "Master Orletylar already informed us of your attempt to get rid of the body. If you insist he is alive, then by all accounts, you must be a necromancer."

"But that was a lie," Caelfel insisted, struggling to keep her voice from shaking. "Feraan never died. Thoroth was unable to save him, so I took Feraan home with me. *I* saved him."

The other Councilors exchanged expressions of confusion, but Uthruil never wavered. "Miss Gyssedlues, I'm rather uncertain of the details. How could you possibly cure the poison in his body?"

"I never completely cured it. I had a protection amulet, given to me by my mother when I was a youngling. It has several magical properties, one being resistance to poison. I gave that to him," Caelfel admitted begrudgingly. She was reluctant to reveal her methods to the Council who were so eager to have Feraan murdered. Divulging the existence of her amulet would only expose Feraan's weakness to them.

The Councilors shared their surprise with each other. "Where did your mother receive such an amulet?" Uthruil asked.

"My mother was Sylaera Ambrosius before she married. She was a member of the Sal'Sumarathar Family. The amulet was an heirloom given to her before she married my father."

Uthruil rose to his feet, a new intrigue to his features. "May we see this amulet?"

Caelfel shook her head, feeling more confident since the accusations had left Uthruil's voice. "I'm afraid not. The amulet is with Feraan."

"And where is Feraan Auvrearaheal now?" he asked.

Caelfel's pulse quickened, and she feared the only interest Uthruil or the Council had in the matter was finishing the work she had stopped them from completing. "I do not know," she said carefully. "I took him to my house that night after the hunting party. I left him in the garden while I stepped inside for a few minutes. By the time I returned outside, he was gone. I assumed he awoke and left for his home."

Uthruil leaned forward, placing his hands on the stone table before him. "Where is his home, Miss Gyssedlues?"

Caelfel leveled her face with the Head Councilor's and kept her voice even as she answered him. "I do not know, Councilor."

Uthruil took his seat again and then watched Caelfel for a few minutes. Then he released a sigh. "Miss Gyssedlues, I am afraid that without Master Auvrearaheal or the amulet, there is no way we can confirm your story."

Her mouth fell open, and she stammered before forming a coherent question. "Can't you bring him here?"

"No one knows where he lives. Our Chief Executor has been unsuccessful in locating his home. Contacting Feraan Auvrearaheal is no small feat."

"Then how did you invite him to the hunting party?" Caelfel asked.

Uthruil scoffed derisively. "Master Auvrearaheal volunteered to join, just before the party left."

Caelfel exhaled through her nose and tugged at her sleeves again. "What happens now?"

"Miss Gyssedlues, you are left with very few choices. Without evidence, there is no way to refute the charges that accuse you as a necromancer—"

"But that's ridiculous! I am only seventy-six years old! Mastering that scale of necromancy takes centuries. Not to mention, I've only just started at the College of Sal'Sumarathar. I can't even perform magic yet!" Caelfel said, feeling herself slipping into hysterics.

Uthruil patiently waited for her to finish. "Normally, it would take centuries to master necromancy, which is why the Council believes you were not alone in this endeavor. The other necromancer is standing to your right."

Caelfell glanced at Thoroth. "He's not a necromancer either."

"In the time since his birth, nearly four centuries ago, Master Orletylar would have had plenty of time to master it. When you saw the dead elf in the forest, you saw a perfect opportunity to practice your art. Here was a fine and powerful specimen for your master's magical prowess, and as his apprentice, you brought Feraan's body to him. Since you are unable to provide the necessary evidence, this is the only story the Council will believe. Now, Master Orletylar and Miss Gyssedlues, you have two options."

Uthruil paused to wait for their response, but the two of them remained silent.

"One, you will be convicted as necromancers. As criminals, you will be taken to Yamalvon for execution. In the simple case of treason we would perform our own executions here in Sal'Sumarathar, but the Empress has set aside specific protocols for the crime of necromancy."

Caelfel tried not to show her fear in the face of the Council. "And our second choice?"

"You will provide the Council with a body."

"You mean show you Feraan?" she asked.

She saw Markis moving again. The Chief Executor stepped to her, holding out a dagger on a velvet pillow. Caelfel stared at the dagger and felt herself grow deaf to everything but Uthruil's voice.

"No, I mean you show us his body, his corpse. As necromancers, you must reverse the act against nature that you have committed and put to rest the soul you revived."

Eventually Caelfel was able to tear her gaze away from Markis's gift. "You want me to kill Feraan?"

"Feraan Auvrearaheal is already considered dead by the Council. We are simply asking you to purge our city of the undead."

Her eyes went to the dagger again. "If you cannot even find him, how do you expect me to?"

Uthruil grinned, but Caelfel thought it looked more like a smirk. "Necromancers usually have a special link to their creations. I'm sure finding him will not prove difficult for you."

Caelfel looked up at the expectant Markis holding the dagger on its pillow. His head turned marginally, and sunlight glinted off the silver paint on his face. She remembered the sight from Feraan's attack, and it filled her with a new rage. With the back of her hand, she knocked the dagger out of the Chief Executor's hands where it clattered to the floor some distance away.

She tried to be brave and rebellious with her blatant refusal, but the Council did not appear particularly shocked with her decision. "You refuse this option?" Uthruil asked.

Caelfel merely nodded.

"Then you shall be escorted to Yamalvon immediately."

She heard the elves behind her gasp in unison, and it felt like all the air had left the Hall of Court. Caelfel's knees began to buckle as she saw Markis approach, flanked by four guards. Markis's features were arranged in an eerily smug expression that made her feel sick.

"Wait! What about the life debt?" Caelfel cried out desperately, thinking back to the book she had read.

"What of it, Miss Gyssedlues?" Uthruil asked, his voice sounding unimpressed.

"If I saved Feraan's life, then that would mean he's required to do the same for me. It would not benefit me to kill him now like you have asked me."

"The life debt does not extend to the practice of necromancy, because it only gives you the motivation to commit the crime. That doesn't prove that you are innocent."

"What if I find him and bring him to you? Would that prove our innocence?" Caelfel asked, thinking quickly. Her heart raced as she watched Markis draw closer.

"If you bring Feraan Auvrearaheal before the Council, we might consider this proposal, dependent on his condition."

"His condition?"

"If he proves to be a victim of necromancy, you will be taken to Yamalvon for execution. If he is how you claim, you may retain your innocence."

Caelfel nodded quickly. "I don't know where he is. I'll need time to look for him."

"We will give you one week to return with him. During that time, Master Orletylar will remain under our custody."

"You can't keep him for that long," Caelfel protested. "He has done nothing wrong."

"Neither of you have proved your innocence as of yet, Miss Gyssedlues. As penance, he will be enlisted in the militia for community service. Even if the two of you are not necromancers, Thoroth Orletylar still lied, providing false information to the Council. A week in the militia will serve as adequate punishment."

Caelfel looked to the healer and tried imagining him dressed in the armor of the militia. The thought unsettled her. Thoroth was a healer; he was not suited for combat.

"Miss Gyssedlues, you are free to leave under the condition that you will bring Master Auvrearaheal to us in a week's time," Uthruil said, rising. Markis approached her with keys in his hands. Caelfel resisted the urge to recoil from him as he reached for her hands to release her from the chains.

"I missed you in the forest," he said again in a voice only she could hear.

Caelfel saw the sun glinting off the High Executor's face and once more recalled the flash of silver she'd seen that day of the goblin hunt when Feraan was attacked. "I didn't quite miss you, even though I was attacked by that goblin. Convenient timing," she muttered back.

He chuckled. "Plucky, aren't you?"

Caelfel said nothing, mutely watching as they escorted Thoroth away and wondered suspiciously at her own luck for getting off so easily. When the Council left the hall, Caelfel was suddenly surrounded by a number of elves. She turned, pushing through the crowds that were all anxious to see the suspected necromancers. She saw her parents leaving, accompanied by a third figure, the tall one from the previous night. Caelfel knew it was Feraan and pushed harder through the crowd to reach him before he disappeared. She glimpsed her parents pausing beyond the entranceway to wait for her, and then someone caught Caelfel's shoulder and spun her around. An angry face framed by copper hair was suddenly inches away.

"This is *your* fault," Garvanna spat. "Thoroth is going into the militia because of you."

Caelfel's face slipped into a frown, and she pushed Garvanna's hand off of her. "I think it's preferable to an execution."

"You best turn in that damn traitor. It sickens me to think that you even saved him. You should have just killed him like Uthruil wanted and been done with it."

Caelfel turned to leave, but Garvanna stubbornly followed her. "I'm sorry," Caelfel said. "I'm not sure if I know you. I thought I was just a baby and fool to you."

"You are a baby and a fool if you're sticking your neck out for that murderer."

Caelfel paused and turned to look at Garvanna. This was not the first time someone had referred to Feraan as a murderer. "Who has he murdered?"

But someone else caught her by the elbow and steered her away. "You should have waited, Miss Gyssedlues. I would have gladly escorted you outside." Markis, she realized.

"I don't need an escort," Caelfel hissed at him, trying to wrench her arm free from his grasp. He didn't release her until she was standing before her parents.

"Master and Lady Gyssedlues," Markis greeted with a wide grin as he delivered their daughter to them.

Caelfel didn't see a third figure or any sign of Feraan so she forced herself to look at Markis.

"Thank you, Chief Executor," she said through tight lips. "We'll be leaving now."

"Watch yourself, Miss Gyssedlues. I'll be keeping an eye on you, so stay out of trouble." Markis winked, smirking at his own thinly veiled threat, and left.

Caelfel wanted to ask her parents about Feraan, but a glimpse of Garvanna's face made Caelfel usher the three of them home. She had no desire to stay near a crowd of elves when they all thought she was a necromancer.

"Let's just hurry home," Caelfel said as she prodded her parents along. She glanced behind her when they passed the street of merchants and, seeing no sign of Garvanna, slowed down. She sighed in relief.

Caelfel confronted her parents when they reached the safety of their home. "That was Feraan last night, and he was at the trial today," she said, getting straight to the point.

Father nodded.

"Did he say anything?" she pressed when they remained silent.

"He was insistent on giving you that book himself last night," Mother explained. "He went to the trial with us this morning but never said anything. He didn't even move. It seemed like he was about to stand up when it looked as though they were going to send you to Yamalvon."

Caelfel pressed her fingers to her temples. "He was at the trial, but no one saw him?"

"He wore a hood, saying that there was a cloaking spell on it. I didn't think it would work," Sylaera admitted.

"Then he left? He didn't say anything about what I should do?" Caelfel asked, growing impatient. She was beginning to feel quite abandoned by him.

"I assumed he had some elaborate plan written in that book he gave you," Sylaera said. "One thing is for certain. He has no intention of showing himself to the Council."

Caelfel's knees felt weak, and she slowly sank to the floor. "What am I supposed to do? I don't want to be executed."

"Go see him," Mother suggested.

"You heard Markis. He's probably watching me now, waiting for me to show him the way to Feraan. I can't risk that."

"It's not like Feraan's left you with much choice. I say show the Council where he lives. That's what he gets for putting you in this mess."

Eviat shot her mother a look, and Sylaera fell silent. "We'll think of something," Father amended. "I don't believe Feraan will just let them take you to your execution."

Then Father touched her shoulder lightly, and it was a reassuring gesture, quite unlike when Garvanna grabbed her. Caelfel smiled at him, feeling slightly comforted. She left her parents and went to her bedroom to change out of the dress. Before she reached her wardrobe, something dark sitting on her bed caught her attention. She paused to look at it.

It was the same book she had spent the night studying. Caelfel gave it to her mother that morning, and Sylaera had not returned home before now. The book was flipped open, and a note Caelfel knew had not been there the previous night was scrawled onto the page.

Go to the college. Meet Sir Kennyratear.

Caelfel hurried to leave without even changing out of her dress. When her parents asked what she was doing, she told them an excuse about meeting Sir Kennyratear to catch up on her lessons. She took the book with her, aware of Eviat and Sylaera's confused glances. They let her leave without another word.

6. Auras

The gate to the college grounds was closed but not locked. It was never locked. Caelfel hesitated, opened it slowly, and jumped when it made a loud, rusted creak. She quickly slipped through and closed it behind her. The grounds were silent with no one in sight, so Caelfel skipped nervously into a slight run as she searched for Sir Kennyratear's room.

Once she was inside the hall of the college, she passed by the Eye of Ewyn which hummed softly. Caelfel paused beside it and wondered if it would give her another vision if she touched it. She quickly decided against the idea, hurrying to the staircase.

"I wonder if it's really an eye," Caelfel muttered to herself. "I wouldn't think so, but it seems strange to call it one."

The college looked empty, but she knew that the second level held most of the instructors' quarters. Caelfel crossed the rotunda and turned a corridor before freezing in her tracks. At the end of the hall, she saw light streaming from the only open door. Caelfel assumed it belonged to Sir Kennyratear and approached it.

She shielded her eyes as she looked inside. "Sir Kennyratear?" she called. The expansive silence of the college grounds made her voice sound unnaturally loud.

The greyling appeared in the doorway as a silhouette. "Miss Gyssedlues," he greeted. "You have been absent from some very important lessons." Slowly, her teacher came into focus.

"I was arrested and put on trial for necromancy," she explained uneasily.

"Yes, so I've heard. I won't accept excuses though. Hurry inside and I will catch you up to speed with your classmates."

Caelfel made a move inside just as Sir Kennyratear left the room. She paused, watching him walk away.

He briefly looked back to her. "Well, go on in. We shan't be kept waiting."

Caelfel wanted to ask where he was going, but Sir Kennyratear disappeared along the hallway before she could formulate her question. She entered his office alone.

The bright light was quickly extinguished once she stepped inside, and Caelfel's eyes took some time adjusting to the darkness again. She blinked rapidly, eventually discerning the outline of an elf.

"Took you long enough," remarked a voice that was undeniably Feraan's. He stood at the other end of the small room beside a window with drawn curtains.

"What are we doing here?" she asked.

"I figured this was a safe place to talk. No doubt you are being followed. I didn't want you bringing the Chief Executor to my house."

"Right," Caelfel sighed uneasily.

"You read the book I gave you last night," Feraan observed, a hint of pride in his voice.

"Not that it did any good," Caelfel said, crossing her arms and frowning.

"No, you did well," Feraan said. "You gave us some time, and once the necromancy issue is cast aside, the life debt gives you motivation for saving my life. Perhaps it will be enough to satisfy the Council for a while."

"You think they'll still try to kill you?" Caelfel asked.

"Know that this is not the first attempt they've made," Feraan said, fixing her with a hard stare.

"What do we do now?" she asked.

"I'm still trying to figure that out."

Caelfel hesitated. "Mother says you won't show yourself to the Council."

"She's right. I won't."

"How else am I supposed to prove that you are alive, then?"

"I am open for suggestions."

Caelfel pressed her back to the wall and slid to the floor. Something in her belly churned. "I don't want to be executed," she mumbled miserably.

"Caelfel," Feraan started.

Caelfel shook her head and buried her face in her hands. She held her breath as she tried to block the sudden panic and despair she felt swelling within her. "I don't want to be executed," she repeated softly.

And suddenly Feraan was on the floor beside her. She felt his hand on her shoulder but it did not feel the way either Garvanna's or her father's did. There was warmth to his touch Caelfel had never felt from anyone else. She looked up at him and saw his face was very close to hers. When he spoke, it was with a severe tone that Caelfel assumed was supposed to comfort her.

"I will not let them take you to Yamalvon. I will not let them execute you. They won't even get to lay a finger on you. If it comes down to it and we've no other choice, I will take you as far away from Sal'Sumarathar as I possibly can."

"And where would we go?" Caelfel asked, her throat thick with misery.

She felt his arm moving as he shrugged. "Maybe I will take you to the coast, so you can see the sea."

Caelfel pushed her hair back, recovering from her panic and despair. "What of Thoroth?"

Feraan's face turned guarded. and he dropped his hand from her shoulder. "What about him?"

"We have to help him too."

"Why should I help *him*?"

"He helped you too and he's been imprisoned for it," Caelfel pointed out.

Feraan leaned back. "That is his fault. He's done nothing to help me."

Caelfel rolled her eyes. "Aren't you older than I am?"

"Of course I am."

"Then you shouldn't be so childish."

Feraan sighed, a sound of reluctance and disgust. "You are currently my priority. Thoroth is not. Perhaps you should have thought of that before getting him involved."

Caelfel sighed. "What do I do now?"

"Keep going to the college. We'll talk again, I'm sure. If you need to see me, speak to Sir Kennyratear. Do *not* go to my house for any reason. Understand?"

"Do you trust Sir Kennyratear?"

"I trust him more than most. He's been a good friend."

"Is Markis here now?"

"I've no doubt he is."

"How will you leave?"

Feraan looked around the room with feigned interest. "I'll wait until you draw him off or I might just stay here."

Caelfel got to her feet, brushing off her dress. She went to the door and threw a last furtive glance in Feraan's direction, feeling as though she should say something to him but was at a loss for words. She left the room in silence, coming across Sir Kennyratear down the hall.

"I shall see you tomorrow morning, Miss Gyssedlues," he bid.

Caelfel offered him a smile and left the college grounds. On the way home, she searched continuously for any sign of Markis but saw none. She had no doubt that he was there and only wished she had her bow with her. The thought of being followed made her nervous.

She paused as she passed the horse meadow. She allowed herself to stop there. She found her horse Rowan grazing by the lake, Rumfel Lake. The lake was surrounded by thick trees on all but one side, and its water stretched further than the length of Sal'Sumarathar's square. Caelfel sat on its bank with Rowan by her side.

Her mother had told her once that this lake was Caelfel's namesake. Caelfel was never sure why her parents would name her after a lake but she did know that the water had special healing properties that helped aging elves find sleep, her father included. If she had her waterskin with her, Caelfel would have brought some water home to her father. However as she did not, Caelfel said goodbye to Rowan and was about to leave the water's edge when she saw odd shadows dancing on the lake's surface. She blinked to clear her vision, and the dancing shadows vanished.

As she turned towards home, the fine hairs at the base of her neck prickled as her thoughts returned to the elf that was surely following her, even now. Markis had to have excellent training as a tracker to be so undetectable.

She left for the college early the next morning, and a tiny voice inside her head reminded Caelfel she had six days left to prove her innocence to the Council. As she squeezed her way through the other students to reach the college grounds, more carefree voices, those belonging to the other students, reminded Caelfel that another important date was fast approaching.

"I wonder who will be crowned Beauty of Spring this year?" trilled a nearby she-elf.

The Spring Festival was a celebration of the new season, held only once every century. It was an enormous gathering of elves full of feasting, drinking, and dancing. A contest was held to determine the most beautiful she-elf, who would be crowned as the Beauty of Spring. Having never been, the Spring Festival was an event that Caelfel had anticipated since she was a youngling along with the whole of Sal'Sumarathar. Now however, she could not muster the excitement for it. She swallowed, dreading what would happen in a week's time, and pushed through to reach Sir Kennyratear's class.

"Caelfel!" called a voice before she could reach the proper archway. Caelfel's heart surged into her throat until she saw it was only Garvanna.

"What is it?" she asked, doing little to hide her displeasure upon seeing the she-elf.

"Please tell me you've solved all this with Thoroth," Garvanna pleaded with an uncharacteristic note of desperation in her voice.

"Not yet," Caelfel admitted quietly.

"You can't abandon him. The military is no place for a healer!" Garvanna yelled, pulling Caelfel away from the stream of students filing in Sir Kennyratear's classroom.

"I didn't abandon him. Talk to Daerad. His father is Head Councilor," Caelfel countered irritably.

"As far as I'm concerned, you left him in there," Garvanna said, face tight.

Caelfel pressed her lips into a thin line, feeling a wave of anger as she looked at Garvanna's face. "I will do everything I can to help Thoroth."

"If you really want to help him, just hand Feraan over to the Council."

Caelfel focused on the wall next to them, her eyes following the line of blue crystals embedded within the glassy surface. "I don't know where he is," she admitted through clenched teeth.

"Caelfel, Garvanna would you like to join the rest of the class?" Sir Kennyratear asked, stepping into the hall with them. "We're going to be dueling again today. The two of you will be on a team with

Daerad."

"Dueling?" Caelfel repeated, rather confused. Sir Kennyratear disappeared into the classroom again, and Garvanna rolled her eyes.

"You've missed the past two days. Sir Kennyratear divides us into teams so everyone can practice using their auras," Garvanna explained, herding Caelfel into the room.

"What are we doing? I haven't been able to use my aura yet."

Garvanna gave Caelfel a wide-eyed look. "Do you mean that?"

Caelfel nodded as Daerad approached them with a smug smirk. She realized her team consisted of an insufferable she-elf and an elf whose father nearly had her executed. The realization did nothing to calm her nerves.

Caelfel quickly learned that Sir Kennyratear had each team facing off against one another. There were ten teams each with three elves. Every team had to learn to attack and defend themselves with their own aura. Before it was their turn, Caelfel watched other teams easily manipulate their auras. She stared at her hands, willing her own aura to appear.

Sir Kennyratear called for Caelfel, Garvanna, and Daerad, and the three of them stood up from the benches that were pushed up against the walls to provide space for the dueling area. Caelfel willed herself to follow the other two and tried not to stumble when her legs suddenly refused to obey her.

"Garvanna, your team is at a serious disadvantage since one of your team members has not been able to fully access her aura," Sir Kennyratear said.

Caelfel's stomach sank as Sir Kennyratear exposed her as the weakest link. Garvanna threw a glare over her shoulder before stepping in front of Caelfel to shield her.

There wasn't a clear scoring system. It seemed that Sir Kennyratear let the students bash each other until he had had his fill of entertainment. Caelfel was careful to stay behind either Garvanna or Daerad, but since the opposing team had three fully functional players, it placed Garvanna and Daerad at an obvious inconvenience. They were too preoccupied with charging their aura shields to fight the others back. Daerad grunted loudly every time his shield was depleted. Garvanna did not mask her impatience so mildly.

"At least try to use your aura!" she screamed over the whizzing auric balls of energy.

"I'm trying!" Caelfel screamed back.

Caelfel was actually impressed with how well the other two held up on their own, but Garvanna wasn't satisfied. She threw Caelfel to the ground in front of them, and Caelfel became an easy target. She raised her arms to shield her face as the opposing team hurled more energy blasts at her. They didn't burn like she expected but they could deliver a solid punch. As she scrambled to her feet, Caelfel could feel bruises forming.

For a brief moment, green light had filled her vision but it quickly ebbed away. Caelfel tried summoning it again but was knocked back to the ground before she had a chance to stand. The sounds of the nearby laughing students filled her ears, and her face burned with embarrassment.

"That's enough," Sir Kennyratear barked, and the room instantly became still. Caelfel's panting was the loudest noise in the room as she got to her feet once again. Garvanna surprised her by offering a helping hand. Caelfel took it without question and hastily dusted herself off before realizing that everyone's attention was focused, not on her, but on a certain visitor.

"You run such an entertaining class, Sir Kennyratear," Markis remarked, stepping further into the room.

"My exercise is designed to teach them to defend themselves," Sir Kennyratear said in a hard voice. "But I'm afraid my classroom isn't open for public viewing." Caelfel shuffled to hide behind Garvanna even though Markis had already seen her.

"I think you'll find Councilor Uthruil has granted me special permission," Markis said, eyes falling on Caelfel.

"The Council of Sal'Sumarathar has no authority over the college. We are protected by the Board of Wizardry in Yamalvon. You can go speak with Headmaster Nimuath, if you like."

"I'm afraid you are wrong, Sir Kennyratear. The Council reserves the right to maintain a presence on the grounds while the college harbors a suspected necromancer. You may speak with the Headmaster yourself if you need further convincing of the legality of the situation."

Caelfel felt everyone in the room look at her, the convicted necromancer, except Sir Kennyratear who kept his glare on Markis. "I will not tolerate any more disruptions," he said at length.

Markis held his palms out, as if trying Sir Kennyratear's patience was the last thing he wanted to do. "Of course. I am here merely to observe one elf for the safety of you and your students."

Sir Kennyratear merely grumbled something inaudible before he commenced ignoring Markis altogether. He told the students to switch teams, and Caelfel returned to her seat on the bench for a break. She did her best to keep her attention on the dueling students on the floor, but Markis's presence distracted her from everything else. Several more teams faced off against each other, and Caelfel began to suspect Sir Kennyratear deliberately kept her team seated.

Caelfel was not the only one to notice this. Markis spoke up. "Sir Kennyratear, I do believe you're not distributing turns evenly. Every team, save for the one Miss Gyssedlues is on, has seen at least two turns in dueling."

Sir Kennyratear rounded on the tracker. "Master Rilynnzea, I thought I asked for no more interruptions."

"I believe my suggestion is for the benefit of your class," Markis said with a wide smile. "I think all of your students should receive equal attention."

Sir Kennyratear frowned but nodded all the same for Caelfel and the other two to take their place on the floor. Then the onslaught continued. In the face of Markis, Garvanna made more of an attempt to shield Caelfel from the attacks that felt more ruthless than before. Several minutes passed, and Caelfel landed on the ground once more, arms around her stomach where she had just been hit. It took her a moment to find her breath again, but by then, Markis had stopped the class a third time.

"One of your students has not learned to utilize her aura." Caelfel wondered if the tracker enjoyed annoying the instructor.

"She will learn in her own time."

"Your teaching methods do not appear effective or efficient for the needs of your students."

"My teaching method is one that has satisfied all of my capable students for centuries," Sir Kennyratear snapped.

"And what of the incapable ones?" Markis asked smoothly.

Caelfel gritted her teeth. "I am not incapable," she retorted. "I am only behind the others because I lost two days of class for a ridiculous trial."

Garvanna whistled beside her, and Caelfel wondered if she had managed to impress the she-elf with her nerve. Markis was not bothered by her words and stepped closer to Caelfel with the grin still on his face.

"Miss Gyssedlues, I sense that you blame me for your lack of progress. Allow me to make it up to you." He walked toward her with his hand outstretched. Sir Kennyratear hurried to block his path.

"That mode of aura activation is outdated."

Markis tilted his head. "It is the quickest method, and the choice ultimately belongs to Caelfel."

"What is?" Caelfel asked.

Markis pushed past Sir Kennyratear and drew closer to Caelfel. "With the spark of another, active aura, your aura can instantly become active to use without the long wait of waking it naturally. Your aura at present remains in a dormant state. It is only a simple matter of waking it up."

Caelfel remembered Feraan mentioning this method in passing and remembered his refusal to help her that way. "Is it dangerous?" she asked. Feraan had given the impression that it was.

"If you are the capable student you claim you are, it should prove no problem to you," Markis said.

"It is *very* dangerous," Sir Kennyratear interrupted.

"There is always some measure of risk with any practice of magic," Markis brushed off.

Sir Kennyratear grew angry, but Caelfel spoke before he could argue further. "It won't kill me, though," she guessed. Even Feraan could not admit that it would.

Markis's grin deepened. "Since you have been proven with the Eye of Ewyn, there is little chance of that happening."

Caelfel did not like how Markis left room for doubt, but she took a sharp breath and nodded for Markis to proceed. He held out his hand again, and Caelfel heard Garvanna's voice next to her ear.

"He could take the opportunity and try to kill you," Garvanna pointed out, voice pitched so that the approaching Markis would not overhear.

Caelfel considered this. "I doubt he would risk it with a room full of witnesses."

"But he could always play it off as an accident."

"He needs me to find Feraan." But Caelfel's resolve faltered, and she could not find the words to stop the advancing Markis. When he was in front of her, the tracker touched two fingers to her forehead.

At first, Caelfel felt nothing. Then she saw red smoke curling down his arm. A surge of electricity coursed through her body a moment later. A loud, delayed *boom* resounded through the room. Caelfel tried to scream, but the energy clamped her mouth shut. No scream came from her throat. A combination of red and green smoke clouded her vision.

Markis removed his fingers and stepped back. All the energy abruptly disappeared from Caelfel's body, and she fell to her knees in a state of indescribable exhaustion. She saw the room tilt dangerously as her head hit the floor. Then came Sir Kennyratear's sharp command, *"Get her to the infirmary!"*

Caelfel made an effort to tell them that she was fine, but no words came to her lips, which made her consider the possibility that she was not fine at all. She tried searching for familiar faces among the sea of confusion. Only one stood out to her addled mind, though she knew he could not be there.

"Feraan?"

But then he was gone, and she succumbed to the dark void of unconsciousness.

***

"How incredibly stupid," hissed a voice that sounded none too happy.

It took a while for Caelfel to recognize the voice as Feraan's. She wondered where she was and how long she had been there. She thought it must have been nighttime but then realized that her eyes were closed. She didn't feel the need to open them just yet, content to listen to the conversation around her.

"Markis left her very little choice in the matter. She was cornered." This was Sir Kennyratear, and Caelfel became aware of the greyling's fingers at her temples. They moved when he spoke. He must have been healing her or conducting some sort of energy transfer.

But then Caelfel slowly remembered the red and green smoke. Sir Kennyratear was wrong. It was her choice to let Markis help her. She hadn't felt cornered at all. The foolish decision was entirely hers, but perhaps Sir Kennyratear was only trying to defend her. It only garnered a scoff from Feraan. There was a rhythmic fall of footsteps on stone, and Caelfel guessed that Feraan was pacing.

"Sit down," Sir Kennyratear told him. "You're making me

nervous."

"I hate feeling so *useless*," Feraan hissed. "I should have done something."

Sir Kennyratear's fingers moved, and Caelfel imagined him shrugging. "If you showed yourself to the Council, none of this would have happened," he noted mildly.

"They are trying to draw me out, Markis and the Council," Feraan said. His pacing increased. "They think that I will come to them if they attack her."

"Has it not worked? You did not take very long to get here after I sent my message." Caelfel was amused how Sir Kennyratear remained calm in complete contrast to Feraan's anxiety.

Something metal clattered loudly to the stone floor, and Caelfel wondered what Feraan had knocked over. She twitched at the noise.

"That's fine. Just alert everyone in the college that you are here," Sir Kennyratear said.

"It's night. Everyone has already left."

"I don't think Markis has. He's been circling the grounds all afternoon. How did you get here anyway?"

"Don't worry about it," Feraan grumbled. The pacing ceased.

"You act just like a mother. Worry makes you careless."

"I'm not worried," Feraan snapped. "I'm only restless."

"Then, here. You can take over this for me." Sir Kennyratear removed his fingertips, and the warmth of his pulsing aura suddenly vanished.

There was a measurable space of silence. Then Feraan quietly said, "I'm not a healer."

Sir Kennyratear laughed. "I know you are not as clueless as you make yourself out to be." A softer pair of footsteps left the room. Feraan's impatient sigh came next, and she heard his footsteps draw closer. A new set of fingertips pressed gently against her temples, and the warm energy returned, flowing from her head to the rest of her body.

"You're awake," Feraan remarked.

She opened her eyes to see his face hovering above hers. "How long have I been here?" she asked.

"The entire day. I told you that exploding your aura wouldn't be worth it," he answered.

"Exploding my aura?" she repeated.

"That's what Markis did to you today. It's not very safe."

"Where are my parents? Do they know what happened?"

"They were here earlier. Then your mother decided to file a complaint with the Council. Your father went with her to make sure she didn't get into too much trouble."

"You came," she noted.

"Someone had to watch over you when Sir Kennyratear left."

"You're very kind," she said. Caelfel lifted her hand and inspected the black smoke curling around her fingers. "Is your aura black?"

He made a noise of derision. "It is."

"Can I use my aura?" she asked.

"Wasn't it the whole reason you did this?" he retorted. "Don't try to use it now."

Caelfel lowered her hand. "Did you find a solution to our necromancy problem?"

"I haven't, but Sir Kennyratear had an idea. He's leaving for Yamalvon now."

"Why is he going to Yamalvon?"

"He is looking for help. He believes he will find someone who can prove your innocence to the Council."

"Who could do that?" she asked.

"I suppose we will find out."

Caelfel sighed and allowed herself to relax against the cot in the infirmary. She felt her eyelids grow heavy. "I want to go home."

"That's not an option until your parents come back for you. You're still too weak to move on your own," Feraan said.

She closed her eyes completely and realized how suddenly aware she was of her surroundings. She imagined the feeling as gaining an additional sense. She felt the fluctuations of energy within Feraan's aura. Then another presence moved into the field of her perception. It felt distant but was swiftly approaching. Nervous tremors ran along her frame.

Feraan noticed. "What's wrong?"

Caelfel struggled to name the disturbance. "I can feel *everything*."

"You'll eventually grow accustomed to the sensation. When the aura awakens, everything feels new and overwhelming."

Caelfel frowned, thinking that was why Feraan noticed nothing. "Is anyone else here?"

"No, we're the only ones."

"Didn't Sir Kennyratear say Markis was outside the college?"

"Yes."

"Wouldn't Markis think it strange if Sir Kennyratear left me alone in here?"

Feraan's aura immediately retracted from Caelfel, and he issued a low curse.

"That's him coming, isn't it?" she guessed.

"Don't panic," Feraan instructed as he resumed pacing.

Caelfel tried sitting up.

"Don't get up either!" he snapped.

Caelfel slowly lay back down. "Lock the door," she suggested.

Feraan gave her a sharp look. "A locked door would hardly stop a tracker who also happens to be the Chief Executor." But Feraan locked the door anyway.

"Does he already know that you are here?" Caelfel asked.

"No." Feraan thought a moment and then amended. "Yes, he more than likely does."

Caelfel lifted her head to watch Feraan pace.

"There's a window," Feraan observed, rushing to the far end of the infirmary. He tried opening it.

Caelfel followed him with her eyes. "I don't see how a window is helpful."

"With the Chief Executor about to bang on our door, I'm hardly going to use it to air out the room," he said with a ridiculously huge smile as he opened the window.

Caelfel propped herself up on her elbows and when Feraan's back was turned, she went to stand on her own. She sensed Markis was only a corridor away from them. "He's coming."

"I'm well aware of that." Feraan turned to look at her, and his brow furrowed. "You're not supposed to be standing," he said, snapping at her again.

"To be fair, you're not supposed to be alive," said Markis's voice from the doorway. Caelfel tried to turn to face the tracker but the sudden movement made her dizzy. Her knees began to buckle.

Feraan lifted his arm and black smoke billowed around his hand, instantly enveloping the room in complete darkness. The smoke wasn't thick like the type that came from a fire. It chilled her skin like a damp layer of cloth. It was a rain cloud that blotted out her newly gained and altogether overwhelming hyper-awareness. Then Feraan was beside her, securing an arm around her waist as they made their escape through the window. The infirmary was in a tower that overlooked the college gardens. Caelfel would have screamed but she had no sense of falling. Their feet touched the ground without a jolt. Were they not being pursued by Markis, Caelfel would have admitted how impressed she was. "You have got to show me how you did that," Caelfel said.

"Perhaps now is not the best time," he grunted impatiently. Feraan reached down and, lifting Caelfel under her knees and around her waist, he began running with her in his arms. She squeezed her eyes shut, because the trees rushing past made her feel sick. With her eyes closed, she felt Feraan's aura shrouding them like an invisible cloak. Beyond that, Markis's aura followed them.

"He's running through the treetops," Caelfel informed Feraan. Normally, Caelfel was a fast runner and very adept in the sport of tree-running.

"There's a problem" he muttered.

Feraan turned and circled several times, and the maneuvers seemed successful in throwing Markis off their trail, if only slightly.

"Where are we going?" Caelfel asked.

"I can't lose him," said Feraan.

Caelfel didn't find that reassuring.

He squinted at her. "Your aura is too loud."

"I haven't said anything."

"No, your aura is newly activated so it shines like a pulsating beacon."

"How do I stop it?"

"You could try meditating."

The faster Feraan ran, the more jostled and uninclined towards meditation Caelfel became. "I don't see that happening if you keep running."

"I could always kill you," he suggested mildly.

"I vote against that idea."

Feraan struggled to keep his breathing steady. "It's a matter of concentration. You just need to focus your mind."

But even with her eyes closed, Markis's aura consumed her attention. It pressed on her mind like a fiery torch. The more she shied away from it, the larger it became.

"Stop it!" Feraan yelled. "You're getting louder."

"I'm sorry," she cried helplessly. "I can't help it."

Feraan turned sharply and suddenly dropped her to the ground. Caelfel opened her eyes and blinked furiously in the dark. Feraan crouched in front of her and without warning or explanation, he kissed her.

Her eyes went wide, and her mind went blank. They were frozen for several minutes as Feraan crushed her body to his. A new warmth rose to Caelfel's cheeks.

At last, Feraan pulled away and he didn't hide the devious smirk from his features. "Now you're very quiet."

Caelfel blinked again, just realizing that they were in the meadow. Everything else was still numb to her. "What?"

"No, thinking will get us killed." And he kissed her again.

When he broke away again, she released a slow breath, doing a poor job of focusing on nothing, her mind bouncing around erratically. Instead she silently watched Feraan hurry away and then return with a dark horse, the same horse she had first seen him with.

"This is Firnis," he said by way of introductions. Firnis was already saddled and Feraan set about tightening the cinch.

"What's going on?" Caelfel asked, sitting herself up.

Feraan sounded reluctant to answer. "Remember how I told you I would protect you, even if it meant leaving?"

Caelfel blinked. "We're leaving Sal'Sumarathar?" she asked. Her voice was strained, and she tried in vain to keep the panic from bubbling up within her.

Feraan stared at her forcefully. "More than that, we're leaving the Fey Forest and the rest of Honey Water with it."

"Leaving?" Caelfel repeated, though Feraan continued as if he hadn't heard her. She went to stand on her own, ignoring how lightheaded she felt. "Where would we go?"

"Umfeld, Umfang. The choice is yours once we leave the forest," Feraan said, holding out his hand for her.

Caelfel had heard of the realms of Umfeld and Umfang. The former was a vast kingdom of humans while Umfang was home to a diversity of races. Elves typically thought the two realms inferior to Honey Water as they were almost always at war with each other. They did not have the longevity of the elves, so the humans, werefolk, and all manner of sorcerers were unable to maintain the patience necessary to avoid war. But the way Feraan suggested fleeing to one of them was odd. He did not speak of Umfeld or Umfang with scorn. "You've been there before?"

He nodded.

"You've left the Fey Forest?" she asked again. She longed to question Feraan further, to discover what the outside world was like, to know why he had left the Fey Forest, but Feraan was impatient.

"We must hurry."

But this was a decision that could not be rushed, because Eviat and Sylaera flashed suddenly through her mind. Caelfel shook her head and stepped back. "I can't leave."

It was evident that Feraan was not prepared for a refusal. "Why not?"

"I have my parents—"

"Caelfel, we do not have the luxury to worry about your parents. We must leave the Fey Forest. I told you it might come down to this."

"It hasn't come down to anything yet," she protested.

Feraan grew angry as his impatience increased. "Markis is looking for us. He will not stop looking for you, no matter what happens. He saw you with me, and that only puts you at risk. You're not safe here."

"You mean *you* are not safe here?" Caelfel asked, glaring. "You said Sir Kennyratear has a plan."

"Sir Kennyratear has an *idea*."

"We should wait to see if it works. There is no point in leaving if Sir Kennyratear can prove my innocence tomorrow."

Feraan stepped closer to her and began moving his hands around emphatically. "It does not matter what Sir Kennyratear proves tomorrow. You saved *my* life and for that, no matter the circumstances, you will always be guilty in the eyes of the Council." He scoffed scathingly. "That is the price for befriending the most hated elf of the empire."

Caelfel crossed her arms and plopped herself on the ground again. "If it turns out that you are right, we can leave the Fey Forest then."

Feraan sighed, exasperated. "We might not have another opportunity to leave."

"We have to try something before leaving the Fey Forest," Caelfel insisted stubbornly. "Trying is better than not trying at all."

So then it was decided that they would try, much to Feraan's reluctance. He must have sensed that there was little point in arguing with her further, because as he sullenly led her home, he didn't press the matter or speak much at all. They must have successfully evaded Markis too, because Feraan was no longer concerned with running away. Caelfel stayed closed to him and focused on keeping her aura contained. It prevented her from sensing where Markis was, but she hoped it would also hide their presence from the tracker. Feraan led her to the back through her parents' garden, avoiding the front entrance altogether.

"Is he gone, then?" Caelfel asked.

"He's still searching but has probably figured we would be gone now." His eyes drifted down Caefel's body and to the door behind her. "Hopefully he does not think to look here."

"Do you think he will?"

"It's hard to be certain."

Feraan turned to leave and Caelfel brought her fingers to her lips. Her mind drifted to before when he had kissed her. She called him back before he disappeared from the garden. "Why did you kiss me?"

Feraan paused at the gate. She could tell by how his anxious fingers ran across the metal bars that he just wanted to leave without facing the question. His defeated sigh was acceptance that he had not escaped in time. "Isn't it obvious? It cleared your mind and helped us to hide from Markis. Outside of that, it meant nothing."

"Oh," was all Caelfel could say. This did not come as a surprise, but nonetheless, as she watched him leave, she could not shake an overwhelming disappointment.

Couriers arrived the following morning to inform all of Sir Kennyratear's students that he was presently occupied away from Sal'Sumarathar, so they would not be meeting for class. Caelfel saw the courier briefly, noting that because the elf was courier to the college and not the Council, he wore blue robes instead of green. She wondered when Sir Kennyratear would return but thought it better that class had been cancelled. Since she had awoken in the college infirmary, Caelfel had never fully recovered from her aura incident. Her head throbbed constantly, and she was unable to keep food in her stomach. Her parents didn't bother her much, saying she needed her rest, but the headache wouldn't allow her any. She began sweating and tossing around on her mattress.

At some point, Eviat entered her room and all but forced her to drink some potion he had brewed. After she drank it, her head felt very heavy, and she slipped into a sleep-deprived, comatose state that allowed minimal speech.

"What is this?" she mumbled to Eviat before he disappeared.

"It will help you feel normal again," he answered softly.

"No, what's wrong with me?"

"It's a sickness. You will feel better soon," her father assured her. Caelfel hoped he was right but didn't have the energy to say so.

The following morning brought a new knock to the door. Behind the knock was another courier, clad in green and flanked by two soldiers who were also wearing green. Sylaera had answered the door, and Caelfel could hear her mother protesting loudly.

"It has not been a week yet," she argued. "You cannot take her."

"My lady, new evidence has been presented for your daughter's case. We must escort her to the Hall of Court immediately."

"I'm afraid she is ill and unable to attend a trial," Sylaera said stubbornly. "You can thank your Chief Executor for that."

Caelfel smiled to herself at her mother's cheek and pushed herself out of bed to meet the courier. "I am fine, Mother," Caelfel said, entering the room. She was well enough to walk and talk even though her head still felt weak.

Sylaera frowned but there was no point in arguing. The courier held out his hand for her, and Caelfel stepped after him. Her parents followed behind, and Caelfel noticed how no one locked her wrists into iron cuffs like before. At the end of their street, she saw Thoroth being similarly led away from the holding cells with Garvanna trailing behind him. Caelfel thought he looked rather pale and then remembered he had been in custody since their trial. She went to walk beside him, and her guards moved with her.

"Do you know what this is about? It hasn't been a week yet," Thoroth asked, his fear quite evident.

Caelfel wanted to comfort him but decided mentioning Sir Kennyratear's efforts in front of the guards would be a bad idea. She winked at him instead, offering a half smile as she could easily imagine Garvanna putting up a similar fight on Thoroth's behalf as Sylaera had done for Caelfel.

It eased his mind. "You don't look very well, Caelfel. Garvanna told me what Markis did."

The smile Caelfel mustered for him faltered. She looked away and held his hand. His skin felt cool against hers, and Thoroth gave a gentle squeeze as they entered the Hall of Court.

There was no audience to witness this new presentation of evidence, save for Caelfel's parents and Garvanna. All five Councilors were there as well as a new circle of soldiers before them. They wore purple livery, signifying that they were soldiers from Yamalvon's imperial army. Caelfel did not feel as confident upon seeing them. As they approached the bench, Caelfel saw that the imperial soldiers made Uthruil nervous as well.

"And here we have our convicted necromancers," said Uthruil, gesturing to Caelfel and Thoroth.

Suddenly, the imperial soldiers parted, revealing the she-elf that they had surrounded. The she-elf turned to them slowly. Her wild, honey hair curled down the length of her back, and her bright green eyes added to the wild air about her. Caelfel found she was more afraid of the she-elf than the she-elf's soldiers. A pulsating energy crackled around her and it made Caelfel's head hurt even more. Thoroth recoiled beside her.

"What are their names?" the she-elf asked.

"Thoroth Orletylar and Caelfel Gyssedlues," Uthruil answered for them.

The she-elf smiled brightly and held out her hands in a welcoming gesture. "Hello Thoroth and Caelfel. My name is Gwyndolyn. Don't be afraid. Come closer."

Caelfel and Thoroth were ushered to enter the circle of soldiers with Gwyndolyn and they did so hesitantly. The soldiers closed ranks as soon as they were in the circle. One of the soldiers stepped closer to Gwyndolyn, and Caelfel suspected this soldier was the leader of the others.

"What's going on?" Thoroth asked. Gwyndolyn started moving as she spoke, pacing in aimless circles. It made her look as though she was always fidgeting.

"There are specific procedures that are used in dealing with necromancers. Normally all suspected necromancers are immediately sent to Yamalvon for investigation, because of the seriousness of the crime, you see. In the past, we have had many false convictions, so Yamalvon prefers to take extra measures in proving a necromancer's guilt.

"I have special abilities that allow me to look into another elf's aura and determine if they have committed necromancy."

"How do you have this ability?" Thoroth asked nervously.

Gwyndolyn paused her pacing to emit a sparkling peal of laughter. "You can't tell? I have a very powerful aura myself. It allows me to be a master of auras, you could say."

Gwyndolyn continued laughing, and the sound made everyone in the room visibly nervous. The soldier behind her placed a hand on her shoulder. "My lady," he said quietly.

She stopped laughing and waved the soldier away. "Oh, Blaes." She turned back to them. "Don't mind him. He always worries. If I'm not careful with my aura, I could destroy an entire city." She laughed again, but stopped herself with a glance from Blaes.

Thoroth and Caelfel exchanged looks as they patiently waited for Gwyndolyn to recover herself.

She tugged at some hair over her ears before speaking. "It is a very simple procedure. I only touch you to read your aura. Very simple, like I said. However, the act is considered intrusive, so normally I would need prior consent. But, seeing as the both of you are convicted criminals, I do not. Now, who is first?" She clapped her hands together eagerly, but her amicable personality did not settle Caelfel's nerves. Something about Gwyndolyn felt *off*.

"Will it hurt?" Caelfel asked, remembering how the last incident of someone touching her aura had ended and how she was still suffering its repercussions.

Gwyndolyn laughed at her expression. "Goodness, no. I'm not *exploding* your aura."

Then without warning, Gwyndolyn reached out to touch Caelfel's forehead. Caelfel tensed but realized she felt no pain as Gwyndolyn had promised. She relaxed and then squinted at Gwyndolyn whose bright eyes appeared very bright and interested.

Gwyndolyn frowned. "Your aura *has* been exploded, and quite recently."

She removed her hand from Caelfel's brow and turned to Thoroth without pause. Thoroth started when she touched her fingers to his head as well. Seconds later, her hand dropped to her side, and she faced the Council, all signs of her humor gone.

"These two are not necromancers. You may release them from your custody as soon as it is possible. For any future cases of necromancy, send them directly to Yamalvon."

Uthruil stood. "Thank you, Lady Ernmas. We shall regard your opinion with the highest of authority."

"Of course it is with the highest authority. My word holds the power of the Empress," Gwyndolyn said, quickly losing her patience.

"Is that all, my lady?" Uthruil asked.

"It isn't, Councilor. It has become evident to me that there is an inner working of abuse Sal'Sumarathar shows its citizens."

"Please explain yourself, Lady Ernmas," Uthruil said.

"I'm assuming Miss Gyssedlues is a student of your college. I advise seeking out the one responsible for exploding her aura. You should know that the practice is outdated and unethical."

Uthruil's mouth flickered. "We will definitely investigate the matter. Markis, will you please escort Master Orletylar and Miss Gyssedlues to their homes?"

Markis stepped from the peripheral of the room but was stopped by a glare from Gwyndolyn.

"There is no need for your services, Chief Executor. My imperial officers shall escort them home instead." She smiled. "Be aware, Councilor, that I will be informing the Board of Wizardry of everything I've seen here today."

"I wouldn't expect anything else of you."

Gwyndolyn threw one last grin toward Uthruil before leading Caelfel and her parents, Thoroth and Garvanna, and her procession of purple-clad soldiers away from the Hall of Court. The elf she had addressed as Blaes hurried to keep pace.

"My lady, it would not be wise to tarry in Sal'Sumarathar for long," he said urgently to her. Gwyndolyn waited until they passed Sal'Sumarathar's center plaza before responding.

"Oh, Blaes," she sighed dismissively. She turned to the rest of them. "Bless him, he's always worrying about my safety."

"And not without good reason," Blaes insisted.

Gwyndolyn said, "He thinks someone is after me, always trying to get me. Centuries in the army have made him paranoid, but Blaes means well. Now, where are we stopping first?"

"Thoroth's house is closest," Caelfel volunteered when no one said anything.

Thoroth directed Gwyndolyn and her troops where to turn and which street to take, and soon they all stood before his familiar green door. Garvanna hurried inside without a second glance behind her.

"Thank you," Thoroth said to Gwyndolyn.

"The pleasure is all mine, Master Healer," she said, but her eyes focused on the door where Garvanna just disappeared. "Was that your wife?"

"No, Garvana has been my friend for many years. You must forgive her. Her nerves make her uneasy around others."

Gwyndolyn nodded slowly before transferring her gaze to Caelfel. "Well if she is not your wife, then the two of *you* must hug each other. It is obvious that the two of you are in love."

Caelfel felt her mouth hang open. "But I'm not—" She looked to Thoroth, unable to finish.

"Caelfel and I are just friends too," Thoroth said, but there was something in his tone that sounded uncertain.

"Friends can always fall in love. Sometimes they are meant to," Gwyndolyn said, laughing.

It soon became clear that she would not leave until they did hug. So Caelfel made her embrace quick until Thoroth squeezed tighter, making her freeze. She untangled herself from Thoroth with awkward movements. Gwyndolyn laughed at their expressions until Blaes reminded her of his desire to leave Sal'Sumarathar as soon as possible.

"Tell me something, Caelfel," Gwyndolyn said as they made their way to the Gyssedlues home. "Why did the Council of Sal'Sumarathar think you and Thoroth were necromancers?"

"It's complicated," Caelfel said. "There is someone they believed was dead, and he wasn't."

"It's not difficult to prove someone is alive. Whatever their reasoning, the case should have been immediately referred to Yamalvon."

"They were going to execute us if they sent us to Yamalvon," Caelfel said.

"The two of you would have never been executed. Something smells sour in Sal'Sumarathar. The Council should be reminded that they're not irreplaceable. Who was this elf they wanted dead?" Gwyndolyn asked.

Caelfel hesitated and watched her closely. "His name is Feraan Auvrearaheal."

Recognition flashed through Gwyndolyn's green eyes. "The elusive one. I think he's often referred to as the most hated elf of the empire." Gwyndolyn returned to her restless pacing and chewed on her bottom lip, thinking.

The imperial soldiers around them stopped with their lady, and Caelfel felt her stomach twist anxiously. "Is there something wrong?"

Gwyndolyn looked to Eviat and Sylaera. "I must speak to your daughter in private."

"You're welcome inside our home," Sylaera offered.

Gwyndolyn nodded and said nothing more until they reached the Gyssedlues home. She preferred using their garden as it was large enough to hold her company of soldiers. Blaes checked the perimeters before drawing the privacy curtain closed around the bathing area where he, Gwyndolyn, and Caelfel stood. The rest of the soldiers stood guard beyond the curtain.

"What happened to cause your ridiculous trial?"

Caelfel steeled herself against the penetrating eyes of Gwyndolyn and wondered if she could trust the she-elf who seemed so interested in their plight. "There was a hunting party. Feraan was injured, and I saved him. Unbeknownst to me, he was already reported as dead. They said what I did was necromancy unless I proved Feraan was alive."

"So why didn't you? That would make things so much simpler," Gwyndolyn asked.

"Because he refused to see the Council."

Gwyndolyn flashed a dangerous grin. "Because the Council is trying to kill him," she guessed.

Caelfel kept her face guarded.

"Why did you save him, Miss Gyssedlues?" Gwyndolyn asked. "Haven't you ever considered that perhaps he deserved to die? Have you ever asked why he has his reputation?"

Caelfel said nothing because, in truth, she hadn't.

Gwyndolyn laughed again, and Caelfel was beginning to loathe the sound. "I've heard he's quite handsome," Gwyndolyn said with a knowing smirk.

Caelfel recalled Feraan's brooding stature, the dark hair, and the sharp planes of his face. Again she said nothing, but the thought of Feraan stirred something within her. Gwyndolyn must have seen the reaction through Caelfel's aura because she didn't press the question further.

"The next time you see each other, you should ask him why he has that reputation and see what he says. Perhaps your feelings for him will change. It's been nice meeting you, Caelfel."

Gwyndolyn offered Caelfel a short curtsy before complying with Blaes's impatient prodding. Caelfel heard Gwyndolyn mention something about a sister before she disappeared from the garden entirely with her guard. Caelfel waited a full minute after the she-elf was gone before allowing herself to relax.

She might have imagined it, but Caelfel could have sworn that the ears that poked through Gwyndolyn's hair were round instead of pointed.

7. Black Crows

No couriers arrived to cancel Sir Kennyratear's class, so Caelfel left early the following morning. A lingering weakness clouded her head as she made her way to the college. Caelfel filed into the classroom with the other students but with her thoughts so focused on the previous day's encounter with Gwyndolyn, she could not meet anyone's eyes. That changed when everyone fell silent for the lesson.

"Settle down, everyone. I am your new instructor."

Caelfel's head shot up to join the confused faces around her. Sir Kennyratear did not stand before them. In his stead was a tall she-elf with thick, raven black hair. A small smile touched her lips as she surveyed everyone in front of her. Caelfel felt very small in her presence, and the feeling irritated her.

"Who are you?" someone asked. Caelfel could easily tell by the audible self-assurance that the voice belonged to Garvanna.

"I am Lady Luewyn," the new she-elf answered smoothly.

"Where is Sir Kennyratear?" Caelfel demanded impatiently.

Lady Luewyn's soft smile did not falter. "Nadeth Kennyratear has been dismissed from his classes for the time being."

Caelfel could not match Luewyn's smile as she scowled, stepping closer. "Why?"

Luewyn took two measured steps. "I do not have the authority to discuss the matter. You may ask Headmaster Nimuath about the nature of his dismissal on your own time, but I suspect Sir Kennyratear took a voluntary leave of absence. Will there be any more questions?"

The students exchanged uncertain glances, Caelfel among them, but no one asked anything else. Lady Luewyn's smile grew wider.

"I am native to the city of Sal'Sumarathar. My husband was from Amasel and he died with its fall. Since then, I have been living the last century in Yamalvon. But I tell you this to demonstrate my versatile range of magic. I have trained in Amasel and Yamalvon, and Rasaen and the Port City. I have even ventured as far as the Baetic Mountains to increase my knowledge of the mystical arts. As you no doubt have assumed, I am very qualified to be your instructor."

She waited, as if expecting a response and continued when no one said anything.

"No matter what occurred in this classroom with your previous instructor, you may take comfort in the fact that under my tutelage, you shall *safely* learn the mechanics of magic."

"Safely?" Garvanna repeated. She stood next to Caelfel and crossed her arms. "I have also studied magic at Amasel and Yamalvon. There is not an elf who provided a safer environment than Sir Kennyratear." Caelfel flinched at Garvanna's brave impetuousness but felt smug that Garvanna had the coherency to properly stand up to Lady Luewyn.

"Miss Hunithrae, is that correct?" Luewyn asked, confirming her name. "My remark was not a comment on Sir Kennyratear's teaching methods. I did not come here to replace him. Headmaster Nimuathar had asked me to come to Sal'Sumarathar."

Luewyn stared at Garvanna for the longest time, and Garvanna did not so much as shrink back. The tension between the two was all but tangible.

Luewyn broke the silence first. "I will not deny that your education history is impressive, Miss Hunithrae, but my classroom does not have a place for your pride."

"Sir Kennyratear's classroom," Caelfel corrected, squaring her shoulders next to Garvanna.

The room fell so silent that Caelfel could not even hear anyone breathe. Luewyn's green eyes flickered between Garvanna and Caelfel, assessing the opposition, before she laughed. The noise reminded Caelfel of Gwyndolyn's unsettling presence, and a shiver ran down her spine.

"I refuse to waste time on this show of insolence. Take all of your issues to Headmaster Nimuath."

Luewyn raised her hand and pointed to the door. The motion sent the door banging open.

"His office is on the top floor," Luewyn said with a smile.

Caelfel hesitated with Luewyn's dismissal, but Garvanna did not.

The taller she-elf marched to the door, and Caelfel hurried to follow. They passed in front of Luewyn on their way to the door, and Caelfel felt Luewyn's finger brush against her arm. She felt a sudden shock and Caelfel gasped, turning to see Luewyn smirking back at her. The expression struck Caelfel with a sudden sense of familiarity, but she was unable to place it.

"Who are you?" she asked, dumbfounded.

"My name is Luewyn Cyredathem. The door is over there, Miss Gyssedlues."

Caelfel hurried after Garvanna, a new trepidation settling over her as she rubbed the spot where Luewyn had touched her.

Garvanna flew up the staircase, but Caelfel was equally fast and had no trouble keeping up. Even so, she preferred Garvanna taking the lead.

"I don't trust her," was all Garvanna said before bursting into Nimuath's office uninvited. She froze suddenly, and Caelfel bumped into her, falling to the ground. She peeked around the older she-elf to see what had made her stop.

It was the scene of a deeply engrossed conversation being interrupted. Uthruil, Nimuath's younger brother, stood in front of the Headmaster who looked quite angry. Markis prowled around the edge of the room. He smiled when he saw Caelfel, and she glared at him.

Nimuath continued to look angry. "Miss Hunithrae, Miss Gyssedlues, please return to your class."

"It's urgent," Garvanna insisted.

"I am busy with matters of state. Come by tomorrow and next time you have an urgent matter, I suggest you try knocking."

His word ended the dispute, and Garvanna gave a noise of disgust before slamming the doors to his office. When she turned around to see Caelfel still on the ground, she looked irritable. "Get up. What are you doing on the floor?"

Caelfel frowned. "I fell when you stopped."

Garvanna shook her head and helped Caelfel to her feet. "Come on."

Lady Luewyn met them with a smirk but otherwise said nothing of their reappearance. Caelfel and Garvanna rejoined their classmates silently. Luewyn lectured for some time on the various branches of magic such as conjuring, obliteration, illusion, and healing. Caelfel was attentive, but Garvanna remained unimpressed, making occasional clucking noises with her tongue whenever she disagreed with Luewyn, which proved to be quite often.

When morning turned into afternoon, Luewyn had them stand and make shapes out of their auras. "Your aura is an extension of your life force and it bends to your will," Luewyn said pacing among the students. "It can take the shape of anything you desire. Weapon, clothing."

Caelfel hated to admit it but she found this portion of Luewyn's lesson enjoyable. The sickness of activating her aura had faded at last, allowing her to finally use her aura. She created simple shapes at first, cloudy and incorporeal versions of small animals. When Luewyn mentioned weapons, she had the idea to make a bow and it appeared in her hand, a hazy copy of the one she had at home.

By then, Luewyn passed her, pausing to admire Caelfel's work. She offered Caelfel a small smile. "Focus on it, and it will become real in your hands."

Caelfel concentrated harder, and as Luewyn promised, the bow fully materialized in her hands. It was warm to the touch and looked to be made of green metal, though it felt nothing like any metal she was familiar with.

Luewyn nodded her approval and moved on.

When Luewyn dismissed class, Caelfel felt pleasantly tired from using the energy of her aura. Meanwhile, Garvanna had stubbornly refused to take part in any of the activities, insisting that it was an insult to her intelligence.

"You are an expert mage, but you insist on taking novice classes," Caelfel pointed out to her as they followed the rest of the students out of the classroom. Garvanna hesitated just outside the doorway, and Caelfel stopped with her. Through the sea of faces, Caelfel noticed Markis leaving the college grounds among them. Caelfel tensed when his eyes met hers but relaxed when he continued on his way.

"I'm going to the library," Garvanna announced slowly. "I want to research our new professor. Try not to get yourself into trouble," she said, looking at Caelfel meaningfully.

Caelfel agreed, rolling her eyes. She left through the college gates alone, intending to visit the archery range and test the use of her aura bow.

She went home to retrieve her arrows first before making her way to the field. The archery range sat on the edge of town, near the horse meadow, in a small glen. When she arrived, it was empty, which was fine for Caelfel. She preferred practicing alone.

She fixed her quiver at her side and summoned her magic bow. The metal was smooth to the touch, and the string felt as though it had no resistance. She tried shooting one arrow, but the dimensions of her bow were off. The arrow went flying above the target and disappeared in the forest.

Caelfel adjusted the size and shape of the bow and nocked another arrow. This time, the arrow embedded itself in the dead center of the target. Caelfel smiled and shot a few more with similar results.

Then an idea occurred to her. She set her quiver to the side and focused on bringing an auric arrow to being. It appeared in her hand and went sailing smoothly into the air when shot. When it landed on the target, it erupted in a shower of green sparks.

Pleased with herself, Caelfel decided to end things and went to dislodge the arrows embedded in her target. When she had claimed all of her arrows in the target, she looked past the clearing, peering through the trees. She left the archery range to find the first misfired arrow that had flown into the forest.

She walked for some distance, until the field behind her was out of sight, kicking over dead leaves and underbrush in her search. Then she paused, feeling an ominous prickle on the back of her neck. She looked behind her but saw nothing there.

She stepped cautiously around the trees but saw no sign of her lost arrow. Her neck continued to prickle uncomfortably, so she decided it was a lost cause. One arrow was not worth the trouble, so she turned around to head back.

Caelfel saw a faint glinting in the distance and ducked in time to dodge an arrow flying towards her. It buried itself deeply in the tree behind her, and Caelfel saw it was one of hers.

Instantly she brought her aura bow to her hands and aimed in the direction the arrow came from. "Who is there?" she demanded of the silent forest, heart hammering in her chest. Her first thought was of Markis, and she would have no qualms about firing at him.

A dark figure stepped from the trees. The feminine curves of a dress was telling of a she-elf, and Caelfel struggled to focus on it with its shifting form that blinked in and out of her vision.

"*Take your best shot,*" the figure challenged.

And Caelfel did, releasing her magic arrow as she aimed for the figure's head.

Then strangely, the figure reached out and caught Caelfel's arrow, which reverted to a mass of shimmering green light. When the figure touched it, encasing it in a purple light, Caelfel felt a mildly painful shock. Her instinct caused her to draw back this portion of her aura, but the purple light followed it in a straight line.

When the figure's purple aura touched her, it produced an electric shock so powerful, Caelfel was sure her scream should have been heard for miles.

***

The steward was not one that fancied the desert, despite being there for the past six years. He anticipated the long-awaited day when he could turn his back on the desert and its black stone fortress for good. That day, he sensed, was close. Handling the affairs of the desert princeling did not suit his superior talents, and as a human, the steward had a rare talent indeed.

Instead he found himself presenting a rare and mysterious guest for an audience with the princeling. As instructed, he led the hooded horseman through the metal gates of the fortress. The cowl and cloak that shrouded the horseman from sight would not be a cause for concern, but the sexless creature astride its blasphemous steed made the horses restless and the dogs uneasy. Even the hired soldiers shied from its presence. This was a messenger from the Blind Seer.

Glancing black, the steward saw that the messenger took no notice of its surroundings. It kept its hidden gaze locked straight ahead, so the steward did the same, opening the castle doors. The messenger proceeded inside, still atop its horse. The princeling rose from his metal-fashioned throne to greet the visitor, a revolting smile touching his sand-puckered face. The steward had been in service to this princeling for nearly a decade, and the princeling disgusted him. Still, the steward preferred his largely arrogant desert prince over servants of the Seer.

"Welcome emissary of Sibylla!" the princeling boomed, holding his thick arms wide as he waited for a response.

The messenger turned to the steward and handed him a slip of dirty paper. The steward read over the foreign runes with a practiced eye. The messenger would not speak, servants of the Seer rarely did, so it was the steward's job to voice their intentions.

"My lord, the Blind Seer has sent this messenger to stay with us. She says that the time draws near and she wishes for her servant to be here when the time comes."

The princeling was delighted with the news and anxious to show the uninterested messenger the expanse of his fortress, a sign of his great wealth. The steward was left alone in the hall, annoyed at the princeling for readily welcoming a creature he had no true comprehension of. A servant of the Blind Seer had no concern with material surroundings.

The steward would have followed behind his master to lightly reprimand him for his imprudent behavior, but there was something on the parchment the messenger handed him that caught his eye. It was a note specifically for him from the Blind Seer.

I know what you plan, Lisiek. Fear the Black Crow, for she will take your life.

The steward detested the prophetic arts of divination. His brother had once dabbled in them, and it only brought him ruin. The incident left him without a brother, and because of it he now avoided seers and the like. He had warned the princeling against using the services of the Blind Seer, but the princeling was blinded by his own grief, determined to avenge the murder of his love. The steward didn't understand the devotion; he had never been connected that deeply to his brother or anyone else. He thought it silly.

But the warnings of the Blind Seer, though unwarranted, should never be taken lightly. He folded the paper and tucked it into his sleeve before leaving the hall to patrol the fortress walls. The steward trained his eyes on the hazy horizon of the desert, his shoulders tense. His instinct searched for a black raven, but his mind told him that such animals were not native to the desert.

"Unless it's not an animal at all," he muttered to himself. The Blind Seer was fond of speaking cryptically.

From the top of the wall, the steward could see all the training companies of soldiers. On the other side, he could see the sudden drop off the edge of the plateau that the fortress sat upon and mentally, he cursed the place. He didn't see the use of building such a large fortress in the middle of an uninhabited desert. It did not seem wise to him, but then again, the princeling owned over half the desert. He would have had little other choice in choosing a location.

Plus, crows weren't native to the desert. The steward had convinced himself of this fact until, turning, he saw one flitting from the turrets of the west wall.

***

"Caelfel?"

Garvanna?

Caelfel struggled to move or to open her eyes or mouth, and her body refused to work properly. She felt the ghost of an immense electrical shock coursing through her blood vessels, and its wake left her muscles quivering involuntarily. Her head hurt, and there were large black spots in her memory. She had no recollection of where she was, but she felt damp ground pressing into her cheek.

Someone rolled her over—that's right, she had heard Garvanna's voice—so then her back felt the soggy ground.

She was too focused on trying to regain control of her body to hear what Garvanna said next. She only caught a name—Thoroth. And then she blacked out from her own mental exertion.

The next time she woke up, things were much simpler. She had more control over her own body so she finally opened her eyes.

She had moved. The soggy ground had been replaced with something warmer—a bed, she realized belatedly. But it was not her own, though she struggled to remember what her bed looked like.

A face hovered over her, and she wanted to call it Garvanna though she knew that was not right. Her mind hummed, casting around for a different name. There *had* been another name, and this face belonged to it.

"Thoroth," she said slowly.

"How are you feeling?" he asked in a throaty voice.

"Tired," she said, blinking at him. She was in a bed so she must have been tired. But the restless trembling of her limbs told her otherwise. She wanted to move.

"Caelfel?" said a new voice.

It took extraordinary effort to turn her neck, but she was rewarded with the sight of the other one. Garvanna. It brought her some relief, because Garvanna had been her first thought.

Then she realized Garvanna was addressing her, and that this *Caelfel* must have been her all along. It made sense, seeing as that was what she responded to.

Yes, Caelfel. That was right.

She did not see the tall she-elf as a maternal figure, but Garvanna crossed the room and touched her fingers to Caelfel's cheek.

"What happened?" Garvanna asked.

Garvanna's fingers felt strange against her face, so Caelfel swatted them away. She didn't have the faintest notion of what Garvanna was talking about. Her only answer was a puzzled expression.

Thoroth and Garvanna exchanged glances. Garvanna met Caelfel's gaze again and said, "Caelfel, your aura is gone."

Caelfel's eyebrows furrowed and she shook her head, not comprehending. Her jaw locked again, and she knew she should be concerned. But Caelfel couldn't focus her mind to understand.

"I found you in the forest, and your aura was already gone," Garvanna tried again.

Aura. College. Magic. Bow. Arrow. "Archery field?" Caelfel asked, as small nuances slowly came back to her.

Garvanna nodded. "I found *this* with you." She handed Caelfel a quiver of arrows.

Caelfel sat up in the bed and took it into her hands, studying it closely. She held onto it so tightly that her fingers went white.

"Do you remember anything?" Thoroth asked.

She focused on the soft leather in her hand, running her fingers on the feather fletching. She had had a green bow, but that was gone now thanks to the mysterious figure.

"There was a figure." She paused, pursing her lips. "How did you find me?" she asked, looking to Garvanna.

"Your mother had said you left home with your quiver, and I remembered seeing you use your aura to create a bow in class. So I looked at the archery field."

Caelfel shook her head; that was not the answer she had wanted. "How did you know to look for me?" she insisted.

"I wanted to speak to you after I left the library. I tried your house first before I went to the field."

Caelfel looked down at her hands. "I have no aura," she repeated quietly. The bow, the magic refused to come to her hands. "How is that possible?"

"What was the figure that you saw?" Garvanna asked.

Caelfel shook her head. "All I remember is a dark cloud. The figure must have taken it."

Garvanna and Thoroth both nodded sympathetically, but Caelfel eyed them cautiously. She wondered if they thought her mad and were only agreeing to humor her.

"*It was there!*" she insisted to them.

"I believe you," Garvanna said, but Caelfel was not convinced.

"Can I get it back?" Caelfel asked, unable to suppress a glimmer of hope. Elves were supposed to have auras. That was what made them elves.

Thoroth shifted in his seat, drawing Caelfel's attention to him. "When I studied to become a healer, my master taught me a re-ignition technique. It's never been completed successfully. The idea is to ignite a dying aura, if it can be done. It's only a theory, but, Caelfel, you didn't have any sort of aura left for me to grow."

"And there is nothing else you can do?" Garvanna asked him.

"I'm sorry, Anna. I don't know what else to do."

Garvanna sniffed. "Don't apologize to me. I'm not the one who lost an aura." She turned her back and disappeared from the room. Caelfel looked up to Thoroth, at a loss for words.

Thoroth offered a partial smile. "Don't mind her. I'm quite used to her temper by now."

Caelfel released a large sigh. "She was much worse earlier with Lady Luewyn."

"Who?"

Caelfel's mouth fell open, surprising herself with the reference. The new instructor had not been on her mind, and Caelfel had all but forgotten her. "Lady Luewyn," Caelfel said slowly as she remembered it herself. "She is Sir Kennyratear's replacement."

Thoroth's eyebrows creased into a dark brown knot. "Why does Sir Kennyratear need a replacement?"

Several large books slammed on the table next to Thoroth. Caelfel jumped and saw that Garvanna had rejoined them. "That's what I want to know. Unfortunately, I had a more pressing matter to deal with."

"Was he dismissed or did he leave of his own accord?" Thoroth asked.

"Lady Luewyn mentioned he took a voluntary leave of absence, but I'm not so sure," Garvanna answered. "We have two problems, though. Caelfel's missing aura and Sir Kennyratear's absence. Which should we focus on?"

"What about Lady Gwyndolyn? She called herself a master of auras. Perhaps she can help or shed some light on this matter," Thoroth offered. "I would assume she is on the Board of Wizardry but I wouldn't know where to find her."

"Sir Kennyratear went to Yamalvon for help. He was the one that found her," Caelfel pointed out.

Garvanna nodded at this. "So first we find Sir Kennyratear."

Garvanna volunteered to look for Sir Kennyratear while Caelfel and Thoroth waited for her return. Caelfel sank back into the mattress when she had left.

"Gwyndolyn makes me nervous. I'm not sure if I trust her," Caelfel confided to Thoroth.

"I don't like her any more than you do, but she may be the only elf able to help us."

Caelfel folded her arms and shifted even lower into the bed. Thoroth turned his head and fixed his eyes on her.

"Caelfel, you have something on your arm."

She absently scratched at her wrist and followed his gaze to a spot on her arm just below her elbow. The spot was black, as if she were stained by soot, and sensitive to the touch. Caelfel was shocked and tried wiping it off with no success. "That was where Lady Luewyn's hand brushed against my arm when I walked past her in class."

Thoroth took her arm into his hands as he examined the black mark. "That was where she touched you?" he reaffirmed.

When Caelfel nodded, he tried healing it with his aura, but the mark refused to disappear. He smeared a salve on it instead and wrapped bandages around her arm. Thoroth muttered darkly to himself for minutes afterward until Garvanna arrived with Sir Kennyratear.

"That was rather quick," Thoroth remarked. "I remember Sir Kennyratear living further away from Sal'Sumarathar."

"I came across him walking through the center of the city. He was leaving the Hall of Court," Garvanna answered, angling her face pointedly.

"What were you doing in the Hall of Court?" Caelfel asked Sir Kennyratear.

Nadeth waved her question away. "That matters little. Miss Hunithrae said your aura is gone."

He stepped in front of her, placing his fingers on her temples. His skin felt warm to the touch, but the warmth did not spread as it had when she was in the college infirmary.

"We thought about retrieving Gwyndolyn. She said she was a master of auras," Thoroth suggested to him.

Without removing his hands, Sir Kennyratear grumbled back, "I would not trust Lady Gwyndolyn with such a delicate matter."

"But she proved our innocence," Caelfel pointed out. "You were the one that went to Yamalvon for her."

Sir Kennyratear scoffed, removing his hands "I went to the Board of Wizardry, and they gave me *her.*" He shuddered at the thought.

"You don't trust her," Thoroth said.

"She's insane. You must have seen that. Someone that unstable should not be placed in such a position just because of her bloodlines."

"She was certainly odd, but I'm not sure if I would call her insane," Caelfel said.

Sir Kennyratear went on muttering under his breath and turned his eyes to her arm. "Were you injured?"

Without waiting for an answer, he ripped the bandage from her arm, revealing the mysterious black spot.

He frowned. "Where did you get that?"

She chafed the mark with her thumb. "I'm not entirely sure. It's where Luewyn touched me."

"Before you lost your aura?" he asked.

Caelfel hesitated, considering how the two events were related. She glanced at Thoroth and Garvanna for their input, but Sir Kennyratear held her gaze as though he was trying to tell her something.

"You need to have this checked," he told her severely. Caelfel stared back at him, slowly realizing that he was trying to send her a message without alerting Thoroth or Garvanna.

"I've done what I can for it," Thoroth pointed out, completely oblivious to their silent exchange.

"She doesn't need the useless cream you've smeared all over her arm," Sir Kennyratear snapped.

"Then what does she need?" Garvanna asked him impatiently.

"Something that is not here," said Sir Kennyratear.

"Then tell us so we can bring it here," Garvanna said.

Sir Kennyratear hesitated, still staring at Caelfel intently.

Sudden recognition caused her to take a sharp breath. "Oh."

Sir Kennyratear meant Feraan.

She pushed herself from the bed and staggered out of the house without pausing for Garvanna's or Thoroth's reaction. Garvanna followed her to the street, though. "Where are you going?" she demanded.

Caelfel briefly turned to face her, scrambling for a plausible excuse for leaving so abruptly. "I'm going home to tell my parents."

Garvanna scowled. "You're lying. You shouldn't be stumbling around right now."

Caelfel didn't offer a response to the other she-elf and took off down the street.

Having little concern if she was being followed, Caelfel decided to walk to Feraan's house. She took the same path that ran along the Blaidd River and passed over the familiar boulders. When the river curved sharply, she knew his house sat just beyond the overlook. Caelfel made quick work of scaling it and rushed to his door, only to pause when she saw Feraan in his garden. Smoke curled over his head and coalesced into a magical black cloud that hovered in the corner of his garden, and as she drew closer, she saw bright red sparks flying around him. He paused to inspect a blade he had been sharpening on his grindstone.

Caelfel found that she was content to simply watch him unnoticed for a few moments. Ash smeared his face and blackened his fingers. She had never taken him for a blacksmith but found that she was not surprised to discover he had a wide range of talents. Feraan was certainly an odd elf, and the more she looked at him, the more Caelfel thought he looked much too large compared to the normally slender shape of an elf. Feraan possessed unusually broad shoulders.

The moment passed when he looked up suddenly, as if sensing he was the subject of her thoughts. Caelfel froze, hesitating when he saw her. The black cloud disappeared when their eyes met. His expression held surprise at her appearance but not anger, so she felt it safe to enter the garden.

"What brings you here?" he asked, setting his work aside.

By way of answer, she showed him her arm with its mysterious blemish.

He took her arm and inspected the spot more closely, rubbing his thumb across the surface. His brow furrowed as he stared at the offensive mark. Then he turned his concentrated glare onto her face.

"This happened today?" he asked.

Caelfel nodded.

He dropped her arm and ran his fingers through his dark hair, all the while muttering inaudibly to himself. A minute passed, and Caelfel was sure he had quite forgotten she was there.

"Do you know what it is?" she asked.

"I've seen it before," he answered. "It was about eighty years ago."

"What happened?"

"It still remains a mystery to me," he sighed. "And your aura is gone too, I see."

Caelfel suddenly realized that her missing aura should have taken top priority. "Do you think it is connected?" she asked.

"How did you receive that mark?" Feraan asked impatiently.

"It appeared on my arm where Lady Luewyn's hand touched me. But also—"

Recognition flashed through Feraan's eyes. "Lady Luewyn?" he repeated with a hiss.

"Do you know her?" Caelfel asked.

"Know her? Luewyn is my sister."

Caelfel stepped back to look at Feraan. The dark hair and green eyes were certainly the same, but the relation still surprised her. "I didn't realize you had a sister." But as she said it, Caelfel realized she didn't know very much about Feraan at all, chiefly why he had his infamous reputation.

Feraan gave her a thin smile. "We have the same mother."

"But not the same father?" Caelfel asked.

"Her father was a noble from Amasel. I don't know who my father is. But that's not important right now. When did you meet Luewyn?"

"She's Sir Kennyratear's replacement at the college," Caelfel answered. "But you should also know—"

Feraan appeared confused. "I did not realize he was being replaced. How did his venture from Yamalvon end?"

Caelfel sighed at being interrupted again and gave Feraan a strange look, thinking Feraan must lock himself in his house so much he was unaware of everything around him. "Thoroth and I were proven innocent."

"So an escape from Honey Water would be unnecessary. How?"

"There was a she-elf from Yamalvon. She called herself a master of auras. She inspected our auras and said we were innocent of necromancy. She didn't appear very happy with the Council."

"Do you remember her name?"

"It was Gwyndolyn. They also called her Lady Ernmas."

Feraan scowled. "I don't recognize her name, but Ernmas is a name of royalty. She must be related to Empress Haelyn."

"Something was off with her. Sir Kennyratear called her insane, but I'm not sure if I would go quite that far."

"Since Sir Kennyratear was the one to retrieve her from Yamalvon, he doesn't have much room to complain about her sanity."

"But it's more than that," Caelfel insisted. "She made strange comments rather frequently. Her head guard thinks someone is after her, and she told us she was powerful enough to destroy an entire city."

Feraan paused at the information and without warning, he darted into his house. Caelfel followed after him in time to witness him pacing the room anxiously and tearing through his shelves as he frantically searched for something. He took no notice of her standing in the doorway as he searched.

"Is there something wrong?"

"I have it written down somewhere," Feraan growled, refusing to explain what he was referring to. He grunted impatiently and moved to the next room, pouring over books and odd scrolls. Caelfel merely stood in the doorway, feeling a shade impatient herself as she waited for Feraan to complete his strange search.

"Can I tell you something?" she asked and as she settled against the doorframe as she suddenly felt exhausted. Her head felt heavy, but she was too afraid to close her eyes. It reminded her of the electrical currents that had shot through her body hours before.

Feraan didn't pause to look up. "Go ahead."

"I left the college this afternoon with my aura. I went to the archery range to practice with my aura. I lost an arrow in the forest and when I went looking for it, I was attacked."

This finally made Feraan pause. "Attacked?" Feraan repeated.

"There was a figure in a dark cloud with a purple aura," Caelfel said, recalling the events sluggishly. "When this aura touched my aura, it almost killed me. I couldn't stop screaming, and after that I didn't remember anything for a while. I was unconscious when Garvanna found me. *I couldn't even remember my name when I woke up.*"

Feraan stood and crossed the room toward her. He placed his hands on either side of her face and looked deep into her eyes. "But you remember now? You remember everything?"

Caelfel shook her head. "I don't know if I'm forgetting anything else but I still see black spots in my head. My hands are still shaking." To prove her point, she lifted them for his inspection.

Feraan gave her an odd look and lowered his hands. "Why didn't you tell me this sooner?"

"I tried, but you were too concerned with Gwyndolyn and Luewyn," she sighed, her exhaustion returning. She didn't want to sleep, though, so she forced herself to watch as Feraan resumed his wild search. "Can I ask you something now?"

Feraan only nodded.

"Why are you the most hated elf?"

This made him freeze. He slowly returned the book he was holding to the floor. "Why do you ask that?"

She offered a slight shrug. "I think it's a fair question. Everyone knows, except me. I think I have a right to know."

He gradually straightened up. "You have a right to know the fabricated story of an unfortunate scapegoat?" he asked critically.

"What's the fabricated story?" she asked.

"It's nothing, and you shouldn't worry about it." He paused. "Do you love Thoroth?"

It was such an odd question, that Caelfel could only grow red in the face as she vehemently denied having any such feelings. Feraan didn't seem convinced, but Caelfel was annoyed with how he changed the subject.

He sent her away then, insisting that she should see her parents and inform them about her aura. Caelfel left reluctantly but not fully deterred from the subject. If anything, his resistance made her all the more curious as she heard Gwyndolyn's words ring through her head.

Perhaps your feelings for him will change.

But Caelfel was quite uncertain what those feelings were. She remembered his kiss fondly even though he had assured her there was no meaning behind it. She had been learning to trust Feraan, but it was quite evident he did not yet trust her.

8. Lost Shadow

Caelfel returned home exhausted from the day's events. Her parents greeted her cheerfully, having no idea of the tragedy that had befallen her. Caelfel did not have the energy to force a smile so her expression remained downcast and exhausted. Sylaera noticed her daughter's forlorn mood and grabbed Caelfel by the shoulders, but Caelfel didn't have to explain.

"You've lost your aura," Sylaera stated accurately.

Caelfel nodded, and her mother gave Eviat a meaningful look.

"You should comfort her," Sylaera told him.

Caelfel wasn't sure how her father could comfort better than anyone else, but Eviat led her through the back door and into the garden. He settled against the lavender bushes, which were Caelfel's favorite. He didn't speak at first, instead running his fingers against the silvery leaves. Caelfel waited patiently, watching her father and taking in the ash-gray hair and the miniscule creases around his eyes. Her father was a greyling. She knew him to be over thousands of years old, but something other than time had made him age so. Sir Kennyratear was older than her father, and he showed less signs of aging.

"Caelfel, you are not the first to lose your aura," Eviat began.

She knew this already from what Feraan had told her but she did not interrupt.

Eviat kept his attention focused on the lavender leaves but his words were meant for her. "I lost my aura as well."

Caelfel's mouth fell slightly agape. "When did this happen?" She felt stupid for not already knowing this.

"It was less than a century ago, just before you were born."

She counted the years. Caelfel was seventy-six years old, and Feraan mentioned a time of this happening eighty years ago. She suspected the two were related. "Was Feraan involved?"

This took Eviat by surprise, and he turned his gaze from the plant to face her. "Why do you ask that?"

She showed him the mark on her arm, and Eviat stroked it gently with his two fingers before returning to the leaves. "Feraan said he saw marks similar to this one eighty years ago. How did you lose your aura?"

"It was taken from me." He rolled up his sleeve to reveal a twin mark on his shoulder.

Caelfel looked at it with wide eyes. "Who took it?"

Eviat shook his head. "I don't know. Ever since the incident, I haven't been able to practice healing as I used to."

Something stuck in Caelfel's throat. "Will I age too?" She was younger than most elves and had had a difficult time being taken seriously. She did not want to look older than them.

"I don't believe so. I think I aged because I've lived over two millennia using my aura."

"How did it happen?" Caelfel asked, drawing her knees to her chest. "Surely you did not wake up one day with it missing."

"I don't remember most of it, Caelfel," Eviat admitted sadly.

Caelfel suppressed an impatient sigh. It was not her father's fault that his memory failed him. That was the product of living such a long life; elves would forget things. "Is there nothing I can do to get it back?"

Eviat smiled sadly. "If there is a way, I have not found it. Where is your amulet?"

Caelfel reached for the pendant that was not there. "I gave it to Feraan to save his life. You should remember that; you were at my trial," she recalled.

Eviat nodded at this information and departed, leaving Caelfel alone with her thoughts in the silent garden.

"There is no help," she said to herself bitterly.

Caelfel had had dreams of becoming a battlemage. She wanted nothing more than to experience the thrill of battle, protecting her elfkind and homeland. But such dreams were dashed now. After all the trouble she went through to use her aura, it was gone from her.

Forever. She was useless, defenseless. Powerless. And the thought weighed heavily in her stomach. She still had her bow, which was what she had been exceptionally talented at, but magic was one of the marks of being an elf. Without it, she could hardly be called one, she thought to herself grimly.

Defenseless and powerless.

She wondered at the usefulness of taking her aura away. Feraan seemed so certain Luewyn was responsible, but Caelfel couldn't understand how the callous she-elf would benefit. Then she remembered Markis's pursuit of her and Feraan only a few nights before and the memory raised the hairs on the back of her neck. She wouldn't peg Markis as one to give up so easily, so perhaps he hadn't.

Caelfel was suddenly alert and aware of every detail around her. Her sharp eyes noted the birds flitting through the tree branches, and her pointed ears picked up the muted sound of the river nearby, the same river that ran alongside Feraan's house. Feraan had been paranoid about someone following her to his home, and she wondered if someone was still following her in spite of her newly proven innocence.

She had been proven innocent of necromancy. Her name had been cleared in front of the Council, even though they had not been pleased with the one who cleared it. Gwyndolyn was suspicious of the Council herself. Gwyndolyn wanted justice against the elf that had exploded Caelfel's aura.

And that elf was Markis.

And then Sir Kennyratear was dismissed from the college, shortly before Garvanna saw him leaving the Hall of Court. A thought occurred to Caelfel. Perhaps Sir Kennyratear had had his own trial, charged with the crimes Markis had committed.

Caelfel rose from her position in the garden and went inside, not feeling very safe while being exposed in their garden. She locked herself in her room, heart racing the entire time. She wasn't sure why Luewyn or anyone else would take her aura. Maybe after Gwyndolyn came to investigate, the Council felt it necessary to remove any auric evidence.

It was not even close to dark, but Caelfel bolted her window shut and strategically placed all of her weapons around her in a circle, positioning each one within reach. She had her short-sword in front of her while her bow rested carefully on the floor to her left side, her quiver on the right. An assortment of knives, mostly throwing knives and two hunting knives, dotted the spaces between them. She had her legs crossed neatly with a hand on each knee. Tremors of anticipation made her fingers twitch nervously for several long minutes.

A sudden urgency seized her, and Caelfel sprang up from her place on the floor and began pacing her room. She grabbed the first object that she could reach, her bow, and she set about polishing its already pristine wood. When she had exhausted that task, she began handcrafting new arrows. She was in a frenzy, which did not subside even hours later when she ran out of swan feathers. Caelfel demanded her parents that more be brought to her. Father told her that he did not like her tone, but within the hour, more had been delivered to her by Thoroth.

"Your parents are concerned with your behavior," Thoroth said, his eyes sweeping the messy array of wood shavings.

"I have been busy."

"With feathers?"

"I've been making arrows," she said defensively.

"What truly bothers you, Caelfel?"

"I am not bothered," she lied, thinking of Feraan, of Sir Kennyratear, of the chilling expression she saw every time she thought of Markis.

Thoroth did not look convinced. Feraan's odd question from earlier crossed her mind. Caelfel came very close to mentioning it to Thoroth, but her face grew red at the mere thought of it. She returned her attention to her work.

"They're worried about you, Caelfel. *I'm* worried," Thoroth attempted when she said nothing. This only brought Feraan's question back to the forefront of her mind, despite her attempts to dismiss it.

She settled instead on biting sarcasm. "What's there to worry about? My aura has only mysteriously disappeared with no explanation. A sinister she-elf has replaced Sir Kennyratear at the college. And *why* is Feraan the most hated elf of Honey Water?" she hissed, turning her glare on Thoroth. She had lost her feeble attempt at humor as her irritation bested her.

Thoroth was not prepared for her ranting and was visibly taken aback. "I don't think you want me to answer that," he said cautiously.

"And why not?" Caelfel demanded, bristling.

"Because as much as I believe he is dangerous, I think you are besotted with him."

"I am not—" Caelfel began indignantly.

"*And* you wouldn't take well to such information," Thoroth continued as if he had not heard her.

"I still think I should know," Caelfel muttered darkly.

"I am not one for breaking hearts. You should ask Garvanna, because she has no qualms about it."

"You don't like him, so why should you care?"

"I care about you, Caelfel," Thoroth said timidly. He crouched next to her. "I have no wish to break your heart, even though I have no reservations about breaking his."

Before she could process that, Thoroth touched his forehead to hers and then angled his face slightly to meet her lips. His kiss was swift and flushed her cheeks. Caelfel sat, blinking in its wake. Before she could properly react, Thoroth excused himself and left her alone in her room with the swan feathers he had delivered.

Caelfel decided she was annoyed with Thoroth then. She had wanted to ask after Sir Kennyratear, but he had distracted her with a silly kiss and a refusal to answer her questions before abandoning her altogether. In her frustration, she pushed her arrow work aside and resumed her pacing.

***

Feraan would have expected to be confronted by anyone else, except Eviat Gyssedlues, and yet, it was Eviat Gyssedlues who approached him.

It was Feraan's own fault, really, for leaving the safety of his home and braving the world of Sal'Sumarathar. He had once been able to roam the streets without fear of being pelted by rocks, or worse, but that was when he had been very young and innocent of the crimes that now plagued his conscience. A different time, altogether.

He had been on his way to the home of Sir Kennyratear and, as was his habit, he was avoiding the streets. How he had even managed to cross paths with Eviat was beyond his understanding. But there he was, making his way around Rumfel Lake, when the greyling stopped him.

Eviat asked only a simple question, "Can you return her amulet?"

There was no need to specify which amulet he referred to because Feraan possessed only one, and it didn't even belong to him. He involuntarily clutched at the burdensome thing that dangled from his neck. He didn't like wearing it and he felt as though it gave him away while he attempted to remain unseen. If he had a choice, Feraan would have ridden himself of it at the first opportunity.

But that wasn't a viable option. He had tried removing it once, for the briefest of moments, only to find himself suffocating on his own frozen blood. Without a certain, extinct antidote, the poison remained lethal to him. Wearing Caelfel's amulet had turned into an unwelcome necessity.

Eviat must have assumed as much from Feraan's expression because he sighed and began searching the Rumfel banks for another solution to his problem. Feraan was about to continue on his way to Nadeth's home but curiosity stayed his feet as he watched Caelfel's father stride through the meadow in agitation.

"Why do you ask?" Feraan called before Eviat ventured out of earshot.

Eviat heaved another sigh and eventually returned to the lake's edge to finish his conversation with the most hated elf of the empire. He explained that he had taken the amulet to Yamalvon, shortly before Caelfel was born, and had it enchanted so that his daughter would not suffer his same fate, the loss of an aura. The enchantments placed on it also provided protection from poisons, which accounted for Feraan's current need for it.

"I gave it to her when she was born so she would be protected for the rest of her life."

Feraan watched him carefully. "You were awfully paranoid."

"And not without good reason," Eviat pointed out. "Look at what's happened now."

Feraan nodded his agreement but said nothing.

"I remember what you said before, that my aura is completely lost."

Feraan angled his eyes suspiciously. "And I still stand by that statement."

"Since Caelfel's situation differs from mine, I thought that there might be a chance to salvage hers."

Feraan considered this for a long minute. "You are right. There is one responsible—"

"You found them?" Eviat hastily interrupted.

Feraan's expression hardened as he remembered the past eighty years of endless searching. "No, I have not found them. I have found my sister, who seems to be responsible for what happened to Caelfel."

"So does she have a chance?" Eviat asked.

Feraan did not want to agree with the greyling to offer him false hope, but he gave Eviat the truth anyway. "There is a slight chance."

"Then what stops you?" Eviat asked, his face darkening.

"Because I am not so eager to confront my sister as you might think," Feraan said.

Eviat was angry. "You even know who is responsible yet you do nothing," the greyling hissed.

"Now Eviat, I've long since learned that involving myself in such matters is not wise."

"I might laugh at that if it were not my daughter in danger."

"You're overreacting because you're afraid. I simply can't do everything."

"You've turned into a coward hiding in your cave all this time. Do you not think the two incidents could be related? Caelfel's missing aura is relevant to your search."

"I don't live in a cave," Feraan protested indignantly.

Eviat shook his head. "My daughter stared in the face of the Council when they threatened her with execution. She did that for you. She didn't hesitate. She didn't even blink. I thought you would at least return the favor."

Eviat stormed off then, and Feraan stared after him. He would have shrugged off this conversation without a second thought except Eviat had reminded him of Caelfel's trial. Feraan had been there. He had seen Caelfel ready to accept death instead of handing Feraan over to the Council. He had thought nothing of honoring his life debt to her, but witnessing her unwavering loyalty was not something he could ignore. He was not accustomed to seeing such passionate devotion in elves.

If only she knew what had happened eighty years ago. Perhaps she would not be so willing to be his friend.

So Feraan changed direction and made his way towards the College of Sal'Sumarathar. A visit to Nadeth would have to wait.

It did not take him long to reach the wrought iron gate that barred the entrance to the college grounds. He stared through the bars for a moment, remembering the last time he had passed through them as a student. It had been centuries ago, and he had just been expelled for kidnapping the Headmaster and setting the grounds on fire. Feraan's mouth twitched into a smile at the memory. He had always had a penchant for mischief, unlike other elves.

But it had been that incident that compelled the Board of Wizardry to take action to protect their colleges. Wards were erected around the grounds, much like the ones that protected the Fey Forest from intruders. An elf could not enter the grounds if he or she had violent intentions, and if things should turn violent inside the gates, the wards would ensnare all offenders within confining, magical bindings until they were promptly dealt with by the Headmaster. Feraan felt honored that he personally inspired the Board to secure the safety of the students of the college.

He focused on nonviolent thoughts and proceeded through the gate cautiously. The wards did not worry him; he had smuggled an entire army through the ones that surrounded the Fey Forest. After all, he had no wish to harm Luewyn. For the moment.

All the instructors of the college were offered their own dormitories. Feraan could easily guess that Luewyn now occupied the room that once belonged to Sir Kennyratear. When Feraan reached the door, he did not bother with knocking and went inside.

When the room belonged to Sir Kennyratear there had been a desk, several bookcases, and two cushioned chairs. All of his possessions had been completely cleared out, and the room was bare except for a single, locked chest. Luewyn herself sat by the window and did not notice his entrance. Feraan went to stand next to her, folding his hands behind his back.

"It has been a while Luewyn," he greeted.

If he surprised her, she did not show it. She turned her face a fraction until he saw the tip of her nose. "I was hoping that it would continue to be so." She gathered her skirts to stand.

"Please, don't get up on my account," Feraan said, putting some distance between him and his sister. "What brings you here to Sal'Sumarathar?"

She turned to face him, and the setting sun illuminated the smirk on her face. "Nimuath offered me a position at his college, so I took it."

"That is quite uncharacteristic of you, considering how much you hate Sal'Sumarathar."

Luewyn kept her smile in place, but Feraan saw that it was

forced. "I hate *you*. I don't hate this city."

Feraan nodded. "I appreciate the clarification—"

"If you're wondering about your friend, the greyling, I have nothing to tell you," Luewyn interrupted.

"What makes you think I am here about him?"

"I know Sir Kennyratear's always been a friend to you. He is the only thing I can think of that would draw you so quickly out of hiding."

Luewyn was wrong; he wasn't there about Sir Kennyratear, but he would jump on any opportunity presented to him. "So what do you know about Nadeth?"

"As I just told you, I know nothing. Nimuath only said there was a problem with the Council. I don't even know if he left voluntarily or if Nimuath dismissed him." Luewyn sighed impatiently, as if she had grown tired of repeating the message of Sir Kennyratear's absence.

But Feraan thought that was odd. He had not realized Sir Kennyratear was dealing with problems from the Council. Perhaps it was a mistake to not visit him first. "And how did your first day of class go?" Feraan asked mildly.

"It went well. There was a concern among the students about replacing Sir Kennyratear. It was to be expected, of course, since Nadeth is a respected instructor at this institution." Luewyn sighed again, bristling at some memory. "I had a tiresome argument with some ignorant she-elf, but once that dispute was settled, the class continued smoothly."

Feraan picked up on the reference and had little doubt she referred to Caelfel. "Did it ease your frustration to take her aura?"

There was a long silence as Luewyn deliberated on his question. At length she said, "I've no idea what you mean."

"Come now, sister. You know I've been researching the matter extensively. Did you think I would not notice?"

"There is nothing to notice. Hiding in your hole has made you paranoid and suspicious of everything. You should rejoin the world one day and see how elves live among each other without fear of being murdered."

Feraan's smile was empty. "If only I had the luxury."

"It is your own fault, little brother," Luewyn said, rising. "You shouldn't have destroyed all of those people. Maybe then you would find it easier to make friends rather than seek the company of animals."

"I didn't destroy those people, and you are changing the subject."

Luewyn clapped her hands together. "Yes, I'd nearly forgotten. I shan't forget your ridiculous tales and silly accusations. I'll play along with your story this time, brother. Whose aura was I supposed to have taken? You think it was the one that annoyed me with her misguided defense of Sir Kennyratear."

Feraan said nothing, folding his arms as he waited for her to continue.

Luewyn tapped her crimson lips in mock thought. A moment passed and her eyes widened as though she suddenly realized something. "This girl was tall and loud with copper colored hair. I do not think she was your type. But there was another one, a quiet one who followed the other around like a lost shadow. She seemed pathetic to me and she must have been weak if her aura disappeared so easily."

A muscle in his arm flexed involuntarily. Feraan briefly considered strangling his sister, but he quickly rejected the idea, reminding himself of the wards that protected the college. He tried to relax himself by pacing. "I have heard of a remote place hidden in the peaks of the Baetic Mountains where the Twin Crows teach you dark magic. They specialize in the sorcery that rivals elven magic. I wonder if this is where you learned the practice of stealing auras."

Luewyn offered a thin smile. "You are misinformed then. It is their mother that teaches such magic. You might like them. Are you not fond of the humans and werefolk, anything that is not elvish?"

Feraan ignored the question and fixed her with a hard expression. "Return what you've stolen."

Luewyn examined his face carefully, a look of puzzlement furrowing her perfect brow. "I know you, Feraan. I know you wouldn't seek me out and confront me on a mere whim. I know you do your best to avoid me at all costs. So tell me, what is this she-elf to you?"

"That is none of your concern. Give it back to her," Feraan said evenly. He focused his breathing through his nose, but Luewyn saw something in his expression that lit up her face with inspiration.

She started circling him. "I had heard about your accident on a hunting party. It was her heroic efforts that saved your life. Still, I would not take you as one to honor the life debt."

Feraan said nothing as he simply watched his sister.

"Uthruil told me of her valiant determination to protect you in court, how she refused to reveal you to the Council. I am surprised you showed her where you live. You did not always trust other elves so easily, even if they did have a pretty face."

Feraan stuck on one detail. "I never showed her where I live."

"Oh?" Luewyn said, as if waiting for an explanation.

Feraan decided not to reveal that it was the Eye of Ewyn that showed Caelfel where his house was. Luewyn might attempt the same thing, and though he doubted she would be successful, he wasn't about to risk it.

"I can't imagine that she would be your champion if she knew why you have your reputation," Luewyn continued, hedging around the subject of Caelfel. Feraan sighed at his sister's prying.

"She was born after it happened," he volunteered reluctantly. "And her parents did not feel the need to tell her."

Luewyn stepped closer to him, and it took everything Feraan had to not back away. He would not show weakness in the face of his sister. "I see. She is enamored with you, then. You must be rather lonely to accept the companionship of one so young."

Feraan felt the corner of his mouth twitch and he chose his next words carefully. "Caelfel is over her half-century mark, so she is not so young as you might think. In any case, I am not so lonely as to seek the companionship of a married Head Councilor even before my husband met his tragic end in the fires of Amasel." Feraan clicked his tongue disapprovingly. "Never have I been that lonely."

Luewyn's smirk faltered, and she turned her back to him to return to the window. The light in the sky outside was fading. "As your sister, I'm offering you one last favor. Take my suggestion and leave."

"What about her aura?"

Luewyn twisted her body to gaze at him malevolently. "Which do you care about more—her aura or her life?"

Feraan felt himself grow angry and he kept his clenched fists at his sides, shaking. "What did you do?"

"Leave before the gate locks and the wards seal you in."

So Feraan turned on his heel and rushed from the college grounds.

9. Tragedy

Caelfel decided she had occupied herself with arrows long enough. She scrubbed the memory of Thoroth's kiss from her lips with the back of her hand and stood up. She needed to see Sir Kennyratear. She had so many questions for the greyling. As Caelfel departed, she said goodbye only to her mother, because her father had left the house and hadn't returned yet.

"Where are you going?" Sylaera asked.

"I'm going to see Sir Kennyratear," Caelfel answered.

"Are you sure that's a wise idea?"

Caelfel couldn't fathom why it wouldn't be, so she nodded to her mother and left with her bow and a quiver full of new arrows.

Sunset would not occur for another few hours, and Caelfel easily remembered the way to Sir Kennyratear's house even though she had been there only once before. Her father had taken her for a visit when she had been a youngling that had just learned how to walk. She remembered it well because the long walk had been atrocious. She had complained the entire way, so Eviat thought twice before bringing her along again.

Sir Kennyratear lived outside the city like Feraan did. Unlike Feraan, the greyling's house was not hidden. It sat surrounded by thick trees on a small hill south of Sal'Sumarathar, and a curving dirt path led directly to his front door. It took Caelfel an hour to reach the dirt path, and she knew it would take another to reach its end. She paused before continuing, her mother's question suddenly resurfacing in her thoughts. Gripping her bow, Caelfel pushed her thoughts away and made a run for the house.

She remembered a remark made by her father some time ago. The purpose of the winding pathway was to allow Sir Kennyratear plenty of time to assess his unexpected visitors. He should have seen her coming, but surprisingly his small front door was bolted shut. She considered the possibility that he might not be at home, and for some strange reason, that made her nervous. In an attempt to dislodge unwelcome thoughts, she began pounding on his door and calling his name.

"*Hush you silly girl!*" said Sir Kennyratear's muffled voice from the other side.

Caelfel paused as she heard his faint footsteps and the sound of locks turning and bolts sliding back. When the door opened, he grabbed her collar and yanked Caelfel unceremoniously inside.

"Breaking down my door is not necessary," he muttered darkly as he set about locking the door once again.

Caelfel straightened her tunic and set her bow by the door, immediately aware of Sir Kennyrayear's agitation. "What makes you so nervous?" she asked as he finished the locks.

Sir Kennyratear turned to face her briefly before retreating to the far end of the room. It wasn't a large house by any means, but his front room had enough space to hold a clutter of books and scrolls that rivaled the clutter in Feraan's front room. Caelfel had to push some of the clutter away with her foot to see the blue-tile floor.

"What brings you here?" Sir Kennyratear asked, ignoring her question and snapping Caelfel's attention away from a scroll intricately decorated with entwining vines.

She frowned. "What brings *you* here? Why are you not at the college?"

Sir Kennyratear sighed, and his face fell slack. In that moment, the greyling's true age showed in the weary lines of his face. The moment passed quickly. "I was put on trial."

"Why?" Caelfel asked, fearing her suspicions were about to be proved correct.

"Endangering my students," he scoffed. Nadeth lowered himself into a chair she had not previously noticed because it had been completely covered in papers. "Particularly the exploding of your aura."

"That wasn't your fault. Markis did that."

"And who do you think ran the trial?" Sir Kennyratear spat. "They had a witness, one of my other students, to testify against me."

"Who?" Caelfel asked.

"The son of the Head Councilor."

Daerad. Caelfel didn't have to say it and nodded slowly instead. She didn't recall Daerad being present at Luewyn's class. "We should gather the rest of your students, at least Garvanna and me. We can testify that Daerad lied."

But Sir Kennyratear wasn't convinced. "The trial is already over. There's no use for it anyway."

Caelfel's frown deepened at Nadeth's refusal to accept help, but she let the matter pass. "They needed a scapegoat, because Gwyndolyn told Uthruil to investigate who had exploded my aura."

"And Gwyndolyn sent Luewyn who relieved you of your aura."

There was a small stool on the floor next to her, and Caelfel sank into it slowly, burying her face in her hands. Gwyndolyn sent Luewyn because she thought Sir Kennyratear was to blame. "So Luewyn did this."

Sir Kennyratear nodded. "I don't know anyone else who would have that capability."

Caelfel ran her fingers through her hair. "I feel so vulnerable without it."

"And right you should," Sir Kennyratear interjected. "They've stripped you of your powers and made you all but defenseless."

"Is there any way I can get it back?" Caelfel asked, setting to work nervously tying back her hair.

"I would not think that Luewyn would know that ability or use it to help you if she did. You first need to know if she saved it."

Caelfel gave him an odd look. "If she saved it?" she repeated.

"Your aura is a field of pure energy," Sir Kennyratear began explaining. "Without a host—*you*—it would short itself out unless Luewyn has devised a way to store or harness it."

"How would I know that?" Caelfel asked.

"One of her possessions would radiate with energy. Perhaps it is in a gemstone, like the Eye of Ewyn. I imagine that if you touched it, there would be some sort of reaction. Maybe it would shock you or maybe it would kill you. Of course, this is supposing your aura is still there. She might have used it or lost it."

"But there is still a chance?" Caelfel pressed.

Sir Kennyratear angled his gaze. "There is only a very small chance that it even still exists and an even smaller chance you would get it back. You can't just release a physical mass of pure energy; it would kill you."

Caelfel chewed on her bottom lip as she considered the unfavorable odds. "Then how could I have it returned to me?"

"You would need to find someone who has the knowledge and ability. It's not a heavily explored field of elven magic, so I don't know of any elf that has the proper skills."

Caelfel sighed but wouldn't allow herself to grow disappointed. Gwyndolyn had called herself a master of auras, so Caelfel decided she would seek help from her, even though Gwyndolyn did prove to be a touch strange. She did not tell Sir Kennyratear of her plans, remembering his reaction the last time she had mentioned Gwyndolyn to him.

"Don't waste the rest of your life away on something that is so highly improbable. Your father gets on without his aura. Do you want to be like Feraan, so focused on some meaningless search that he's lost everything around him? He's hardly left his house in eighty years."

Caelfel perked up at the mention of eighty years. Eighty years ago was before she had been born. Eighty years ago was when her father lost his aura. Eighty years ago Feraan had been a part of something. Sir Kennyratear's words reminded her of her other question for him. "Why is Feraan called the most hated elf of Honey Water?"

Sir Kennyratear's expression changed, and Caelfel immediately knew he would be reluctant to answer. He smiled. "So your curiosity has won out," came his observation.

"I have always been curious," she pointed out to him softly.

"But the dreadful reputation has not scared you away yet," Sir Kennyratear countered. "And he has not told you."

"I've asked him," Caelfel said.

"But he does not want you to find out. He needs you, more than he might think. Feraan has always isolated himself from others, but aside from me, he has been starved for personal interaction these past eighty years. I believe you are a blessing to him."

Caelfel felt her face grow warm, having often noticed Feraan's loneliness. "What happened eighty years ago?"

Sir Kennyratear's smile turned sad. "I do not have the heart to tell you, Miss Gyssedlues. It was an awful day that I am sure he would rather forget. I would rather not spoil your opinion of him."

Caelfel pressed her lips into a thin line, suppressing the wave of impatience that buzzed through her tense shoulders. "Tahlmus and Garvanna have both called him a murderer," she pressed.

"Does he seem like a murderer to you?"

Caelfel could have answered that question when Feraan first handed her the medicine during the goblin raid, and her opinion hadn't much changed since then. "No, but I also do not think they would call him a murderer so lightly."

Sir Kennyratear leaned forward and maintained his gaze with her. "Feraan Auvrearaheal has done things he is not proud of. You will not wring the reason behind his shame from me, but if you find out on your own, know that he had no choice. Feraan is not a murderer."

Caelfel scowled at the cryptic remark. She didn't appreciate secrets being kept from her, even if Feraan supposedly didn't deserve his reputation.

She was about to protest further when Sir Kennyratear suddenly jumped to his feet and moved to the window to investigate outside. Her words stuck in her throat as she watched him. He lingered by the glass panes for an inexorably long minute before he yanked the curtains back over them. When he turned to look at her again, there was a dangerous shine to his eyes, and he took an even breath through his nose.

"This is when you leave," was all he said.

He took her arm with a surprisingly strong grip. With his other hand he grabbed her bow where it rested against the doorframe. She complained about the force he used but did not resist. "What do you mean?"

He pulled her into a small closet that held cloaks and winter coats. The floor there was made of wooden planks. He released her momentarily to test each plank with a few, selective light taps. Soon he found one and lifted it, raising a sizable trapdoor. Caelfel peered over his shoulder at the dank tunnel entrance hidden in the floor of the cloakroom. "I told you about my trial," he said.

"What of it?" she asked, eyeing the tunnel suspiciously.

"I didn't tell you how it concluded. Daerad testified against me, and I was found guilty."

"And your punishment?" she pushed, just now hearing the distant and ominous monotone of marching footsteps. She had no comparison for the sound but she imagined that it belonged to an army.

Before he answered, he pushed Caelfel through the tunnel. She tumbled a short distance before coming to rest on the cool earth at the bottom. The wind had been knocked out of her, and she struggled to catch her breath. She squinted through the darkness as her eyes adjusted and she got to her feet. The trapdoor hovered beyond her head, and she saw Sir Kennyratear silhouetted in the glowing square.

"What are you doing?" she demanded.

"I was to report for my imprisonment by sunset," he said.

"The sun has not set yet!" she pointed out desperately.

He threw in her bow after her. "I did not think they would wait that long. It's an execution for me."

"*What?!*"

She jumped and hurled herself at the trapdoor, but he had anticipated this and slammed it shut. It hit her hands, and she fell back to the ground again, rubbing her fingers. The sound of the rug being pushed back over of the door was muffled. Sir Kennyratear's voice was even fainter. "Follow the tunnel. It will lead you away from the house and surfaces amongst the roots of a large tree. Hurry and escape before they discover you are here."

"I'm not going to leave you to die!" she screamed back.

"*Keep your voice down,*" he hissed. "They were going to kill me anyway. I'd rather go in my own house, but you need to leave before they find you here."

"You can't let them kill you!"

"You shouldn't have come. I've got to go now. You need to leave. *Now.*"

His footsteps were hard against the floor as he hurried away from the closet. Caelfel stood and waited with bated breath for a few moments before she heard Markis's voice unusually loud in her tunnel, probably amplified by magic.

"Master Greyling Nadeth Kennyratear, you have been tried and found guilty by the Council of Sal'Sumarathar for treasonous crimes against Her Majesty's Scepter and Book. Since you have failed to appear before the Council for your sentencing, your punishment is death by execution. Show yourself to the militia behind me and face your death with dignity. If not, we will burn—*everything.*"

"My dignity will remain preserved in my own dwelling," was Sir

Kennyratear's response.

Caelfel wasn't sure what happened next. There was a sound of terrible crashing from above. Glass broke and wooden planks snapped. Caelfel smelled the acrid stench of smoke before she felt the immense heat of a mage-fire drifting from the floorboards above her. She stifled a cough with her hand, her eyes watering, and grabbing her bow, she ran to the end of the tunnel. The distance would have cleared the length of the house, but she still felt the powerful heat. The fire didn't breach the tunnel but it engulfed the closet with its trapdoor quickly, and the flames illuminated a small rope at the other end. She pulled on it, and another hatch opened, dropping a rope ladder. She climbed it and quickly found herself outside.

The smoke from the fire swirled in black, menacing billows. It was nothing like the white smoke of goblin-fires. Just as Sir Kennyratear said, there was a tree planted right next to the secret tunnel. She climbed it to get a better view, and what she saw sickened her.

Markis was easy to spot, even from Caelfel's vantage point, and she could clearly make out the cold smirk on his face. The mages of the militia that had set fire to Sir Kennyratear's home stepped back to let their magic run its course. Caelfel watched in horror. Her nose stung, and her eyes pricked. She waited for the impossible to happen; she waited for Sir Kennyratear to follow her through the trapdoor.

Minutes passed, and the sky turned red from the sinking sun and thick with churning smoke. She realized rather belatedly that Nadeth Kennyratear would not follow her. He would die in his home. Sir Kennyratear had chosen his fate, and Markis had gladly supplied it to him. She had an urge to cry out for him in her grief but suppressed that, knowing it would not be favorable to reveal her location.

"He is dead," she heard one of the militia say.

Sir Kennyratear's words ran through her head. Caelfel should leave, run away at once or risk exposure to a vicious murderer.

"Yes," Markis agreed. "But I do not think his visitor is. *Am I right, Miss Gyssedlues?*" he called in a louder voice, looking in the trees around them. He held his arms wide in a welcoming gesture.

Caelfel crouched, placing a tighter grip on her bow as she watched him from the safety of the dense foliage. She wondered how Markis could know that she was there. With a surge of fear, she realized that her earlier hunch about Markis still watching her must have been true.

He continued pacing around the soldiers. "You are always found in the wrong places, Caelfel."

A shiver worked its way up her spine when he said her name. She tensed to stop the tremor and watched Markis. Caelfel crouched further out of sight.

"You've come to see the greyling in his final hour, hoping he would help you find something you've lost. Did you find it, Caelfel? Or has your search led you nowhere? Show yourself, so we can meet each other honorably before the hunt."

Caelfel's fingers tightened around the tree branch she held.

"You must be wondering what hunt I could mean. You are a master huntress, I know. I have heard of you. It would be a tremendous joy to hunt with you this night. It might be your last."

The last sentence was mumbled darkly, but she wasn't foolish enough to believe his words. He had exploded her aura and placed the blame on Sir Kennyratear, and she had just witnessed him executing the greyling for it.

"Will you not speak to me? Will you not allow me a glimpse of your beautiful face?"

A violent tremor shook her frame as she continued watching Markis, unable to tear her eyes away.

"Come see me Caelfel, and I will tell you what we are hunting." But Caelfel knew what he was hunting. She didn't believe herself to be a master huntress but she was skilled enough to know when a predator was luring their prey.

"Perhaps she is not here," another a member of the militia said, approaching Markis.

Something changed in Caelfel. Her fear transformed into a thrilling rush of excitement. She twitched restlessly, wanting to tell Markis that she was indeed there and that she could escape him. Logic told her that her pride was folly and would only put her in danger.

"She *is* here," Markis hissed to the guard. "She has to be. I saw her, I felt her. I can still feel her."

"You can feel her?" asked the same guard dubiously.

Marks grinned dangerously. He lifted a finger in the air as if it would reveal her location. Then without hesitation, he turned, staring straight at her. "She is there."

Caelfel shouldered her bow and ran.

Tree-running was an exercise Caelfel had mastered many years ago, jumping from tree to tree and limb to limb, dodging the drooping brush of sharp leaves and branches. Her excitement and her fear, though, made her feet heavy, turning tree-running into an arduous task. The limbs and the branches clawed at her face as she ran desperately. She wasn't sure where she was going. They would look for her at home. They would know where to find her. They might even hurt her parents.

But they didn't know where Feraan lived, and though he might have committed some ancient, deplorable crime, he was her only chance.

With the thickness of the trees and the sinking of the sun, the canopy soon grew dark. She began running through the trees next to the Blaidd River that she knew would eventually wind its way toward the meadow and beyond that to the north side of Sal'Sumarathar where Feraan lived. She relied on the water's bubbling voice to guide her. It would take her to Feraan.

But it was also the long route, and if she was not fast enough, the militia, with their advantage of torchlight and clear roads, might easily catch up. If she were to take refuge at Feraan's house, she could not lead the militia to his doorstep.

"Why do you run? You will only hurt yourself."

Markis's voice sounded dangerously close. She pressed herself harder, using her weight to bounce forward. Caelfel focused on remaining nearly airborne, mentally pinpointing her location in relation to the forest around her. With her heart feeling as though it would burst, it would do no good to get herself lost.

In the waning light, she detected a gap ahead in the trees. Caelfel didn't hesitate or slow. Drawing a short breath, she pushed tremendously on the last branch to jump across.

The tree was unexpectedly wet. Her boot lost traction, and Caelfel fell.

Caelfel had fallen many times in her youth and had taught herself to stop the fall by reaching out with splayed and hooking fingers as the branch passed before her face. There was the sound of her clothes ripping, and Caelfel felt a branch scrape down her side. She cried out in pain.

As she dangled above the river, Caelfel tried focusing her strength to pull herself back up. The damp fungus that grew on the wood was slick, and she was unable to secure her grip. She realized with a wave of panic that her hands were slipping.

"Grab my hand," said a voice hovering above. She glanced up at the white hand Markis offered her. Caelfel glared, furrowing her eyebrows in contempt. When he saw she would not accept his help, Markis reached for her wrist.

"Get away," she snapped.

"I am trying to pull you to safety."

"I don't believe you."

"Come now, I really must tie up all these loose ends. There wasn't supposed to be any witnesses."

She dug her fingernails into the wet bark. "You cannot hide the smoke. Anyone in Sal'Sumarathar can see it. They will know what happened."

"It was an execution."

"*It was murder*," she hissed back.

Seeing no other choice, Caelfel let herself fall, and the freezing water swallowed her up greedily.

The cold hit her like a frozen wall, completely numbing all of her senses. She fought with the dregs of her strength to pull her head above the water to breathe. Her entire body hurt from the impact of the fall and the cold, but she swam away from Markis.

To her relief, he did not follow her into the river, and she was grateful her destination was downstream. Crosscurrents tugged at her, and eddies made it difficult to maintain her speed—

***

—*She was hardly an elf at all*—

***

—She propelled herself onward, gritting her teeth against the freezing cold. She was surprised that the water was as cold as it was, but then she realized it was still thawing from winter ice—

***

—*She was a snake with the way she wove around the trees and swam through the water.*

***

She didn't fight the current and used it to move herself faster until it deposited her at a small embankment, bashing her against the rocks. Shaking, she managed to pull herself to land.

She pushed her hair from her face, trying to think quickly. Her heavy, wet clothes stuck everywhere to her skin. She still had her bow, but all of her arrows were gone, lost in the stream. Powerless, the only thing she could think to do was to climb a tree, and she did. She continued running and left the riverside for the heart of Sal'Sumarathar. The night was silent, but Caelfel's ears were filled with the sound of rushing water. Her muscles ached and spasmed, but she ignored the pain and continued running.

She didn't allow herself to think of time, but her weariness made her head pound and her bones ache. She only stopped when the innocent, twinkling lights of Sal'Sumarathar rested below her. The tree where she took her break guarded a crossway that intersected between empty forges on the fringes of Sal'Sumarathar. She slowed her breathing, looking around for the militia.

She felt alone but Caelfel did not trust her senses. She watched for movement.

But then a breeze blew, and everything shifted in its wake. Caelfel tensed, muscles clenching painfully, and wished her clothes would dry.

Something sharp pierced the flesh on the back of her right calf. A gasp stuck in her throat as she fell out of the tree. She collided with the ground face first, the rest of her body crashing into the earth a moment later. Caelfel stayed still, only aware of the dull throbbing that she felt pulsing through her entire body. Her vision blurred.

The voices that had risen up around her in the forest town were quickly silenced with a shrill command of, *"Find her!"*

The patterned cadence of marching boots sounded as if it came from everywhere, all looking for her. The militia, she realized. She had to move.

She struggled to lift herself from the ground, first her head and then pushing herself up with her arms. She steadied her left foot on flat ground. It held her weight as she dragged the right foot.

Her knee buckled, and a sickening wave of pain caused her to sink to the ground again. She bit down on a groan and reached around to feel an arrow protruding from her calf, rivulets of blood coating her fingertips.

She couldn't walk; the arrow embedded deep in her muscle made sure of that. Caelfel could only lamely drag herself along the ground in a feeble attempt to escape the clearing. The nearby sound of approaching warriors told her she would not make it in time. She resigned herself to capture and stood as tall and straight as she could.

Her leg shook violently and then crumpled beneath her. Caelfel plunged toward the ground again.

But she never hit the ground. Instead, something—*someone* caught her, wrapping their strong arms around her. They pressed a hand over her mouth to silence the instinctive scream that rose in her throat. Caelfel couldn't see their face.

For a brief moment, she thought she had fallen into Markis's clutches at last, but when the figure carried her away from the exposed intersection and into the protected crevice between two buildings, Caelfel realized that this was not the case.

She did not know whether to fight or to trust this person, but her weakened and injured position left her little choice. Rendered immobile, all she could do was wait.

She began to formulate a string of muffled questions. The elf—at least she assumed it was an elf—pressed a hand harder against her mouth, though not threateningly, and pointed a gloved finger to the open space they were just at moments ago.

Caelfel watched.

Markis entered the clearing, an expression of utter rage on his face. He paced the spot where she had been moments before, and Caelfel did not dare to even breathe as members of the militia joined him.

"She was here—*right here!* Only seconds ago. She disappeared. No one can vanish like that."

"Perhaps you were mistaken," someone suggested. When Markis angrily whirled to face him, holding a sword to his throat, Caelfel instinctually moved to defend the nameless soldier, but the elf who held onto her kept Caelfel securely in place. She only managed to twitch slightly.

"I know I'm not mistaken. Do you know why? *Because I shot her out of the tree.* Wherever she went, she could not have gone far with an arrow sticking out of her leg. Maybe if we're lucky, she is bleeding to death at this moment." Something in the soldier's face made Markis smirk. "Find her," the Chief Executor spat.

The soldiers automatically fanned out across the clearing and the surrounding area, combing the city and forest for her. In moments, only Markis remained, pacing the very spot where she had landed. He inspected the ground, crouching over spots of blood Caelfel had left behind, and then he inspected the trees before disappearing into the night himself.

Caelfel could not help but wonder why no one searched the crevice where they were hiding. She wanted to turn and confront her rescuer, but no matter how much she moved, the elf kept her firmly in place. Eventually—after several long minutes—the grip on her relaxed. Realizing that the elf had held her pinned upright against their chest, Caelfel now tried to stand on her own.

But her injured leg could not support her weight, and she fell again. The elf caught her before she could hit the ground. They deftly wrapped her arm around their neck and then half-supported-half-carried her away from their hiding spot. She realized that they were headed to the horse meadow but Caelfel did not dare to speak until she had been safely deposited in a grove of trees.

"Why the meadow? Don't you think they could easily find us here?" she asked. The hooded figure turned from her before her eyes could penetrate the shadows of the hood and identify the face.

"They won't think to look here," her rescuer said. "You can't ride a horse with a lame leg."

Caelfel blinked. "*Feraan?*"

He lowered his hood, revealing his familiar hair. She had to admit to herself that she wasn't very surprised.

"How did you—" But Caelfel did not have the words to voice her shock. He turned to meet her face with a characteristic smirk in place.

"I imagined you would be happier to see me," he mused with a twinge of disappointment.

Caelfel was reminded of Sir Kennyratear's words about Feraan's loneliness and she saw it reflected for that moment in his distant face. She shivered in the night. "I'm not unhappy about seeing you. I am surprised. I am grateful that you showed up, because I don't know what I would have done otherwise." Caelfel shivered again but not because of the cold.

A smile touched his face.

"*But,*" she interrupted harshly, before he could change subjects. "I want to know how you found me." She struggled to keep her voice even, for it came very close to erupting in short, gasping hiccups. The smell of smoke from Sir Kennyratear's burning house still smoldered in her memory.

Feraan seemed to notice how close she was to hysteria because for once, he was quick to explain things. "I confronted Luewyn about your aura," he said. "She dropped the hint that you could be in danger, so I went looking."

Caelfel exhaled shakily and kept her eyes trained on his knees. She was admittedly impressed he confronted Luewyn instead of hiding in his house. "Then do you know about Sir Kennyratear?" she asked.

Feraan said nothing, so Caelfel was forced to look at his expression, which suggested he knew nothing of the fate of his greyling friend. Caelfel angrily wondered how he could not; the smoke from the fire should have been seen for miles around.

But his confusion garnered her pity, so she tried to explain what had happened in a series of teary gasps that quickly turned into uncontrollable sobs. Her teacher, her father's friend, *her* friend had been murdered, and she felt largely responsible. She could not voice this to Feraan, reduced to irrepressible shaking as she was, but to her astonishment, she felt his hand touch her shoulder lightly in what she assumed was a comforting gesture. The contact made her hold her breath for a long time, hiding her face with her hands. Feraan did not say anything until she finally regained the nerve to look back at him.

His expression was endearingly soft. "Right now, I need to look at your leg."

Sudden apprehension replaced her moment of grief. She dragged her lame leg protectively to her chest, feeling the hot stickiness congeal on her pants. She winced when her hand brushed past the arrow. "Why?"

"You've got an arrow lodged in your muscle and you can't walk. I'm not a healer like your precious Thoroth but I know that it's not good for you."

"We *should* take it to Thoroth. You're not a healer, so I don't want you touching it," she said aggressively.

"We don't have that option," he told her. "The city is swarming with the militia. I'm afraid you'll have to settle with me as your healer."

She remembered their first encounter and the medicine he had given her then. She sighed and nodded her consent.

"On your stomach," he merely instructed. After a while, Caelfel relented and bit down on the folded layers of her cloak as Feraan pried the arrow from her calf. It was a long process that made tears stream down her face and her legs jerk about violently. She only had to kick him in the nose once before he tied her legs together to restrain them. When he finally released the arrow, the mangled nerves in Caelfel's leg made it shake horribly.

Caelfel wanted to curse his name and all his ancestors but remained silent to not betray her tears. He was surprisingly gentle after that, using a warm liquid he had in his pocket to numb the trembling pain. He ripped something—Caelfel didn't see what it was—into long strips and wrapped the bandages tightly around her leg. When he tightened her boot laces and helped Caelfel to her feet, she hardly felt any pain. Standing on her own still proved difficult, however, so Feraan kept an arm around her.

"We need to leave the meadow," he said quietly, his eyes darting about. "They may not suspect you to take a horse, but it's only a matter of time before they check."

"Where are we going?" she asked.

He turned to look at her slowly, and a smile lifted half his mouth. "I'll take you back to my house. You can't ride with that leg, so there's no point in leaving the Fey Forest just yet."

Caelfel remembered their conversation about leaving and although she still did not want to leave Honey Water, she did not have the energy to put up an argument.

So he carried her away from the meadow, too impatient to let her limp on her own. He seemed to know where guards patrolled and expertly dodged certain streets and corners until they were safely out of Sal'Sumarathar. When they reached his dwelling, he didn't use the front door, entering the back way through the garden.

"What if the militia comes here?" she asked as he squeezed through a library.

"Even if they managed to find it, the entire house is protected. It's even safer than the college."

"How can you be so certain?"

"Because I set up the wards myself."

They entered a dark room, and Caelfel was momentarily unable to see through the shadows. He set her down on a soft mattress, and she realized just how exhausted she was. He sat on the other end of the bed, doing nothing to illuminate the dark room.

"You saw Sir Kennyratear today," he prompted carefully.

She nodded but hesitated when she realized he could not see her. "Yes," came her hoarse whisper. "Markis and the militia killed him today, executed they claim."

"For what crime?" Feraan asked, sounding bewildered.

"He was put on trial for endangering his students, because Markis exploded my aura." She breathed through her nose then, and it felt sharp.

"But you got out safely," Feraan pointed out.

Caelfel wasn't sure if he was being curious or suspicious. "I had an arrow sticking out of my leg and I fell in a half-frozen river. I hardly call that safe." She tried rubbing the warmth back into her arms.

Feraan left the bed and went to retrieve something on the far end of the room. When he draped it over her shoulders, she realized it was a blanket. She felt his hand linger against her neck before he drew back.

"You might want to take off your wet clothes."

She turned her horror-struck face where she thought he was standing and drew the blanket tighter around herself.

The words hung awkwardly in the air after he said them, and he must have sensed that because he quickly amended them. "No, it will help your body warm up if you're dry. Besides your clothes are ripped to pieces. I'll leave the room and find you something dry."

He did as he promised, giving her privacy. She tried to settle her nerves by breathing deeply and, keeping the blanket firmly wrapped around her, she wriggled out of her sodden, ruined clothes and threw them to the floor. She was about to remove her breast band before deciding to leave it on. The thought made her wonder how exposed her ripped shirt had left her. She knew he should have noticed, although he never mentioned it. Eventually, Feraan returned, cracking open the door.

"I found some clothes for you, but they may be a bit big. Do you want me to bring them to you?"

Caelfel almost banned him from entering the room but then realized she would not be able to get off the bed to retrieve the clothes. She nestled deeper into the blanket and summoned him.

He crept into the room and set the clothes beside her. "You should sleep and give your leg time to heal. You must be exhausted."

"I want to know about my aura. Did Luewyn give it to you? Can I get it back?" she pressed stubbornly.

With her eyes adjusted to the darkness, she saw his outline heading for the door. "We can talk about that later," he dismissed. "I haven't gotten everything figured out yet."

Caelfel knew he was prolonging an inevitable conversation, but there was some truth to his words. The longer she settled on the bed, the more she felt her own exhaustion. Her eyelids felt heavy, until they flew open with a sudden realization. "This is *your* bed," she realized rather slowly.

"It is."

"I can't sleep here," she whispered in the darkness.

"Would you rather sleep in the garden?"

"Yes," she answered automatically, sitting up. She heard him draw near, and he gently pushed her down by the shoulder

"You are ridiculous. You need sleep."

"What about you?"

"I can sleep with you, if it will make you feel better."

She felt her body grow warm with the thought but fiercely rejected the offer. Caelfel heard him laugh quietly as he left the room.

10. Underground

Caelfel awoke two days later.

She was surprised by how much she had slept. Obviously Feraan was worried too, because when she finally opened her eyes, he was hovering over her. She kicked herself free of the blankets and suddenly realized her leg had completely healed. She gingerly touched the back of her calf for inspection.

"You slept an entire day and night," he said. "There were a few times when you started babbling, but I don't think you were conscious."

"What did I say?" she asked warily.

"Nothing coherent. Something about a wolf."

Caelfel rubbed her head, having no memory of dreaming about wolves. "And that was enough reason for you to spy on me while I slept?"

Feraan visibly shrank. "I was only worried."

She swung herself out of bed and tested her walking abilities. To her surprise, she found her bow leaning against the wall. She thought she had lost it during her flight. She turned a questioning gaze onto Feraan.

"You left it at the meadow. I went back for it, but I didn't find your quiver or any arrows."

Caelfel sluggishly recalled the events of the night Sir Kennyratear was murdered. "I dropped all of them in the river." She tugged at the baggy shirt, recalling it did not belong to her, given to her by Feraan. She turned to him. "I want to know about my aura."

He sighed and tensed, as if he were bracing himself. "I do not

137

know where it is."

"Did Luewyn not have it?" Caelfel asked, confused.

"I suspect she does, but when I spoke with her, I had to make a choice between you or your aura. Logically, I chose you."

"Why did you have to choose?"

"Because Luewyn dropped obvious hints that you were in danger. Good thing for you too, because I don't know what Markis would have done to you if I had not come along."

"But Luewyn still has it?" Caelfel insisted impatiently.

Feraan hesitated, and his expression suggested he was hiding something from her.

"We can go back and get it now—"

"No." Feraan stood and blocked her path to the door.

Caelfel gave him an odd look. "No?"

"We can't leave the house," he told her.

She blinked. "What about my parents?"

"You can't see your parents. Markis had the entire militia searching Sal'Sumarathar for you. It's too dangerous. If your leg wasn't injured that night, we would have left the Fey Forest altogether."

Caelfel breathed through her nose, mustering all of her patience to face this dreaded and unwelcome conversation. "So we are supposed to hide out in your house?" she asked crossly. "For how long?"

Feraan gave an irritatingly uncertain shrug. "Until I feel it is safe."

Caelfel felt her face slip into a glare. "I don't have my aura, and you won't get it back. I can't see my parents and I'm stuck here for however long you see fit. Does that mean I'll be here for about eighty years?"

Her sharp words stung him, but Feraan quickly recovered. "That sounds about right," he retorted. "And there are benefits to missing an aura. It makes you more difficult to detect."

"My aura isn't missing. My aura was *stolen* from me," she hissed

Feraan shrugged again, and this time the movement felt callous. "Humans aren't even born with auras. Be grateful that you aren't dead."

He turned his back and left the room then. Caelfel trailed after him. "*But why?*" she demanded of his back.

He stopped and turned so suddenly that Caelfel ran into him. He caught her by the elbow before she could fall, and there was a flash of amusement in his eyes. "Why aren't you dead?" he asked.

"No. Why are you keeping me here? Why would you take me away from Honey Water?" she asked.

"I'm protecting you," he answered, as if it were obvious.

"But *why* are you protecting me?"

His eyes grew distant as he gazed over her shoulder. Then he turned his bewildered expression on her, and for that moment, Caelfel saw the centuries line his face. "Because I'm responsible for you."

He released her elbow and continued down the hall, but Caelfel wasn't finished with him yet. "You mean the life debt?" she asked.

"I don't believe in the life debt."

Days later, Caelfel would have argued that point with the way he stubbornly kept her in his house. He would let her venture to the garden but no further, so after she pestered him for an entire day, Feraan set up an archery range for her to practice. But Caelfel's aim was flawless, and she soon grew bored with the pastime. She resorted to following him around the surprisingly enormous house and harassing him with questions about himself. This was how she learned Feraan was five hundred and thirty-six years old. For some reason, she expected him to be older, although he certainly didn't act like it. He had also attended the college during his first century, like she had, except he had been expelled for kidnapping the headmaster—*twice*—and setting the grounds on fire.

"I am the reason they have wards around the college now," he told her proudly, though she wasn't sure why that would make him proud. He refused to elaborate why he did those things.

Her endless questions didn't seem to truly annoy him, and he picked up on the habit of calling her Hen. When she inquired on the reason behind the nickname, he only shrugged and smiled to himself. Caelfel rolled her eyes and just hoped it wasn't an insult. She had plenty of experience with being called hurtful names; it came with being the youngest of a city. It was an arduous task to prove to everyone that she should be taken seriously. But what surprised her with Feraan was that he did not seem to mind her young age. Although he enjoyed teasing her to no end, he spoke to her in a way that did not sound condescending or suggested that he thought her inferior. Caelfel slowly found herself craving their conversations because of it.

Since Feraan had made it clear on numerous occasions that he had travelled abroad, she pleaded for him to share stories of his travels.

The request initially made Feraan reluctant, but it was that night he told her about the werewolves.

"Since I had been expelled from the College of Sal'Sumarathar, the Board of Wizardry would not allow me to learn magic in the other colleges. I left Honey Water, hoping to learn magic elsewhere. I was greatly surprised when I learned that there were very few places outside of Honey Water that taught magic," he began.

"Why's that?" Caelfel asked, resting her chin on her hands. They sat outside in his garden next to his forge that offered warmth in the waning winter.

"I've told you that humans aren't born with auras, Hen," he said. "Because they don't have auras, very few practice magic. The ones that do only know the mundane magic—alchemy and such. More or less, I taught myself to use my aura on my own. During my travels, I encountered a pack of werewolves. I met their leader, Lycaon, and he took me in like a brother. Lycaon is perhaps the closest friend I've ever had. He lives in a city called Haradrop, a fortress he keeps to protect the werefolk of Umfeld."

"Why would the werefolk of Umfeld need protecting?"

Feraan's face turned grim. "The people of Umfeld are prejudiced and hateful towards the werefolk, particularly the werewolves. Most of it is based on a misconception of the race. Humans tend to fear things they do not understand. People with the ability to transform into various animals confuse them, frighten them. The humans of Umfeld still hold up one of their own as a god—Saint Hubertus. Hubertus was just a man, but a famous werewolf slayer. He all but exterminated the race in Umfeld. His efforts spurred this bloodbath against the Haradrop fortress. Many did not survive. Lycaon was one of the lucky few. Unfortunately, Refurinn was not."

"Who is Refurinn?" Caelfel asked.

"Refurinn was the wife of Saint Hubertus. She did not approve of his werewolf raids and often rebuked his actions. Then one day, she discovered Hubertus had been unfaithful to her, so Refurinn revealed her true nature. Refurinn was a werewolf. Hubertus grew angry and murdered her. In his rage, he led an assault against Haradrop where many werewolves were killed. The battle ultimately took his life."

Feraan fell silent, pondering on the events that played through his mind. Caelfel looked at her hands and eventually mused, "The irony of it is that he married a werewolf in the first place."

Feraan smiled back at her. "And Hubertus could not see past his blind hatred to realize that werewolves were people—extraordinarily gifted people, but people all the same."

He released a sigh, and Caelfel was reminded of the blind hatred the people of Sal'Sumarathar harbored for Feraan. She didn't understand it, though she desperately wanted to. The time she spent with Feraan showed her that Feraan was not a person who deserved the burden of a scornful people.

Then again, if she knew what happened eighty years ago, perhaps she would feel differently about him.

The amulet hanging from his neck caught her eye. She remembered it belonged to her. "Why do you stay here?" she asked him suddenly.

Feraan's smile was erased by his confusion. "Because it is dangerous to leave the house now."

"That's not what I meant. From what you've told me, you are fond of your werewolf friend in Haradrop. Why do you stay here in Honey Water where all the elves hate you when you could be elsewhere?" she asked.

The light of the forge embers reflected in Feraan's eyes, and Caelfel saw something dark and unreadable in them. He took a while to answer. "I am here because this is where I belong."

Caelfel didn't believe that. "You belong to a place that makes you happy," she countered.

He considered her words for a few minutes. "You are insightful for one so young, Hen. However, you are wrong. I've done many things in my life. I have interfered in the affairs of humans and I have paid for it. I have a duty to pay my penance."

"I don't understand what you mean," she sighed. "Is this about your reputation?"

His responding silence told her it was.

Caelfel had taken to sleeping in Feraan's bed, though she was unsure of where he slept. She had also picked up the habit of wearing his clothes. The clothes she had worn her first night were ruined from when Markis had chased her through the forest, but she didn't mind, preferring the comfort of Feraan's baggy clothes. Secretly, she had grown attached to their smell.

The next morning she found him already in the garden, bent over something. He straightened when he saw her.

"For someone who was such a pest about having those archery targets, I have not seen you use them," he said.

"I used them once," she said defensively.

He looked at her pointedly, and rolling her eyes, she retrieved her bow to practice target shooting some more. She shot three arrows but quickly grew bored. The practice was not challenging for her. She glanced in Feraan's direction and saw him hunched over again, this time black sparks flying above his shoulders. Curious, she continued watching him until he finally rose and came to join her. He stood in front of the target.

"Shoot me," he instructed.

Caelfel gave him a mystified look. "I'm not doing that."

"It's all right. I've been working on something. You won't hurt me."

Caelfel wasn't convinced, so she aimed above his shoulder. The arrow seemed to glance off an invisible shield. "What was that?"

Feraan looked pleased with himself. He removed something from his neck, and Caelfel panicked when she saw an amulet in hands. Then she realized it was not the same amulet she had given him, so her nerves settled. He handed her the new amulet for her to wear. "I had an idea. Without your aura, you are largely defenseless against other magical attacks. The humans are aware that they are at a disadvantage when it comes to magic as well. They developed protective charms, but those don't usually work. I decided I could make another amulet for you that would protect you from magic or other projectile attacks."

Caelfel smiled at his proud expression. "That was very thoughtful of you."

He looked sheepishly to the ground. "I'm sure I could develop it some more to protect you against other things or maybe even enchant it with offensive spells. It's not a complete substitute for an aura, but it's better than nothing."

Caelfel looked down at the amulet which looked much different than her first one. It was silver, and the pendant had been crafted into the shape of a crescent moon. She appreciated his gift and pressed the cool metal of the pendant to her face.

He gave her a strange look and told her to take his place by the target. She did, feeling less confident than he had. He took her bow and fired an arrow. Caelfel flinched when it came into contact with her invisible shield and screamed when he sent a ball of fire after it. Feraan laughed at her just as the fire disintegrated when it came in contact with the amulet's shield.

Even with her personal archery range set up and the gift of a new protective amulet, Caelfel often found herself wandering around his house with little to do. Feraan began to instruct her in the basics of blacksmithing, which she discovered was strangely liberating work as she pounded metal into shapes. The monotony and exertion of the movements she found much more enjoyable than when her father had attempted to teach her alchemy.

Feraan started by helping her make the blade of a dagger. At first, Caelfel had felt ambitious and wanted to try making a sword. Feraan discouraged her, which was well enough because even the smaller blade of the dagger took a great amount of time and effort. He instructed what temperature the metal had to be for shaping by judging the color it turned. He taught her to quench her work to prevent the metal turning brittle. By the time she had a chunk of metal remotely shaped into a dagger, an entire day had passed. She was pleased with her work until she saw some of his creations, which were far more elaborate and superior than what she made.

But her energy had been spent on the endeavor and after a meal of tubers and mushrooms from Feraan's garden, she climbed gratefully into his bed to await sleep.

Only sleep did not immediately greet her. She fingered her new necklace with a captivated restlessness. She speculated at the effort it took Feraan to make and the consideration he put into it. She knew of many who called him a murderer, but Caelfel could not bring herself to believe such accusations. Feraan was a quiet and often lonely elf, but she did not think those were the qualities that defined a murderer.

Then she remembered his stories of mischief at the college. To the elves, he had a history of mischief and arson. Perhaps that was enough for the making of a murderer, not to mention his myriad ventures among humans. Humans were always fond of war and bloodshed, as evinced by his story of Hubertus.

Feraan has always isolated himself from others. I believe you are a blessing to him.

Despite Sir Kennyratear's pleas, Caelfel's curiosity bested her, and she crept out of the room.

Sometimes Feraan would eat with her in the evenings, whenever he did eat. Caelfel did not often see him eating alone so she usually took pride in reminding him to take his meals. That night, he had joined her silently with his soup of tubers but slipped away on his own when he had finished. Caelfel did not bother him then; she noticed he turned rather pensive at night.

His house was larger than what it looked from the outside. There were numerous rooms, spare bedrooms and several libraries. They mostly appeared unoccupied, so Caelfel thought Feraan did not frequent them often. She never saw where he went to sleep, but when she went to bed, she had seen him slip out to the garden on various occasions. She had never followed him before tonight.

She imagined a secret entrance somewhere in his garden that led to a small room or chamber and when she didn't find him as she wandered the house, Caelfel was certain that was where he was. The trouble was finding it.

Night in the garden was alive with the sound of insects. The approaching spring warmed the forest, and creatures of all sorts would venture from their winter slumber. A breeze wafted through the garden, but it brought warm air instead of the cold winds characteristic of winter. She scanned through the darkness to search for an entrance to the room she suspected Feraan retreated to. The only logical answer her search found was a tree.

Part of the reason Feraan's house so well hidden was that it was concealed on all sides. The front side was protected by the rising hummock of rock and deracinated roots. The back and left side was guarded by the river, and the last side was surrounded by his garden which was home to a massive tree. The branches and foliage of the tree concealed the structure of the house completely. The only way the house would be visible by someone from Sal'Sumarathar was if they climbed the hummock as she had done on her first visit. Caelfel often found herself admiring the ingenuity of the architecture and location but then began to recognize that the tree served another purpose.

She approached its colossal trunk, and her fingers traced the edges of the rough bark. Caelfel circled the tree, keeping her hand on it. Then on the back side, where the bark touched the house, she discovered a small space tucked in the tight corner large enough for an elf to squeeze through. She wedged herself in and found herself at the top of a spiral staircase. She peered through the darkness and descended the stairs.

It led her to a basement under the house that was the same dimensions of the floor plan. The underground room was dim, having only one torch to illuminate its wall. From what Caelfel could see, his basement held more shelves for even more books, as if the two libraries he had above ground weren't enough. She couldn't see the rest of the basement except for faint outlines of other structures and furniture.

Feraan sat by the only torch next to the nearest bookcase. With the way he reclined in his lounge chair, Caelfel assumed he was asleep. She picked her way past him, doing her best to avoid stepping on something that might be hidden in the darkness. A book was open in his hand, and Caelfel gazed at his open-mouthed, quiet snoring. She couldn't imagine someone sleeping like that every night. He had to sleep elsewhere.

But she didn't want to wake him so Caelfel took the open book in his hands to return it to the shelf. The title caught her eye. *Reign of Firescales*. Remembering Sir Kennyratear mention such an event in his lecture, she briefly thumbed through the illustrated pages to see it was a book of the ormr occupation of the Vinius Islands. Caelfel thought it a strange choice for a bedtime story, but she settled at Feraan's feet and began reading.

She quickly learned that the Reign of Firescales was more than a simple occupation in the Vinius Islands. The ormr were a hostile strain of dragons that terrorized the nations of Ariang'ron—Honey Water, Umfeld, and Umfang. Eventually the ormr were defeated, and the elves reclaimed the islands for their empire. Since the war's end, the elves purposefully took measures to isolate themselves from the other races, seeing the ruthless devastation of their bloodthirsty temperaments, and the elves permanently sealed themselves away in the Fey Forest.

Caelfel glanced at the cover again to read the author's name. There were two. *Thamil Kennyratear and Feraan Auvrearaheal*. Caelfel quietly laughed to herself, thinking that Feraan *would* read a book he had written. She wondered if Thamil Kennyratear had any relation to Nadeth and resumed her place in the book. It detailed the number of casualties, asserting that no other single event had claimed the lives of so many elves.

Behind her came the sound of a nasally snort. Feraan started into awareness. "Did you follow me down here?" His voice was thick with sleep, and Caelfel hid a smile at the sound. She found it pleasing.

"Who is Thamil?"

Feraan peered at the book in her hands. "That is Sir Kennyratear's familiar name."

Caelfel nodded, recalling that *nadeth* was a term generally granted for greylings. She held out the book to him. "I didn't realize you wrote books," she said as he took it.

"Of course, my books are the only ones I can stand to read." He stretched, producing a wide yawn.

"What made you write about the Reign of Firescales?" she asked. "I've only heard it mentioned one time, and that was in Sir Kennyratear's class."

"It was a terrible war that happened over a thousand years ago. During my travels abroad, I found remnants of the war scattered across the world of humans. Huge, complicated weaponry buried beneath centuries of dirt. Various relief paintings that depicted widespread fires across the land were with them. Humans have such a weak memory, you see, that they had no record of such a war ever happening. I decided to research the subject, and my efforts led me to the race with the longest memory. The elves. Only, I soon discovered many elves did not remember the war either."

Caelfel's brow furrowed. "Why was that?"

"Elves can live to be thousands of years old. Your father is living proof of that. But if you actually look around, there aren't many elves over a thousand, and those that are are considered greylings. Greylings used to be tens of thousands of years old. The war decimated the population of Honey Water. It completely eradicated the race of mountain elves. Many elves today weren't alive during the Reign of Firescales, except for our current greylings. There were only three greylings I knew of personally."

Caelfel glanced at the first name on the book cover. "Sir Kennyratear," she easily guessed.

Feraan nodded. "He was my teacher when I first attended to the college. When I returned to Honey Water, my ventures led me back to him. He was always fond of me, trying to get me out of trouble. There wasn't much he could do when I kidnapped that Headmaster, though." Feraan's voice trailed off at the memory.

"I'm having trouble justifying that decision," Caelfel told him.

Feraan continued as if he hadn't heard her. "I conducted an interview with Thamil. As it turns out, elves do not have such a strong memory as they gloat about. After you've existed for a millennium, memories tend to fade, particularly traumatic ones. Sir Kennyratear did his best, though, and we pieced that book together. As you can probably imagine, it was not very popular with readers. The Board of Wizardry voiced their condemnation to Sir Kennyratear for upsetting the public and associating with inferiors."

"Associating with inferiors?" Caelfel repeated, squinting at Feraan.

"That would be me," he clarified.

Caelfel felt a pang of pity for him once more. The feeling made her uncomfortable, so she pushed it away and avoided Feraan's eyes. "How can you be upsetting the public by recounting history?"

"It is not a favorable time in history for elves. The Board disapproved because they did not see the use in remembering the tyrannical ormr if all the dragons were dead."

Caelfel wasn't sure if she agreed with this ruling. Her troubled expression must have reflected this, because Feraan's face broke out into a small smile. He handed the book back to her.

"Don't let it trouble you too much. They disapproved because I was a co-writer. You should read it and become my first fan."

Caelfel did a poor job of hiding her snort when she took it back. Feraan gave an odd look at the noise. She quickly covered it with, "I'm sorry about Sir Kennyratear. I did not realize how close you were to him."

But the distraction only turned Feraan somber. He didn't look at her and silently left Caelfel pressing the book to her chest in the dark basement.

***

Gwyndolyn snapped the book shut and looked across her own vast library. Guards were posted at all entrances, as always, and faithful Blaes hovered a few feet away like a loyal shadow. She sighed theatrically, and it was the despairing sound of boredom. She tossed the red leather book to Blaes who caught it easily with his free hand. His other stayed permanently stationed at the sword on his belt.

"What do you think of this book, Blaes?" she asked, humming another sigh.

"I've not read it, my lady," he said, setting it to the side on the granite table next to him. "Your mother suggested that you should help with the planning of the Spring Festival."

Gwyndolyn was too impatient to sigh again. She detested being given mindless chores to do. Preoccupation did not improve her condition. "I find the Spring Festival boring." It wasn't entirely untrue. Its preparation and organization she thought to be loathsome. She wouldn't mind attending the festival itself. "You should really read that book, Blaes. It might prove helpful."

"Why is that, my lady?" asked ever-patient Blaes.

"Look at its author."

He picked up the book and read, "Thamil Kennyratear."

"*And?*" she insisted sharply for him to continue.

"Feraan Auvrearaheal."

"*Exactly*," she trilled gleefully.

"My lady, I refuse to see the importance of Master Auvrearaheal."

"You're the one that is always paranoid, Blaes. Make the connections and while you are at it, read his writing. He has a personality quite unlike any elf I've seen."

When Blaes disapproved of her pastimes, he was always gentle. He abandoned the book once more to the granite table, purposely pushing it away from him. Gwyndolyn imagined others would have tossed it across the room. "I cannot approve of your ladyship's obsession with the Wandering Elf."

"I just wonder what compelled him to write about Firescales. What are Firescales anyway?" she asked, rising from her lounging position on the elegant chair that was constructed to her preference. It was tall to resemble a throne and wide so she could drape her feet over the arm. And she had it padded with Vinius threads for when she sat for long periods of reading.

"Firescales are a specific breed of dragon that razed the land during the war," he answered quickly. She loved how Blaes was like a walking reference book.

"What other books has Master Auvrearaheal written?" she asked, pushing herself up to meet Blaes on eye level.

"There was a volume on werewolves called *The Dirus Clan* and another of a different subject called *Mountainfolk*."

Gwyndolyn frowned, troubled. "He's lived for over five hundred years and he's only managed to write three books?" she asked.

Blaes was trained in the military. He was commander of Empress Haelyn's armies, yet his primary job was to babysit the royal, illegitimate daughter. Gwyndolyn often wondered if he regretted giving up his military career for her. But for the rarest moments, she would see a shine of humor in his eyes. She saw it now as he said, "I apologize for Master Auvrearaheal's inefficiency."

She giggled at his wit and allowed herself to snake her arms around his neck. Blaes stared down at her as impassively as ever. She felt familiarly wounded as she usually did when he did not respond to her affection. She always blamed it on his venerated military service, but there was always that doubt that the problem rested within her.

The moment was interrupted by the entrance of the empress. "Gwyn, stop flirting with Blaes and get off of him. You make him uncomfortable."

Gwyndolyn sighed again, but this time it was an annoyed sound. She slipped from Blaes and slid sinuously to her chair, arranging her features into a pout. She did not look up at her mother. The painting she had of Empress Haelyn in her library did not do justice to the flawless ebony skin and the midnight black tresses of the elven empress.

Haelyn stopped when she stood in front of Gwyndolyn. "You should not sulk all day, my dear. It is not good for your health."

"I am not sulking, mother. I am *researching*," Gwyndolyn clarified.

"I cannot approve of such brooding. Please, my darling, you should help arrange the Spring Festival. There are four cities that could use your help."

"There were *five* cities that did well enough without my help a hundred years ago," Gwyndolyn countered.

Empress Haelyn rolled her eyes, but seemed to miss the reference. "Did you enjoy your time in Sal'Sumarathar?" Gwyndolyn watched as the empress's eyes traveled to Blaes, as if waiting for some confirmation. The action annoyed her. Gwyndolyn could answer for herself.

"I did not like Sal'Sumarathar. The Head Councilor acts as though he owns the city. He wanted nothing but for me to leave."

"It is always a matter of how you present yourself, Gwyndolyn," Haelyn reprimanded softly. "You are a noble dignitary of the House of Ernmas. You should act like it for once. If your grandmother were here—"

"I never knew Grandmother Clytemeria, so I doubt she would have that much of an effect on me."

Haelyn fell suddenly silent. Gwyndolyn could tell the empress was not accustomed to being interrupted. Gwyndolyn took satisfaction that she was the only one who could be rude to the empress without fear of consequence.

Except there was a hidden consequence this time. "If you do not pick a city to attend for the Spring Festival, I will pick one for you," the empress said coolly, giving Gwyndolyn no choice on the matter. Empress Haelyn turned to take her leave, pausing briefly at the door. "Please, Gwyn. If you stay in this library all the time, you will give yourself another headache."

"Yes, mother," Gwyndolyn huffed impatiently.

"You remember what I said if that happens again?"

"Yes, you will send me to the castles of the Baetic Mountains," Gwyndolyn snapped.

Haelyn left silently, and Gwyndolyn took comfort in her absence. She turned to Blaes who asked her, "What city would you choose, my lady?"

Gwyndolyn thought for a moment. She did not care to stay in Yamalvon for the festival. Elewyr was a beautiful city next to the seaside, perhaps the most tempting. Rasaen was home to the fetching diplomat Lanslak. Otherwise, Rasaen was not of marked importance.

And then there was Sal'Sumarathar, with the councilors who feared her and the elf with the infamous reputation who had written only three books. And Gwyndolyn had made her decision.

***

It was dangerous to leave the house, Feraan knew, but when he sensed someone searching relentlessly for him, he decided it would be best to meet Luewyn at the college grounds again. At least the wards there would protect him, and it was better than Luewyn discovering his home. He left at night, when he was sure Caelfel was deeply asleep, making it easier to escape his house and brave the streets of Sal'Sumarathar.

"So you came," Luewyn breathed, standing from her desk. She went to retrieve something from the far side of the room.

"And what do you want with me?" Feraan asked from the doorway.

"I am leaving Sal'Sumarathar. My job is finished, so I thought you might like to have this." She handed him a small, ivory chest with a silver clasp. When he held it, Feraan felt the soft thrum of auric energy—Caelfel's aura.

"Why?" he demanded suddenly suspicious.

Luewyn's answering smile was sweetly malevolent. "Uthruil agreed to give it back. Taking it was only a warning."

"You have never been so generous before. What more than that?"

"The box is small, and her aura is trapped. Open it, and it will kill her, unless she is wearing the amulet Eviat had modified specifically to contain her aura."

At this, Feraan visibly stiffened. There was a flash of teeth as Luewyn's smile widened.

"But you know you cannot take off the amulet. The poison from your *accident* can never leave your body without that extinct flower from Amasel. That amulet is the only thing keeping you alive. Uthruil knows this and agrees to return her aura."

"So he told you what poison they used for me."

"Uthruil described it as lead in your blood that would freeze your veins. I wish I could see it kill you." Luewyn closed her eyes in mock ecstasy.

"Thank you, sister. You have been remarkably kind."

Luewyn's eyes flew open. "Do you care for the she-elf? Do you love her?"

Feraan didn't answer.

"You can't love anything without killing it. Look at your greyling friend. The same will happen to her," Luewyn hissed, turning her back to him.

Feraan moved to leave, and Luewyn called back to him.

"I have seen the Blind Seer, and she has a message for you," Luewyn said in her deceptively pleasant voice.

Feraan paused at this. "The Blind Seer is no concern of mine."

"Sibylla feels otherwise. She says you've procrastinated too long in your task. There is a force in the desert that moves against you."

Feraan ground his teeth together from frustration. Damn the Blind Seer. Out of spite, he remarked to his sister, "Your princeling screamed like a child when he died."

Luewyn froze, and Feraan could see her shaking fists. She looked at him from over her shoulder. "Her aura is beautiful—shimmering, green, and innocent. Yours is black with all the souls you've murdered. The Seer tells me Caelfel Gyssedlues will join the rest."

11. Moonlight

Caelfel grew restless in the days that followed. She found it increasingly difficult to occupy herself and often ended up wandering the length of the garden. The days turned imperceptibly warmer. After a week of this weather change, Caelfel remembered the fast approaching Spring Festival.

Being seventy-six, Caelfel had never seen a Spring Festival but she recalled the celebrated event from her parents' fondly narrated memories. Elves flocked from any and all of the cities to take part. Caelfel and her mother had spent the past few months designing her dress, and the thought sent a dull pain throbbing within her chest. She had not seen her parents since Sir Kennyratear's death. They must have worried or fretted over her absence, but Feraan would not even allow Caelfel to see them. He insisted it would not be necessary, that they would know she was safe. Caelfel didn't see how.

"Don't worry about them," Feraan repeated. Caelfel would sigh wearily, shrinking back into her seat and wondering if she would waste the rest of her days at Feraan's house. When she would ask him this, Feraan would only say, "Not forever. It isn't time yet." He always refused to elaborate what he was waiting for.

But the thought of the Spring Festival raised Caelfel's spirits. She thought of the dress Sylaera had made for her and the stories her parents often told, detailing the glittering lights of firefaeries and the heady odor of gin and honey wine what would waft through the trees. It was supposedly a romantic night, a magical night that would be unforgettable. The event was so sacred even the criminals of Honey Water were permitted to join in its revelry without fear of retribution.

It would be her first festival, and she thought endlessly of attending with Feraan. The thought was enough to make her blush faintly as she summoned the courage to ask Feraan about the festival.

"We should go to the Spring Festival," she tried arguing one day. "Everyone is allowed to attend, even suspected criminals. We can't be harmed there."

But all Feraan would do was shake his head. "It is too dangerous. I won't risk it."

She placed a pleading hand on his arm. "When was the last time you visited the festival? It is only held once every hundred years."

He gave her an odd look at the question. "I don't see where that matters. The whole of Sal'Sumarathar will be there," he pointed out to her.

"Yes, and I can see my parents and my friends." Her mind flashed to Garvanna, and Caelfel deliberated on the irony of considering Garvanna a friend.

Feraan looked away from her begging eyes. "I'm sorry, Hen. I can't agree to it. I promise you, soon, you may be able to leave."

She felt herself grow impatient but Caelfel was too reticent to show him her temper, so she took it elsewhere. Attempting to get as far away from him as possible, she locked herself in his bedroom where she slept. She sat with her knees drawn up to her face, and as she pushed her hair back and chewed on her lip in frustration, a dangerous idea came to her. This plan took shape in her mind as she eyed the door cagily, and when it was fully formed, her head fell against his pillow. She closed her eyes and inhaled deeply, disappointed that Feraan's scent was fading.

Then she counted the days and waited.

She waited until the day of the Spring Festival, the first day of spring. She bid her time until Feraan wandered off to his secret basement for a time, and then she snuck away.

It was before dusk, and the sun was still fiery orange in the sky. She avoided going into Sal'Sumarathar, making her way home through the forest by following the river. She entered the house through her parent's garden, easing herself quietly through the doorway. The house was still, and Caelfel wondered where her parents were. The house appeared completely deserted, and a short search of the rooms proved this to be so.

She went into her dark bedroom and opened her wardrobe. The

dress she and her mother had worked on all year hung from the center. Caelfel touched the light, iridescent material of the jagged edged skirt. She had admired the dress for weeks since her mother had finished it, and it was just as beautiful as she remembered.

She washed herself in the bathing fountain, letting her wet hair fall loose and dripping down her back as she brushed it out. Putting on the dress was slightly more difficult now that she was alone. Tying the corset was the worst, especially when the sleeves fell off the shoulder, but she managed to fix it right. The hemline of the skirt fell above her knees, and the crescent moon amulet Feraan had made for her rested above the bustline.

Gazing at her reflection in the mirror, Caelfel fidgeted, all previous excitement replaced by nervousness. She wasn't sure who she would see or what she would do at the festival, though she wanted nothing more than for Feraan to attend with her. She wondered if he had noticed her absence by now, if it would even trouble him. She imagined he would come looking for her, and they would find each other at the festival. But that was an unlikely fantasy, so she drove it from her mind.

Pushing down her skirts once more, she left the house, reminding herself she would be safe at the festival. There was nothing Markis or the Council could do to her there.

She joined the long lines of elves streaming toward Sal'Sumarathar's plaza and Caelfel was amazed by the number of elves that lived in the area. While most elves tended to keep to themselves, nearly all would attend the Spring Festival.

Except for Feraan, of course.

"Caelfel"

She turned to meet the shrill cry and found herself with a mouthful of copper hair as Garvanna embraced her. Then the embrace was over, and Garvanna stepped back to show Caelfel her cross expression. Caelfel knew Garvanna could not wait to scold Caelfel for her absence but Caelfel looked around uneasily and tapped a finger to her lips. Garvanna received the message and kept her silence. She slipped her arm through Caelfel's, and they made their way to the festival.

They came upon the site of the night's festivities, and the sight of it all made Caelfel momentarily forget her anxiety. There were firefaeries in glass spheres, floating and dancing while casting a warm orange light upon all those near. Spyder silk braided into thick cords and dyed bright colors swayed from trees, glowing with muted lights whenever a glass orb passed. The music on the reedy elvish instruments was delicate and deliberate. Then, there was great amounts of food on large silver and bronze platters—steaming soups and crisp vegetables decked with spices, ripe, pomaceous fruits and mushrooms. The mushrooms were always served with gin or wine— red, white, or spiced. Mulled wine and honey wine. Members of the Council served mushrooms as the entering elves filed in queue for their turn at the Great Fountain where their feet would be customarily washed before being allowed admittance into the Festival.

Garvanna pulled Caelfel along when it was their turn at the Great Fountain. The water in the fountain was warm to the touch and scented with rose petals and lavender. Caelfel made swirls in the water with her feet and watched the ripples gently rolling all across the surface. She focused on them and kept her attention away from the tittering elves around her. But Garvanna could not keep her silence forever.

"What happened?" she whispered urgently.

Caelfel turned to the she-elf who had strangely become her friend. Garvanna was wearing a red dress that matched her strong cheekbones nicely. Garvanna's sleeves were off-the-shoulder too, but they fell down the length of her waist, splitting at the shoulder. "Did you hear about Sir Kennyratear?" Caelfel asked, though immediately regretting it. The Spring Festival was a time of revelry, so she did not want to think or grieve for her old professor.

Garvanna nodded slowly, though Caelfel wasn't sure if she knew the entire story. Caelfel promised Garvanna to detail the entire incident later. Garvanna insisted, "Where have you *been*?"

At this, Caelfel could not meet Garvanna's eyes, and she felt a slight blush reach her cheeks. Mercifully, their turn at the Great Fountain was over before Caelfel had a chance to answer.

Garvanna led them to a secluded corner of the festival, next to the circle of musicians, but not before Caelfel grabbed a handful of mushrooms for herself. As she nibbled, Caelfel found the music relaxing. "Explain yourself," Garvanna demanded.

"I don't want to talk about what happened with Sir Kennyratear now," Caelfel told her.

"But where have you been? Your parents, Thoroth, and I have

been looking for you."

"I was safe."

"Safe *where?*" she challenged sharply.

Caelfel glanced around uneasily to see if anyone was listening. When she was satisfied that they were alone, Caelfel admitted in a low voice, "I was with Feraan."

The look of horror that followed on Garvanna's face was predictable, but then her eyes skewed into a look of suspicion that Caelfel did not understand. "Did you?"

"Did I *what?*" Caelfel asked, losing her patience.

Garvanna looked her over some more and found some unspoken answer that satisfied her. She shook her head. "I doubt that you have."

"I don't know what you mean," Caelfel said, crossing her arms.

"But it all matters naught now," Garvanna said, brushing herself off. "Your parents will be glad to see you, and you will never have to see him again."

There was something about the casual indifference to her tone that made Caelfel's face fall, and disappointment seeded in her stomach. Garvanna did not overlook the reaction, and her face twisted up again. "You will miss him?" she asked in disbelief.

"Perhaps I will," Caelfel defended.

Garvanna laughed. "Then you are positively mad."

Caelfel said nothing. Conversation began gradually filling the plaza. Some elves began dancing, and the pace of the music quickened.

Garvanna stood up from her seat. "I'm going to find Thoroth. He will want to see you."

Caelfel nodded and watched her leave, content to listen to the music and stare at a nearby cluster of firefaeries.

"Normally they live in a volcano," interrupted a voice some moments later.

Caelfel stood suddenly to see Markis approaching her.

"What?" she asked, feeling her heart race with fear as she remembered the night in the forest.

"The firefaeries, they live in a volcano, specifically Mount Ormr, the one near Yamalvon. I caught them myself for the Festival." He smiled, his face turning smug. Caelfel thought he looked considerably different without his silver paint.

"Oh," was all she could say. He sat down on the stone bench she had previously occupied and gestured for her to join him. She didn't.

156

Seeing this, he changed the subject.

"I'm quite impressed with your endeavors from the other night. You eluded me rather well."

"You can't do anything to me here," she told him firmly, though it took an extraordinary effort to stop her knees from shaking.

His eyes raked the length of her dress. "I would not dream of doing anything to harm you."

She clenched her hands at her sides and said nothing.

Markis stood. "I see you as my equal. It would be a pity to see anything happen to the Master Huntress." He looked her over again and stepped closer, reaching for her face with two fingers. "I wonder, has something happened to your aura?"

Caelfel took an equal step back, clutching at Feraan's amulet. "Don't you know?" she hissed.

He lowered his hand and tilted his head. "It is a crime to deform a beautiful creature such as yourself. Our auras met when I activated yours. Imagine the essence of our life forces touching. I had hoped our relationship would progress beyond that."

Before Caelfel could fully express her disgust, they were interrupted by an enormous wave of laughter that rippled through the crowd of elves that Uthruil now spoke to, standing above them on top of the plaza platform. Caelfel assumed he had recited a joke that Markis had distracted her from. Uthruil continued when it had quieted, "Begin the Festival."

The music took a livelier form and the cheering elves began dancing to it. Caelfel watched them dolefully for a moment before Markis suddenly stepped in front of her.

"Do you feel like dancing, Miss Caelfel?" he asked.

She loved dancing but not with Markis. He seemed to sense her rejection.

"How about a fortune reading, then?" Without waiting for an answer, Markis took her by the crook of her elbow and led her to a low table where a priestess sat with her incense and her basin. When she saw the two of them approaching, she smiled, showing the dark lines of makeup on her face that marked her as a vessel of the gods.

"I'm apprenticed to an oracle and know the ways of foresight. Who shall be first?"

"Just her, thank you," said Markis, pushing Caelfel to sit on the ground. The priestess blinked at her and continued smiling.

"Beautiful as Elewyr herself," the priestess commented.

Caelfel did not respond. Her neck prickled ominously as she felt Markis standing closely behind. She was not certain how she remained with him when she could think of nothing other than getting away.

"How about a card reading?" he asked.

The priestess flashed her smile to Markis. "Of course."

She presented a deck of paper cards with ancient runes painted on them that Caelfel recognized as Daemona ones. Primal Daemona runes at that, the language of the Ormr Masters, an ancient race that supposedly lived before the elves. The priestess held the cards before her.

"Select three cards, my dear."

Caelfel reached for the deck, hesitated, and then chose three cards at random. She gave them back to the priestess without looking and took a deep breath. The sharp scents of the priestess made her head sick.

The priestess revealed the first. On it was an elf with a bow and a hood that concealed his face.

"The Ranger. Something or *someone* has been pursuing you." The priestess cocked an eyebrow between the two of them. "Has this mysterious pursuer been successful?" asked the priestess. Markis chuckled above her, and it sounded closer than Caelfel realized.

"In a manner of speaking," Markis replied. His answer made Caelfel's face warm with an uncomfortable heat. She longed to be away.

The second card was turned, and the image of two ravens sitting on a stick made the priestess frown. "Twin Crows with the Wand. A traitor lurks near you, waiting to strike with death. Not very appropriate for the Festival. Let's try the third one—"

"I would rather not," Caelfel said as she tried standing. Markis pushed her shoulder back down.

The priestess flipped the third card, the one that represented her future. Caelfel averted her eyes, holding a superstitious feeling that she should not know her future before it happened. She managed to slip from Markis's grip just as she heard the priestess identify the subject of the card.

"It's the Wolf!" the priestess called behind her, but Caelfel pressed forward, determined not to look back.

She pushed past thrusting elbows and swaying shoulders, looking for Garvanna and getting away from Markis. She stumbled through a small gap of elves and happened upon another elf altogether. Thoroth had caught her by the elbow before she could fall. He laughed at her without any trace of the frown Garvanna would reserve for her, and Caelfel found herself genuinely smiling back.

She let him take her hand, and he swept her away with the dance. They circled other elves until they ended up at the bar that held the gin, wine, and other spirits. Caelfel, determined to have a nice time, drank the worth of several glasses while Thoroth chatted amicably away. By her third glass, Garvanna appeared next to Thoroth. She cast a strange look at Caelfel before pulling Thoroth away for herself. Caelfel glowered at being left alone. Being inebriated did not cure loneliness.

She reached for her half-finished glass and brought it to her lips, only belatedly registering that the previously golden liquid should not be the deep red that it was now. The taste was fruity, and the heady liqueur traced a fiery path down her throat and seemed to blossom in her core. It brought a strange tingling, yearning to her fingertips. Caelfel turned to see Markis standing beside her, and to her immense surprise, it wasn't an unwelcome sight.

He smirked, holding out his hand for her to dance.

And she didn't know why, but her body accepted the invitation.

Markis had hands only for her, and she felt them against her waist and against her shoulders. She leaned into his touch and moved with his lead. His caresses only made her crave for more, and she found herself swaying to the same rhythm other elves around them were moving. She tilted her head against his neck and squinted at him through heavy eyelids. Markis was not unattractive, particularly without his silver paint. Markis was strong and dangerous and he held her hips with a sure grip while she flirtatiously rustled with the hem of her skirt.

His hand followed hers, and she had it brush against her thigh. His other hand trailed against her waist. She turned her head to see Markis's hand glowing red and she felt it tracing a line to the small of her back, playing with the ties of her corset. The red light burned in her eyes, and she felt a primal craving burn inside of her.

It was then that she was pried away from Markis. Caelfel protested, struggling against this new elf even when, after looking up, she saw it was Feraan. The redness inside her still burned for Markis even while Feraan looked her over coolly. She ached for the Chief Executor, but Feraan held fast, tethering her in place by the waist. Feraan leaned toward her until his lips were only a hair's breadth away from hers and he whispered something urgently against her mouth, eyes closed in concentration.

"What?" Caelfel breathed, rather confused.

His eyes flew open and he pressed his mouth to hers. Caelfel protested at first, resisting Feraan's touch but eventually the memory of Markis's caresses was overpowered by the sensation of Feraan's lips on her own. She hungrily responded in kind, wrapping her arms around his neck as she pulled herself closer to him. Only Feraan wasn't kissing her. It felt as though he was sucking the very air out of her lungs, but he was drawing something more than that. When he broke away, Caelfel was left gasping for air, and Feraan stumbled away in a fit of coughing.

Dazed, Caelfel blinked at him, following him through the crowd. She reached him in time to see Feraan spitting up what looked to be black bile. When he had recovered, he turned to look at her. A number of conflicting emotions ran through her too quickly to reconcile so she elected to remain silent.

"I realize getting drunk is one of the festival's appeals, but did you have to get yourself poisoned?" he asked, having some difficulty catching his breath.

"Poisoned?" she repeated.

"More like charmed or bewitched, but as much a poison as any fatal drug." He wiped his mouth, giving her a sideways smirk.

He had probably just saved her then, she realized. She felt fatigue, but the burning desire for Markis had completely left her, fortunately. She looked Feraan over with a new interest.

"Thank you," she said slowly, but her head still swam with drink. She obviously needed more.

***

Feraan straightened. "You snuck away just to throw yourself at Markis?" He was too out of breath to laugh.

"I didn't—I tried avoiding him," she desperately insisted to him.

He knew it wasn't by her choice; he had only meant to tease. But Feraan enjoyed watching her face turn red as she became flustered. It did not take him long to relent and describe the mechanics of the enchantment. "It's an unfair spell that he used. It forces the subject to become unbearably physically attracted to the caster. From the looks of it, I would wager Markis intended on leaving with you soon."

She shuddered at the thought, and Feraan didn't pause to think about how well Caelfel would take the information. The whole idea of Markis using the spell infuriated him. His eyes scanned the crowd of dancing elves for the Chief Executor, murder boiling beneath his skin. Caelfel Gyssedlues was not a prize to be won or dominated.

Then Feraan stopped himself, looking back down at Caelfel, wondering why he had just felt the sudden urge to protect her. He would not doubt if the poor girl had no idea about the significance of the Victory Dance that came after the crowning of the Spring Beauty.

A hush fell over the mass of elves, and Feraan turned to see Uthruil standing before the whole of Sal'Sumarathar. The councilor spoke, and his amplified voice was heard by all.

"We have a special guest from Yamalvon to present the Snowdrop Crown to Sal'Sumarathar's Beauty of Spring," Uthruil said. "We welcome Lady Gwyndolyn to our festivities."

There was an applause, and Feraan turned to see a second figure accompanying Uthruil. She was shadowed by a tall guard that Feraan recognized after a moment as Blaes Llychlin, general of the imperial army. Feraan blinked at the general's presence and turned to the girl who was identified as Gwyndolyn. He remembered Caelfel talking about her. Gwyndolyn was related to the empress somehow, but it did not explain why an experienced general was demoted to be the bodyguard of one she-elf. Feraan watched her closely, sensing the undercurrents of a dangerously powerful aura emanating from her.

Gwyndolyn took Uthruil's place and smiled brightly at the crowd before her. "First I am thankful for Sal'Sumarathar's hospitality. The empress sent me to watch over the festival preparations, and I am happy to report that Sal'Sumarathar's festival did not disappoint."

The elves clapped politely, and Gwyndolyn pulled at some of her hair nervously before continuing.

"I have personally chosen your Spring Beauty. When I announce her name, the she-elf will of course, as per custom, receive the Snowdrop Crown as well as a political pardon signed by the empress herself."

She gestured to Blaes who held a silver tray on which sat the Snowdrop Crown and a scroll wrapped in red leather. Feraan did not recall that a political pardon came with the crowning and, judging from the excited murmurs from the elves around them, he easily guessed Lady Gwyndolyn was starting a new trend.

"And now time for the naming of our queen, Sal'Sumarathar's Beauty of Spring who will lead everyone in our Victory Dance. This crown belongs to Caelfel Gyssedlues!"

The announcement was met with a deafening roar, and Feraan watched mutely as Caelfel slowly left him for the stage. Then Feraan's senses began to shift. Everything around Caelfel faded and as she stepped further away, she pressed into his awareness even more.

When she turned to accept her crown from Gwyndolyn, Feraan saw that her face was flushed with drink and excitement. Her pale hair cascaded over her shoulders, shining like glittering moonlight. She was warm and soft, and he knew that because he had felt her lips moments before. The green stems from her flower crown rested above her pointed ears, and though Caelfel was not the picture of nobility, Feraan could admit she was beautiful.

After the crown had been placed on her head, Caelfel accepted a drink of honeyed mead from a silver chalice, the pride of Honey Water with its famous Honey Dew plant. Caelfel drained the goblet quickly, and her cheeks flushed a deeper red.

Then Gwyndolyn told her, "Choose your partner."

And the whole of Sal'Sumarathar fell silent, waiting for Caelfel's decision. He saw her eyes scan the crowd, searching, until they rested on him. She left the stage, walking a straight path until she unwaveringly stood before him.

She chose him. Feraan Auvrearaheal, the most hated elf of the empire. The decision was met with a unanimous gasp from all around.

Feraan sucked in a sharp breath and nearly choked on it. Gwyndolyn must have thought highly of Caelfel to give her a political pardon, only for Caelfel to risk it all on him. After keeping himself mostly out of sight for the past eighty years, Feraan was now the focus of attention of every elf in Sal'Sumarathar. Over Caelfel's shoulder, he saw Gwyndolyn's eyes meet his with a smug expression.

But Feraan pushed everything else away from his mind and focused on Caelfel before him. He had not answered her invitation to the dance, and his silence seemed to trouble her as though he was refusing her. He watched her bottom lip quiver uncertainly. In an uncharacteristic moment of indecision, he looked down Caelfel's striking frame once more before offering a curt nod. Music began, and a gentle smile graced her face before he swept her away by the waist.

It was interesting, because Feraan had never led a mass of elves into a dance before.

He found something pleasing in the way he touched her and pressed his body into hers, and she did not shy from it. Soon his breathing became heavy, and the blood throbbed uncomfortably in his ears. His body was warm, and he recalled Caelfel's dance with Markis with a touch of envy.

She blossomed in the Victory Dance, and he ran his hands from her shoulders to grasp her hips. She moved into his touch in time with the music, and he felt her light breath against his neck. He inhaled, relishing her scent, an earthy yet floral fragrance.

"Do you know what the Victory Dance is?" Feraan asked in a husky voice.

Caelfel's eyes fluttered open. "Is it not a dance to celebrate the victory of the Beauty of Spring?"

Feraan laughed thickly. "Not quite."

He pulled her away from the center of the crowd, twirling her until they reached the fringes. When she didn't protest, he took her even further away from the festival until they were alone, surrounded by nothing but silence from the forest. He stopped them, and she leaned against a tree.

He avoided her eyes as he explained. "The Victory Dance is for choosing a partner with whom to celebrate the meaning of the festival."

"You couldn't tell me that back there?" Caelfel asked skeptically. "What is the meaning of the festival?"

"You know this. The festival celebrates fertility, specifically elvish fertility." Feraan hesitated. "Particularly the fertility of she-elves." Caelfel's eyes still held confusion. "It's a festival for sex," he stated bluntly, looking at her.

Caelfel's mouth parted, finally comprehending. "Oh." Then her eyes met his, and she did not blush with shame as he expected. "You mean I—in front of everyone—you agreed to dance with me," she pointed out stubbornly.

Feraan was taken aback by the direction her mind went. "I did." Then cupping her face, he decided to make the best of it.

He was acutely aware of the labored rise and fall of her chest, how she breathed so heavily. The alcohol he smelled on her breath did not surprise or repulse him. Instead, he crushed his mouth over hers, lasting for a fiery moment before briefly pulling away to gauge her reaction. They smiled at each other through the darkness, but, being elves, they could see each other perfectly. He touched her shimmering moonlight hair before passionately meeting her lips again.

Her mouth tasted sweet, and her delicate hands brushed his face before tightening around his neck. She pulled herself up to him, and he anchored her against the tree, tangling his fingers into her hair. He felt a great heat surging through him, and it proved unbearable. Centuries had passed since his last Spring Festival, and here Caelfel was offering herself to him. His hand went to her thigh, and his mouth moved down her neck.

Something happened. Something suddenly locked him into place. He glanced down to see the amulet he had fashioned for Caelfel glowing brightly. Feraan twisted his body around to shield Caelfel and turned in time to see an arrow freeze in midair, centimeters away from his face. The amulet had done its work, protecting both the wearer and one that stood so close to her.

A member of the militia, wearing the black robes of the assassin division, lowered his bow some feet away and backed away a few paces uncertainly. Feraan had been generals of armies in centuries past so he could easily guess this was the work of a lone dispatcher, Markis testing the extent of his abilities.

But the heat within Feraan warped itself into a violent rage. He stalked toward the assassin, black fire appearing around his hands as he approached the now shaking attacker.

Feraan rushed him, sending waves of black fire towards the desecrator of his night. When the smoke cleared, his opponent had fled through the night, leaving the smell of burnt flesh behind him.

He turned back to Caelfel, intending to make the best of what happened, but her wide eyes were horrified at what had just transpired. It ruined his mood.

Feraan sighed heavily, grabbing her hand as he passed her. "Let's go home. Coming to the festival was idiotic," he grumbled, scolding her.

She didn't object as he pulled her along. "You didn't enjoy yourself?" she asked dubiously.

"No," he said through gritted teeth, too incensed to admit the truth.

12. Unmasked

Caelfel eagerly followed Feraan home, twitching with anticipation, but it quickly became apparent that Feraan's mood had been spoiled for the night. It seemed to sour her mood too, so by the time they reached his house, she was already frowning. He glanced at her briefly, and though she knew he saw her expression, Feraan said nothing as he continued through the house.

"Did I have to come back here?" she pouted. "I haven't even seen my parents yet."

"You don't have to do anything. You're the one that has a political pardon now," he pointed out evenly.

Caelfel grew quiet as she thought that over. For days, her forced confinement within Feraan's house had made her bored and listless. She had yearned for her freedom. Now she had the opportunity to leave, and she found she would rather not.

"Why did you come to the Spring Festival?" she asked somberly. Her head buzzed as she felt increasingly sleepy.

"I went looking for you," he snapped, as if it should be obvious. He scratched his arm absently, and Caelfel looked at him more closely. He was restless from anxiety. The attack might not have shaken him, but it clearly weighed heavily on his mind.

"Are you all right?" Caelfel asked tentatively.

Feraan nodded, rubbing at his nose, and left the room. She shadowed him through the narrow library. His agitation only grew worse in the limited space. "The she-elf who crowned you tonight. Was this the same one that proved your innocence?"

Caelfel nodded. Just now remembering her crown, she picked the snowdrops from her hair.

Feraan said nothing for a while, seemingly satisfied with her silent nod. He moved further down the library, scanning the dirty titles. He chose one and pulled it from the shelf to peruse its contents.

When she peeked over his shoulder, she saw it was a book on the elvish royalty before he moved to hide it from her. Caelfel sighed, tiring of his secretive antics before retiring to the bedroom. She was too exhausted to change out of her dress, so she stretched on the bed fully clothed.

She recalled what Garvanna said about her parents. She regretted not seeing them at the festival but decided it might have been for the best if assassins were attacking her and Feraan so close to the festivities. She hoped they were there to see the Beauty of Spring crowning, so they would know she was safe.

Despite fretting over her parents, Caelfel's last thoughts before drifting off to sleep were of Feraan's rough, desperate kiss. She replayed it countless times in her mind, touching her lips as she remembered the way he tasted. There was nothing he could say to convince her that that one meant nothing.

So she drifted into unconsciousness with a small smile on her lips.

She could not have been asleep for more than a few hours when she was jolted awake. Her heart hammered in her chest, unsure what had woken her up.

Then the loud *bang* came again, and Caelfel jumped out of bed, thinking that perhaps the militia was attacking the house. They had come to kill her off like Sir Kennyratear—

Bang.

But as Caelfel scrambled out of the bedroom, she realized that the noise came from somewhere inside. She turned a corner to investigate a hall when the sound of Feraan's scream pierced the thick air of the dark house. Caelfel raced to the narrow library where she found him on the floor, back arched as though he struggled with some immense pain. A quick scan of the room told her that he had fallen asleep in the midst of his research.

He was still asleep, and the banging came from him pounding the floors with his own fists. Caelfel hovered over him uselessly, uncertain how to help him. "Feraan?" she said loudly, trying to be heard over his screaming.

The screaming stopped, but he clenched his teeth together as he struggled to moan some syllables. His eyes remained closed, and

Caelfel guessed he was still asleep, facing some horrible night terror. She firmly pushed down on his shoulders to restrain him.

"*Wake up!*" she pleaded sharply.

"*I destroyed the monsters!*" he responded clearly in his sleep.

"What monsters?" Caelfel began shaking him. "Wake *up.*"

"*The monsters of Amasel are no more.*"

"Amasel? What does—" she started to ask.

Then there was a unified gasp from both. Feraan broke the surface into awareness, and he panted, looking around frenziedly. Meanwhile Caelfel covered her mouth with her hand as she finally understood. She stared at Feraan with wide eyes, leaning away from him. Feraan quickly regained his composure and retained his confusion as he met her gaze.

"What is it?" he snapped, impatient. The cadence of his voice suggested terror.

But Caelfel looked Feraan over in a new, darker light. "You destroyed Amasel."

The color drained from his face, and when he didn't deny it, Caelfel knew she was right.

The destruction of Amasel occurred eighty years ago, only a few years before she was born. Garvanna's and Thoroth's family had lived in Amasel. It all made *sense* now, why everyone hated him. But with this revelation came the realization that Feraan had kept this from her. Everyone kept this from her. It burned deep in her chest and stung her eyes. She lifted herself from the floor and turned her back to Feraan.

"Caelfel, wait!" Feraan called behind her.

But she ran from the narrow library, gathering her bow and the few personal items she had, mostly a bundle of ruined clothes. She rushed for the front door, but Feraan was waiting and he cut her off, placing a firm hand on her wrist.

"Will you let me explain?" he asked desperately.

The exact details on Amasel's sacking remained a mystery to everyone, but its results were evident. The brutal carnage littered the street. Burnt bodies scattered everywhere with no discrimination between elf, she-elf, youngling or greyling. Death was not common among the elves and it was so debilitating that Caelfel had seen some rip their hair from its roots and moan for days. Some elves would sing, and their songs would be so heartbreaking the petals of the Honey

Dew would supposedly shrivel and die. The Years of Mourning for Amasel had lasted through the celebration of Caelfel's first decade. But when everyone thought of the fate of Amasel, they also thought of Feraan's face.

How could I have not known?

And this elf that stood before her, begging her not to leave, was responsible for all of those deaths. This elf she had been prepared to give everything to had a darker side, a heavy shame that he carried everywhere with him. Sir Kennyratear had mentioned Feraan was not responsible, but Feraan made no attempt to deny the claim. He only wanted to explain himself, to justify the mass murder of elves.

Her eyes stung again as she asked, "What if I had been there?"

The question stunned him. "You weren't," he said lamely, as if that dismissed the subject.

Caelfel angrily pried his fingers from her wrist, and when Feraan did not resist, she ran from his house.

The sky was bleak and gray from dawn. The fiery sun peered over the horizon, casting bright shafts of light through the trees. But Caelfel did not pause to enjoy the scenery. She flew over the boulders and the gnarled roots of ancient trees and foliage. The babbling river next to her did nothing to quiet her nerves. She ran the entire way home, bursting through the door with tears in her eyes. As if expecting her appearance, both Eviat and Sylaera sat in the front room with heads bent toward each other.

Caelfel eyed their clasped hands with resentment before demanding, "Why didn't you tell me?"

It had been over a week since she had seen her parents. She had missed them, and they had probably worried over her absence. But Caelfel wouldn't allow them a peaceful moment to ensure that their only daughter was safe, for Caelfel felt betrayed. They exchanged glances in ignorance.

But Caelfel wouldn't even allow them a moment for confusion. "You've told me about Amasel before," she clarified, furiously wiping her face. "You taught me about the one of the single most reproachful incidents of our history. *The death of an entire city.*" She took a breath to steel herself. "Yet you did not tell me who was responsible. You did not tell me *he* was responsible," Caelfel all but screamed at her parents in her tearful rage.

Their impassive faces only irritated her. She wanted to scream

169

some more, but her anger seemed to drain the fight out of her. She sagged against the wall, still staring them down with hurt eyes.

"I am the only elf in the empire to be kept in ignorance about this. You made me stupid and foolish and—" She broke off, unable to form the words to adequately express the dull pain eating at her core. Her hands flew around. "I trusted him. I trusted *you*. No wonder the Council wants me dead. I've been in the company of a *mass murderer*, and the both of you never so much as bothered to tell me that."

They finally reacted, Sylaera squeezing the bridge of her nose. Eviat sighed, rising to cross the room for his precious daughter. He placed his hands on her shoulders, and while that was usually comforting, Caelfel irritably shrugged them off. Eviat would have to work with what he had.

"How much did Feraan tell you?" he asked carefully.

Caelfel glared at her father. "He didn't deny it."

Sylaera left the room, and Caelfel didn't miss her departure. She seethed at her mother's absence and would not even be consoled when Sylaera brought in tea for all them. Caelfel refused hers, so Sylaera set the cup nearby, returning to her seat.

"You must let us explain," Sylaera said.

Caelfel continued glaring. She had not allowed Feraan that opportunity but she would relent now, for they were her parents. Even so, her parents had lied to her for seventy-six years.

Eviat sighed heavily again. "We kept the secret from you, simply because Feraan saved my life."

This had not been the direction Caelfel expected. It shocked some of her resolve, but she refused to show it, folding her arms tightly around herself. "One life excuses the death of hundreds?" she asked sharply.

"Feraan didn't kill those people, Caelfel. He saved them."

She rolled her eyes but didn't interrupt this time.

"Before you were born, I visited Amasel for some alchemy ingredients." Eviat's eyes darkened at the memory. "Amasel had already been lost for some time."

"I don't understand," Caelfel insisted petulantly.

"The elves of Amasel were possessed—*all* of them—by some sort of evil spirits I had never seen before. They inhabit the bodies of elves, feeding off auras until there is no aura left. Then they turn hostile and use the bodies to attack other elves so they can grow."

"They take elf bodies and pretend to be elves?" she asked.

He nodded. "They feed off our auras and eventually our life force until there is nothing left except a walking corpse." Eviat struggled to swallow. "It is the ultimate form of blasphemy for elves—murdering masses of elves for necromancy."

"What are these things? Why has no one noticed them before?"

"I don't know where they came from, but by the time I had arrived at Amasel, they had already exhausted their food source. They came at me like magnificent, black orbs. They chased after me, and I lost my aura permanently to them that day."

"They took your aura?" Caelfel said, her wrath dissolving.

Eviat turned grim. "I don't remember much after that. I couldn't have gone far before passing out. Then I woke up to Feraan healing me. He had saved my life, and I told him everything about the menacing orbs that plagued Amasel.

"Feraan reasoned that the parasites only feed off of elves because our race possesses auras so he led an army of humans—who have no auras—and sacked the city. He was right. The parasites in their elemental state couldn't harm the humans so they assumed the bodies of the elves and tried to fight back. Feraan's army won, and they burned all the elf bodies. They were already dead, Caelfel," he added when horror flashed through her face.

"And Feraan, he fought in this battle, even though he is an elf too?" she asked skeptically.

"He is either the bravest or the most foolish elf I ever met."

"So why does everyone hate him?"

"No one else knows about the parasites. Feraan attempted to go to the Council about Amasel, but no one believed him. When they went to investigate for themselves, all they saw was a smoldering city with only the word of the strangest elf who admitted to destroying it. They had no proof against him, no way to explain how the human army breached our borders, but they saw an opportunity to frame him for the incident. And so Feraan's name lives on in infamy."

Caelfel slid to the floor, sighing. "And why didn't you just tell me that about Feraan and Amasel? It would have been better than telling me nothing."

"It was Feraan's wish," Sylaera interjected. "Without him, your father would not have been alive. Without your father, you would not have been born. Feraan is, in his own right, responsible for your life."

"While that may be a romantic notion," Caelfel said, hoping her face did not look as warm as it felt. "It does not explain why he did not want me to know."

Sylaera rose from her seat and joined her husband in front of Caelfel. "We know of Feraan's true nature. He performed an unsolicited act of kindness. He saved your father's life and probably the lives of countless elves by stopping those parasitic orbs. If they had gone in hunt of new prey after desecrating Amasel, our city Sal'Sumarathar would have experienced the same fate."

"Why did he not want me to know?" Caelfel insisted impatiently. "I'm not questioning his goodness, only his secrecy."

Sylaera smiled softly. "Do you not remember the reactions of Garvanna, Thoroth, the Council, when they all learned you had helped him? He used to have a house here in the city, but many elves burned it to the ground when they learned of Amasel. He fled the city. He did not want to tell you the truth because he did not think you would believe it."

"I believe it now," Caelfel told her. "I would have believed it if you told me, instead of hiding it from me."

"That is a quarrel you should reserve for him and not us, my daughter."

But Caelfel was not ready to face to Feraan yet. She thought of Sir Kennyratear's words to her. *It was an awful day that I am sure he would rather forget. I would rather not spoil your opinion of him.* And she felt shame for running from Feraan as she had. *I believe you are a blessing to him.* He had kept a secret of this magnitude from her because he was afraid. That touched her in an odd way. She felt a need to apologize but also an urge to demand his explanation. She was sure he would give her one.

But for now, Caelfel spent the morning with her parents. She told them of Sir Kennyratear's death with fresh tears, her face hidden in her hands. She had never really permitted herself a moment to mourn his death before, and it felt appropriate with her parents, since her father had been close friends with Nadeth. Then she ate with them, Sylaera passing around slices of bread smeared with blackberry jam. Caelfel enjoyed the company of her parents. Eviat commented how they had witnessed the Beauty of Spring celebration, that they were proud of her and happy for her. Sylaera was by no means modest when she spoke of the work she had put into the dress that Caelfel realized she still wore.

But before the morning was over, Caelfel voiced her need to leave the house. Her parents, shared a glance, obliged, and gave their daughter a last parting hug before Caelfel headed out.

"Do not leave us for too long," Sylaera called before Caelfel was out of earshot.

Caelfel cast her parents a furtive glance, not wanting to think about how much stress she had put them under during her absence. Now as they both waved her goodbye, Caelfel saw how happy they looked and she had no wish to spoil their happiness.

However she had an unfinished matter. She had pulled a shawl over her dress, belting it at the waist, to ward off the morning chill from her exposed shoulders and braced herself to meet Feraan again.

She was nervous now, in light of their most recent encounter. She had hurt him and she was just now realizing the significance of Sir Kennyratear's preemptive warning. But before she could allow the guilt to mercilessly clench her stomach, she pushed the sense of blame from her. Caelfel had not lied; everyone else had lied to her. She had nothing to be ashamed of.

All the same, she took a quick, deep breath to steel herself and prepared to meet Feraan again. She hesitated before his door, fist held in midair as she prepared to knock. When she did, the dull pounding sounded muted to her ears. She raised her hand to try again.

Then the door open, and Feraan stood before her in a disheveled and incorrigible state. When he saw it was her, for no one else knew the location of his home, he released a steady breath, running his fingers through his unkempt hair. She wondered at this. Caelfel had only left for a few hours. Feraan opened his mouth to begin what she supposed was a rehearsed explanation or excuse for his actions, but she raised a finger to silence him.

"Before you say anything," she began, steering the conversation with a newfound authority. "I want you to tell me exactly what happened eighty years ago."

Feraan paused at this. Apparently it was not the reaction he had been expecting. "You want me to tell you what happened?" he repeated, considering her question a moment. "Can I show you instead?"

Something in Caelfel's stomach twitched, stirring a mixture of dread and anticipation. She nodded. Feraan took her hand, leading her to the horse meadow. Caelfel found herself delighting at the feel of her hand in his, but the sensation was short-lived, for she quickly found herself in front of Feraan's steed. Firnis, the black stallion with the unnerving red eyes.

"Why does he have red eyes?" Caelfel asked.

"Because Firnis is not like any other horse," was all Feraan would say.

Caelfel frowned. "I don't want any more secrets to be kept from me."

"I can understand that, but this is not my secret to share." Feraan mounted his horse, holding his hand out for Caelfel.

She wasn't sure if she believed him but accepted his hand anyway.

They set off through the forest, Caelfel sitting behind Feraan. She wrapped her arms around him, resting her head against his back. They traveled swiftly, but the rocking motion of Firnis's gait and the repetitive cadence of his hoofbeats lulled Caelfel into a trance and she vaguely recalled that she'd gotten very little sleep the previous night. She closed her eyes.

When she opened them again, the stiffness in her joints told her a few hours had passed. The sinking sun confirmed this.

***

One of the steward's duties was to entertain guests, not that they received many. Very few ventured through the perilous desert. Those that did were usually hired. Mostly women.

This time there were three, and the steward thought the practice to be a waste of money. It was obvious that the desert princeling had only brought them in as a pretense, especially since he would stubbornly ignore all of their advances. This time the princeling arranged a woman for himself, one for his steward, and one for the Blind Seer's messenger. Had the steward not been there, the result might have turned disastrous.

The messenger remained in the west wing that the princeling allocated for it. And there it stayed and would not be drawn out of hiding with invitations to dinner or the seductive, alluring promise of female companionship. The steward knew the attempt to be futile, because servants of the Seer did not partake in secular pleasures. Besides, the messenger might have been female herself, or a being that did not enjoy the company of women.

And so the messenger voiced its refusal to spend an evening with the princeling by obstinately ignoring any call at the door to the west wing. Offended and irate, the princeling stormed to his own chambers, leaving the steward to see after the three women. They were flirtatious enough, and the steward had no qualms with devoting an evening with one of them. He chose the fair one with the azure-colored eyes for his own, and sent the other two to the tent of higher ranking officers. The colonels there could contest for their attention. He took his choice to his bed chamber, which was arguably far too lavish for a mere steward. But he was not a mere steward.

She called herself Wystaria and she was pale enough to belong to a home far away from the desert. He gently pushed her to the bed, and she complied. When his lips met the skin at the crook of her neck, it tasted sweet and icy. He guessed her home had seen blistering winters for unseasonably long months. He imagined her beautiful face framed by a fur-lined hood as a biting wind stung her cheeks bright red. He kissed them and her nose, and a smiled curled her mouth, showing small, perfect teeth.

Her wide, glassy eyes were too innocent to belong to hired companionship, but he enjoyed that about her. However, he had barely tasted her saccharine lips before she lifted herself to meet him at eye level, immediately stopping things. The steward never had one to hesitate before, so he drew back, cautious.

"I've never done this before," she admitted quietly to him.

He might have loved her for that, Wystaria baring all of her innocence for him to take. He fantasized keeping her as his own treasured gem. He would pledge himself to no other, if she would have him. The thought terrified him. He had only been with her for the span of a few minutes. He opened his mouth to offer her some words of consolation, but she stopped him, pressing a cold finger to his lips.

"I didn't come here as one of *them*," she said. "I snuck in."

His shoulders straightened. Wystaria was admitting to be a stowaway. He crossed his arms. "Continue." All tenderness he had felt moments before vanished.

"I have heard tales. I wanted to see the great sorcerer." Her eyes dropped from his, and the finger she had previously used to silence him traced the muscular lines of his bare chest. He tried not to shudder, but it was inevitable. She was beautiful and half-naked.

His mouth lifted into a cocky half-smile. He spread his arms wide. "Well here I am." He held his palm out between them, producing a blue flame with his aura.

Wystaria marveled at it, the light matching her own eyes. Then, to his immense surprise, she touched the tip of the flame.

He was about to warn her against it—

Only there was a shock and a blinding light. The flame had frozen into lavender-colored ice, dropping heavily into his hand. He looked between it and her with a renewed interest.

Wystaria was a sorceress.

"I've never met another human capable of magic," he said, allowing his surprise. Then, thinking of his brother, he amended, "At least one who is born with the ability. Why have you come?"

"Because I have not met one either," she said with a sheepish smile. "And I sense that you have much you can teach me."

The grin that touched his face was genuine. When he lowered himself over her, it was with a new warmth, a new feeling. A reassurance that he would never be alone as he had felt all his life. She made no protest this time, eagerly knotting her fingers into his hair. His mouth moved against her collarbone, and then suddenly it was his turn to interrupt things.

Hanging from her neck was a charm, a talisman crafted in the shape of a black crow.

Wystaria had no time to question his abrupt indecision before he jumped away from her. He backed to the wall, blue magic coating his hands.

And though it broke his heart, he issued a single, hoarse command. "Leave."

Her face shattered, but she obeyed without complaint. She probably would not understand his harsh refusal, but Lisiek could not risk his life for the possibility of companionship.

Strangely, her departure made him feel even more alone than before.

***

Caelfel's arms drifted to her sides as Feraan quickly dismounted. She rubbed the sleep from her eyes, and Feraan held out a hand to help her. She took it.

"Where are we?" The trees of the forest gave way to a clearing, allowing the sun, now sinking to the horizon, to be clearly visible.

"See for yourself." But when she looked, she saw nothing, save for the trees and the clearing.

So she turned and saw the toppled ruins of a crumbling city that was the obvious victim of nearly a century of abandonment. Though Caelfel had never been here, she could easily identify the place, and it made her stomach fall to the ground.

Amasel.

Caelfel stepped past Feraan to approach the city. She raised her hand to her quivering lips, and a deep sadness overcame her. Elves were instinctually saddened in places of mourning, tears flowing with or without consent, and Amasel was certainly still a place to be mourned.

Then, without knowing why, Caelfel ran into the city.

Amasel was a city made of stone, and the great walls remained mostly intact from what Caelfel saw beneath the scorch marks that blackened the once white pillars of the elvish city. Caelfel ran, aware of the saplings that had taken root in the empty streets and a faint smell of smoke and ash that shifted and stirred with her feet, trapped within the walls. She heard Feraan chasing after her, but the only thing that filled her ears was the ghostly screams of a city of elves dying. The tears flowed hot from her eyes.

She didn't know where she was running, but her feet eventually stopped at Amasel's center where a giant, majestic mausoleum stood, untouched by any rampant fires or stampeding soldiers. Caelfel gingerly climbed the steps before falling to her knees halfway up. The crypt was a new construction, built to house the citizens of Amasel. Their names were written all along the walls in endless lines. When she blinked, she found herself lying face down on the steps, sobbing silently, her shoulders shaking. Footsteps padded quietly behind her, loud against the fading screams.

"We don't have to stay in the city," Feraan said quietly.

Though she had made her peace with the truth her father revealed to her, Caelfel still found herself fighting the anger of grief. It was a natural instinct to mourn for them, and many souls had suffered here. It wrenched a primal pain through her chest as she ineffectively wiped the tears away. "Why did you bring me here?" she asked, wondering why this elvish instinct that gripped her so passionately held no effect on him.

Feraan held a hand out for her and when she took it, he helped pull Caelfel to her feet. "I wanted to show you what happened here eighty years ago."

He led her to the edge of the city where Firnis remained waiting for them. Then he had her sit on the grass of the clearing and he sat facing her, the city sitting on her right and his left.

"Close your eyes," he instructed.

She did just before feeling his fingertips touch her brow. At first, there was only darkness from the inside of her eyelids. Then something shifted.

Through the dimness of moonlight, she saw Eviat Gyssedlues staggering away from the city, obviously injured with blinking orbs flying after him. The orbs appeared non-threatening, but Eviat's frightened expression suggested otherwise. Then Feraan entered the scene, rushing to her father. The vision faded as Feraan half-carried Eviat to a horse with glowing red eyes.

"When I found your father," Feraan's voice explained briefly, cutting through her thoughts.

Caelfel nodded as the vision continued.

Feraan stood before Amasel once more against the dazzling light of high noon. When Caelfel turned slightly, she could see an army behind him, an army of rugged and hairy men that numbered in the hundreds. Their movements were slow and cumbersome when compared to the grace of elves, so Caelfel knew that they were humans. But even more appalling and horrifying was the decaying bodies of elves that lumbered through the city toward the army. They glowed with a dull, gray light, and Caelfel knew that they were possessed by the malicious, parasitic orbs.

Feraan, astride Firnis, yelled, and the sound was distant to her ears. Snarls ripped through the air next, and Caelfel saw the army behind Feraan transform into huge wolves. *Werewolves*, she realized.

Then the bloodbath ensued. Feraan ended the scene before Caelfel could properly see the slaughter wrought by the army. When she opened her eyes, she was drenched with a cold sweat, and Feraan did not appear to fare any better.

"Werewolves? You brought an army of werewolves?" Caelfel asked panting, wiping her forehead. "Father said you brought humans."

A small smile touched Feraan's face. "I am close friends with Lycaon."

"Lycaon?" Caelfel repeated, faintly remembering the name.

"He is the head of the Dirus Clan of werewolves," Feraan explained. "The alpha." Feraan waved his hand, and the portrait of a man appeared in the air. Lycaon was darkly tanned, pale white scars stretching across his face. His hair was long and gray, and his equally long beard was braided and white. Caelfel remembered seeing him stand closest to Feraan before the battle began. After a moment, the image dissolved with the breeze.

Caelfel eyed the city next to them warily. "And those things, those orbs? Are they all gone?"

"I did not leave until every last one was destroyed. When they die, they look like rotten fruit and they smell just as bad." Feraan grimaced at the memory.

"Where did they come from?" Caelfel asked.

"That is what I have been trying to solve for almost a century." He stood up. "We should head back before it gets dark. Being this close to the city unsettles me."

Caelfel got to her feet, realizing something. "It still bothers you," she said with a gasp of discovery. "That battle. You have nightmares about it and you strike out when you are surprised. That is why—" But Caelfel couldn't bring herself to bring up the incident when he had violently pinned her against the wall.

Feraan avoided her gaze, but there was something sad about his features. "Let's leave."

Caelfel held her palms out. "I want to know why you didn't tell me about Amasel in the first place."

"There was nothing to tell you," Feraan said bitterly. "I've committed no wrong."

He refused to say any more until they left Amasel's clearing. Soon she found her arms wrapped around his waist again. This time, it felt as though Feraan urged Firnis to go faster. Caelfel could not blame him; standing in the shadow of the city made her skin crawl.

"I had a right to know," Caelfel insisted during the ride.

"It was not your problem," Feraan said dismissively.

"It became my problem when I risked execution for you," she pointed out indignantly.

"And how did you react when you first found out? You ran away without even allowing me a chance to explain," Feraan shot back.

"Perhaps if you were honest with me from the start, I would not have felt compelled to run away," Caelfel grumbled back. Inevitably, her sore limbs took precedent, and Caelfel found herself burying her face into Feraan's back. She felt something tense in him relax at the touch. "My father said that those parasites took his aura."

"Yes," she heard Feraan say, his voice reverberating through his torso.

She still gripped him tightly with one arm and examined the black mark on her other arm. "Do you think one of those orbs took my aura as well? I don't remembering seeing an orb before it happened."

She felt him stiffen again. "I have long considered it."

"So that means the orbs are still alive?"

"It means," Feraan corrected harshly. "That whoever created the orbs still lives."

13. Trouble at Home

"**I** feel sorry for you," she volunteered after some time. "I'm not sure what keeps you here."

They had arrived back at Sal'Sumarathar and returned Firnis to the meadow after their long journey. It was decidedly late, and Caelfel was having a hard time keeping her patience. She was groggy and ill-tempered. Her harried mind had kept her awake throughout the ride from Amasel, until finally she had thought of that question to ask Feraan. By then, they had reached his house, and he helped her weary body through the doorway.

It was a question that he considered deeply. "I have been charged with the duty of finding the one truly responsible for destroying Amasel."

Caelfel sank to the floor once she was inside, picking at the dirt that had stained the gauzy skirt of her Spring Festival dress. Somewhere in the back of her mind, she was surprised she was still wearing it. "Mother said the elves of Sal'Sumarathar burned down your house when you told the Council what happened." She sniffed. "If I were you, I'm not sure if I would have stuck around to find out who was responsible. You should have left the ungrateful bastards to die."

He gave a soft chuckle at her irritation, but Caelfel saw nothing funny about it.

"Do you think the Council was involved with Amasel?" she asked him.

"I had suspicions of their involvement when they were so quick to accuse me and Eviat and then cover up the whole event as if it were a mere accident when they discovered they couldn't rightly pin charges against me. The Tree-Talker told them what happened, so they could only spread rumors that I was an evil sorcerer that learned the darkest secrets and spells on my travels."

"Tree-Talker? What is that?" Caelfel asked. Feraan turned to stare disbelievingly at her before comprehension dawned on him.

"Of course you wouldn't know. I forget that you are so young."

Caelfel's cheeks burned, but she ignored the comment. "Know what?"

"The Tree-Talker is the guardian of the forest. He can communicate with the trees, and as unbiased, absolute witnesses, the trees recount everything that they witness to their guardian. The Council demanded the truth from the Tree-Talker, but when he told it to them, they refused to accept it. They declared the Tree-Talker untrustworthy, which is why they no longer consult him. Your trial, for instance. They already knew the truth of what happened in the forest. They hired Markis to kill me. It would not do well for them and their agenda to have the Tree-Talker speak the truth, so they spread rumors that, with my dark secrets, I confounded the Tree-Talker with lies."

"Where is the Tree-Talker now?"

"Anywhere. No one keeps up with him." Feraan sighed, changing subjects. "So perhaps the Council was responsible for those parasites and they could harness the orbs to take away the aura of a meddlesome she-elf when she saved a life that was not meant to be saved."

"My aura? You said Luewyn took it."

"Luewyn knows many more dark secrets than I. It does not surprise me to think she learned to harness that power."

"Does that mean I can't get it back?" she asked. Feraan avoided her gaze, looking at his own palms instead.

"I should think not," he said quietly. They were silent for some time.

Caelfel yawned, stretching from her position in the floor. She guessed the time to be around midnight, her eyelids drooping heavily. "It is late. I should go home," she said, thinking of her bedroom that she had not seen for days. Caelfel pushed herself to her feet.

"You can stay here," he said quietly, his gaze dropping to the floor.

Caelfel felt the sudden desire to accept his offer, her mind veering to the bed she had primarily been using as of late. It was far more comfortable for sleeping than the one she had at her parent's house.

"Perhaps I want you to stay," he mused mildly. "I've grown so used to your presence here. I might miss it."

Caelfel said nothing, wandering over to his desk, and touched the book he had authored with Sir Kennyratear. "Well, now it seems as though I know nearly everything about you, at least more than other elves," she said quietly at length.

"Yes, you do," Feraan admitted quietly. "And you are not angry with me?"

She turned around leaning against the desk to find him inexplicably closer to her. There was a thought that flashed through his eyes, and though she had no possible way of knowing, she guessed it mirrored her own. "No," she managed to answer breathlessly. There was a loud thrumming in her ears that obliterated every sound except Feraan's voice.

His gaze was penetrating as he looked her over with calculating eyes. Her festival dress might have been too formal to wear on a casual outing with him, but Caelfel was secretly glad she still wore it. Her mother's work proved very flattering for her frame. Feraan's eyes held hers as he said, "There is still the matter of last night's dance."

Her mind whirred through her sluggish thoughts as she struggled to recall the Victory Dance and his explanation of its meaning. The tips of her ears turned awfully hot. "Yes," she all but whispered.

Her hands clenched tightly, nervously at her sides. Her throat went dry as he easily pried open her fingers and put his own through the spaces. A new, burning question filled her mind. It had obviously been her first Spring Festival, and Caelfel had never before shared a moment of intimacy with another elf, Feraan being the first. She could not expect the same went for him.

"Has there been anyone—"

But he silenced her with a finger to her lips. "You are the most beautiful," was all he would assure her.

She found it unlikely but smiled at him all the same. His bright eyes shone brilliantly just as the house grew dark, the candles extinguished as if by some mystical wind. No doubt he was the cause of it. Caelfel tenderly squeezed his hand in response.

He tilted his head curiously. "Does that mean you are not refusing me?" His other hand trailed from her shoulder to her waist, and she was grateful to discover he was supporting her weight against the desk. He transferred her hand to the nape of his neck. She clung to him desperately, her suddenly accelerating heartbeat making her lightheaded and breathless.

Caelfel shuddered with anticipation, unable to say anything that would resemble coherency, so she merely nodded. He brushed his fingers against her lips and then traced them along her cheek, pushing some hair behind her ear and cradling her neck. She delighted in the sensation.

"Then be still, my fair lady," he murmured. His breath tickled against her ear, sending tiny tremors down her spine. His fingers pressed against her skin.

Caelfel stretched on her toes and kissed him.

The heat that emanated from his body would have normally been unbearable, but Caelfel soaked in it, matching it with her own heat that burned intensely. She wanted Feraan, she *needed* him. He must have felt the same, for he held her face and pulled her closer to him.

He pushed against her, shoving her against the desk. She heard an inkwell knocking over and felt the liquid staining her fingers and hair as she groped around for support.

When they finally broke apart, they separated barely a hair's breadth away from each other. He said but one word before meeting her lips fiercely again.

"Remember."

***

The Blind Seer's messenger emerged from the west wing, clad in all black with the cowl that always masked its face. The desert princeling stood outside, overseeing training regiments and perpetually listening to the never-ending complaints about the blasted desert heat from his steward. Without acknowledging anything around it, the messenger strode up to the desert princeling on its ungodly steed and silently handed him the letter.

The time is now.

"Ready the armies," he commanded his steward with a wide grin. "I will be bringing back a treasure of its own sort of rarity." Laughing, the princeling went to mount his own horse.

"The Seer expects her payment," the messenger rumbled in an indeterminate voice of ancient magic. The princeling froze at this, having not heard the messenger's voice before. He paused at the words, not expecting to pay the Blind Seer any type of required compensation.

"What does she expect?"

"She wants the bow and the Bastard's sword. She also requires a servant, someone who will learn the Ways and do her service, like myself."

"Choose any person you see fit," said the princeling with a forced smile and a desperate wish that the Seer would not require his invaluable steward.

Instead, the messenger turned its head to a stable boy, no older than ten years, and said, "He will do." The messenger pointed, and the princeling watched as the boy was suddenly enveloped by black and purple fire. The child screamed before disappearing entirely.

***

"There have been sightings," reported the scout.

"Sightings of *what?*" Markis snapped.

The scout hesitated. "Wolves, sir, but not ordinary ones. I believe these are *dire wolves.*"

Markis thought for a moment. The dire wolf was not a creature native to the Fey Forest and one had not been sighted in several centuries. "How large were they?"

The scout indicated with his hand, ranging from his shoulder to above his head. "Even taller than Head Councilor Uthruil and Headmaster Nimuath."

Markis was only able to hide his surprise because of his centuries of experience with politics and diplomacy. Uthruil Killelvris and his brother were notably the tallest elves recorded in Sal'Sumarathar's recent history. They had no equal save for the diplomat Lanslak from Rasaen. For wolves to be *that* tall indicted beings of marked intelligence, above a mere animal. Markis immediately suspected *werewolves*, and *that* was certainly troubling. "Where were they seen? What were they doing?"

"They were spotted roaming the southern border, where the Fey Forest connects to the Pirinac Forest of Umfeld."

"Then perhaps Rasaen would be better suited to dealing with this matter, as the Pirinac Forest is closer to them," Markis pointed out harshly.

The scout humbly bowed his head. "Sir, Sal'Sumarathar has been asked specifically to address this matter. Rasaen has struggled as of late, and they've no formal militia or training. Simply put, sir, they are not qualified."

This bit of news surprised Markis. He had not visited the city of Rasaen for some time. He knew that in the way of development and industry, Rasaen suffered in comparison to the sister cities. But to be completely inept to address a potential threat? Rasaen must have fallen so far to be bypassed by the imperial army.

"Very well," Markis sighed. "We will gather volunteers for a response party."

The scout made a move to leave when Markis, upon receiving sudden inspiration, stopped him once more.

"Directly invite Eviat Gyssedlues," he said with a devilish smile. "I would very much like it if he attended."

The scout nodded at his orders, and Markis felt that much closer to relieving greylings of their long memories.

***

Caelfel awoke at dawn to find Feraan twisting strands of her hair around his fingers with a distant look in his eyes. When he noticed she was awake, he kissed her once on the brow and twice more on the lips.

It was in a panic when she remembered her promise to Eviat to be home before dawn, though as she walked home, Caelfel realized that the promise never occurred. Instead, Sylaera had asked Caelfel to not leave them for very long. In either case, Caelfel decided it would not be a poor decision to relate to Eviat and Sylaera her wish to be with Feraan. She assumed they would not be surprised, but the prospect of doing so made her stomach twitch with nervousness. Such thoughts vanished when she was accosted just outside her home by a despondent Garvanna who had her long hair tied up uncharacteristically.

Caelflel's perfect happiness was instantly marred when she saw Garvanna's forlorn expression. Caelfel crossed the distance to meet her. "Garvanna, what is the matter?"

But Garvanna numbly shook her head, brushing Caelfel's hands from her shoulders. The she-elf smoothed her hair back into place, though no strand had flown astray. Caelfel pressed the issue, and eventually, Garvanna divulged. "I will no longer be staying with

Thoroth," she announced as proudly as she was able, squaring her shoulders.

Caelfel's hand flew to her mouth. "Why not?"

Garvanna set her chin high. "We've had our differences, but I've felt it is time to relieve him of the burden of handling me."

"You're not a burden, Garvanna," Caelfel tried comforting.

Garvanna's eyes suddenly turned to daggers as she looked Caelfel over sharply. "Perhaps I am not, but it is difficult to compare to the *queen of beauty*," she hissed venomously.

Caelfel was startled by Garvanna's sudden turn of hostility. "What are you on about?"

"It is not enough for you to be pleased with your *murderer*. You must have Thoroth, too?" Garvanna demanded.

Caelfel ungracefully gaped at her friend. "Thoroth is only a friend to me—"

But Garvanna would hear none of it and fled from their conversation, her face red with anger. Caelfel resumed the walk home, utterly confused at what had just transpired. Caelfel was still mumbling to herself as she walked into her house, nearly running into her father.

"Good morning, Caelfel. Why do you look so sour?" Eviat asked.

"I ran into Garvanna, and we had a disagreement. Did you not wonder where I was last night?"

"I assumed you were with Feraan," he said, shrugging his bow over his shoulder. Caelfel blinked and noticed how he was dressed.

"Where are you going?" Caelfel asked. Her father usually did not start his routine hunting in the spring without inviting her.

"A courier came yesterday. I have been summoned to a hunting party for this morning. There have been sightings of dire wolves along the borders."

"A hunting party?" she repeated, uneasy with the idea of her greyling father facing a dire wolf. "I should go instead."

"No, Caelfel. The invitation specifically requests my presence this time." He chuckled. "They probably don't want you saving another condemned elf." But something in his words made Caelfel freeze, and she did not share Eviat's humor.

"Do you know who your hunting partner is?" she asked.

"We have not been assigned them yet. They will tell us in the meadow, I suspect."

Caelfel nodded at this but it did not soothe her anxiety. "I'll go with you, to see you off."

Eviat nodded at this, and they left for the meadow in silence. She noticed he did not seem disturbed when she felt he had every reason to be. Caelfel could not stay quiet the entire walk to the meadow.

"I don't think you should go on this hunting expedition," she said.

"Why is that?" he asked patiently, though it was evident that he did not see the danger she did.

"Dire wolves are dangerous. What if something happens to you?"

"There is a possibility of something happening to me every day. I will not wait around for my death just because you are paranoid."

"No, Father. What if something happens to you like what happened to Feraan on the last hunting party? Or Sir Kennyratear?" Eviat's face turned solemn, and Caelfel thought he looked mutely angry. She had a strong feeling that there was something he was not telling her, but neither spoke the rest of the way.

Uthruil was handing out assignments to arriving members of the party. He was referencing names on a list in his hands when he saw Eviat standing nearby.

"Ah, the Venerable Eviat Gyssedlues. You are with Markis Rilynnzea today."

Caelfel found she could not swallow as her eyes darted about for the tracker. "Is there any way I could take my father's place? I have never seen a dire wolf before."

Uthruil forced a smile. "Unfortunately, not today, Lady of Spring. You would not want to ruin your beautiful dress," he said, appraising her figure.

Caelfel grit her teeth, realizing once more she had not changed. She felt her face slip into a glare at the irrelevant and abrupt subject change. She did not bother to dignify Uthruil with a response and led Eviat off to the side to speak with him instead.

"I really do not think you should go," she pleaded. He didn't meet her gaze as he saddled his horse.

"It is my duty to Sal'Sumarathar."

"It is not your duty to let them kill you!"

"Oh, Caelfel. *Stop.*"

"Your partner is Markis. You know what happened to his last hunting partner. He was abandoned to die in the forest. If not for me, he would still be there. *Markis kills his partners!*" she hissed.

"Go home to your mother. She can use your worthless fretting more than I can," Eviat said gruffly. But even as he said it, Eviat refused to look at her.

Caelfel stared at him, repressing the urge to shake him. "Tell me you at least see there is something suspicious about this. Remember what happened to Sir Kennyratear—"

"How beautiful," interrupted the approaching Markis. "The lovely huntress worries over her father."

Caelfel ignored him. She couldn't fathom her father's reasoning for behaving this way, especially when the truth was so obvious to her.

"What is the matter with you?" she asked.

"Please leave, Caelfel. I do not need you worrying over me. I'm perfectly capable of handling myself if something were to happen."

Caelfel didn't want to believe her father had turned stubborn over a matter of pride, but she could do nothing as she watched Eviat resolutely gallop away. Perhaps he knew his fate though, and they were merely holding something against him to force his hand. Caelfel glared at the back of Markis's cloak as he disappeared beyond the forest line with the rest of the hunting party. She waited three full heartbeats before sprinting away from the meadow to find Feraan.

He hadn't left his house since she had seen him that morning. When she returned, Caelfel saw that he remained on his bed with the same thoughtful expression she had awoken to that morning. His features instantly changed, however, as he noticed something was amiss.

"I didn't expect you to return so soon," he said uneasily.

"It's Father. They summoned him to a hunting party this morning."

Feraan arched an eyebrow and stepped closer. "There are always hunting parties, Caelfel."

"But Markis is his hunting partner," she insisted impatiently. It took only an instant for Feraan to reach that same conclusion she had. He was alert and suddenly on his feet.

"I'll follow after him," he said, rushing through the house and grabbing his weather cloak.

"I want to go with you too," she said, following Feraan's heels as he bounded out the front door.

"No," he said firmly. "Go find your mother and bring her to my house to wait for us. The two of you should be safe here."

Caelfel frowned, not fond of the idea of being left behind. She told him this as she followed him to the meadow, but he didn't answer until he was on top of Firnis.

"Time is very critical right now, Caelfel. Your father may not have the luxury of waiting on you to retrieve your mother, but if your father is being targeted, it's essential to make sure you and your mother are safe. Understand?"

Caelfel nodded, trying to hide her disappointment. "Are you sure you will be safe, since—if not for me—you would not have left the forest the last time?"

Feraan offered her a sympathetic expression and allowed his hand to cradle the side of her face for a second before spurring Firnis into the forest. She lingered only a moment before rushing away from the meadow to find her mother. It did not take her long. Sylaera was sitting in her garden, her face uplifted to the sun with its rising warmth. Caelfel dreaded ruining her would-be peaceful day.

"What's going on?" she asked when Caelfel had warily approached without a word.

"Father has gone to the hunting party."

"Yes, I know. I saw him leave just minutes ago."

"His hunting partner is Markis."

"Your father has had many hunting partners in the past."

"Even one that will attempt to kill him?" Caelfel shot back. Sylaera arched an eyebrow skeptically.

"You are paranoid because of what happened to Feraan."

"Perhaps I am cautious because of what happened to him and Sir Kennyratear. I saw that for myself; Markis did not hesitate to annihilate the oldest elf of Sal'Sumarathar. I doubt he would hesitate with Father." Sylaera slowly got to her feet, gauging Caelfel from head to toe.

"Did you not warn Eviat?"

"He would not listen. Feraan has left to find him. He told me to bring you to his house and wait for him to return with Father."

"Why Feraan's house?"

"It is safe there."

"And you trust Feraan on that? You trust him with Eviat's life?" Sylaera asked, measuring the depth of Caelfel's devotion.

"He has proven himself with it once, has he not?"

Sylaera nodded, having no response for that. Caelfel led the way to Feraan's house. With Markis gone from the city, they did not need to worry about being followed. And soon enough, they reached the last boulder that overlooked Feraan's home. Sylaera assessed it silently before following Caelfel inside.

And there they waited.

Caelfel glanced at the tips of her hair that had been dyed black. She would have mumbled an excuse, but Sylaera's eyes wisely drifted to the ink puddle on the desk. Her mother moved to clean it.

Whenever Sylaera was worried, she would often be seen flitting from room to room, scouring the house clean of any offensive mess. Feraan's house stood as no exception. Caelfel had long since learned to avoid the hurricane known as Sylaera so she hid out in Feraan's narrow library, hoping Feraan would not be too upset with the way Sylaera decided to organize his things.

She settled sideways with her legs crossed in the small corridor. There was a small pile of books sitting on the floor that had not been returned to their proper places. Caelfel estimated, with the dust wiped freshly from their covers, that these were the books Feraan had recently read. The ones on top were about dreamrealms and auras, but Caelfel slid them away to read the title of the bottommost book—*The Dirus Clan*. But it was Feraan's name on the cover that intrigued her the most.

She picked this one up and began reading. It began by explaining how a human named Hubertus had become a saint and martyr to the people of Kanetalm, a kingdom within Umfeld. He led many battles against evil and those who dealt in evil magic. He was famous for defeating necromancers and sorcerers. Caelfel recalled Feraan telling her about it, but the book continued, discussing how the Temple of Saint Hubertus was located in a city named Sorasaen, an elvish name, she realized, though she did not know what it meant. There was a separate cult of Hubertus worshippers called the Reclaimers of Hubertus that had tasked themselves to eradicate the forces of evil, as Saint Hubertus had once done, specifically by exterminating the race of werewolves.

Caelfel imagined Markis as a Reclaimer, riding through the forest, chasing huge, man-sized wolves she thought would be dire wolves. The vision continued until she saw Eviat appear among the wolves, riding his white horse. Markis's attention shifted from the wolves to the greyling, and Caelfel saw a sudden fire in his eyes as Markis spurred his own horse on to quickly strike down Eviat. Her father fell face down to the ground, and his blood pooled around him. The scene reminded Caelfel of the way she found Feraan unconscious in the forest.

A cold shiver ran through her body as she screamed, and suddenly she was blinking in the dark library with a warm hand on her shoulder.

"Caelfel, your father," said Feraan. Caelfel blinked herself into awareness was suddenly on her feet and following Feraan to a spare bedroom where her father lay limp and unconscious on a bed.

Sylaera had her head bent over Eviat's hand.

"What happened?" Caelfel asked as her pulse accelerated with her panic.

"I followed them for a while. Then Markis and Eviat separated from the rest of the group. I didn't think it was intentional at first—others had separated—but when I found them again it was too late. Eviat had fallen, and Markis had disappeared."

"Is he still breathing?"

"Just barely," answered Sylaera.

"He needs a healer," Caelfel said, feeling herself grow closer and closer to hysteria.

Feraan nodded and, without another word, left the room.

14. Missive

He didn't fancy a visit to Thoroth, but he had little choice. The healer had proven himself to be the only one of his kind who would possibly break royal decree to save the condemned and Thoroth had a way of keeping his mouth shut on such matters. Still, as Feraan tugged his hood over his face, he did not look forward to seeing Thoroth's smug expression, and Thoroth was not one to disappoint.

"I've just received notice of Eviat's death, and any attempt to revive him will be considered an act of necromancy."

"Such grave news should not be delivered with such a large grin, Master Orletylar."

"Where is he?"

"He is at my house, if you are up for the task."

"You are going to show the way to your house?" Thoroth asked skeptically.

Feraan's grin was mischievous. "Only because your services are needed. Do not expect an extended invitation. You will have to be blindfolded."

Thoroth was initially disinclined but, since he was fond of Eviat and didn't want to see Caelfel crushed by her father's death if he could prevent it, he eventually and reluctantly agreed. It made Feraan think that Thoroth's friendship with Caelfel ran deeper than the healer would let on. But Feraan prodded Thoroth along, hiding his enjoyment as the healer ran into trees and various other obstacles. Feraan particularly liked it when the path wound uphill, forcing

Thoroth on all fours to grope his way along. Whenever pity won out, Feraan would give less-than-helpful instructions on how to avoid upturned roots and loose stones.

"How is Caelfel taking it?" Thoroth asked, doing little to conceal his agitation.

Feraan's amusement waned as he thought about Caelfel's broken expression. "She is devastated, but I don't believe she has come to terms with it yet."

"I suspect his condition will be the same as yours."

Feraan sighed heavily through his nose and touched the amulet hidden beneath his shirt. "As do I."

When they reached his house, Feraan would not remove Thoroth's magical blindfold until they were safely inside. He gave strict orders to the healer that he was not to leave the house under any circumstance unless Feraan permitted it. For good measure, Feraan adjusted the wards around his house so they would prevent Thoroth from leaving, though the spell drained some of his own energy. Feraan would not risk revealing where he lived.

When they reached the room where Eviat was, Feraan saw that Caelfel and Sylaera had not moved. Thoroth hurried to examine Eviat's wounds, and Feraan watched as some color returned to Caelfel's face as Thoroth set to work.

The assessment came shortly. "He's been poisoned."

Feraan watched calmly as the news was received. As expected, Eviat's wife and daughter did not take the information well. From the corner of his eye, he saw Caelfel reach for the place on her neck where her new pendant sat. Feraan felt the amulet around his own neck weigh heavily. Thoroth stood, gazing steadily at Feraan as he approached him.

"A poison not unlike your own," he said, dipping his chin and not blinking.

"Is there anything you can do?" Sylaera asked, standing.

"I can ease his pain but nothing more," Thoroth said. Feraan kept his breathing even as he avoided Thoroth's piercing eyes to scratch the nape of his neck. The twine he touched there felt unusually thick. He could not tell if he had the courage or the will to give up Caelfel's amulet for Eviat, for it only meant his own death. One life or the other, and *that* would be an unfair decision to put on Caelfel. He looked at her once more, very aware of her wild eyes darting about for some hidden solution. He would have liked to imagine Caelfel being as fretful in the face of his own near demise. He thought it unlikely; she barely knew him then.

Then she turned her pleading eyes onto him, and he found it very unsettling. "You saved him once when he was near death. You have helped me when my aura exploded and then when it disappeared. There must be something you can do," Caelfel pleaded.

He sighed and could not bear to face her. "Those were not caused by poison. I have many things and many abilities, but curing poison is not one of them."

"What do you need to cure poison, then?" Sylaera pressed.

Thoroth answered her. "There is a flower that used to grow in Amasel that was the base for all antidotes. I have not seen it for the last half-century."

"Who would have this flower? Would there be any left at Amasel?"

"I have not seen any but I could ride there and search for some," Feraan offered.

"That may be a waste of time," Thoroth countered smoothly.

"We talk on borrowed time!" Feraan shot back, voice rising dangerously. "We don't have many alternatives."

Thoroth's gaze shifted to the famous amulet that resisted the effects of poison, and Feraan read his thoughts perfectly. *Give the amulet to Eviat. Die. Leave Caelfel to me. Spare everyone in Honey Water of your existence.*

"I may still have some high connections to the nobility. Could one of the Families have some hidden away?" Sylaera asked.

Thoroth turned to her slowly, unconvinced of the probability. "If there is, I have not heard of it. Then again, I doubt they would allow such a secret to slip. If you rode to Yamalvon, I doubt Eviat would have the time to wait for your return."

"I would start with the Families of Sal'Sumarathar. I will see my sister. Then I will go to Rasean."

"I doubt you will find anything in Rasean," Feraan muttered bitterly. They all looked at him curiously, but he explained nothing of his contempt for the city of elvish squalor.

"I can still try, just as you will at Amasel," Sylaera said.

They left Eviat's room, and Sylaera threw a weather cloak over her shoulders when they were in the front room.

"I would like to meet my aunt," Caelfel said weakly.

Sylaera turned around and briefly touched Caelfel's cheek. "I do not think that would be wise," Sylaera said.

Caelfel's disappointment was tangible, and Feraan immediately understood that she needed a distraction or an escape from the house that held her dying father.

"You can help me look for flowers at Amasel," he suggested with a small grin. "If that is a suitable alternative for you." Caelfel stretched on her toes to reach him, and something in Feraan's chest froze.

But she did not kiss him. Instead she whispered sheepishly into his ear, "I do not know what to look for."

Smiling, he whispered back, "I will help you."

She nodded with an odd, grateful smile, and the three filed out of the house. From the door, Thoroth called, "I will stay, then, and look after him."

Feraan smirked but did not answer. Secretly, he was glad to have Caelfel accompany him. It was better than leaving her alone with pernicious Thoroth who would only poison her against him.

They parted in front of Feraan's door, Caelfel and Feraan heading towards the meadow and Sylaera going her own way. Feraan resisted the urge to stare after her, for nothing would answer the mysteries that surrounded the she-elf who voluntarily exiled herself from the Sal'Sumarathar nobility. He wondered if she had passed any of that mystery to Caelfel but found he truly did not know which qualities in Caelfel were Sylaera's and which were Eviat's.

"What's on your mind?" Caelfel asked when they reached the edge of the meadow. He glanced down at her, realizing Caelfel and Sylaera looked the same in their grief, just as they looked the same in other expressions.

"Your mother is a puzzling elf."

Caelfel managed a small chuckle. "Father says it's because she belonged to the Family."

"But you never met them?"

"No, just as I have never met Father's family."

"I remember. Eviat and Travin had a disagreement."

"Travin?"

"That's the name of your uncle. He's an interesting person, but it has been a while since I have seen him."

"You know more about my family than I do. I'm not even allowed to mentioned I have an uncle. What did they disagree about?"

"Travin was in love with a vampire. Eviat was against them marrying. Travin argued that Eviat had married a vampire as well. Eviat was quite insulted."

Caelfel sighed. "It's a shame."

Feraan whistled, and Firnis came trotting up faithfully. He mounted first and then held out a hand for Caelfel.

"I have Rowan," she began to protest uncertainly.

"You should ride with me."

It took Caelfel no further convincing to accept his hand, and when she had secured his arms around his waist, they were off.

The ride to Amasel was long, as always, and as uneventful as the last time he had taken Caelfel there. He would have thought she had fallen asleep again, except she remained firmly upright despite the rather long ride. He had discouraged her from riding by herself because of how preoccupied she was. He pushed Firnis on faster, and they arrived at the site of the decimated ruins hours later. He jumped easily to the ground, and Caelfel slowly slid off after him.

"We don't need to go into the actual city. The flower grew outside of it."

"What does the flower look like? What was it called?"

"It's yellow and shines like gold even in darkness. The humans call it Ruxlitta's Light."

"What do the elves call it?"

"Haelyn's Honey, but I much prefer the story of Ruxlitta."

"Tell me." They walked in long circles and looping arches. Feraan was disinclined to leave Caelfel's side, even at the risk of not covering more ground. He was reluctant to tell the story of the goddess Ruxlitta because he had specifically intended to save it, should he ever take her to the mountains of Umfeld.

"Ruxlitta was the goddess of happiness, love, sunlight, magic, and women. She lived in the deepest mountain, where no light penetrated and created life from her own light. Her breath supposedly became the flower, a cure to all mystical ailments."

"So, how did it become Haelyn's Honey?"

"Because Haelyn is our Empress and Honey Water her empire."

They continued searching, and strangely enough, Feraan began noticing how Caelfel made an effort, whether consciously or no, to remain within his shadow. It moved something in him, but when the urge came to reach for her hand, he suppressed it.

"Why did the flower become extinct?" she asked.

Feraan looked in the sun and became momentarily blinded. "Because the parasites were creatures of darkness that consumed everything with light in it," he said grimly. "That's how they feed off auras."

"And it grows in no other place?" she pressed.

"This was the only place it could be found in all of the Fey Forest."

She circled around him, stopping when she stood in front of him. "What would happen if you took the amulet off?" she asked.

He didn't want to answer but eventually did. "I would die."

Caelfel nodded at this and said nothing more of her amulet. She continued searching, but Feraan stood, staring after her, and felt inexplicably annoyed.

"If your father wore it, it would save him," he told her.

"I'm not going to ask you to sacrifice yourself for him."

"You would only be asking for something that is rightfully yours. You could save your father."

Caelfel angled her gaze to him, trying to discern the reasoning behind his behavior. Feraan wasn't sure of it himself. "And what of you?" she asked. "If you want to sacrifice that to save Eviat, go ahead. That's your decision."

"And if I decided to keep it for myself, how much would you hate me?"

"I wouldn't," Caelfel said defensively. "Saving one life does not justify giving one life in return." She suddenly snapped her body around to face him and with a passion that did not fully suit her now, she said, "Do not *dare* remove that amulet from your neck."

The unspoken threat in her voice was so strong, that any notion he had of giving away her amulet was suddenly dashed. Feraan decided he would deal with the matter later when it was more pressing. Their search for Ruxlitta's Light continued for a while longer before Caelfel declared it was hopeless. Feraan could only agree silently but did not voice his thoughts. They mounted Firnis and left for Sal'Sumarathar, hoping Sylaera's ventures would prove more fruitful.

***

The small army stopped their roving convoy through the desert to rest at a small oasis. The desert princeling gauged the distance ahead with a naked eye. He estimated they had a few days yet before they reached the magical, forbidden forest. His steward approached him with a nervous edge that was quite unlike his usual calm demeanor.

"What troubles you, Lisiek?" the princeling asked.

"Our destination, sir. How will we enter the realm of the elves with an entire army? What's more, what do we look for once or if we get there?"

"Humans have entered the Forest before."

"*Rumor* tells us that they have. I've not seen any proof," his steward insisted.

"Lisiek, have you any proof that we cannot enter the forest?"

Lisiek only shifted uncomfortably, unconvinced.

"The Blind Seer has revealed the secrets to me. She has shown me the way and what we are looking for."

"What about Kanetalm?"

"We will not go through Kanetalm. Why risk worrying the noble Prince Brenin? He has his own problems to look after. We will ride for the mountain pass instead, Farpass. Trust me on this, Lisiek. The Seer gave me all the answers."

"There's something else, my lord," Lisiek volunteered uneasily.

"Oh?"

"There was a deserter. At least, we thought he was. Further investigation proved he was an undercover agent of the Chthonic Order. I would wager he attempted to escape to warn others of our plans."

"How did you discover he was of the Order?"

"The tattoo, of course. It was behind his left shoulder."

"Is he elf or human?"

"Human. You know there is only one elf of the Order."

"Bring me to him, Lisiek. I wish to speak to him."

Lisiek led him through the encampment of soldiers, many of whom took refuge under stunted, malnourished trees, the only kind that grew in the desert. They all dropped their gaze to the ground appropriately as the princeling passed. The Chthonic prisoner was chained between two of these trees near the camp's center, beside the watering hole but just out of its reach. The prisoner did not move and only hung his head submissively in accepted defeat.

"What is your name?" the princeling asked. The prisoner lifted his—*her* face.

"Macha," she said in a strange, lilting accent. She had short, black hair that fell over her face and ice blue eyes.

"Lisiek, I thought you said the prisoner was a *he*."

Lisiek was not concerned with the issue. "A trivial detail, my lord."

"Where are you from, Macha? Umfeld, I would presume."

"I was born in the Baetic Mountains," she said curtly, glaring at Lisiek all the while.

"While you are being cooperative, may I ask how you infiltrated my army?" the princeling asked. Keeping her eyes trained on Lisiek, Macha's glare turned into a smirk.

"Your security detail is not as fortified as you may wish."

"And when you attempted to escape, where were you planning to go?"

Macha didn't answer, only continued smiling at Lisiek with a malevolent gleam to her eyes. The princeling began circling her and he saw the exposed tattoo on her left shoulder blade.

"Tell me how you received this tattoo, Macha," the princeling tried instead. He pointed at it with his sword, catching her skin in the process. Macha inhaled sharply with the pain, and the princeling moved again to face her.

"It is the mark all of my people are given once they reach the Age."

"What age is that?"

"It is different for every person. My sister was nineteen. I was sixteen."

"I don't quite believe that, Macha. I know that tattoo isn't the mark of a people. It is the mark of the Order," said the princeling.

Macha grinned. "And who do you think my people are, my *lord*?" she hissed.

The princeling wasn't sure what she meant. He asked, "I'll try once more, but my patience wears thin. Where did you plan to go once you escaped here?"

"There are only so many places I can go. But I will show you."

Macha convulsed into herself, shrinking, and with a swirl of black smoke and feathers, she transformed into a raven. The chains slipped from her wings, and Macha took off towards the east. The princeling growled and chased after her a few feet before stopping.

"*Follow that bird!*" he screamed. A handful of soldiers around him took up their horses and chased Macha the crow. A few archers tried to bring her down with their arrows. He knew it was a futile attempt just as calm Lisiek stepped up beside him.

"You appear better now," the princeling snarled at him.

"She made me nervous," Lisiek replied simply. "It's best that she's gone. There's not much she can do to change things."

"Your confidence may be back, but you've lost your reason. She will spoil our surprise. She will warn him."

"Even if she does warn Feraan Auvrearaheal, there's not much he can do to stop your *army*. If you do not even know what we're after yet, there's little chance he does either."

"I'm not so certain, Lisiek. But remember why we are here. I do not want to risk anything to chance."

Lisiek looked at him gravely. "My lord, you are relying on the Blind Seer. *Everything* has been put to chance. The elves do not call her the Traitor of the World for nothing."

***

It was to everyone's immense relief when Sylaera returned with a small, measured amount of Ruxlitta's Light. She wouldn't say what it required of her to get it, but Feraan was under the impression that Sylaera gave up something of great value.

"It was worth it," she said to Feraan as Thoroth set to work brewing the elixir. "I'm sorry there wasn't enough for you as well."

Feraan shook his head, as if it were of no consequence. Caelfel remained glued to her father's side, and as much as Feraan wanted to, he didn't have the heart to disturb her. He let her be, with Thoroth working his alchemy magic, and went to occupy himself outside in the corner of his garden where he kept his small forge. He took a whetstone and some oil and went to work sharpening his sword with slow, methodical strokes. He wondered off-handedly where Sylaera had gone but he didn't want to think of Sylaera or Thoroth or even Eviat and Caelfel. He had already deemed himself incompetent in helping others with their grief.

Sometime after dark, Feraan sheathed the sword and put away the whetstone, throwing some charcoal in the forge to warm up the garden. The orange embers provided little light but when he turned, it was enough to see the curious black bird sitting on a nearby drooping branch. The sight made Feraan freeze as he watched the bird tilt her head first to one side, then the other, watching him inquisitively. The shockingly bright blue eyes told Feraan she wasn't a mere animal.

"Where did you come from?" he asked it.

The raven tittered, jumping from the branch to the forest floor outside the forge. Feraan rose just as a face appeared over the stone, garden wall. Her hair was cropped short, except for the fringe in front, and her eyes were the color of ice, but, most notably, her ears were rounded.

"Where is your tattoo?" she asked suspiciously.

"Tattoo?" he repeated. "Who are you? You're human, not an elf. Are you a werebird?"

"I need to see your tattoo first," she insisted. "You are one of us, are you not? The elf wanderer that lived among humans and found himself a family of misfits that would claim him?"

"I'm certain that I would be the only elf that would marginally fit that description."

"Prove it. Show me your tattoo."

"I never took the tattoo. I am an elf. It would not be appropriate."

She narrowed her eyes, having little choice but to trust him. "What is your name?"

"Feraan Auvrearaheal."

She frowned, and he knew she would not to try to pronounce his name. "I'm Macha."

"Macha. What brings you to the Fey Forest?"

"I was put on an assignment for suspicious activity in the Amhsis Desert of Umfang. I went undercover as a soldier in some commander's army where the admiral of the fortress struts around and calls himself a desert princeling."

With the mention of the princeling, Feraan suddenly became alert. "So why are you here?"

"To warn you of his intentions," Macha said impatiently. "He was building and training his army. Then one day, a messenger emerged from his castle with some sort of signal. When they disappeared, the princeling mobilized his army. They have been trekking across the desert, past the Baetic Mountains. He's bringing the army here, to the Fey Forest."

"Why? He wouldn't make it past the borders," Feraan said.

The excitement didn't leave her bright eyes. "He spoke of

obtaining revenge from an elf, rumored to be descended from gods, if I remember my elvish correctly."

"So he's out for revenge against me. How does he plan to do this with an army that can't even march through the trees?" Feraan asked with a light smile, crossing his arms over his chest. He would have laughed at the princeling's attempts but thought better of it. The princeling wasn't an idiot, or at least, his advising steward would be smarter than that. He didn't mention to Macha that, even with an army that could penetrate the forest, the princeling or his steward wouldn't be able to find him.

"I didn't know at first. When I found out, I tried escaping, but they captured me. I flew away before they could really interrogate me."

"So what did you find out?"

"The princeling doesn't intend to attack you or other elves. He's after a different elf entirely. An oracle told him what to do."

"Another elf?" The arms unfolded and hung limply at his sides.

She nodded. "There was a conversation about being unable to find you, so they settled on a different elf they could find. A she-elf, if I'm not mistaken, that would force *you* to find *him*."

Feraan purposely kept his face neutral and unchanged. "I'm not aware of any elf or she-elf that could do that." He eased a smile to his face. "Perhaps this oracle of theirs is mistaken. They will find nothing."

Macha tilted her head curiously. "I do not think the Blind Seer is often mistaken. They are very certain of their efforts. I don't know who the she-elf is. The only one who would know is the princeling, but if what you say is true, then my warning has come for nothing."

"The Blind Seer?" he repeated. He kept his external features calm but secretly, Feraan panicked. The Blind Seer didn't have the power to break past his wards, but she could give the desert princeling everything else he wanted. He wondered what the princeling had paid her. He couldn't imagine the steward approving the utilization of her services.

"I haven't seen her, but she sent a messenger who had the Voice of the Unknown. The princeling and the steward disagreed over it though. Lisiek wasn't fond of her methods."

Lisiek the steward. Feraan committed the name to memory. "And why do they think that targeting this supposed she-elf would help? What do they plan to do with her?"

"I can't imagine the purpose of the army if they only mean to kidnap her," Macha pointed out. "The princeling believes that you would care so much for this she-elf, you would reveal yourself to him. That's what he wants—to bypass your curse."

"It's not a curse," Feraan corrected. "It's a protection spell. And they're wrong. I wouldn't reveal myself to him for any purpose. Their journey has been in vain."

Macha narrowed her eyes suspiciously until they caught something behind him. "So there is no she-elf, then?" she repeated with a light smirk.

Feraan spun around to see Caelfel carefully approaching. The sound of beating wings followed, and when Feraan turned again, Macha was gone.

"Who was that?"

"That was no one," Feraan said quickly. "No one important."

"She just turned into a bird."

"She is a werebird."

"What did she say?"

"She came to warn me of an army gathering in the desert. I told her there is nothing to worry about. Did you need something?" Feraan asked, changing subjects when Caelfel's brow only furrowed deeper in confusion and concern.

"Father woke briefly. He groaned some but didn't say anything."

"Did Thoroth give him the antidote?"

"Yes, Thoroth has been very helpful," she said. The remark made something in Feraan prick uncomfortably, but he pushed the feeling away.

"I am sorry I have not been very helpful, then."

Caelfel shook her head numbly. "Don't be. There is not much any of us can do. I wanted to ask if you wanted to come inside to see him or to eat."

"Offering me my own food? How generous of you."

Feraan was thrilled to see the small smile that touched her face. "Mother took the liberty of preparing dinner. What was that girl's name?"

"She said it was Macha."

"Do you know her?"

"That was the first time I have ever seen her."

"She didn't look elvish. Is she from Honey Water?"

"I would venture not."

Caelfel nodded but still appeared troubled as she hesitated before the door. "She was naked."

"I did not notice."

She shot him a disapproving look, angling her eyebrows suspiciously. "I have trouble believing that."

"It's a trademark of the werefolk. Clothes do not fit them properly in animal form."

Caelfel rolled her eyes and went inside.

Nobody ate in the kitchen. Thoroth and Sylaera took their food to Eviat's room while Caelfel and Feraan went to sit in the narrow library. He was aware of a book she had been reading, disturbed from the pile he left on the floor, but she hid the title from him before he could read it.

"Have you ever been to Kanetalm?" she asked suddenly.

He blinked. "It's been a few decades, but yes. Why do you ask?"

"I thought you moved back to Sal'Sumarathar a century ago."

"I visit Sorasaen on the rare occasion. I left the Fey Forest briefly, about twenty years ago now. There was a priest there, and I taught him some elvish magic. He worked in the temple of Hubertus." Feraan paused at the memory. "He wanted me to find a cure for werewolves."

"Did you find one?"

"Not yet," he said uneasily. If Feraan was being honest to himself, he hadn't spent much time looking for one. Perhaps he should put some effort into that task. Twenty years was longer for humans than elves.

"I didn't know that there was a cure. I thought werefolk were *born* being part animal," she said, her brow wrinkling.

Feraan leaned against the bookshelf. "It's complicated. Some are born and some are created, from my understanding of it. They are very secretive about the process."

Caelfel was silent a moment as her gaze slipped and became unfocused. "What about that army Macha warned you about? Aren't you worried?"

Feraan smiled to reassure her. "Not at all. To bring an entire army in the forest? It's impossible."

"You did," she pointed out.

"Because I am capable of the impossible. Wards surround the Fey Forest, similar to the ones that surround the college."

Caelfel hesitated to say something on her mind. She succeeded after a moment of mouthing syllables silently. "Will we go to trial for saving Father, like I did with you?"

Feraan did not have an answer for her. He looked at her empty bowl. "I'll take that if you're finished with it."

Caelfel handed it to him, and Feraan went to return it to the kitchen.

Feraan found sleep difficult that night and doubted it came to the others any easier. Sylaera stayed in an empty room next to Eviat's, and Thoroth had been offered the room across the hall. Caelfel preferred staying by Eviat's side. In the few hours before dawn, Feraan roamed the house, until he realized that he still had his sword belted at his waist. He turned to put it away, passing by Eviat's room. He paused, seeing Caelfel asleep with her head on her arms next to her father. Thoroth was in there too, which made Feraan pause to watch.

He was washing and bandaging the open wounds that dotted Eviat's chest, and Feraan briefly wondered if the arrows had penetrated the flesh on his back. Thoroth moved quietly to gather his instruments, wrapping the excess bandages into a single wad. Thoroth made a motion to leave the room, but the unconscious Caelfel caught his attention. The satchel of utensils fell silently to the floor, and Thoroth crouched to place a hand on her shoulder.

Feraan hardly registered his movements but suddenly he had drawn his sword and held it to Thoroth's throat. "Do not touch her," came the even warning.

Thoroth froze. "I was just comforting her. She *is* having a bad day."

"You comfort her by using your hands to heal her father, not by touching her."

"Don't be so insecure of yourself that you fear my hand on her shoulder will take her away from you," Thoroth hissed irritably but did not argue with the sword as he got to his feet.

"I don't care what you may think. You are in *my* house under *my* generosity. Don't risk my hospitality over something stupid."

"I thought I was here for Caelfel."

Feraan cocked an eyebrow at him and looked at Thoroth as if he were mad. "You're here for Eviat and you will soon overstay your usefulness." He followed Thoroth to his room as if he were a misbehaved child and only sheathed the sword when they reached his door.

"Why did you suddenly care for her? Before she brought you to me that day, you never spared her a passing glance."

"And when did you suddenly decide to care for her yourself?"

"It was only the realization that was sudden. I have cared for her for many years."

"Exactly. Your only problem is that you never decided to act upon it until her attention turned elsewhere."

"Perhaps this is only a small distraction. She is still rather young and you have a reputation of disappointing people."

Feraan scoffed. "I've not disappointed anyone. Perhaps in time, you will accept her decision. Good morning, healer."

Thoroth grumbled something inaudible and left Feraan in the hallway, shutting the door in his face. Feraan looked at the door a moment and briefly considered locking Thoroth in his room before deciding against it.

He returned to his room, thinking over Macha's warnings of the desert army marching for him right now. But then he remembered Macha saying they weren't after him. They were after a she-elf. It was no question who that she-elf was, Feraan knew. His concern was if the princeling or his army could penetrate the trees.

You did.

Caelfel's insightful words rang through his head. He did lead his own army of werewolves through the Fey Forest, because the intention had not been to harm elves. In this way, the princeling could make his way through elvish land, and Feraan doubted they would even attempt to make their way across the desert if they were not completely certain of their efforts. He wondered if the Blind Seer had truly shown them how to reach him or, worse yet, how to find Caelfel.

He decided he couldn't rely on the magical barriers around the forest. Their journey alone proved they had found a way to bypass them. How they had discovered Caelfel completely baffled him, but Feraan supposed that the Blind Seer wasn't necessarily blind to her own gift. The discovery must have been recent, since they had not come sooner, or perhaps the Seer had been waiting for him to make a decision, to subconsciously will the significance of Caelfel into existence and to allow them the opportunity to snatch her away.

Why did you suddenly care for her?

It was Thoroth's words this time that repeated themselves, and Feraan pondered on them. Perhaps Thoroth was right, and the decision had been instantaneous and sudden. Perhaps even when Caelfel had kissed him. That was when Feraan had made the conscious and deliberate decision to act on his desire for her.

It then became apparent that Feraan's only option was to be resolute in his next decision to not care for Caelfel at all. He waited for the verdict to settle on him and he nearly choked on the decision. He swallowed past it, deciding Caelfel and her family should leave once Eviat was well again.

Feraan locked his bedroom door to allow himself privacy as he came to terms with this. He should have left her alone long ago and not deviated from the task the Blind Seer had originally charged him with. Feraan had no business involving himself with other elves. He had no place in pursuing romance or companionship. He was the Wandering Elf, doomed to an eternity of duty and solitude. His only consolation he found in this new loneliness was that Caelfel should be safe from the Blind Seer's sight.

Never mind the fact that she would more than likely turn to Thoroth when Feraan no longer had affection to give her.

15. Call to Arms

Caelfel was woken by a greyling ruffling her hair, and it was an especially welcome sight since the greyling was her very alert father looking down on her with bright eyes. She jumped to her feet and raced to tell Feraan about his recovery. The door was shut, but she didn't think much of it, figuring he wanted his privacy in a house full of elves.

However when she went to open it, Caelfel found it locked. This puzzled her. She wondered if she was supposed to knock and tried doing so. The sound was met with faint shuffling from the other side of the door. A moment passed, and Feraan appeared before her, looking haggard with disheveled hair and oppressive, dark circles beneath his eyes, as if he had no sleep at all last night. He looked at her expectantly, and Caelfel found she didn't know which concern to address. She decided to fall back on her initial purpose for coming to him.

"Father is awake—*really* awake. He's been completely healed." But even her excitement did not seem to reach through Feraan's weariness, and it took him a great deal of effort to manage a small smile.

"That's wonderful," he said. She expected him to inquire further on Eviat or to walk past her to see for himself, but Feraan remained where he was. Something curled in the pit of her stomach, but she tried convincing herself that she shouldn't be worried. Anyone would act uncharacteristically without a night's sleep, but this did not explain why something with Feraan felt inexplicably *off.*

"Your door was locked," she tried conversation again, her stomach twisting itself into knots.

"I locked it," he merely agreed.

Something in Caelfel's chest clenched at his words. "Would you like to see him?" she asked finally after they had stood in awkward silence for what felt like an eternity.

"Perhaps later," he said before retreating again to his room. Caelfel heard a lock clicking into place once the door was shut.

She stared at the door as something thick settled on her chest, making her throat swell up. She combed a hand through her hair and pushed the discomforts down as she slowly returned to her father's room. Sylaera had already been by her husband's side before Eviat had disturbed Caelfel, and now Caelfel saw her parents smiling and muttering sweet nothings to one another. The tightness in her chest moved to her stomach as she was reminded of Feraan's coldness. Something was wrong.

Caelfel hardly saw Feraan again for the rest of the morning. She only caught a glimpse of him as he escorted Thoroth home with a cold shoulder. She sat with her parents in the spare room where Eviat was staying, feeling mostly invisible because Sylaera and Eviat were so absorbed with each other.

"So your sister found it? Well, they don't entirely hate me."

"Of course not. They never have. They just hated *me*," said Sylaera. There was a giggle and a chortle, but Caelfel didn't bother to notice who they belonged to. She grew impatient.

"But *what happened?* In the forest, with Markis?" Caelfel asked. They both turned, as if noticing her for the first time. Eviat had a look that indicated he was not ready to discuss the encounter with Markis yet.

"I've decided to retire from hunting."

And the sweet nothings continued between her parents.

When it was determined that Eviat was strong enough to return home, Feraan was there to see them off. Eviat thanked him profusely, to which Feraan responded with a thin smile. He still had the dark smudges under his eyes.

She let her parents go on ahead as she lingered by the doorway, staring at him first before fixing her gaze on the floor. When she realized that she was wringing her hands nervously, she hid them behind her back.

"You should be with them," Feraan said at length. He didn't cross the room to be with her. She felt as though she should kiss him, given everything that had transpired between them. Caelfel felt as though she needed it then to assure herself nothing was amiss. But his stony expression told her he wasn't interested in kissing, and this was rather damaging to her confidence.

"I will see you later, then," she said. As was her habit, she fled before he could respond, thus avoiding the risk of Feraan declining the offer.

She had planned to leave Feraan alone for the rest of the day, thinking he probably needed time to himself. She tried to take the opportunity to catch up on her own sleep, but sleep did not find her as she was constantly reminded of Feraan's indifferent expression. By afternoon, she could only sit at her window and stare dejectedly outside. Her position gave her a wide scope of the main street which was deserted.

Minutes passed and suddenly Caelfel saw royal couriers flooding the street, some stopping at houses while the rest continued to the next city. When one turned for their house, Caelfel ran to answer the door. Her parents were in the garden, completely oblivious to what was happening.

The courier that called was tall and clad in imperial armor. His hair was pale and swept into a long braid draped over his shoulder. He handed Caelfel the scroll with a ruby ribbon.

"Urgent response requested," he said, folding his hands behind his back, waiting as patiently as any impatient elf could.

Caelfel tore open the scroll.

Empress Haelyn calls upon the house Gyssedlues to join the militia forces and protect Honey Water as a ranger *due to a sudden threat of war that approaches our borders.*

Signed.

It was a summons to war. She thought of her father who was the only properly trained ranger of the family, but Caelfel knew all the secrets he had taught her. Eviat was in no condition to leave or volunteer. Not only that, he had just announced his retirement from such matters and was probably considered as officially dead.

"I will go," Caelfel said.

The courier, who was probably a commander of rangers, did not argue. "We meet in the meadow in half an hour. Pack your bow and light essentials. The rest will be explained there." Without further question, he left for the next house.

Caelfel approached her parents hesitantly. The pair hid among the lavender bushes, near the very same spot Gwyndolyn had discussed Feraan with her. But that seemed ages ago, and now her parents had noticed her and fallen silent. She took one look at Eviat and despite his recent recovery, saw that he was still quite weak. She looked away and decided news of wartime would not be suitable for him.

"Mother, may I speak privately with you?"

Sylaera, confused but obliging, followed Caelfel to her room. Without a word, Caelfel showed her mother the scroll the royal courier gave her. It did not take long for her to read it.

"He cannot go to war!" Sylaera hissed venomously. "He's only just survived that damn hunting party. The empire just tried to murder him and now they want him to fight—"

"I've volunteered to go," Caelfel interrupted before Sylaera could finish her tirade.

Her mother was stunned. "You *volunteered?*"

"Yes, and I'm supposed to meet them in the meadow in thirty minutes. I don't know how long I'll be gone."

"You did not need to, Caelfel. They're merely gathering volunteers. This isn't a draft. It is only an investigative recruitment."

"I want to go," Caelfel insisted. "I've always wanted to fight in battles as a battlemage, but I can't do that now. A ranger, though? I can be the perfect archer. I already am."

Sylaera looked doubtful. "Your father will not be pleased."

"Then don't tell him I'm going. Say nothing about it at all."

"He *will* notice your absence, especially if you don't return to us." She arched an eyebrow, glaring quite pointedly.

"If it turns into a war, then tell him once I've already gone. Tell him it was what I wanted."

"What about Feraan?" Sylaera asked.

Caelfel's shoulders shifted uncomfortably. "I will tell Feraan myself."

She packed her things quickly, kissed her mother on the cheek, and soon stood before Feraan's door with time to spare. She knocked, and he answered shortly.

"It seems as though Macha's army might be more dangerous than you thought," she said, shoving the scroll into his hands.

"It's a preemptive measure," he said after reading it. "It's only natural for the empire to meet an army gathering at their borders. It doesn't necessarily mean war."

"They have an army, we have an army. I'm not going to ignore the inevitable."

"No, but is Eviat going?"

"No, but—"

"Then there is nothing to worry about. It is only a voluntary recruitment, not a draft."

Caelfel exhaled through her nostrils impatiently. "You are not listening."

"There is nothing to listen to. You're safe. And as long as you're safe, you have no business here," he said. Caelfel's twitching stomach froze, and the weight felt too much for her knees.

"What do you mean?" Her voice sounded hollow and distant to her own ears.

"I've helped save your father and yourself many times. Don't you think that settles my life debt to you?"

"Your life debt?"

"Don't you remember saving me from the forest and being called to trial for it?"

"Of course I do."

"Then wouldn't you agree I've done plenty for you in return?"

Caelfel gaped at him. "Well, yes. I don't understand what you mean."

"I was always alone before you picked me up from the forest. Since then, I haven't been. I'd like to return to that. I want to be alone."

Caelfel's mind reared about wildly. "But I thought—"

"I don't need you. I've spent enough of my time taking care of you."

"But we went to the festival together—" But Caelfel couldn't muster the heart to finish her thoughts.

"You insisted on going to the festival, like a child, and it was you who picked me for the Victory Dance."

Caelfel searched desperately for the words that would bring sense to his but she was left fighting to swallow air. "Do you not like me?" she asked.

Feraan smiled, but Caelfel could not read its intention. "If you truly care enough about my opinion of you, then you will stay away from me, because I do not want you."

Caelfel couldn't respond; she didn't know how to. He stepped closer, his face much kinder than his cold manner and words. She managed, "This isn't about the debt."

"No, you're right. The life debt is my own pathetic excuse, but, Caelfel," he began uneasily. "I have decided I don't want what's between us. It's not a lifestyle for me to settle down."

"I never asked you to settle down. I want to go places."

"And I don't want to be responsible for you. You're like an infant, always need watching, saving, or protecting. I'm tired of it."

"I'm not like that," Caelfel protested, hurt that he thought her so immature. "What has suddenly changed with you? Why are you so different now?"

"I'm not different. Only, I've had a realization. I don't want to dedicate the rest of my life to looking after you—"

"*I'm not a child!*" Caelfel hissed, face turning red as something hot dangerously pricked at her eyes.

Feraan checked himself. "You still have some aging to do," he pointed out. "But I'm incapable of making you happy. I'm too different and I've never had that sort of companionship before. I don't *want* to. It puts you at danger and makes me unhappy. I'm sorry. I don't want to see you anymore. Return to your home, spend time with your family, and forget about that desert army." Feraan's voice had become threateningly low, as if he were warning her of something.

But Caelfel's chest felt like it was shattering, and it took a great deal of effort to draw breath. So she heeded no such warning. She was hurting and breaking, crumbling before him. Her wide eyes must have shown this, because, as if from mercy, Feraan touched his forehead to hers. She thought the gesture must have meant he didn't mean what he said, but his next words were not so comforting.

"I'm sorry. I know this must hurt you, but I cannot continue caring for you. Feel free to pursue someone else."

Caelfel's throat tightened, and her breathing became even more difficult. "But I don't *want* anyone else," she managed breathlessly.

"Then perhaps someone else will want you."

"And you?" she shot back angrily, glaring at him. It was much easier to be angry than sad. She had been sad too much as of late.

"Remember the other night? Remember what I said after?"

"No," she said darkly.

"Remember it. Remember it like I do."

Caelfel shook her head with a single, violent movement. She didn't understand what Feraan meant nor did she want to. She stepped back from him, understanding only one thing.

He didn't want her. He didn't love her. And though he never said it, she was nearly sure he had. She knew she loved him. But that didn't matter now.

"Goodbye then? Forever?" she asked bitterly.

He smiled, sadly, regretfully, or perhaps spitefully, and didn't answer her question. "Forget about the desert army," he reminded her as she bounded down the front steps.

"Not likely," she muttered under her breath.

She left for the meadow, seeing all sorts of elves streaming along with her. She caught sight of Garvanna and Markis. Caelfel wondered what assignments they were called for. She would have asked Garvanna, but the royal courier with the blond braid raised his hand and called for the archers. Caelfel went toward him as another asked for battlemages. She glanced over her shoulder to see Garvanna moving toward the battlemage line.

There were two others in the group of archers from Sal'Sumarathar, one of them Winwaloe, and Caelfel remembered him from the hunting party and the college exams. She kept watching for Markis from the corner of her eye. He floated about from group to group, as if everything was under his charge. The idea made Caelfel's stomach turn.

"My name is Sanddef, and I am the Captain of Archers. I am the commanding officer you will report to. We of the Royal Militia and the honorable Empress Haelyn appreciate your contributions to the Imperial Army and whatever else you may sacrifice."

Captain Sanddef paused, as if waiting for questions. When none were asked, he continued.

"A military threat has been seen approaching our borders. We know not what this threat wants or hopes to achieve. Your commanding officers suspect that they are not here for simple negotiations. The plan will be to confront them at the treeline border in the shadow of the mountain. We will raise the white flag and demand their purpose. If a settlement cannot be reached, we will engage them in battle and we will win."

Caelfel swallowed, her throat feeling immensely dry, and could not bring herself to question Captain Sanddef's confidence in their victory. He simply flashed them a brilliant smile and instructed them to mount their horses and to ride for the border.

"A camp is being prepared for our small outfit at this moment. We shall not be away for long. This engagement should not last a week. When we arrive, you will be sent to the smith to be fitted for your new imperial armor. We ride with our divisions, the archers behind the swordsmen and battlemages. The healers are behind us. Tomorrow begins your training."

Caelfel called Rowan and saw her sunbathing at a distance. Beside her was the dark stallion Firnis. Caelfel stared at the pair as her fingers turned cold and something caught in her throat. She coughed to clear the feeling and whistled for Rowan once more. The mare trotted up to her faithfully, and Caelfel saddled her, preparing to join the line. "We're going to be in battles now, Rowan," Caelfel murmured excitedly.

The mare, not moved by her feigned excitement, only snorted. Caelfel looked up to see Garvanna mounting her own dark bay horse nearby. She neared them cautiously, adjusting Rowan's reigns.

"What is his name?" Caelfel asked.

Garvanna peeked at her sideways. "Nerium."

"He is beautiful."

"He was my mother's. She gave him to me so I could go to Yamalvon and the other cities to study magic at their colleges, before Amasel was destroyed."

Caelfel blinked, realizing that leaving Amasel had probably saved Garvanna's life, though she would probably never accept the truth of her family's death.

They rode, heading southwest. Caelfel was behind Winwaloe and the other archer the entire way and she concentrated on keeping speed to prevent her mind from wandering. She wasn't sure how long they had been riding, but darkness had fallen by the time they stopped the procession of volunteers in the designated glen. She dismounted with the others, and there was a deep soreness in her legs. She was tired, but as promised, Sanddef urged them to the blacksmith tent. She waited in line to have her measurements taken.

The blacksmith was a she-elf who introduced herself as Adar. Her fumbling apprentice was an elf called Olwen. She turned Caelfel this way and that with quick movements, measuring her sizes with her eye and bits of string she threw at Olwen for cataloging.

"Your name?"

"Caelfel Gyssedlues," Caelfel said, holding her arms out.

"Good name for an archer. Do you know Sylaera?" Adar asked, stretching the string from Caelfel's underarm to her waist.

"She's my mother. How do you know her?"

Adar froze, then barked at Olwen to write something down. "Have you ever worn armor before?" she asked, either ignoring or avoiding Caelfel's question.

"No."

"As an archer, you will be given standard issue leather. How does that sound?"

"That's fine," Caelfel answered uncertainly. "Where do you get your leather from?"

"The militia tanners provide it for me. If there will be no further questions, you are free to go. Your armor and a new set of arrows will be delivered to you by morning."

"Will you not sleep?" Caelfel asked, astonished.

Adar offered a thin smile. "I have an army to arm and protect. Sleep can come later."

She next met Captain Sanddef with six other archers, the two from Sal'Sumarathar, three archers from Yamalvon, and one from Rasaen.

"As archers, you will sleep in hammocks among the trees. There are seven of you, so space yourselves out around the clearing. Once you've set up your hammock, you may sleep. Training begins at dawn. I recommend that you get to know each other. If this threat becomes real, you will have to depend on one other. Sleep well, archers."

"Where will you sleep?" Caelfel asked.

"In the Captain's quarters, of course," Sanddef answered.

No one else commented, merely giving Caelfel odd looks until she turned her gaze to the ground.

"Get to know each other then?" one of the she-elves offered brightly when Sanddef left them. "I'm Fódla from Yamalvon."

"Winwaloe from Sal'Sumarathar," said Winwaloe.

"Caelfel, also from Sal'Sumarathar."

But the other archers became impatient and wandered off to claim a tree, except Winwaloe, Fódla, and the silent elf from Rasaen.

"What's your name?" Fódla asked him.

He looked at the three of them, eyes resting on Caelfel. "Galath." He pointed at her. "You're not very old, are you?" he asked.

Caelfel's face burned, and she didn't know if she should be timid or angry. "I'm seventy-six," she answered quietly.

"I ask because I am the youngest of my city. I am only sixty-three."

The instant relief she felt surprised Caelfel. "How can you tell I'm so young?" she asked.

Galath offered a noncommittal shrug. "It's something you notice. At least now you know you are not the youngest of Honey Water."

She smiled at him. "If it helps, you do not look so young to me."

Fódla shifted as a small breeze blew through the encampment. "Shall we find our trees?" she asked.

Everyone nodded in agreement and scattered to find a tree. Caelfel picked one she thought closest to the border and after she set up her hammock, she climbed to the topmost branches to try to see the desert army. When she reached the thin branches in the crown, she could pick out the army's campfires twinkling at the base of the Baetic Mountains that rose above the Fey Forest. Her nerves quivered at the sight of the dormant camp of soldiers she may soon be fighting. She had never seen an army, save for the Sal'Sumarathar militia.

Then a ruffle of feathers and leaves interrupted the silence of the forest. Caelfel adjusted her footing and watched as a black mess of feathers flew from the grasp of the trees and soared as high as the peak of the mountain. Caelfel thought back to the previous evening and wondered if the bird was Macha, the werebird who had first brought news of the army. A thought crossed Caelfel's mind, and it suggested that Macha had divulged more to Feraan than he initially led her to believe. Perhaps it was Macha's word that had turned Feraan so suddenly cold.

Caelfel shivered as an unseasonable wind whistled through the trees. She decided to return to the forest floor and her hammock for the night.

***

"They're preparing an army," Lisiek remarked to the princeling, hunching his shoulders even in the protective shield of the commanding tent. It had been a long time since Lisiek had left the desert.

"Would you expect anything else? It is only a small recruitment."

"What did the Seer tell you about the army?"

"It is not a surprise, Lisiek. Honestly, if an army showed upon our doorstep, would you not feel inclined to respond appropriately? Besides, it only proves something in our favor."

"Pray tell, what is that?"

"They are worried we will enter the forest, which only means that we can," the princeling explained. Lisiek opened his mouth to speak, but someone else answered.

"Just because you can does not mean you should. There is a reason why others have not entered our forest before you."

Lisiek turned to see that two figures, undoubtedly elvish, had entered the tent.

"Forgive us for the late hour of our intrusion," the one continued. Lisiek could not decipher the purpose of the silver tattoos on his face. Were they merely decorative or indicative of something else, rank perhaps? The elf continued, "But I'm sure you understand. We're not overly fond of visitors, particularly the kind ready to make war."

"We mean no harm to any of you," the princeling said.

"Your army would suggest otherwise."

The desert princeling stepped forward. "I am the admiral, the commanding officer of this outfit."

The elf with the silver tattoos tilted his head. "The admiral? Then why does everyone call you a princeling?"

"I inherited some land and donated a section of it to the Umfang military," said the princeling. Lisiek checked himself, unsure if he would call nearly half the desert '*some land.*'

"And what is your name, oh desert princeling?"

"Admiral Grimault."

"And I am Markis Rilynnzea. My companion here is called Blaes Llychlin, but don't be fooled by his silence. He is no fan of uninvited guests either."

Lisiek looked to the princeling. He hoped Grimault had maintained some shred of sense over the years, considering they were standing before two possibly hostile elves with unknown magical abilities.

But, as Lisiek knew, Grimault was infamous for his pride and bravado. Grimault continued, "Then invite us into your forest so we shall not be uninvited guests."

"We do not allow strangers, particularly bloodthirsty ones into our home," Blaes interjected. "Tell us your purpose for coming. We've gathered our own army, and its soldiers are waiting beyond the trees. We will not hesitate to defend ourselves or destroy you."

Markis grinned gleefully at his elfkin's words. "Blaes does not fancy idle chatter," he explained.

"We are here on behalf of the Blind Seer," said the admiral.

Markis nodded in consideration and looked about the tent. "I do not see her here."

"That was why Admiral Grimault clarified that our presence is on behalf of hers," Lisiek countered, annoyed with Markis's show.

"And what mission has she put you to?" Blaes asked.

The princeling answered him. "We are set on a course of revenge."

"Who do you seek revenge against?"

"Another elf, the Wandering Elf who intervenes in the affairs of humans."

The two elves exchanged glances, and Lisiek might have wagered they knew which elf the princeling spoke of.

"And what do you intend to do with him?" Markis asked.

"We want nothing with him. We are after an elf he cares about. Are you aware of any such elf?"

It was Blaes that looked to Markis in confusion, but Markis did not seem to share the feeling, instead looking between Grimault and Lisiek carefully. "And should you find this elf, what do you plan to do with them?"

"That has yet to be determined."

"We will not surrender one of our own to a hostile force," Blaes said.

"It is already foreseen," Grimault argued.

"The elves are not popular for favoring prophecy, admiral," Markis pointed out. "You may find your task slightly more difficult than you might have imagined."

Grimault spread his arms wide, smiling. "And that is why I have brought my own army for the occasion."

For the first time, Markis appeared uneasy. "Allow us time to relay your intentions to our superiors—"

"We will *not* negotiate the life of another elf," Blaes interrupted angrily.

"I did not say negotiate. We are merely messengers now, Blaes," Markis responded calmly.

"Certainly," the princeling agreed. "You are free to visit us tomorrow with their response."

Markis nodded and turned to leave. Blaes lingered, taking a step towards Grimault. Lisiek did not feel inclined to interfere, even for the princeling's safety.

"Know this, little human. Just as Markis said at our entrance, there is a reason no one has disturbed the elves for centuries. We decimate armies, leaving nothing but ash and smoke behind."

The princeling said nothing, and the two elves disappeared into the night.

***

"Come on, then. Wake up, it's time to go for training."

When Caelfel opened her eyes, she instantly recognized the flaming red hair of Fódla.

They descended the tree together, and the pre-dawn horizon made the sky a shocking purple. Caelfel was secretly glad Fódla had come to retrieve her; she wasn't certain if she would have been able to get up on her own. But then, Fódla revealed her true interest for visiting Caelfel.

"So, you and Winwaloe are both from Sal'Sumarathar."

"Yes," Caelfel replied.

"What is he like?"

"I do not know him much. He is quiet, loyal, and a talented archer. Why do you ask?"

"I find him attractive." She paused. "Perhaps Galath finds you attractive as well."

Caelfel wanted to laugh but thought that might be rude. As they walked to the training grounds, bows in hand, Caelfel was consciously aware of Galath standing nearby, just out of earshot. "Has he said

221

something?" she asked carefully.

"Perhaps he confides to me," Fódla teased conspiratorially. "There is a chance that he wonders if you have someone waiting for you back home."

Caelfel's chest tightened, and she found herself irritated with Fódla's fixation on matchmaking. They were about to train for an upcoming battle, and Caelfel wanted matters of the heart to be far from her mind.

Mercifully, they were then approached by a breathless Olwen, delivering their armor. "Right. Names, please?"

"Caelfel Gyssedlues." Olwen handed her a set of neatly bundled leather armor.

"So you must be Fódla Danann."

Fódla took her armor silently, and Caelfel watched Olwen hurry on to Galath next. He took it with a word of thanks, and they all made their way to the archery field.

Captain Sanddef was there, personally issuing them their new quivers full of arrows. Caelfel inspected the fletching on hers and saw that they were all swan feathers. Their quality was unsurpassed and made Caelfel's own work look shoddy in comparison. Sanddef lined them all up with their own targets and instructed them to begin shooting. After five rounds, he told them to take ten paces back for another five shots.

They continued this process for four rounds of five arrows each. Caelfel noted that the arrows had sharpened wooden ends instead of flint or steel, probably to conserve materials for when they were no longer practicing. All the while, Captain Sanddef strolled between them all, admiring or commenting when he saw fit. After another five rounds, he told them to pause.

"Olwen! Clear those targets!" he ordered, and Olwen raced to each one, plucking out the practice arrows from the stuffed targets. Sanddef continued, "I'm rather pleased with your skills, but let's change the shape of your targets to resemble bodies."

He held his hand out, gesturing toward Olwen who began changing them on command.

"You will each go in turn as I wish to see your abilities individually."

They waited in line by city, the archers of Yamalvon going first. After that, Caelfel was the first of Sal'Sumarathar and she took a deep breath to calm her nerves, nocking an arrow and drawing it back. She steadied her aim and sent the arrow flying toward the target. It firmly embedded itself in the center of the chest, where Captain Sanddef instructed they should aim. He circled her, studying her target.

"Impressive. You are a Gyssedlues? You are born with the innate talent of ranged weaponry before Eviat honed your skills. Is that right?"

"Yes," Caelfel answered, avoiding eye contact as he continued circling around her.

"How is Eviat doing? I have not seen him for some time."

Caelfel hesitated, remembering the attempt Markis made on her father's life. But a quick glance told her Markis was not around, and Captain Sanddef appeared to respect Eviat all the same. "He is mostly well. His age is catching up to him, but he refuses to admit it."

Captain Sanddef chuckled. "I would expect nothing else of him. Try again please, Caelfel."

He stepped back, and Caelfel aimed and shot her arrow once again, much more quickly this time. Sanddef stood next to her and admired her work.

"You have a gift," he said, nodding in approval. He called for Winwaloe's turn, and Caelfel joined the Yamalvon archers.

When everyone had completed their rounds, Captain Sanddef assigned everyone partners and ordered for Olwen to bring him seven swords from Adar. As they waited for Olwen's return, Captain Sanddef began pacing before them.

"You are not swordsmen, nor do I expect you to possess any extraordinary talent with the blade. However, if we do go to battle, there will possibly come a time when your bow is useless to you, and then you must face the enemy in close combat. We will be sparring, and since there are an odd number of you, I will take on Camlann of Yamalvon myself."

Caelfel stood next to her partner who was Galath, shifting her weight from foot to foot uncertainly as she remembered Fódla's comments. Caelfel wasn't sure if Galath had contributed at all to her thinking that way but she resolved to say nothing to him and peeked toward Fódla who stood merrily next to her partner Winwaloe.

Olwen brought back the swords, and Captain Sanddef began his sparring. He initiated an attack against Camlann and delivered blow after blow relentlessly. Camlann struggled to defend himself. Then

Sanddef made a strike that sent Camlann to the ground with an ugly gash on his arm. Everyone looked to Sanddef, astonished with his ruthlessness.

"I am a highly trained military officer, skilled in many areas of combat. It takes little effort on my part to bring any one of you down. You must be prepared for that. You can be killed. You *will* be killed."

"He's bleeding!" Galath reminded Sanddef who looked to the fallen Camlann, unconcerned.

"He will be fine. *Younglings,*" Sanddef called, pointing to Caelfel and Galath with his sword. "Escort him to the Healer's tent."

Galath hurried to help Camlann, but Caelfel stayed where she was, giving Sanddef a hard look.

"We are *not* younglings," she said in a low but clear voice.

Captain Sanddef turned slowly to face her. "You speak to your commanding officer this way?" The question was casual but there was something else hidden in his tone that told Caelfel she had just done something she wasn't supposed to.

"I only question the way our commanding officer speaks to us. We did not volunteer to be treated as inferior to everyone else."

"Caelfel, it's fine," Galath whispered to her, and then she was suddenly aware of everyone staring at her in shock. Sanddef drew near to her and whispered something only she could hear.

"Watch your pride, little one."

Then Sanddef turned to everyone else, "They will take care of Camlann. The rest of you will begin sparring."

Caelfel went to help Galath with Camlann without another word, her face flaming red. They left their swords with the other archers at Captain Sanddef's command. When they deposited Camlann at the Healer's tent, which was green like their doors, Galath spoke to her, pausing at the tent flaps.

"It is unwise to speak out that way in the military."

Caelfel turned to him. "Do you like being called a youngling?"

Galath shrugged. "I am always called one in Rasaen. I am used to it."

"Does it not trouble you? We stopped being younglings at our half-century year. We could be *two centuries* old and if another elf is not born, they would still call us that." Galath sighed but it was not impatient.

"Caelfel—" Galath started.

"Caelfel?" He was interrupted by another voice, and when Caelfel looked over her shoulder, she saw it was by Thoroth.

"Thoroth? What are you doing here?" she asked. Thoroth eagerly crossed the large tent to meet her.

"I was voluntarily recruited, same as you were, I assume. I am only a healer's assistant here. Why did you come?" he asked. Caelfel chewed her bottom lip nervously as she struggled to remember her original reason for volunteering. Currently she found she appreciated the opportunity to get away from Feraan. If she told Thoroth that, Caelfel guessed the healer would quickly volunteer to fill the new void in her life.

"I came because I could not let my father leave." It was a natural, unsurprising reason that Thoroth believed without question, but Caelfel felt as though she were lying.

"And what about Feraan?" Thoroth asked, accurately naming the topic she had been trying to avoid.

She changed subjects. "Garvanna is here. Did you know?" she asked him. Thoroth reacted strangely, and Caelfel couldn't name why.

"I did not know that. The healers left after everyone else."

"She's enlisted as a battlemage, if you were wondering."

Thoroth folded his arms and bounced on his toes. "She would make an excellent one."

"We better go back," Galath muttered to her. Caelfel nodded and gave a small goodbye wave to Thoroth before departing.

She trailed just slightly behind Galath as they crossed the clearing to return to Captain Sanddef. Caelfel glanced briefly at the bow in her hands and then secured it over her shoulder. When she looked up again, she just barely avoided colliding with someone.

"I'm sorry," she said quickly, only to step back and see Markis standing in front of her.

"I've been looking for you, Caelfel," Markis said quietly.

Galath turned around to see what had stalled her. "Caelfel?"

"Return to your commanding officer. Tell him Markis had business with her and she will rejoin training shortly."

Caelfel tried to tell Galath with her eyes that she did not want to be left alone with Markis, but whatever ranking Markis had here sent Galath away without argument. When they were alone, she crossed her arms. "What do you want?"

"How is Master Feraan doing?" he asked. The condescension she expected from him was gone. He was cautious, and this concerned her.

"I would suspect he has locked himself in his house to continue brooding."

"You have not seen or spoken to him?" Markis was genuinely confused, and Caelfel wondered if she should tell him the truth.

"I have not seen him since yesterday, when he made it quite clear he did not want to see or speak to me again."

"Did he know about the approaching army, then?" Markis asked, pointing vaguely to the border where she knew the desert army was camped. Caelfel bent her head to the ground, unsure of how much would be suitable to reveal to Markis and wondering how he guessed as much correctly.

"A werebird came to warn him," she answered at length.

"Did this werebird tell him *why* that army is here?"

"If she did, Feraan didn't tell me anything." There was an edge to her voice, and she wondered if Markis could understand what had happened between her and Feraan. But this was none of Markis's concern, though she could not possibly fathom the trouble of answering his oddly innocent questions.

"Has something happened between the two of you? I was under the impression—"

Caelfel unleashed a malevolent glare, which seemed to be answer enough for him. Markis fell silent. "Why are you asking this?" she asked him.

He became uncomfortable when it was his turn to answer a direct question. "You were recruited as an archer?"

Caelfel nodded.

"That means they will be sending you, probably tomorrow morning, as scouts to secure our borders before they send a unified force to engage in combat."

"So this battle *is* happening?"

"Caelfel, pay attention. That army has no particular desire to fight but they are certainly not against it. They are only after *one* thing, just one. They will attempt to infiltrate the forest, to sneak through, in which case your job will be very important. You will have to be careful."

"You're telling me to be careful?" she asked with a derisive scoff. She froze when she realized Markis was being serious. "This all seems uncharacteristic of you."

His hand fell heavily on her shoulder, but when he squeezed, it was gentle. This softer side of him disturbed her. "Because, Caelfel, despite my peculiarities, which may appear malicious to you, I still hold my loyalty to the elves, not some spoiled desert human." He started to walk away but Caelfel called out to him.

"What is it they are after?" Markis turned slowly, and when his eyes met hers, they looked up and down her frame, and Caelfel felt as though he could see straight through her.

"We don't know yet."

By the time Caelfel had returned to Captain Sanddef, the sword sparring had ended, and she learned that Markis had been wrong. They were not waiting until tomorrow morning. Captain Sanddef was organizing them into scouting parties to begin their watch that night. Caelfel was unsurprised to learn that her scouting partner was also Galath.

"Go pack your things and get your hammocks. Meet back here as soon as you are ready to receive your assignments. That army intends to enter the forest."

They ran to do as they were told, and Caelfel had her things together in mere minutes. She and Galath were among the first to meet back with Captain Sanddef. They waited for the rest of the archers, the last of whom were Fódla and Winwaloe. Caelfel thought they acted suspiciously, but Captain Sanddef did not comment on their behavior or tardiness.

He pulled out a rough map of the border and indicated where each army was in relation to the other. He explained they were to go to specific locations and to watch for similar scouts from the other army. They were to watch the border and report any suspicious activity.

"Be wary. Under no circumstances should you leave the forest. You will not be protected if you leave the trees, and you are not to attack them unless they cross the border. Understand?"

They all chorused, "Yes sir," and he dismissed them to their duty. Caelfel shouldered her pack and her bow and followed the line to their assigned locations. Before they left the encampment for the forest, they passed Olwen humming and singing in a low, cheery voice that seemed to occupy him as he repaired the straw targets the archers had destroyed earlier.

But something he said caught her attention, and she paused, briefly breaking away from the line. She paid no mind to Galath loyally falling out of line to shadow her.

"We all march to our own destined Fate,
Even the heroic Archer of the Lake
With her bow and a god's sword
No one escapes what is Foretold
That which is predicted by the Blind Seer
Means that their End shall draw Near."

"You said my name," she said, approaching Olwen.

"What?" Olwen looked up.

"Archer of the lake. That's my name," she insisted to him.

"Oh. No, I didn't. I was singing. It's an old lullaby my mother taught me. She told me it used to be a song my father would march to when he went off to war." Olwen's animated features turned solemn. "He died when I was still a youngling."

"I'm sorry about your father, but that song—"

"Caelfel, they're leaving us," Galath interrupted softly. Caelfel exhaled through her nose, her irritation prickling the back of her neck.

"It's just an old story," Olwen assured her. "It doesn't mean anything, so don't think much of it."

One of the archers yelled for them, so Caelfel reluctantly returned to the line, Olwen's song becoming faint with the distance.

"We all march to our own destined Fate,
Even the heroic Archer of the Lake
With her bow and a god's sword.
No one escapes what is Foretold
That which is predicted by the Blind Seer
Means that their End shall draw Near.

We march off to War
Praying
For the Archer of the Lake."

16. My Name is Lisiek

They found their tree, just out of reach of the mountain's shadow, as per Captain Sanddef's directions. Caelfel and Galath were stationed on the fringe of the line with Fódla and Winwaloe some distance away. The other pair of rangers was within shouting distance although Caelfel could not see them.

But what she could see was the thinning of trees that indicated the border and, beyond that, the grassy plains that rolled away to a hazy horizon.

"What do think is over there?" Caelfel asked Galath who was busying himself with the hammock. She wasn't even troubled that Captain Sanddef had purposefully assigned her and Galath furthest away from the army because they were the youngest.

"Desert," he answered, pausing.

Their tree had widely stretching limbs that made it easy to position themselves. The leaves were a light green which would hide Caelfel nicely. She feared Galath with his darker hair would not be masked as easily.

He pointed slightly to the left. "Umfeld is that way while Umfang is a straight shot behind the mountain."

"Have you ever wanted to go see the humans?" Caelfel asked.

"Aren't we about to meet them in battle?"

"I don't mean like that. Would you not like to see their cities, their castles, and their magic?"

Galath thought for a moment. "I should think I prefer to see the elvish cities first. I've never been to Yamalvon."

"Nor have I. My father has been on several occasions."

"It sounds as though you think very highly of him."

Caelfel eased herself down on one of the branches, her legs dangling. "I am very close to him. He's a greyling, been one ever since he met my mother. I was an unexpected miracle to him."

Then Caelfel's throat closed tightly as she remembered the elf they all thought responsible for her life when that elf had saved her father's life, and the name behind the story was one she did not care to think of presently.

"He made me this bow on my fiftieth birthday," she said, unstringing it in her lap. "He taught me how to shoot and hunt."

"What about your mother?"

"My mother and I look alike, and Father swears we act the same. She prefers the magical arts. She was part of the Sal'Sumarathar Family, but her family disowned her for some mysterious reason she has not told me."

"You never thought of practicing magic yourself?"

Caelfel looked away from him. "I started studying at the college, but then I lost my aura."

"Really? I've only ever heard rumors of that happening."

"My father first lost his, which was a shame because he was a highly skilled healer, and then I lost mine not too long ago. It still bothers me."

"I won't bring it up then." He paused. "Is there anyone else at home who's waiting for your return? That healer you spoke to mentioned a name. Though you were probably trying to avoid it, so perhaps I shouldn't have brought it up."

Caelfel sighed, and the sound was weary and sad. "I think I should tell someone. It hurts my head thinking about it. Talking may help, but only if you can keep secrets."

Galath laughed, and strangely enough, the sound made her feel better. "I will heavily guard any secrets you tell me."

Caelfel hesitated to begin. "His name was Feraan, and I found him dying in the forest. I rescued him, even though everyone wanted him dead. I was summoned to trial for saving his life and I defended him in front of the Sal'Sumarathar Council."

"That sounds odd."

"Not many like him. Everyone believes he destroyed Amasel."

Instant recognition flashed through Galath's face. "*That* elf?"

"It's not true, though."

"I believe you."

"Good, because no one else does. The Council had a tracker follow me and he chased me one night through the forest after he murdered the oldest greyling in Sal'Sumarathar. Feraan found me and he protected me. He always seemed to find me when I needed him. Then, it may be that I started falling in love with him."

Caelfel breathed slowly through her mouth, and something pricked her nose. Galath didn't interrupt.

"I snuck away to the Spring Festival, and he followed. He saved me again. We danced. Then I was crowned Beauty of Spring and I chose *him*. Then I found out about Amasel.

"I ran off before he could explain anything. My father told me the truth of what happened. I returned to Feraan, let him explain. And I thought—"

At this point, Caelfel buried her face in her hands. She didn't want to think of her night with Feraan or him wanting to take it back.

Then Galath reached down, putting a hand on her shoulder. "You don't have to continue."

She lifted her face, pushing her hair behind her ears. "No, it's fine."

Caelfel took another deep breath and resumed.

"I felt like we became very close. Then my father was invited to a hunting party, which was created as a poorly disguised mission to kill him. Feraan went after him, but he had already been poisoned. My mother was the one that found the antidote, and we stayed at Feraan's house for two days. Then, this girl came. She was a werebird, a *human*, and she warned Feraan about *this* army."

"How long ago was this?"

"Only the day before we came to the camp. Feraan didn't seem concerned, but I think there was more that Macha told him."

"Macha?"

"The werebird. She gave me this strange look before she disappeared, and I can't get it out of my head. But ever since she left, Feraan started acting strange, like he didn't want anything to do with me. Before I came here, I went to see him, and he explained quite thoroughly how he didn't want to see me anymore."

"*Why?*" Galath asked, sounding just as confused as she felt.

"He said he wanted to be alone, that he didn't care for me—that he didn't *want* to care for me. He said romance and companionship was not for him."

"It sounds as though he is incredibly selfish or hiding something. I am very sorry that happened to you," Galath said quietly. Caelfel set her bow off to the side and wrapped her arms around herself. Her chest felt like it was bleeding and exposed like a pulsating wound. She decided she didn't want to talk about Feraan.

"What about your family? Tell me about your life."

"It's nothing tale-worthy. There's my mother, who's fiercely loyal to our family, and my father who was a banished noble from the Yamalvon court. He still spends most of his time away from home. I don't remember him much from my childhood."

"Why was he banished?"

Galath smiled, but Caelfel could see there was no amusement in it. "Cavorting with the empress, no less. He enjoys his leisure time with she-elves. He was never particularly faithful to my mother."

"She must have been devastated."

Galath shrugged. "If she was, and I would not doubt it, she never allowed herself to show it. I believe she always tried to remain strong for me."

Caelfel smiled at him. "What about the other kind of she-elves? Do you have a special one waiting for you?"

"I'm afraid I have not been fortunate in that area of my life. My father, whenever I do see him, speaks about taking me to Yamalvon to find me a proper wife. The idea upsets my mother, and I don't believe I want to go to Yamalvon for that."

"Then don't," Caelfel said simply. "Why did you volunteer to come here?"

"Being the youngest, I've often waited for an opportunity to prove myself. When the courier came, it just seemed like the right thing to do."

Caelfel didn't respond to that, and they remained in a content silence as the sun sank and darkness began blanketing the sky. Caelfel dug through her pack and offered Galath some dried fruit. He accepted it gratefully, and they both ate in silence until Fódla approached their tree.

"The desert army is moving," she called up to them. "They're coming this way. We've sent for Captain Sanddef. If you spot any suspicious activity or if there is an emergency, sound your alarm."

"What's the alarm?" Caelfel asked when Fódla had left.

"They gave me a horn. It's right here." He patted his chest, and

Caelfel saw its outline in the dim light.

"When did you get that?" she asked.

"Captain Sanddef handed them out while you were speaking to that tracker."

"Oh, I also missed sword sparring," she pointed out.

"That's right," Galath said, remembering. "You were never issued your sword either."

Caelfel glanced at the one belted to Galath's waist enviously. She had a similar blade at home, but it did nothing for her there. "Hopefully I will not need to use one."

The sun had disappeared entirely, but the evening was still pleasantly warm. The flowering trees filled the air with a sweet scent, and Caelfel was reminded of how it was spring. She yawned.

"You can go to sleep," Galath offered.

Caelfel blinked at him. "What?"

"I'll keep watch for the night while you sleep. We can change in the middle of the night, but Captain Sanddef said at least one elf had to be on watch at all times."

"I missed those instructions too." She stifled another yawn. "Are you sure you don't want to go to sleep first?"

Galath shook his head. "I am fine for now. You go on ahead. I doubt anything exciting will happen anyway."

"If you insist, I'll sleep first, but you must wake me up if something happens or if you become tired. Promise?"

He laughed. "I promise."

With that, Caelfel settled in her hammock, just realizing how exhausted she truly was. Telling Galath about Feraan disturbed her with unhappy thoughts as she remembered Feraan's last words to her. However, there was something uniquely comforting about Galath standing watch. It wasn't the same comfort she shared with Feraan, but it was suitable enough to lull her to sleep without the daunting prospect of nightmares.

***

The messenger of the Blind Seer returned to them that night without invitation or harbinger. Its entrance was silent until it spoke with the Voice of the Unknown.

"Everything is in place. You must complete your next instructions precisely and *don't forget her payment.*"

"What must I do?" the princeling asked.

The cowl shook in the messenger's disagreement. "Not you. Everything depends on your sorcerer. He is the only one that can breach the forest."

***

She stretched, feeling oddly rested and thinking it felt awfully warm for a spring night, but when she opened her eyes, she saw that it was not nighttime. The sun hovered brilliantly in the morning sky.

"Galath?" she called, fearing something may have happened to him.

"I'm here," said his voice from behind. She turned to see him lounging against a branch just a short distance from her.

"You didn't wake me," she accused, lifting herself from her hammock.

"You looked rather peaceful, and I wasn't tired. I didn't have the heart to bother you."

"Did anything happen?"

"Nothing that I have noticed. There has been nothing from the desert army and no other news from Fódla."

"Perhaps the danger has passed, and we are here for nothing," she suggested.

"Or it's the calm before the storm."

Caelfel reached for her bow, stringing it, and ran her fingers over the swan fletching of her issued arrows. Her shoulders tensed as they watched the border. The sun was bright, and the air was balmy. Caelfel couldn't determine if something was amiss of if she had already grown bored.

"Did you sleep well?" Galath asked. His voice sounded muted.

"Well enough. Do you want to sleep?"

"I don't feel the need right now. I may doze off later."

Caelfel laughed once. "That would be fine by me."

She kept her eyes diligently trained on the desert's horizon. Around midday, she turned to look at Galath and found him with his head resting against the tree, eyes closed and mouth slightly agape. She smiled at the sight of him sleeping and turned back around, rising to reposition herself.

Caelfel froze when she saw a dark mass against the landscape. It was the desert army nearing their position in the trees and making their

234

way out of the mountain's shadow. Caelfel grabbed her bow and pulled herself onto another branch to get a closer look.

It wasn't the entire army, only a fortified group, and they were closer to Fódla's and Winwaloe's tree than their own. They all gave the forest a wide berth, even if it meant exposure for them.

"Galath?" Caelfel called to him softly. When she heard no response, she returned to his branch, placing her fingers on his cheek.

He awoke instantly. "What?"

She put a finger to her lips, gesturing for him to be quiet, and indicated toward the approaching soldiers.

He was alert, grabbing his bow as well. Caelfel pulled her quiver over her shoulder and climbed onto another limb to get a better view.

"Should we do something?" she asked.

"What *can* we do? The others knew they were coming this way, and Captain Sanddef said we're not to attack them unless they enter the forest. Sounding the alarm would only reveal our position."

"So we wait." She glanced over her shoulder at him.

He nodded. "We wait."

The battalion was making slow progress but soon they came into hearing range. Caelfel detected nervous mutterings rippling through them, and their eyes darted about the forest frantically. Then Caelfel heard the agitated growl of a beast. She scanned the soldiers and found one gripping a chain with a black, monstrous feline secured at the end. Her heart quickened.

"Is that a *panther*?"

Galath joined her on her branch, following her gaze. His surprise was tangible. "I believe so."

Then movement caught Caelfel's attention elsewhere. She crouched suddenly and turned her head to it.

It was a lone man, quite some distance ahead of the other soldiers and unarmored. He looked casually among the trees, unafraid, and felt for something in the pocket of his cloak. He stopped, still outside the forest and directly in front of their tree.

"Galath." Caelfel's breath stuck in her throat but she felt Galath's comforting presence close behind.

"Be still and wait," he whispered to her. "Have your bow ready, but move slowly."

Caelfel did as he said and held her breath just as the man entered the forest.

"We shouldn't attack him unless he proves to be a threat."

She gave a single, curt nod as the man walked among the trees, looking around with marked interest. He stopped just short of their tree and pulled something from his pocket. It was a smooth, black stone that rested in his palm. He held it out before him, and everyone waited with bated breath.

The stone glowed with red tendrils and it spoke with two layering voices, one apparently feminine and the other deep and magical. Its words seemed to shake the very air around them, and Caelfel gripped her bow for reassurance.

"And she will have the Bastard's Sword and the Lake Bow. They will be hers until she delivers them unto the Masters."

With the mention of the *Lake Bow*, the bow in Caelfel's hands began to glow red, matching the stone in the human's palm. Then suddenly and without warning, her bow began to burn Caelfel's hands. Instinctively, she tried to release it, but the bow stuck to her hands, and the shock made Caelfel lose her balance.

Then, she fell.

The fall was not long, the trees being shorter at the borders than in the cities, but she had dropped her bow. Caelfel pushed herself up enough to see that her bow had landed at the feet of the human. He looked at her briefly and then reached to pick it up. He examined it closely, feeling the weight of it in his hands.

Then, he turned to leave the forest.

Caelfel was immediately on her feet and chasing after him. She tried to reach him before he escaped the trees, but he was too quick for her. He slowed his pace once he left the forest.

Caelfel watched him walk across the treeless expanse, holding the bow her father made, and she *knew* she shouldn't leave the forest. But the warning Captain Sanddef had issued was pushed to the back of her mind, and she continued running after the man without slowing.

"*Caelfel, no!*" Galath's scream was audible, but only just.

She broke through the treeline and was nearing the man who had stolen her bow when he finally turned around to face her. There was something so unnerving about the way he looked at her that Caelfel paused.

Then something large knocked her off her feet.

Her head hit the ground, hard enough that it made her vision blur. She blinked furiously and a roaring panther came into focus. It pinned her down with its massive paws and bared its long fangs. Caelfel grimaced at its rancid breath that reeked of rotten flesh.

She pulled her knees up to her chest and kicked at the panther with all her strength. It flew over her with the thrust.

She scrambled to her feet just as the panther's leash followed its momentum. The metal chain clipped Caelfel on the back of the head.

She struggled to regain her balance as a thick wetness throbbed behind her ear. The panther had already righted itself, pacing slowly as its long tail twitched with irritation.

It charged towards her and then pounced, extending its claws as it hurtled through the air. Caelfel dived out of the way, rolling under it as it passed over. She had neither bow nor sword to brandish for her defense.

The chain passed before her face, and seeing no other alternative, Caelfel reached out to grab it. She yanked, and the panther crashed to the ground, instead of landing as it wanted. It recovered and stalked around in circles as far away from Caelfel as the chain allowed.

She dropped the chain when she heard a nearby horn ringing the air around them. She looked around to see the soldiers had all formed a circle around her and the panther, effectively trapping her.

The man who had stolen her bow walked to her, an expression of complete smugness on his face. Caelfel took one step back but did no more to escape from him.

"My name is Lisiek," he greeted. Caelfel narrowed her eyes, thinking his accent strange. "Would you be so kind and come with us?"

Caelfel crossed her arms and saw little other choice since she was staring in the face of an army.

17. Pursuit

Eviat worried about his daughter, even though Sylaera had told him that Caelfel was preoccupied with Feraan. It was not unexpected; neither of them was blind to what was happening between their daughter and Feraan. Still, Sylaera had to admit to herself that she was beginning to worry as well. They had heard nothing from Caelfel or anything about the status of the approaching army for two days now. *Something* should have happened in that time.

Then something did happen and it came in the form of a knock at the door one evening. Sylaera hurried to answer it before Eviat could leave his spot in the garden to investigate.

The knock belonged to Thoroth, and he looked haggard with the look of bad news.

"What is it?" she snapped at him.

He silently handed her a letter, dressed with official, royal ribbons. Sylaera tore it open and read it quickly.

Then she read it again.

When she looked up at Thoroth, he apologetically shook his head.

Sylaera was always rash in her anger but not illogical. She left her home without alarming Eviat and, dragging Thoroth in tow, she marched with as much dignity as any elf to Feraan's house. She did not even bother to concern herself with revealing its location to Thoroth.

Sylaera did not have the patience or the time for politeness. She did not knock but opened the door and invited herself inside. She saw Feraan, who was startled by her appearance, sitting at his puny desk with his insignificant books completing some menial, unimportant task.

"How can you sit there?" she demanded. "How can you do nothing and allow this to happen?"

Thoroth winced at her voice, but Feraan rose to meet her.

"What do you mean?" Feraan asked, matching her anger.

Wordlessly, she handed him the official letter. She watched him read it.

And she watched his eyes travel back to the top to read it again, this time aloud.

"Dear Master Eviat and Lady Sylaera,

We regretfully report that your daughter Caelfel has been taken while in combat. She is currently under the custody of Admiral Grimault of the Umfang army. The nature of her well-being is unknown.

Honey Water's imperial army does not have the resources to reclaim her from enemy hands. Unfortunately, there is nothing we can do, as the Umfang army has departed and no longer poses a threat to elvenkind. We will be withdrawing from the border in a few days' time. You may reclaim her personal items once the army disbands.

We send our best regards.

Captain Sanddef—"

When Feraan looked up, Sylaera saw something dark and unreadable in his eyes. She only saw it for a moment as he ran through his house, gathering things. She followed him.

"Well?" she demanded expectantly. She saw him wrapping his sword before he straightened up to answer.

"What would you have me do, Lady Gyssedlues?"

She did not flinch. "Find her and bring her back."

"That is exactly what I intend to do," he said through clenched teeth. Feraan's voice was deadly, and the cold determination in his eyes sent a shiver of fear down Sylaera's spine. "Even if it kills me."

***

"What is your name?" asked the heavily armored man who sat behind a desk with a large map pinned to its surface.

Caelfel said nothing. The circle of soldiers had managed to herd her to their main encampment, which had not been truly difficult on their part as Caelfel was without weapons and outside the protective enchantments of the forest. She could admit that it was her own folly that put her in this situation but if she was going to be held captive, she refused to give her captors the satisfaction of gracing them with a response.

"She's been silent since we found her, my lord," Lisiek explained to him.

"Maybe she is a mute elf, then. My dear, I am Admiral Grimault. You may hear some call me the princeling. I am the commanding officer of this army. You are probably wondering why we have plucked you from your woodland home to bring you with us. That's right. Now that we have you, there is no longer a reason to stay. We do not want war with your people, but we are more defensible at my castle, should anyone come looking for you."

Caelfel arched an eyebrow at Grimault. As much as she did not like to admit it, Caelfel knew no one would come looking for her. Once Grimault's army left, the elves would retreat further into the Fey Forest, not risking a mission to rescue her.

"Lisiek here will be your personal guard. We will do our best to cater to the needs of an elf, but please, understand if we must resort to unpleasant measures to secure your safety."

Caelfel drummed her fingers against the hardened leather of her armor impatiently. She did not appreciate condescending or cryptic remarks from anyone, much less her kidnapper.

"Forgive me," Grimault said, rising when he noticed her drumming. "You must still be wondering why you're here. Well, my dear, that's because you are possibly the most special elf there ever will be in elven history."

His smile was open and encouraging, but Caelfel only gave him a blank stare.

"You shall understand later. Now, we have a long journey ahead of us through the desert."

***

Feraan reached the camp before the day was over. He dismounted Firnis, who was grateful for the reprieve, and saw that the letter had been true. The imperial army was preparing for its return home. He approached what looked like a group of archers.

"I am looking for Captain Sanddef. Where is he?"

A she-elf with flaming red hair stepped forward. "He's over there by the archery field," she said, pointing.

Feraan nodded his thanks and ran to the archery range where he saw two elves arguing, an archer and his superior. Feraan didn't catch the subject of their debate, too impatient to care. He called out to them as soon as he was in shouting distance.

"*Captain Sanddef?*"

The tallest one with the braided blond hair turned toward him. "And who are you?"

"I am a tracker from Sal'Sumarathar and I am here to attend to a matter that you have neglected."

"I am sorry, but you will have to be more specific. What is your name?" asked the one he assumed was Captain Sanddef.

Feraan was finally standing before them. "My name is Feraan Auvrearaheal, and I am searching for Caelfel Gyssedlues."

The dark haired elf beside Sanddef stirred, and Feraan glanced at him long enough to determine he was young, perhaps around Caelfel's age.

Sanddef answered, "Caelfel Gyssedlues has been unfortunately captured by a division of the Umfang army, which has already disappeared some hours ago. There is nothing more we can do for her. I am very sorry—"

Feraan stepped closer to Sanddef and angrily jabbed his finger against Sanddef's plated armor to stress each word. "I said that I will be searching for her myself. All I am demanding from you is that you give me the last person that saw her."

Sanddef was speechless, taken aback by Feraan's manners, but the elf beside them spoke up.

"That was me. I saw everything. I was there."

Feraan beckoned him to come closer, and Captain Sanddef marched off, leaving them alone.

"My name is Galath. I was Caelfel's training and scouting partner. I didn't think they were going to send anyone to look for her."

Feraan nodded. He had already garnered the fact that Caelfel had volunteered as a ranger from Sylaera. "Please, explain everything to me as quickly as you can."

"We were in our designated scouting area, and this man entered the forest. He didn't wear any armor and he was alone. The rest of the army was remained behind him. He pulled out this rock, and there was a voice saying something about a sword and bow. Something about it made Caelfel lose her balance, and she fell out of the tree. The man picked up her bow and just walked away with it. Caelfel chased him. I yelled for her not to, but she left the forest, trying to get her bow back."

"And then what happened once she left the forest?" Feraan asked, mentally cursing Caelfel's stubbornness.

"Then a *panther* attacked her. By the time she threw it off, they had her completely surrounded."

"That's it?"

"Yes. They just left with her. Why would they take only her?"

"They only needed her. Thank you, Galath," Feraan said.

"You're going to find her? I want to go with you and help."

Feraan sighed. "I will be faster if I do this alone. I know what he wants."

Galath appeared disappointed but did not argue. "You're Feraan? She spoke of you."

This made Feraan pause. "What did she say?"

"I think you broke her heart."

Feraan sighed and he could feel the cracks in his own. "It broke mine to do it."

He found the location of the Umfang army's abandoned camp easily enough. That amount of soldiers left more than a mere footprint, so it would not be hard to follow them. But following them wasn't even a necessity. He remembered the location of Grimault's fortress.

They had less than a day's head start on him. If he pushed through the desert, he might meet Grimault before the princeling became too impatient for Feraan's arrival. Feraan did not dare to allow himself to think what would happen to Caelfel if Grimault turned impatient.

"I'm sorry, Caelfel," he whispered to the breeze before riding Firnis into the desert.

***

The admiral had stayed true to his word, ordering the entire camp to pack and move almost as soon as she arrived. Lisiek had tied Caelfel's hands together with some sort of metal wire and secured the other end around his waist. Caelfel was still bleeding on the back of her head from where the panther's chain had struck her, and even though it throbbed painfully, no one tended to her injury. Lisiek eventually called attention to it during their trek through the desert.

"I had heard a rumor that elves are particularly sensitive to the scent of blood from their own kind. Is this true?"

They had put her on a horse, and the air was unbearably hot and dry. Caelfel didn't believe she had ever been as uncomfortable in her life, so she did not feel inclined to answer him.

"Since you are bleeding, I thought it might be possible for someone of your kind to smell your trail."

She turned her head slowly and met his curiosity with a blank face.

They didn't stop until they reached a hidden oasis well after nightfall. Lisiek tugged her to the admiral's tent where they were discussing something in low voices. Caelfel sat in the corner and tried to pretend that they weren't there. She lifted her hands to discreetly feel around the dried blood on her head. Lisiek looked up immediately, feeling the movement on the chain, and Grimault fell silent with him.

"Is there something wrong, Lisiek?"

"I suspect her wound has probably closed now, scabbed over or something."

"Is this a problem?"

Lisiek straightened, and Caelfel met his ruthless eyes without unwavering. "It is not something I would like to risk. Call in a guard."

Grimault did, and when the guard entered his tent, he received a very clear instruction from the admiral. "Reopen the wound on her head."

The guard did not intend to be gentle about it either. He turned to Caelfel, and holding his sword by the scabbard, bludgeoned her with the hilt. She tried dodging the attack, but Lisiek pulled her to the ground with her leash. The best she could do was bite down on her tongue and taste fresh blood as she forced down any and all vocalizations that started rising in her throat.

"That's enough," came Grimault's command, and the beating ceased. She felt nauseatingly dizzy, but it did not slow her anger as she stood up and lunged for the guard who had senselessly attacked her. She did not have a sword, her bow, or her aura, and Lisiek might have taken her defensive amulet away once he recognized its magical properties, but Caelfel still had her hands, though bound, and she used them like a club on the man's face to knock him to the ground.

The damage she could inflict was minimal. The guard wore his helmet, so she just bent his visor before Lisiek dragged her off of him.

But Caelfel's anger did not stop. She attempted to attack Lisiek by kicking him. However, he stood out of her range, and her kick proved ineffectual. Before she could do anything else, Lisiek held out his hand with the palm facing her, and a glowing blue light twisted from his fingertips. When it touched her, Caelfel found that she could no longer move. She dropped to the ground.

Now that she was no longer a threat, the three men examined the guard's broken helmet curiously. Caelfel watched them silently from the ground as their gazes transferred from her to the misshapen metal and back again.

"How strong are the elves again?" Grimault asked at length, taking the helmet into his own hands. "She must be rather young. Those other two were much larger than her."

Lisiek leaned forward. "She easily pushed the cat off her as if it weighed nothing. Elves do have heightened senses and abilities, which would account for the helmet and the ability to detect blood."

"Then we must be sure we are prepared. I want this camp mobilized before dawn," Grimault ordered.

They left her lying on the coarse sand and although Caelfel's head and eyes throbbed, she was able to deduce something. While she wasn't sure why they picked her over all the elves of Honey Water, they did expect someone to follow them to rescue her.

She did not look forward to the moment when she disappointed them.

***

It was noon when Feraan reached the oasis. Even a cursory inspection made it obvious that this was where Grimault and his army had camped the previous night. Perhaps the most unsettling thing about the campsite was the heavy, lingering odor of elf blood that filled his nostrils and made his stomach roll and his head spin. There was no doubt it belonged to Caelfel, and he didn't want to think what caused this fresh injury.

He walked around some more but then lost his patience for the place, spurring Firnis on in the direction of the princeling's fortress. He didn't want to think about what waited ahead. Instead, Feraan kept his mind trained on the endless stretch of sand. The heat made his head feel heavy, and Feraan periodically reminded himself to take sips from his water skin so he wouldn't suffer from traveler's delusions.

Soon Firnis's fatigue became obvious, and Feraan stopped to

allow his horse to rest even though they had not been able to locate another oasis. He allowed the horse to drink from his water supply, and when he was finished drinking, Firnis eased himself on the ground, nudging him for more.

"We'll find another oasis," Feraan promised as he sat next to him, pushing the heels of his palms against his eyes. He hated the desert.

The pressure of his hands brought sparks of color to his vision. Feraan rubbed at his eyes, but it only brought a clearer image to him.

It was Caelfel sitting on a horse with her hands bound and dried blood caked on her head. She looked angry and tired, and Feraan knew she wasn't fond of the desert either.

He didn't think much of the vision until a human's voice entered the scene. "I know you can speak."

Feraan froze and focused on the vision more closely. He saw Caelfel turn to the voice, and it appeared as though she were staring straight at *him*.

Feraan jumped at this. The vision had disappeared but it still made his heart race, filling him with a renewed sense of urgency. He got Firnis to stand again, and they continued their chase through the desert.

***

The heat coupled with her untended injury made her head sick, so Caelfel didn't bother to concern herself with time. Eventually, the fortress came into sight, and the admiral ushered all of his men inside after she and Lisiek had entered first. They lingered in the outside courtyard while Grimault began ordering the sentries for watch.

"Let me know as soon as you see him." Then he took several guards with him as he led Lisiek and Caelfel into the palace.

No one had touched her since the first night Grimault had ordered the guard to beat her. Now that they were at their destination, Caelfel was apprehensive on what they would do with her. Lisiek still kept her bow on him at all times, so Caelfel spent most of her time glaring at him. But once they were in the main hall with a throne at its end, Lisiek removed the bow from his back and hung it on the wall above the throne.

"Lisiek, can you set the wall for scrying?" Grimault asked, settling himself onto the throne. Caelfel remained standing and preferred to be as far away from Lisiek as the leash allowed. He took them to the side wall where Caelfel noticed jagged crystals lined the corners.

"He would need to have something that would connect us."

"The girl, of course," Grimault said impatiently. Caelfel desperately wanted to know what they were talking about but she still refused to speak to either of them.

Lisiek turned to her, and Caelfel suddenly found herself frozen as soon as their eyes met. She felt the cold, blue fire of his aura pulsing around her skin, and it kept her motionless.

And then with a simple flick of his wrist, he threw her against the scrying wall. The blue light ignited the wall and it sent electric shocks coursing through her veins. Caelfel felt like screaming, and she probably did, but was unable to hear herself over the crackling pain that hazed her mind.

But in the center of her brow, she felt a vibrating light. She focused on it, and something else flooded her vision.

It was Feraan riding through the desert at breakneck speed. Caelfel noticed the amulet around his neck that was outlined in Lisiek's aura. Feraan seemed to see something as well, for he stopped riding and dismounted to approach them.

Caelfel heard Grimault's voice first through the electrifying fog. "I knew you would come. We are waiting for you."

"It seems as though you have taken great measures to find me."

"Then you should not be so hard to find."

"Release the she-elf, and I will come to you willingly and without a fight."

Caelfel's jaw clenched as she desperately longed to disagree with Feraan's proposed plan.

Grimault remained unconvinced. "Come now, Feraan. Do not underestimate my intelligence and expect me to take such a risk."

"I give you my word," Feraan said, angling his gaze.

"I'm not going to gamble anything I've done this far on that. Do not keep me waiting, Feraan, but you would probably appreciate if we keep this conversation short—"

"Show her to me!" Feraan demanded with a strong voice. "I want to see her condition."

"I'm afraid she's preoccupied at the moment. I meant it when I said you would appreciate a brief conversation."

"Grimault—"

"Do you sense a familiarity with our connection? Or have you not even been intimate with her?" Caelfel did not see Grimault but she heard his footsteps and felt his presence grow closer. "How special is she to even draw the wandering elf from hiding in a wasted attempt to save her? How can you rescue her when you cannot even protect her own life force that is supplying the energy for our conversation?"

And Caelfel felt the drain as her muscles weakened and gaping holes disrupted her vision. It made the image of Feraan shimmer slightly.

Then Caelfel felt something against her cheek where Grimault pressed two fingers against her face. The touch brought another vision, a premonition that unmistakably detailed the desert princeling murdering Feraan.

This is what the Blind Seer has shown me, Grimault whispered in her mind. Caelfel blinked, rapidly losing strength, and the faint movement caused Feraan to fade from her vision.

Grimault laughed, and it was an odd choking noise she suppressed from her attention. She focused on Lisiek's magic instead and was somehow able to briefly reroute it so that she was able to speak to Feraan herself.

"Don't come here! If you do, he will kill you!" Her strength had waned so much that Caelfel had to scream to reach Feraan.

"I don't care," was the cold response Caelfel heard from him before collapsing.

***

Feraan did not stop.

Firnis must have known what had occurred or at least sensed Caelfel was in danger because he charged on without protest, even though the strong desert winds threatened to veer them off course. Feraan still did not stop and he would not be swayed. He had seen Caelfel for a moment, and that glimpse of her outlined in ghostly, azure light, haunted him. He could not erase her battered face from his mind even when the sand kicked up into his eyes. It burned in him.

Soon the landscape changed, the sand yielding to the stark basalt crags that signaled the home of the desert princeling. It was here that Feraan slowed. When he stopped, he secured Firnis in a hidden crevice in the rock before continuing on foot. He knew Grimault expected him and would be watching. If Feraan wanted to maintain the element of surprise, he would have to remain undetected for as long as he could, a difficult task in the barren desert.

Feraan began climbing the crags. Ahead of him was the plateau on which stood Grimault's home. There was an easier path that led to the front gate, but they would see him there. He searched for stable footholds and pulled away at loose pebbles. It was dark when he had reached the top, but the darkness did not trouble him, for it made it easier to hide.

He took a moment to catch his breath and plan his next move. He could make out the torchlight of the sentries that patrolled the high walls—

Then the skin on his lower back began burning. It took sheer force of will for him not to cry out in shock. He lifted his shirt to see two runes branded above his hip, and they spelled out his familiar name.

When Feraan went to touch the burns, they disappeared without a lingering mark. Then the sound of Caelfel's scream filled his head. Her pain obliterated everything else, and he was aware of nothing else but Caelfel.

Then she was gone from him again, and Feraan was left sweating and trembling in the wake of the sensation. He regained his composure and pushed on, trying to convince himself that the echo of screams emanating from the castle was his own imagination.

A direct approach would not be fortuitous, because that would all but ensure defeat. Against an entire fortress, Feraan's only ally was stealth and even that approach was likely anticipated by his enemies. Seeing little other choice, he moved silently through the growing darkness until he could press himself against the towering east wall of the fortress. He pulled out a handful of throwing knives and took one in his grip, gauging the distance away from the closest guard.

He arched his arm back and threw it. It landed where he needed it, ahead of the guard who predictably went to investigate the noise of metal scraping against stone, and Feraan was left alone without the worry of sentries.

He hurried while the guard was occupied. He backed away from the wall a few paces, took a running start, and jumped. He caught a protruding stone halfway up the wall and was left dangling a frightening height above the ground.

He used his weight to swing himself and, when he had the right momentum, Feraan jumped high enough to reach the top of the wall.

He pulled himself over the ledge and crouched in the walkway that led to the nearby turret.

Feraan skittered across the length of the wall, ducking his head below the height of the crossway's ledge. He reached the stairwell leading inside the fortress walls and hid behind a corner as an ironclad human passed by. He took the first opportunity to descend the stairs.

When he reached the courtyard, he watched troops marching across the expansive space he assumed was reserved for training grounds. Even at night, Grimault's army remained on alert.

Heavy footsteps told Feraan to take cover behind a nearby wall. He held his breath and watched as a soldier climbed down the stairs after him and went to report something to his superior. Feraan saw the soldier hand over his own throwing knife. Grimault would soon know Feraan was there.

Feraan saw the problem would be crossing the main courtyard. He didn't know if his personal wards would work against Grimault's soldiers or not, but if they weren't functioning, reaching the shadow of the soldier barracks across the walkway, undetected, would take nothing short of a miracle. Feraan didn't like to chance such things but saw little other choice.

The moments he waited were long and painful. He kept his eyes trained on the superior officer that held Feraan's throwing knife as he strolled among the lines of training soldiers. Feraan was about to make his move when someone else approached the officer.

"There is a dust cloud in the east. Something large is coming this way very quickly."

"We're not looking for something large. Remember our target. His horse was discovered at the base of the mesa not long ago."

"But sir, this cloud—"

"We have no quarrel with a dust storm, boy."

The soldier squared his shoulders at attention and looked past his officer. "Whatever is stirring this cloud seems to have quarrel with us, sir."

The officer sighed. "Back to your post—"

"*Something is coming! We are being attacked!*" yelled another soldier from the wall. To prove it, the ground shook with sudden explosions, and orange light briefly illuminated the night sky. The soldiers in the courtyard instantly dispersed as they scrambled to their defensive positions. Feraan took the moment to blend among the chaos. He took slow, purposeful strides to Grimault's castle.

"*Someone inform the admiral. They will be here within the hour.*" Feraan knew of only one thing that resided in the east but he was not sure who would visit the fortress from that direction.

He caught sight of the previous officer, a lieutenant judging by his shoulder markings, weaving his way against the current of pauldrons and breastplates. Feraan followed him at a respectable distance until they were before the great entrance of the castle. The lieutenant entered, and Feraan slipped between the doors before they closed.

He and the lieutenant stood in a shadow, and the princeling sat on his throne in the entrance hall. Grimault rose to see the visitor, and the lieutenant moved towards him. Feraan remained where he was, scanning the length of the room for Caelfel or Lisiek.

"What is the meaning of this noise?" Grimault demanded. "Have you found him?"

"We are being attacked by something—"

"Is it him?"

"No, my lord."

"Then where is he?"

"Sir, scouts sighted his horse earlier, and a guard found a missile of elvish make." The princeling stepped up to his lieutenant. Feraan shifted to the corner of the entryway's shadow and saw a figure off to the side lying motionlessly. A metallic rope leashed her to the darkly clothed Lisiek. The steward looked about the room as if he sensed another presence.

"Return outside until you have found him and dispatch whoever else is trying to attack us," Grimault ordered. The lieutenant hurried outside without another word, oblivious to Feraan as he passed him.

Grimault turned back around to return to his throne and combed his fingers through his sandy hair. Lisiek crossed the short distance to meet him, also turning his back to Feraan. The smell of burnt flesh hung heavily in the air.

"When is he coming, Lisiek?" Grimault hissed. Before Lisiek could respond, the sound of a chain moving caught the steward's attention. Feraan looked to see Caelfel stirring in the dimly lit hall. Feraan left the protective shadow and drew his sword just as he reached Grimault.

"Perhaps he is already here," Feraan answered in Lisiek's stead.

Grimault turned in time to meet Feraan's blow with his own

sword, and the scraping of blades echoed through the castle. Feraan threw off his weight and took one cautious step back. Grimault struggled to regain his balance but then quickly righted himself.

"Feraan, you made it just in time. I was afraid she would not last for long."

"Why would she not?"

"Lisiek, the girl," Grimault commanded.

Feraan watched Lisiek deftly pull Caelfel to her knees and saw there was not much consciousness left in her eyes. Lisiek went to stand behind her, and when he put his hands on her shoulders, the familiar blue light covered Caelfel's entire body. Feraan sensed a parasitic draw on her life force.

"I am here now. Release her," Feraan said, facing Grimault again.

"I don't believe you understand why we brought the two of you here."

Feraan's eyes briefly travelled to the bow resting above Grimault's throne and felt his sword humming in his hands. "You took her so I would come to you. You want to exact your revenge against me."

"Nearly correct. I plan to do the same to you as you've done to me. I will kill the one you love while you witness her death, unable to help her."

"Your friend killed himself by dabbling in magic he did not understand."

"If I recall correctly, it was your sword that pierced his heart. Lisiek is going to kill your she-elf, and I will watch you suffer."

Without pausing, Feraan hurled a throwing knife towards Lisiek. It clipped the sorcerer's shoulder, and Lisiek released Caelfel to grope at his injury. The blue light around her vanished. She fell again to the floor, attempting to break the fall with her elbows. Feraan noticed the chain around her wrists.

Grimault growled with rage, lifting his sword above his head. Feraan dropped to his knees and rolled out of the way, stopping himself when he was next to Caelfel.

He rose to his feet and swung his sword in the same movement, breaking the chain that bound her to Lisiek. It fell slack and dropped to the floor.

Grimault barreled toward him, and Feraan had just enough time to throw him back with the hilt of his sword.

Feraan looked around to see Caelfel struggling to move herself and noticed that Lisiek had recovered from his attack. He did not heed the blood dripping from his shoulder as he strode deliberately toward Feraan, blue fire engulfing his hands.

In a fight against a single human, any elf would easily succeed, but Feraan did not find himself fond of facing an admiral of the Umfang army and one of the few humans that possessed a magical aura. Feraan took calculated steps back as he measured the distance between Grimault and Lisiek.

"I'm curious, Grimault. Why is Lisiek assisting you in this revenge?"

"The man you killed? They were brothers."

"It's strange, because I recall Lisiek helping me kill his own brother."

Grimault's eyes shifted uneasily to his steward who in turn kept his features placid. "You're stalling and trying to distract me."

"Think about it, Grimault. How did I know so much about your friend in the first place? Why would any elf be compelled to leave the forest to kill a human that means nothing to them without first being invited?"

Grimault turned his attention to Lisiek this time who smirked at Feraan's words. "I don't believe you. Lisiek would never betray me."

"You should know your steward better than I do. What is the only thing that interests Lisiek?" Feraan asked.

Lisiek was grinning widely and he answered for the admiral. "Myself."

Grimault turned his stunned gaze to Lisiek. "Your own brother?"

The blue fire dissipated, and Lisiek folded his arms. "My brother was an idiot—"

Feraan charged Lisiek with his sword. The sorcerer reacted and reached out with a lash of fire that singed the weather cloak on Feraan's shoulder.

But Feraan still brought Lisiek to the ground by sinking his blade deeper into steward's battered shoulder. Feraan drew back his sword once more.

Then something sharp sliced his back. Feraan whirled around as his now broken bow and shredded weather cloak fell to the floor. Grimault prepared for another attack as Feraan sensed Lisiek getting to his feet behind him.

Feraan dropped to the ground and rolled away again. When he got to his feet, he ripped his now useless side quiver from his belt and tossed it away. It landed near Caelfel.

He lowered his sword and, calling upon his own aura, raised his hand. Black smoke billowed around Feraan's arm, and he sent a spray of tiny ice shards plunging toward the sorcerer. Lisiek's reflexes were delayed in his defense, and pinpricks of blood dotted his face. The ones that pelted his wounded shoulder made him claw at the open sore in pain.

The black smoke swirled away, and Feraan turned his attention to Grimault. They parried blows for a while, but Feraan was nearly always distracted as he kept his eye on Lisiek.

When Lisiek finally straightened, he pumped his arms from side to side and wiped at the blood on his face. His right arm sagged slightly but it didn't stop him from summoning a wave of blue fire that he hurtled toward Feraan's face.

Feraan retaliated, and the black smoke reappeared to extinguish the fire with a wall of thick frost. Meanwhile, Feraan narrowly dodged another attack from Grimault, and the princeling's blade nicked him in the ribs. The sting of the metal resulted in a wet, red stain that rapidly soaked his clothes and drenched his armor, but Feraan didn't allow himself to think of that.

***

It was hot and then it was cold. She blinked to see a quiver inches from her face—

***

He pushed Grimault away from him again. The princeling stumbled and fell to the ground with the force. Feraan stepped back to Lisiek and raised his blade over his head for a high guard. The black smoke curled around the Bastard's sword, and Feraan sent streaks of electricity running down his blade.

***

—Her hair prickled with the energy in the room as she struggled to maintain consciousness—

***

Lisiek drew closer to him, and Feraan swung the blade forward, sending the man flying into the opposite wall with a bolt of lightning. When the dust settled, Lisiek did not move.

Feraan's hair stood on edge with the shock, but the magic took more of his strength. He had to blink furiously in order to keep Grimault in focus.

"It would appear as though you have destroyed my steward," Grimault observed, leaning on one leg.

"You might as well surrender now before I destroy you."

"Nonsense. I have a whole army waiting outside. I doubt even you could fight this entire fortress alone."

The foundations of the castle rumbled, and Feraan wondered who had arrived to attack the fortress. He didn't want to think about facing another threat once he rescued Caelfel. He tightened his shaking fingers around the hilt of his sword.

If he rescued Caelfel.

He didn't have the energy to call upon more magic, so as he charged Grimault, he left it to sheer force. Grimault lifted his weapon and easily parried Feraan's blow.

***

—He was going to die. Grimault's premonition would come true.
***

Feraan adjusted his grip and delivered a quick series of strikes in rapid succession, first aiming for Grimault's waist, then his head, his chest, and finally his neck. Grimault met every one, a bit slower each time.

Then Feraan reached for Grimault's wrist, and the princeling's sword clattered to the ground, the force of Feraan's blow warping the pommel in an unnatural fashion.

Feraan was panting but smirking as he rendered Grimault defenseless. But Grimault did not appear alarmed as Feraan thought he should. Instead, Grimault retrieved a large battle axe from the wall and its double blades whistled when he swung it through the air.

Feraan crouched and held his sword by both the hilt and the blade as Grimault brought the axe down on him. Feraan's sword caught the attack, but the ringing blade sliced into the palm of his left hand. Blood dripped in long, viscous streaks, staining his arm and his blade.

The princeling brought his axe back. Feraan dropped his sword and saw that blood had completely coated his hand and fingers. His veins continued to spew fresh blood, and Feraan closed his hand into a fist, feeling how deep the cut was. He fell back to the ground and looked up to see the princeling preparing for his final assault.

Then Feraan saw an arrow pierce the princeling's throat. Grimault choked on his own blood before lifelessly falling to his knees. Beyond the fallen princeling stood Caelfel, her bow back in her hands and Feraan's discarded quiver at her feet. Feraan breathed a sigh of relief as he realized, even in her extremely weakened state, Caelfel had proven her namesake as Archer of the Lake.

Then, she fell.

18. Goodbye Anna

It took some time before Caelfel could open her eyes. When she did, all she saw was Feraan, and he filled her with a sense of security and relief. She smiled at him, and he smiled back.

"Is she awake?"

This was another familiar voice Caelfel did not expect. She raised her head to see Thoroth. Behind him, she caught glimpses of her mother, Garvanna, and Galath. But holding her head up quickly became painful, so she let it fall back to the ground. She felt Feraan cradling her neck.

"What happened?" she asked weakly. The dark stone walls told her they were still in Grimault's fortress, but she didn't remember the others being there.

Suddenly, Thoroth's face was beside Feraan's. "I need to heal her."

But Feraan, who was holding her, would not allow this. "I will take care of it. You go tend to the others."

Thoroth looked as though he wanted to disagree, but Feraan picked her up from the ground and carried her off to the corner. When they had settled once more, he touched the back of her head where they had beaten her. She winced but felt warmth spreading from his fingers to the rest of her body. He was healing her, and she was slowly getting her strength back.

"I came here to rescue you, but it was you who ended up saving *my* life."

"Well, of course." She blinked, sluggishly recalling all the events

256

from before. "He was going to kill you."

"He would have killed you too. Fortunately for us, I was not the only rescue team to come after you. Your mother met your friend Galath, and they were able to recruit over half the army to find you."

"But you found me first."

He smiled, and she saw there was something sad about it. "I did."

"How?"

"I'm a tracker, Caelfel."

"But they wanted you to find me. That's the reason they took me. Why?" she asked. Feraan sighed, and Caelfel saw something more than sadness. She saw his exhaustion.

"I am very sorry, Caelfel. I never wanted any of this to happen."

"They knew you," she pressed.

"Admiral Grimault had a very close friend in the Umfang army, and I killed him. Grimault wanted revenge so he sought to take something that was equally precious to me."

"You knew they were coming for me since Macha came to visit you." Caelfel couldn't keep the accusation from her voice and she saw that it bothered him.

"I tried stopping it," he mumbled.

Caelfel wanted to ask how, but she quickly grew tired. She had Feraan, and that made her content for now. For now.

He continued healing her, strengthening her life force with his own aura, and it was a slow process. She delighted in his touch, not caring to wonder why no one else approached them. At some point, he lifted the bottom of her shirt to inspect something on her hip. Feraan's face was grim as he lightly traced the marks Lisiek had burned onto her skin. He looked as though he wanted to say something but didn't.

"How did you know that was there?" she asked.

He met her gaze briefly. "I felt it, when they did that to you. I'm not sure how but I felt everything they did to you. Only, I don't have the permanent scars," he explained. He pulled her shirt back down.

Caelfel shifted, something uncomfortable seeding in the pit of her stomach. "I want to ask you something."

He turned his attention away from her hip and seemed to identify the nature of her question from her face. "Not now, Caelfel. Ask me later when you have your strength back."

She sighed, feeling her eyelids grow heavy. "Is it daylight?" she asked. She felt rather than saw him smile.

"It's just now dawn."

***

Feraan thought it was extraordinarily opportune, though he did not expect it, for the elvish army to attack when they did. They distracted Grimault's soldiers from the fight in the castle and secured Feraan's and Caelfel's safety. Feraan had to admit to himself that if Sylaera had not brought down the doors of the castle, he was not sure if he or Caelfel would have made it back to Sal'Sumarathar.

But going back was another matter that Feraan was not inclined to concern himself with. The present focus was to ensure that Caelfel's health returned to normal, and he personally saw to that. He saw the questions in her eyes but he chose to avoid them, at least until he had made up his own mind about things. He did not know what would happen when they left fortress.

Caelfel had fallen asleep again when Eviat approached him. Despite the greyling's near death experience only days before, Caelfel's father had insisted on accompanying the rescue mission for Caelfel. He looked troubled as he struggled to relay a message to Feraan.

"The sorcerer that took her," Eviat began. "He's still alive. Markis and Blaes wanted your opinion on him."

Feraan nodded, irritated that a spell that took so much out of him did not even manage to kill Lisiek. "I'll be there shortly."

Eviat left, and Feraan scanned the room to find someone he could trust to watch over Caelfel. When he did not immediately see her parents, his eyes fell on Galath, and he beckoned the boy to him.

"Watch over her, please. Don't let anyone except her parents get too close. I mean that."

Galath crouched over Caelfel, looking surprised. "Why trust me with her?"

"I trust you because you wanted to find her first, and you gathered the army to attack the fortress. Because of that, I trust you with her more than anyone else in this room." As Feraan walked away, a notion crossed his thoughts, and he considered that he might accept Galath as his replacement in Caelfel's life. But Feraan did not want to think of being replaced. Not yet, anyway.

As promised, Lisiek was still alive, sitting and blinking between Blaes and Markis. Feraan wondered at Markis being there, since he had

258

never showed interest in protecting another elf before, least of all Caelfel.

"What shall we do with him?" Markis asked, grinning cheerfully. His expression didn't suit the occasion.

"You're asking me?"

"You *were* the one to fight him. You know his capabilities the best out of all us."

"What are his choices?" Feraan asked.

Blaes answered him this time. "He will face execution or he will be interrogated and allowed to make a case for himself."

"The latter seems rather generous, given the first option," Feraan commented.

"Interrogation is not exclusive to torture, and no matter what case he presents, he is all but ensured an execution."

"So what will it be?" Lisiek asked, and Feraan crouched in front of him. "You left a pretty good mark on me," Lisiek noted, indicating the large scorch mark on his chest.

"I'm afraid it wasn't good enough. I would kill you right now with my own hands for what you've done."

Lisiek laughed, and Feraan hated him for it. "Caelfel wouldn't want that. She doesn't like it when you threaten people, much less kill them."

Feraan glared, all but willing Lisiek's own aura to turn him into ash. "*Don't* say her name."

Lisiek whistled sharply through pursed lips. "You don't like that. You probably won't like the present I left on her side. I was only thinking of you."

Feraan's mind went to the new scars on Caelfel's hip, and he straightened. "General Blaes, if you can guarantee his torture, you may interrogate him before his execution."

***

Caelfel wasn't sure how long they had stayed in the desert palace but she found herself wandering its halls. Certainly they had not been there long and certainly they would leave soon. She didn't like being there.

She avoided everyone, including her own mother who she was told was fearsome in battle, wielding her powerful aura to bring down the walls of the fortress. Caelfel could easily imagine it, but she still avoided everyone, looking for only one person.

And eventually, she found him, standing in the open archways that overlooked the west.

"Is the coast that way?" she asked.

Feraan did not turn but he smiled when she approached him. "Yes it is."

"Will you take me to it?"

This time he looked at his feet. "You've only just recovered."

Caelfel scraped the toe of her boot back and forth on the floor impatiently. "Then does that mean I can ask you my question now?"

"I wasn't sure if you would remember it."

"Of course I do. It's all I can think about."

"By all means, then, say what is on your mind."

"Were you lying?"

"You will have to be more specific, Hen," he said. Something in her stomach twitched joyously at the nickname, but she stifled it.

"Our last conversation in Sal'Sumarathar. You said you didn't want me. Were you lying?" she asked. He finally turned to look at her, and Caelfel saw from his face that she knew she would not like the answer.

"I said those things in Sal'Sumarathar to try to prevent all of *this* from happening." He waved his arms around, gesturing to the palace. "If I'm going to be honest, what I said then could not be further from the truth. That's why nothing changed, and it all still happened. And Caelfel, I am sorry for it."

"But?" she prompted, sensing there was more. "You knew Grimault and Lisiek were after me. That was what Macha told you."

"I tried preventing it—"

"No, you abandoned me and left me completely unprepared for something you knew was inevitable." Caelfel was surprised at the accusing conviction in her voice. It made Feraan scowl.

"I suppose you are right, but know that it was not my intention."

"Then what was your intention when you said those things to me on your doorstep?"

"I was trying to force myself to not care about you, so Grimault when Grimault asked the Blind Seer who I loved, your face, your existence wouldn't be revealed to him."

"So you do love me?"

He looked away. "It is not enough."

"Is it enough that I love you, then?"

"You don't understand—"

"I will never understand if you insist on hiding everything from me. You have to make a decision to trust me just as I trust you."

"That's not the decision I have to make. I have to decide to commit myself, to accept you is to accept always putting you in danger and to accept constant responsibility for you. I have found that I cannot make that decision."

"Then I assume I am not worth the responsibility." Even though she had accepted the same responsibility for saving him in the forest. Something stuck in her throat and her eyes pricked. She had to look away this time, blinking back tears. "I wonder who will be worth it to you," she mumbled miserably.

She turned to leave when he gently pulled her back by the hand. Then Feraan held her face and kissed her. "Only you. Always you."

Then the kiss was over, and he gave her a sad, apologetic smile. Caelfel watched the smile, and though she did not want to, she felt as though she understood him.

Feraan was not ready.

But given some time, he may yet be.

She parted from him with this understanding and returned to the makeshift infirmary where she had stayed since the elves invaded the palace. There was a sound of screaming from within, and Caelfel paused to listen to an argument that was largely one-sided before she made her entrance.

"I do not understand!" came Garvanna's devastated shriek. Then brokenly, "I love you."

"I don't know what to tell you, Anna. I do not love you this way. I want Caelfel. I prefer her over you," was Thoroth's agitated response.

"She does not prefer you, though."

"She will. Feraan will not love her, and then Caelfel will see what I can offer her—"

"You're wrong," Caelfel said as she stepped into the room. Garvanna's face was red and tearstained. Caelfel continued, "Perhaps there was a time when I liked you, but I cannot love you. I don't love you, at least not in the way you want me to." Caelfel walked further into the room and she saw how her words finally hit Thoroth. He looked as though he were breaking too.

"Caelfel—"

"No, Thoroth. I know I cannot make you love Garvanna, just as I cannot be forced to love you. But do not break her heart to wait for mine."

Thoroth had no response, so Caelfel turned to Garvanna.

"I want you to come with me."

"What?"

"I want to leave this fortress, but more than that, I want to leave Honey Water. I want to see the world, to meet its people and fight in their battles. There is nothing, really, for me in Sal'Sumarathar, and I suspect the same goes for you. I want you to accompany me, please. I know you've already mastered magic, and since I cannot perform magic, I would appreciate having a friend who can."

Garvanna's answer came slowly but when she spoke, her answer was confident and without hesitation. Caelfel offered a hand to her. Garvanna took it just as Thoroth left the room.

"Where would we go?" Garvanna asked.

Caelfel smiled. "To the coast."

***

Thoroth confronted him during the night. "They are leaving."

"What are you talking about?" Feraan noted that the healer was angry.

"Caelfel went to Garvanna and asked Garvanna to leave with her. Caelfel argued that they had nothing left in Honey Water, and Garvanna *agreed*. Garvanna has *me*—"

"You've never cared about Garvanna, at least not since you've been so concerned with Caelfel," Feraan pointed out. "Perhaps you should have told Garvanna who she had before she decided to leave."

"Will you do nothing, then? After crossing the desert to save her life, you're going to let Caelfel venture into the world of men unprotected?"

"I gave her up Thoroth. She is free to do whatever she wishes."

Thoroth stormed off cursing. Feraan waited until he heard a door slam before he moved to retrieve Firnis.

He had told Caelfel he didn't want to commit, but Feraan found it difficult to commit to *that* decision.

Epilogue

L isiek didn't know where they took him. He could have been in the heart of the Fey Forest or within the caverns of the Baetic Mountains. He had been blindfolded for the journey and when they removed the cloth covering his eyes, he saw that the air was still and dark, permeated by an ancient silence. His guards left him in the cavernous room which he suspected to be something akin to a prison cell, only there were no bars or metal grating, no elvish guards to flank the entryways.

But Lisiek knew better than to try to escape. The elves would not abandon him without purpose, so all he could do was wait. And in his waiting, Lisiek recalled the events that led him where he was, particularly the foolish ventures of Grimault who had blindly followed the Blind Seer's instructions. Grimault was not without retribution, however, because he was dead now, which might have been merciful in its own way.

Because Lisiek's crime had been far worse than the princeling's. Lisiek had brought harm to an elf, and the elves did not look favorably upon such deeds. Grimault only sought revenge against the most hated being in the world, but Lisiek had nearly killed the only person who did not hate Feraan.

Nearly.

And now he stood in a dark cove in some nameless, gods' forsaken place. Lisiek wondered if he regretted his decisions and could not find any sort of guilt in him. Well, that was that.

Lisiek turned around to see three orbs of light hovering in one of the corridors. They illuminated two long lines of elf soldiers that marched silently into his holding place. When they entered, the two lines split, circling the room's perimeter. In the center was a girl with dark green eyes. Her ears were rounded but her movements were as lithe as an elf's. Her wild hair curled down to the small of her back. Lisiek felt something different emanating from her. Wild energy pulsed around her being. The guards trained their eyes on her carefully. Lisiek thought that was strange. He would expect the guards to watch him.

"This is your interrogation," she said. Her voice was smooth and harmonious like water. Her smile was smug.

Then the voice was in his head. *Do not be afraid. The soldiers are here for me.*

Surprised, Lisiek's arms, previously crossed, fell limply to his sides. He watched as the three orbs of light circled about him as if they were sentient beings. And they frightened him.

Her smile deepened. "My name is Gwyndolyn, and I am here to talk to you." *Don't worry. You can answer in your head. I will hear you.*

Lisiek focused his thoughts into a single question. *The soldiers are here for your protection?*

She laughed aloud. *No. For yours.*

Glossary

Characters

Caelfel Gyssedlues—daughter of Eviat & Sylaera Gyssedlues, crowned Beauty of Spring, archer in the Volunteer Regiment, 76 years old

Feraan Auvrearaheal—most hated elf of Honey Water, member of the Chthonic Order, tracker, 536 years old

Eviat Gyssedlues—Caelfel's father, prior training in healing & alchemy, ranger, 2,375 years old, greyling

Sylaera Gyssedlues—Caelfel's mother, estranged member of the Sal'Sumarathar Family, Master Summoner, 589 years old

Thoroth Orletylar—mother was citizen of Amasel, healer & alchemist, 399 years old

Garvanna Hunithrae—originally from Amasel, master of magic with focus in Summoning, battlemage in the Volunteer Regiment, 431 years old

Nadeth Kennyratear—Thamil, master of the arcane and mystic arts, 5,676 years old, greyling, deceased

Markis Rilynnzea—Chief Executor of Sal'Sumarathar, ambassador of the Fey Forest in Foreign Relations, tracker, 293 years old

Uthruil Killelvris—Daerad's father, Head Councilor of Sal'Sumarathar, Conjurer, 591 years old

Daerad Killelvris—student of magic with a focus in Obliteration, 92 years old

<u>Nimuath Killelvris</u>—Uthruil's brother, Headmaster of the College of Sal'Sumarathar, master of the mystic arts with a focus in Illusion, 600 years old

<u>Luewyn Cyredathem</u>—Feraan's sister, widow, master of the mystic arts, master of the Forbidden Magic, 554 years old

<u>Gwyndolyn Ernmas</u>—illegitimate daughter of Empress Haelyn, member of the Board of Wizardry, Warden of the Labyrinth, 100 years old

<u>Blaes Llychlin</u>—general of the elvish imperial army, military advisor to the empress, ambassador of the Vinius Islands in Foreign Relations, swordsman & highly trained obliterator, 874 years old

<u>Empress Haelyn of Ernmas</u>—ruler of the elves, 844 years old

<u>Empress Clytemeria of Ernmas</u>—previous ruler of the elves, mother to Empress Haelyn & grandmother to Gwyndolyn, ruled during the Reign of Firescales

<u>Galath Caerbannic</u>—son of Lanslak, archer, ranger in the Volunteer Regiment, resides in Rasaen, 63 years old

<u>Winwaloe Lannvenec</u>— ranger, archer in the Volunteer Regiment, resides in Sal'Sumarathar, 122 years old

<u>Sanddef Pyrd</u>—ranger captain of the elvish imperial army, 777 years old

<u>Fódla Danann</u>—archer, ranger in the Volunteer Regiment, resides in Yamalvon, 298 years old

<u>Adar Ambrosius</u>— blacksmith for the elvish imperial army, Sylaera's sister, native to Sal'Sumarathar, resides in Yamalvon, Daughter of the Sal'Sumarathar Family, 589 years old

<u>Olwen</u>—Adar's blacksmith apprentice, resides in Yamalvon, 193 years old

<u>Elaine</u>—human name for Sylaera's sister Eleanir, master of Illusion & Healing, Daughter of the Sal'Sumarathar Family, 589 years old

<u>Macha Morrígna</u>—werebird (alternate form is a raven), member of the Chthonic Order, 19 years old

<u>Grimault Cromlech</u>—also known as the 'desert princeling', admiral

of the Umfang army, resided on inherited estate in the Amhsis desert, 37 years old, deceased

Lisiek Darkling—steward of Grimault, prisoner of the Honey Water empire, human sorcerer, 26 years old

Wystaria—human sorceress, 17 years old

Travin Copperlyre (previously Travin Gyssedlues)—blood brother to Eviat, married to a vampire, 1,053 years old, likes to sing

Lycaon—werewolf alpha, head of the Dirus Clan, member of the Chthonic Order

Hubertus—famous werewolf hunter, deceased

Refurinn—wife of Hubertus, werewolf, deceased

Lanslak Caerbannic—exiled diplomat, father of Galath, 609 years old

Ewyn—mother of all elves, the Creator

Yamalvon—eldest child of Ewyn, founded the capital of Honey Water

Elewyr—fourth child of Ewyn, famous for her beauty, briefly betrothed to foreigner Sidhe shortly before her assassination

Sidhe—distant sailor, briefly engaged to Elewyr before her death, fled from the Fey Forest, currently resides in Umfang

Sibylla—the Blind Seer, "Traitor of the World", a feminine being who is physically blind but is able to accurately determine all possible futures and the choices that spur them, she resides in the Center of the World, also called the Middle Tree

Places

Ariang'ron—the Silver Crown World, the world that encompasses the Honey Water Empire, Umfeld & Umfang

Honey Water—empire of the woodland elves

Fey Forest—forest with magical barriers, mainland of the woodland elf empire, primarily deciduous

Vinius Islands—cluster of islands in the Latrielle Sea, north of the Fey Forest, conquered by the elves over 5,000 years ago and then added to the Honey Water empire, originally home to the ormr before the Reign of Firescales resulted in their extinction

Heather Tombs of the Nadeths—section of the Baetic Mountain range where it only borders the Fey Forest, reserved as sacred burial ground for the woodland elves

Latrielle Sea—body of water that borders the Fey Forest to the north, the sediment content in the water prevents natural underwater life

Baetic Mountains—long mountain range that primarily borders the Fey Forest but also extends into Umfeld and Umfang

Pirinac Forest—Umfeld forest in the kingdom of Kanetalm that connects to the border of the Fey Forest, primarily coniferous

Yamalvon—elvish capital of both the Fey Forest and the Honey Water empire

Sal'Sumarathar—elvish city in the Fey Forest

Elewyr—elvish city in the Fey Forest, also commonly referred to as the Port City, center of trade and shipping for the empire

Amasel—once great elvish city in the Fey Forest, now lies in ruin

Rasaen—elvish city in the Fey Forest

Umfeld—realm of the humans, south of Umfang and west of the Fey Forest

Kanetalm—kingdom of Umfeld

Palpses—capital of Kanetalm

Sorasaen—religious center of Kanetalm, previous home to Hubertus

Haradrop—city of Kanetalm, only known residence of a high concentration of civilized werewolves in Umfeld

Onusal—kingdom of Umfeld

Akeonn—capital of Onusal

Temple of Donar—religious center of Onusal, maintains regular correspondence with Sorasaen

Rotariel—city of Onusal

Atalon—city of Onusal, center of trade in Umfeld

Umfang—northern realm of Ariang'ron, home to werefolk, humans, blood drinkers and others, northwest of the Fey Forest, north of Umfeld, governed primarily as a representative democracy

Amhsis desert—desert of Umfang that separates it from Umfeld and the Fey Forest

Terms

<u>youngling</u>—an elf child, an elf less than fifty years old

<u>greyling</u>—an elf that has breached their second millennia

<u>nadeth</u>—title given to the oldest elf in a certain region, usually over 3,000 years old

<u>aura</u>—slightly perceptual field of radiation that allows its owner to perform magic, each person has a distinctive color that may change or disappear over time, usually natural born among elves and rare in the case of humans

<u>ormr</u>—dragons

<u>Reign of Firescales</u>—a long war the ormr waged against all other races that resulted in the extinction of mountain elves and dragons and also the isolation of the Fey Forest from Umfeld and Umfang, the ormr were eventually conquered

<u>Firescales</u>—a special breed of ormr that took pride in terrorizing Ariang'ron

<u>Ormr Masters</u>—a mysterious race that tamed the ormr, were destroyed in the original conquer of the Vinius Islands

<u>Daemona language</u>—language used by the Ormr Masters

<u>Chthonic Order</u>—a secret and mysterious organization, members are usually identified with a unique tattoo behind their left shoulder with one given exception to their sole elf member

<u>Voice of the Unknown</u>—a magical spell used to cloak one's identity (up to user's discretion), the spell is normally detected by the user's voice when using the spell (a dark, rumbling voice that does not hint to the user's original), a typical characteristic of followers and servants of the Blind Seer

<u>Family</u>—as in, Family of Sal'Sumarathar, the nobility of a certain area, usually granted special favors and privileges from the empire, believed they were descended from the original Conquerors of Ormr that established all the elvish cities and as such are born with superior abilities, Caelfel's mother was born into the Family of Sal'Sumarathar

Pronunciation Guide

Familiar Names

Caelfel (KALE-ful)
Feraan (FAIR-in or fur-OHN)
Thoroth (THOR-oth)
Garvanna (gar-VON-uh)
Markis (MAR-kus)
Eviat (EH-ve-ot)
Sylaera (sih-LARE-uh)
Nadeth (NAY-deth)
Thamil (THA-mil)
Galath (Guh-LATH)
Grimault (GRIM-alt)
Lisiek (luh-SEEK)
Daerad (Dare-ad)
Uthruil (OOTH-roo-eel)
Nimuath (NIM-yoo-wath)
Winwaloe (win-WUH-low)
Fódla (FODE-luh)
Blaes (BLAZE)
Sanddef (SAN-def)
Macha (MOCK-uh)

Haelyn (HAY-lin)
Luewyn (loo-WIN)
Ewyn (EE-win)
Lycaon (lie-KAY-in)
Hubertus (hue-BURT-us)
Refurinn (reh-FURR-in)
Lividia (luh-VID-ee-uh)
Tahlmus (TALL-mus)
Ruxlitta (RUX-leht-ta)

Surnames

Gyssedlues (guh-SID-luze)
Auvrearaheal (ov-REAR-a-heel)
Orletylar (or-LEH-tuh-lar)
Hunithrae (HUN-ith-ray)
Rilynnzea (ruh-LAN-zee-uh)
Kennyratear (KEN-nuh-RA-teer)
Caerbannic (CARE-ban-ik)
Cromlech (KROM-leck)
Killelvris (KILL-el-vris)
Lannvenec (LAN-vuh-neck)
Danann (Duh-nan)
Llychlin (LICH-lin)
Pyrd (PIRD)
Morrígna (more-RIG-na)
Ernmas (ERN-mus)
Cyredathem (ky-RED-a-them)

Geographic Names

Ariang'ron (AR-ee-AIN-gron)

Sal'Sumarathar (SAL-soo-ma-RATH-ar)
Yamalvon (yuh-MAL-von)
Amasel (AM-a-sell)
Rasaen (ruh-SAY-in)
Elewyr (ELL-uh-weer)
Umfeld (OOM-feld)
Umfang (OOM-fang)
Baetic (Mountains) (BAY-eh-tic)
Amhsis (Desert) (OHM-sis *or* AM-sis)
Vinius (Islands) (VIN-ee-us)
Kanetalm (KAN-eh-talm)
Rumfel (Lake) (RUM-fell)
Blaidd (River) (BLADE)
(Mount) Ormr (OR-mur)
Haradrop (HAIR-uh-drop)
Sorasaen (SORE-uh-say-in)

Acknowledgements

When initiating the project to write and publish a book independently, one quickly realizes how much of a burden it is to shoulder. It comes as no surprise that there would be others responsible for helping to bring this story to life. I am no exception.

This is my first book and, as it were, it will always hold a special place in my heart. The same goes for the people that suffered through this with me.

The first I shall mention are my brilliant editors. Andy Arnold has become a reliable friend over the years. I trust him and his love for stories of the fancy. Even though I did break his heart with this one. Cow Field shall return! Kelsa Warner is a friend I hope to never lose. Not only is her grounded sense of language irreplaceable, but it is her beauty that graces the cover of *Archer of the Lake*. She was always my vision for Caelfel. It should also be noted that Kelsa's patience is remarkable. I should mention how much she endured through my peculiarities over the years ranging from my high school antics to my indecision during the cover photo shoot. (I can hear her voice reprimanding me now, "You are too kind Kelly-wa!"). I love you Kelsa-la!

There are others who were brave enough to plow through the terrible quality of my original draft. I will list them here: Amanda, Olivia, Mrs. Debbie. And I shan't of course forget Mrs. Lisa who offered so much support. That woman is an invaluable cheerleader.

Other notable people who plowed through the horrid first draft:

Laura and Alyssia. Laura is a friend I've known for many years but have never met in person. She has remained a constant and loyal contact since I slowly recovered from my "Fanfiction Phase" (at least, we will tell everyone I've recovered). Alyssia is a brutally honest friend, who spares no expense for your feelings. And I mean that in a good way. If something did not suit her, she would let me know. Her companionship was invaluable as we endured a THIRTY-EIGHT hour road trip that should not have taken that long, all the while passing the time by rocking out to Die Antwoord and fantasizing about Skyrim characters, critically analyzing the *Lord of the Rings* movies. Anywho.

There is Ms. Denise who relentlessly demanded why I had not produced a finished book yet.

I will never forget Caitlin, my steadfast friend since third grade. Caitlin who is honest beyond measure, who is beautiful and a much more talented writer than I. She also might have been milked for inspiration.

There are my parents. My dad who never gave up on me, though pestering me to always complete something. My dad who proudly bragged about me to his friends and coworkers. Most notably, he never missed one of my band concerts, and I will always love him for that. It is my mother who is the reader, though. My love of stories and their characters was inherited directly from her. My mother, who is always there for me. Always. Who never lets Kathy and I forget that our birth inflicted twenty-four hours of labor, and as such, she missed the finale of *X-Files*. I am only sorry that this story did not have your werewolves. Maybe next time.

There is my maternal grandmother who was my chauffeur throughout school, until I was forced to ride the dreaded cheesewagon. Without my grandmother, my Nanny McPhee, I would not have had the many opportunities granted to me, particularly throughout high school. She encouraged my music-doings and she encouraged my writerly-doings. And there is my paternal grandfather, my aunt, and dearest Makayla. I love you.

To my uncle who is probably the biggest fantasy and sci-fi bookworm I know, I hope this meets your expectations. Thank you for sharing your love and, of course, those *Harry Potter* books that may or may not have been returned.

And almost last but not least. There is a third name to my list of official editors. That name is Halley, pronounced like the comet. Without Halley, simply put, this story would not be before you. Feraan would have turned out differently, among other things. But the most notable thing about Halley is that she cared and the only qualms she ever had with me were for my benefit. She deserves so much more than a simple paragraph. Being the star of a comedic sitcom involving aliens might have sufficed, if I ever finished it. In either case, when reflecting on this book, Halley should not be forgotten.

And to the others who did not make it to witness my accomplishment:

Patsy June Michaels
(1944 – 2009)
&
James Selwyn Hemphill
(1936 – 2014)

requiescat in pace

About the Author

Kelly R. Michaels writes fiction and independently publishes books and novels under the imprint of Little Owl Publishing. Her first book *Archer of the Lake* was released May 23, 2014. The next book of the same series titled *Prince of the Vale* is expected to be released in 2015.

She lives in a small town in southern Tennessee where she graduated in 2013 with her Associate of Art (A.A.) in Foreign Language. After a gap year, she then proceeded to Athens State University to pursue a Bachelors in English with a minor in Education. Aside from school and her part-time job, Kelly usually spends time with her books and her publishing.

FOR MORE INFORMATION
ON KELLY R. MICHAELS OR HER BOOKS
YOU MAY VISIT HER WEBSITE AT:
WWW.KELLYRMICHAELS.COM

The Silver Crown Chronicles
by Kelly R. Michaels

Archer of the Lake

Prince of the Vale

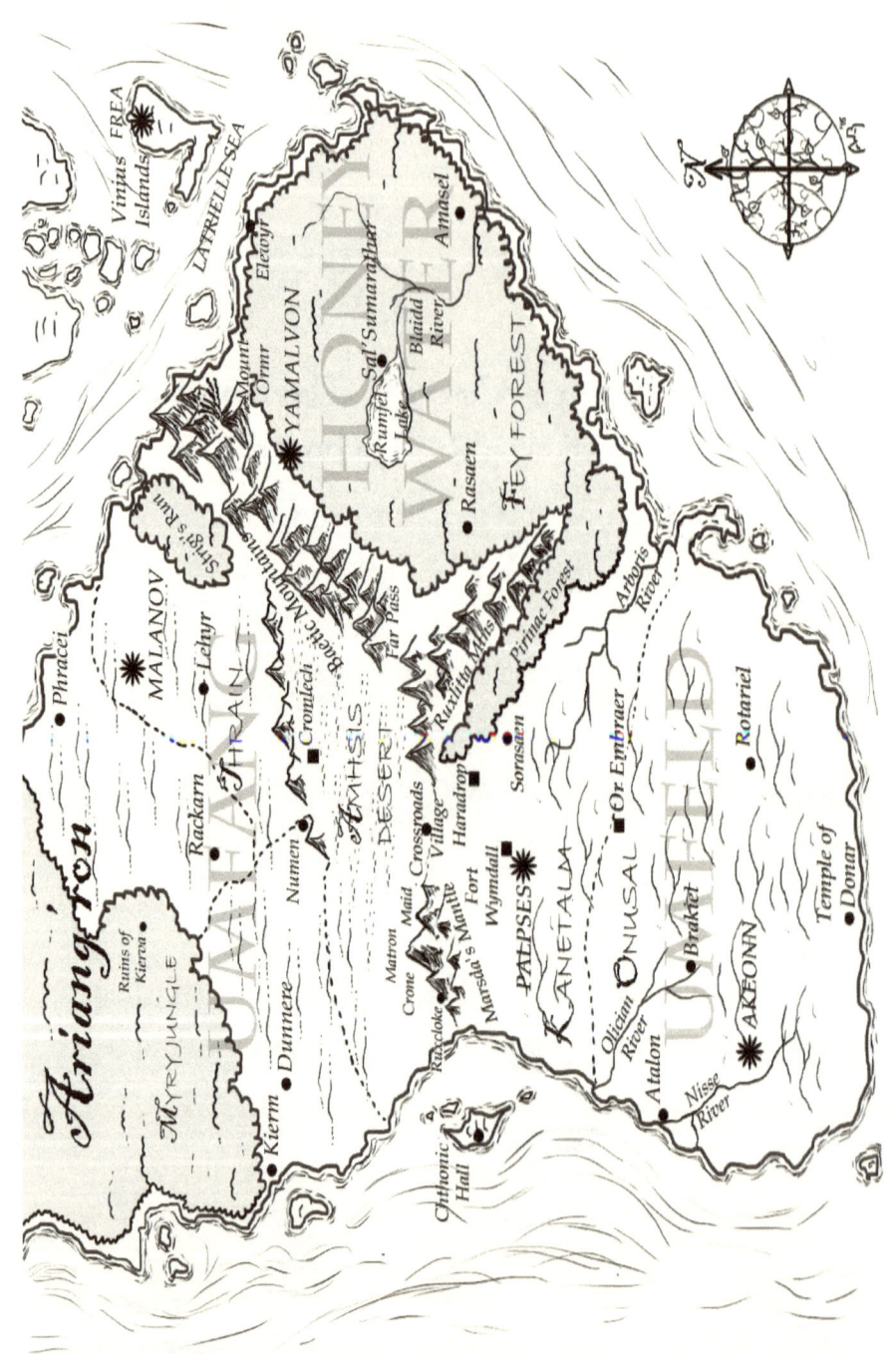

FREA

Vinius
Islands

LATRIELLE SEA

HONEY WATER

Amasel

Mount Omnr

Eleoyl

YAMALVON

Sal'Sumarathar

Blaiidi River

Rumfel Luk

Rasaen

FEY FOREST

Phracei

Lehyr

MALANOV

String's Run

Rackarn

Baelic Mountains

Far Pass

AMSIS DESERT

Pirinae Forest

Ruxlifin MISDIAN

Arboris River

ROTARIEL

Cromlech

Numen

Sorasaen

Or Embraer

Ariangron

Ruins of Kierva

Kiern

Dunnere

Matron Crone

Maid

Crossroads Village

Haradrod

Or Embraer

ONUSAL

UMFELD

Braket

Temple of Donar

MYRYJUNGLE

UAAFANG

Razcloke

Marsa's Mantle

Wyrndall

PATPSES

KANETALM

Olician River

AKEONN

Atalon

Nisse River

Chthonic Hall

Little Owl
Publishing

www.ingramcontent.com/pod-product-compliance
Lightning Source LLC
Chambersburg PA
CBHW031703170626
46808CB00005B/1584